Cynthia Harrod-Eagles is the author of the hugely popular Morland Dynasty novels, which have captivated and enthralled readers for decades. She is also the author of the contemporary Bill Slider mystery series, as well as her recent series, War at Home, which is an epic family drama set against the backdrop of World War I. Cynthia's passions are music, wine, horses, architecture and the English countryside.

The Mistress of
Ashmore Castle

Cynthia Harrod-Eagles

SPHERE

SPHERE

First published in Great Britain in 2023 by Sphere

1 3 5 7 9 10 8 6 4 2

A CIP catalogue record for this book is available from the British Library.

ISBN 978-1-4087-2948-9

Typeset in Plantin by Palimpsest Book Production Limited, Falkirk, Stirlingshire
Printed and bound in Great Britain by Clays Ltd, Elcograf S.p.A.

Papers used by Sphere are from well-managed forests
and other responsible sources.

MIX
Supporting
responsible forestry
FSC
www.fsc.org   FSC® C104740

Sphere
An imprint of
Little, Brown Book Group
Carmelite House
50 Victoria Embankment
London
EC4Y 0DZ

An Hachette UK Company
www.hachette.co.uk

www.littlebrown.co.uk

For Tony, always

DRAMATIS PERSONAE

AT ASHMORE CASTLE

The family

Giles Tallant, 6th Earl of Stainton
  — his wife Kitty, the countess
    — their baby son Louis, Lord Ayton
  — his eldest sister Linda, married to Viscount Cordwell
    — their children Arabella and Arthur
  — his brother Richard
  — his sister Rachel, age 18
  — his sister Alice, age 17
  — his widowed grandmother, Victoire (Grandmère)
  — his grandfather's half-brother Sebastian (Uncle Sebastian)
  — his widowed mother Maud, the dowager countess
    — her brother Fergus, 9th Earl of Leake (Uncle Stuffy)
    — her sister Caroline, widow of Sir James Manningtree (Aunt Caroline)
    — her sister Victoria (Aunt Vicky), Princess of Wittenstein-Glücksberg
    — her cousins Cecily and Gordon Tullamore
      — their children Angus, Beata, Fritz, Gussie, Ben, Mannox, Mary

The male servants
Moss, the butler
Crooks, valet to Mr Sebastian
Speen (deceased), former valet to Mr Richard
Afton, new valet to the earl
Footmen William, Cyril, Sam, James (Hook, former valet to the earl)
House boys Wilfrid, Eddie
Peason, head gardener
Allsuch, under gardener
Cox, Wilf, gardeners' boys

The female servants
Mrs Webster, the housekeeper
Miss Hatto, maid to the countess
Miss Taylor, maid to the dowager
Housemaids Rose, Daisy, Doris, Ellen, Mabel, Tilda, Milly, Addy, Ada, Mildred
Dory, sewing maid
Mrs Oxlea (deceased), former cook
Mrs Terry (Ida), new cook
Brigid, Aggie, Debbie, kitchen maids
Nanny Pawley
Nursery maid Jessie

In the stables
Giddins, head man
Archer, groom to the earl
Josh Brandom, groom to the young ladies
Stable boys Timmy, Oscar, George
Coachmen John Manley, Joe Green

On the estate
Markham, land agent
Adeane, bailiff

Moresby, solicitor
Saddler, gamekeeper
Gale, estate carpenter
Axe Brandom (brother to Josh) woodsman

In the village
Dr Bannister, rector of St Peter's Church

Physician, Dr Arbogast

Police Sergeant Mayhew
Police Constable Tom Holyoak

Miss Violet Eddowes, philanthropist
— her cook Mrs Grape, her maid Betty

IN MARKET HARBOROUGH

Nina, Kitty's best friend
— her husband Joseph Cowling, an industrialist
— Decius Blake, his right-hand man
— her housekeeper Mrs Deering
— her maid Tina
— her groom Daughters
— her friend and neighbour Bobby Wharfedale
— Bobby's husband Aubrey
— Bobby's brother Adam Denbigh
— her friend Lady Clemmie Leacock

IN LONDON

Molly Sands, piano teacher, once lover of the 5th earl
— Chloë, her daughter
Sir Thomas Burton, impresario, Grandmère's cicisbeo
Henry 'Mawes' Morris, cartoonist, Mr Cowling's friend
— his wife Isabel and daughter Lepida

CHAPTER ONE

December 1903

As the butler, Moss, walked down the room, everyone could see that there was a letter with a foreign stamp on his silver salver. But everyone was too polite to stare, and carried on eating breakfast as if nothing interesting were happening.

Moss stopped by Kitty, bowed, and murmured. She took the envelope and, while he paced slowly back, opened it, drew out the sheet and read it. It was only when she folded it back into the envelope without comment that the patience of her sister-in-law Linda snapped. She glared at Kitty, and said, 'Well? I suppose it is from Giles. What does he say?'

'Dear,' Linda's husband, Lord Cordwell, admonished gently.

Even Kitty's mother-in-law, the dowager countess, not known for tact, drew a sharp breath of disapproval.

Linda shrugged it off. 'Oh, don't pretend you don't all want to know,' she addressed the room. 'Kitty! What does he say?'

Kitty didn't answer at once. Her throat had closed. She hadn't expected to hear from her husband. Even if he had time to write, and had anything he wanted to say to her, she didn't suppose there were postboxes in the Valley of the Kings. Her heart had jumped with painful joy when she saw the letter: the disappointment was proportionately great.

'He says one of the other archaeologists at the dig had to come back to Paris on business, and offered to post letters for everyone there,' she said at last.

'Oh, don't be tiresome,' Linda said. 'Is he coming back for Christmas? That's what we want to know.'

Alice and Rachel both looked up at that point, hope in their faces. But Richard said, 'It's the best part of two weeks' travelling to get back here, and he hasn't been gone long. It wouldn't be worth his while.'

Linda gave a snort of disapproval. 'It's disgraceful, going off like that. It looks so *outré*. People will talk if he's not here for Christmas. But that's typical of Giles – he thinks of no-one but himself.'

Kitty pushed back her chair abruptly and got up. Linda threw the rest of the rebuke at her departing back. 'I blame you, Kitty! You've had plenty of opportunity to develop a proper influence over him. If you had exerted yourself, we shouldn't now be in this position.'

'Please may I have the stamp, Aunty Kitty?' Linda's son Arthur pleaded urgently, but had no reply.

The dowager shrivelled Arthur with a look, and said to Linda, 'I cannot understand why the children should eat with us at breakfast. None of *my* children was allowed down until they were twelve.'

'It was Kitty's idea,' Linda said sulkily. 'It's a modern thing, I suppose.'

'It's so that they can learn how to behave at the table,' Richard said, but the veiled rebuke slid off her. She might notice being hit with a brick, but subtlety was wasted on her.

'Stuff and nonsense,' said the dowager to Richard. 'That is what a nanny is for, to teach them manners. And until they have acquired them, they should remain in the nursery. Why did you not bring their nanny with you?' she asked Linda.

'Oh, she left suddenly, just before we came away,' Linda said, buttering a piece of toast so fiercely it shattered. The fact was that they couldn't afford a nanny. The Cordwell finances were in a perilous state, and Linda was hoping for a lengthy stay at Ashmore Castle to tide them over a thin patch.

Cordwell sighed so penetratingly that Sebastian, who had a shrewd idea how things stood at Holme Manor, felt sorry for him, and sought to distract him. 'What do you say to taking a gun out this morning, Cordwell? We could walk down to the Carr and see if there are any duck.'

While they were discussing the possibility, Richard slipped out and went looking for Kitty.

In the Peacock Room, which she had taken as her private sitting-room, Kitty was standing at the window, staring out at the grey winter day. The cloud hung low over the woods like mist; nothing moved but rooks, scraps of black blowing above the trees.

On the wall beside the window was the pencil-and-water-colour likeness of Giles that Alice had done, which he had had framed as a present for her. It showed him three-quarter profile, looking away pensively into the distance. It was appropriate, she thought: his mind, his heart, would always be somewhere else.

She had shed all her tears in the days after he had left for Egypt to join friends at a dig. Archaeology was his passion, as she had always known; but it was his parting words that had crushed her. He had said he felt stifled at home, that he needed to get away. She feared that she was one of the things he wanted to get away from. At any rate, she had no power to keep him with her. She'd had to realise that he did not love her as she loved him. His wife, his child, his home, his family, together had less pull than the dusty sarcophagi and crumbling bones of long-dead strangers.

She heard someone come in behind her, and knew from the aroma of the Paris Pearl lotion he used after shaving that it was Richard. He came up behind her and placed a light hand on her shoulder.

'Poor Pusscat!' he said. 'Don't cry any more. My sister's an ass, and there's nothing to be done about her.'

'I'm not crying,' Kitty said.

'But you sound as though you might. There's nothing to be done about Giles, either, you know.' She turned to face him, showing her eyes bright but dry. 'What did he say in the letter, my impossible brother?'

'That the weather was tolerable, the insects not too troublesome, the dig going well, and they think they are on the brink of exciting discoveries.'

'Abominable! Married to the prettiest woman in England and not one tender word for her?'

'Will people really talk when he's not here for Christmas?' she asked.

'Can't think why they should,' he said. 'In his position he can do whatever he wants. Of course, people would generally prefer an earl to go in for the traditional sins: loose women and high-stakes gambling, like my father – who was much admired, by the by. But if old Giles can't quite rise to full-blooded vice, embracing eccentricity is the next best thing. The only really shocking thing would be for him to behave with Victorian propriety.'

'You're talking nonsense to cheer me up,' Kitty said, beginning to smile.

He gave her a look of shining innocence. 'Not a bit! Look at our dear old King Teddy. Thoroughly naughty before he came to the throne, and everyone loves him for it. They wouldn't feel the same about him at all if he had comported himself like a respectable bank clerk from Sidcup. Now, what we must do is dedicate ourselves to the cause of cheering you up. We should throw the most tremendous Christmas ball.'

'A ball? Really?'

'Really! Let's see . . . It should be on the Saturday before Christmas. The nineteenth.'

'But that's so close – everyone will already be engaged.'

'They'll cancel, for a ball at Ashmore Castle,' he said confidently. 'We'll ask a dozen people to stay for it, and give them a shoot on the Sunday. I'll arrange that part of it with Adeane and Saddler. And invite everyone in the neighbourhood for the dancing.' He looked around. 'You must have paper and ink here. Yes, fetch them, then, and we'll start making lists. Then you can talk to Mrs Webster while I go and see Adeane.'

'I'm so glad I bought new mattresses for all the beds,' she said, crossing the room to her escritoire.

'The mattresses *are* the essential element,' he assured her. 'It's what people will principally come for.'

She smiled. 'You're absurd.'

Mrs Terry had been cook at Ashmore Castle for only seven months. She had been just plain Ida, the head kitchen-maid, under the previous cook, Mrs Oxlea. But after Mrs Oxlea's shocking death, she'd had to take over on an emergency basis. She had been doing a lot of the work anyway – Mrs Oxlea had been a drinker – and she'd long had ambitions. When Mrs Webster, the housekeeper, had relayed the mistress's enquiry as to whether she would like the post permanently, she'd been glad and grateful.

Everyone seemed to think she had done pretty well. But there had not been any major entertaining until now. A ball! And people to stay for it as well! It was a completely new challenge.

Mrs Webster had come straight to see her, before the plan had been officially announced. The news had reached her in the usual roundabout but effective way: Richard had gone from Kitty to see Uncle Sebastian, who had been in his room. Sebastian's valet Crooks had been bumbling about in the background so could hardly help overhearing, and Crooks had lost no time in telling Mrs Webster.

Mrs Webster had no doubts about her own ability to cope, but she realised that Ida would need encouragement. 'The mistress will send for you, and of course you must pretend it's all news to you, but it will be a good thing to have your plans ready, so that you can seem calm and confident.'

Ida was not calm and confident yet. 'A dozen people to stay! Plus the family.'

'Plus their servants, don't forget. It's a lot extra, but Brigid and Aggie can do the cooking for the servants' hall. Don't worry about that.'

'What do people have at a ball? Isn't there always a supper?'

'A buffet,' Mrs Webster said. 'You can make most of it ahead of time. Lobster and oyster patties, bouchées à la reine, that sort of thing. A glazed ham. A cold sirloin for the gentlemen. Soft rolls—'

'When will I have time to make *those*?'

'Buy them in,' Mrs Webster said briskly. 'Toller's in the village can supply them, and nobody will know the difference.'

'If you think it's all right . . . What else?'

'Fruit. Whatever you can get at this time of year – the arrangement is everything. And some kind of sweet. A coffee blancmange, perhaps. You can make that ahead, too. We've got a lot of little glass custard cups somewhere – it'd look pretty in those. And then white soup for the end of the ball.'

'And there'll be a dinner before the ball, I suppose?'

'They won't want too much before dancing. Four or five courses, and you can keep it simple. Then there'll be the shooting luncheon on Sunday, and dinner on Sunday night.'

'And breakfasts.' Ida put her hands to her cheeks, contemplating the mountains of food she must prepare. Her voice wavered. 'However will we manage? Oh, Mrs Webster!'

'You said you wanted the job,' Webster said briskly. 'Now here it is. You'll need more girls, that's obvious, but the mistress has already said I can hire anyone we need, and that includes in the kitchen. Brace up, Mrs Terry. You don't have to cook every single thing yourself, you know. You'll be like a general at a battle, giving orders to the troops. Of course,' she added slyly, half turning away, 'if you really don't think you're up to it . . .'

'Oh, I'm up to it all right,' Ida said quickly. 'Don't you worry about that. I'm going to be the best cook of any big house in the country! They'll talk about me in years to come. I'll be famous – Mrs Terry of Ashmore Castle, they'll say. And when I'm old I'll write my own book, like Mrs Beeton, and everyone'll go to it for reference.'

'That's the spirit,' Mrs Webster said.

The old schoolroom at the top of the house, which was now a sitting-room for the young ladies, was pleasantly warm. Since Kitty had taken over the direction of the house, there had always been a fire lit for them – unlike the days of economy under their mother.

Alice was sitting on the floor, sketch-pad against her knees, drawing Rachel, who was sitting on the window-seat staring dreamily out of the window. Alice had asked her to loose her hair, and it fell in long coils over her shoulders, while the light from the window threw interesting planes and shadows into her lovely face. It was, Alice thought, going to be a nice piece.

The dogs, Tiger and Isaac, were sprawled in front of the fire, giving an occasional groan of comfort. Linda's children, Arabella and Arthur, were quiet for the moment, working on a jigsaw puzzle of the map of Europe, which Alice thought ought to keep them busy since she happened to know that half of Belgium was missing.

Rachel gave a sigh, and Alice thought she was looking particularly pensive. She had been travelling with her mother for most of the year, going to parties and balls and meeting young men,

7

and Alice thought it was most likely that she had fallen in love with someone. She had been in love the year before with Victor Lattery, a most unsatisfactory young man – but at the time, he was almost the only one she had met, and Rachel was the sort of girl who would always be in love with someone.

So to be kind to her, Alice said, 'You look as though you're in a dream. What are you thinking about?'

'The ball, and what I shall wear,' said Rachel.

'Oh,' said Alice blankly. She wasn't 'out' yet, and much preferred riding to dancing.

'I hope Mama doesn't make me wear the white organza again,' Rachel went on.

'Richard's trying to persuade Kitty to wear white – Daisy heard Miss Taylor talking about it.'

'But Kitty's married,' Rachel objected. 'Married women don't wear white.'

'Don't frown – I'm doing your face. Yes, but you know Richard, always trying to shock. He says a countess can do as she likes, and that with Kitty's colouring she'll look stunning in white.'

Rachel sighed again. 'I'm so fair it doesn't suit me.'

Alice agreed. 'Next to Kitty, you'd look like two penn'orth of cold gin.'

Rachel wrinkled her nose. 'Where did you get such a dreadful expression?'

Alice didn't want to say she'd heard Axe Brandom use it. 'Oh, it's what the grooms say,' she said vaguely.

'Well, don't let Mama hear you.'

'Don't look disapproving – still doing your face.'

'You spend too much time in the stables. And you'll never get a husband if you use coarse phrases like that.'

'I don't want a husband,' Alice said, as she had said many times before, whenever she was rebuked for being unladylike, or having untidy hair, or sitting on the floor, or whatever other way she had fallen short of the maidenly ideal.

'Well, you surely can't want to stay here all your life,' said Rachel.

'Why not? I can't see how I'd be happier anywhere else.'

'I like it here,' Arabella said, startling them both – they hadn't realised she'd been listening. 'I'd like to stay for ever. I don't want to go home. Our house is like two penn'orth of cold gin.'

'Two penn'orth of gold chin,' Arthur echoed importantly. 'It's nasty and smelly.'

'Arthur! Don't say such a thing!' Rachel said.

'It is!' Arthur averred. 'Smelly-welly-jelly! I hate it! I want to stay here.'

'Me too!' said Arabella. 'Can we go riding this afternoon, Aunty Alice?'

'Ooh, yes. And can I ride Biscuit?' Arthur said, bouncing on the spot. The dogs woke and raised their heads to look at him, wondering if the movement heralded a walk.

'No, he has to have Goosebumps, doesn't he, Aunty?' Arabella objected quickly. 'I always have Biscuit, cos I'm older and I can ride better. Arthur's only a baby.'

'I'm not a baby!'

'You are!'

'Well, *you* fell off yesterday! I've not fallen off for ages.'

'I won't take either of you if you squabble,' Alice said. They fell silent and, under her stern gaze, went back to the puzzle. The dogs flopped back again. Next to a walk, toasting at the fire was their favourite occupation.

Rachel gave her a look that said, *Now you see what staying here all your life would mean. You'd be the spinster aunt.*

Alice continued working. She was rather looking forward to the children going home, because she did tend to get stuck with them. She felt sorry for them, but having them tagging along meant she couldn't go and see Axe in his woodman's cottage up in Motte Woods. She missed those visits. She missed Dolly, his terrier, and the cats, and Della, his beautiful

9

Suffolk Punch mare, and Cobnut, the rescued pony she had named, and the various injured or orphaned animals he had from time to time.

Most of all she missed Axe. And she wondered . . . Her hand slowed and stopped as her thoughts went travelling. Last time she had visited there had been a strange, palpitating moment when she had thought he was going to kiss her. He had stood so near, stooped his big golden face towards her, and everything in her had reached up to him, like a flower reaching for the sun. But then he had straightened up and turned away, and afterwards had been almost gruff with her. And insisted she left as soon as she had drunk her tea, saying it was going to snow and she must get home before it broke.

The snow hadn't lasted long, and was followed by a thaw; but then Linda had arrived with the children, tying her down, and she had not seen Axe since. Christmas was coming, and it would be impossible to get away for ages. She missed him. And she wondered . . .

There was a tap on the door, and Ellen, one of the house-maids, came in. 'Her ladyship wants to see you, Lady Rachel.'

'Which ladyship?'

'Your mother, my lady.'

Rachel got up obediently, straightened her skirt and was heading for the door.

'Your hair!' Alice cried.

Rachel hated to be told off, and her mother would object to her appearing in that fashion. She looked frightened. 'I'd forgotten it was down!'

'Let me, my lady,' Ellen said. With some clever twists and a few pins gleaned from Alice and Arabella, she got it into a kind of chignon. 'There. Not perfect, but it might pass on a dark night, as they say.'

'Oh, thank you, Ellen! How clever you are! How did you learn to do that?'

'Miss Hatto showed me, my lady. And Rose lets me

practise on her sometimes. I'd like to be a lady's maid one day. And if I can do hair, I can attend visiting ladies that don't have their own maid, and maybe one day—'

'Mama's waiting,' Alice reminded her sister; and Rachel fled.

Ellen followed her out. Alice turned the pages of her sketch-pad. She came to a pencil sketch she had done of Axe, head bent over a piece of harness he was mending. Lovingly she added some more shading, deepening the chiaroscuro. She could have drawn him from memory by now, but it was so much more satisfying to have the subject before her. Perhaps if she could slip away from the children for a few hours . . . She wasn't their governess, after all. Surely someone else could watch them.

'Aunty Alice, can we go riding now?' Arabella broke into her thoughts.

'Riding, riding, riding!' Arthur shouted, bouncing again, and waking the dogs fully. They got up and stretched, and stalked towards Alice with suggestive smiles. They were delighted to find a human face at tongue level for a change.

'All right,' Alice said, sighing, fending them off, and rising. 'Go and get changed.'

'Hooray!' said Arabella. 'We've finished the puzzle, only there's a piece missing.'

'Puzzles are smelly,' Arthur crowed triumphantly. 'Puzzles are penn'orth of cold gin.'

Alice said, 'If you mention "cold gin" once more I shan't take you at all. And stop saying "smelly".'

Arthur clapped his hands over his mouth at the threat. Arabella did the same, but they both shook with giggles behind them.

Mrs Webster found Moss, the butler, in the glass-closet in a sort of slow bustle that spoke more confusion than activity. What was wrong with him these days? she wondered irritably.

Was he getting too old? Was he drinking – well, all butlers drank, but more than usual?

He looked up as she appeared at the door. 'We haven't had a ball for such a long time,' he said. 'And such short notice! There's so much to do, and no time to do it. I hardly know . . . People staying, as well – and a shoot on Sunday.'

'Everything will get done in its turn,' said Mrs Webster, firmly.

'But you have not considered. The ballroom, for instance, so long unused – we don't know the condition of the floor!'

'Don't you remember, we used that firm in Aylesbury last time. They do everything – test the floor, clean and chalk it, tune the chandeliers. They hire out rout chairs as well, and tables for the card room. Mr Richard has already spoken to Giddins about the visiting horses and to Adeane about the shoot. I've spoken to Mrs Terry and she has the menu in hand, and I am hiring extra maids to clean the rooms – they arrive tomorrow. We're short of good sheets, but I'm putting the mended ones on the family's beds and I've ordered new ones from Whiteleys – they've sworn they'll be here by Monday.'

'Dear me,' Moss murmured feebly. 'I don't know how you've managed to do so much already.'

'Method,' she said unkindly. 'If you apply it to any task, order will result. There is never anything to be gained by panicking.'

Moss was hurt. 'I never panic.'

'There isn't so very much left for you to do,' Mrs Webster went on briskly. 'Mr Sebastian will consult you about the wine, and you'll need to talk to Giddins about the transport for the shooting luncheon and for those who want to go to church. Adeane and Saddler will see to the beaters, and loaders for the gentlemen who don't bring their own. You'll have his lordship's guns ready for Mr Richard?'

Moss reached for his dignity. 'Of course,' he said, with

12

faint reproach. 'What was it you wanted to speak to me about? I *am* rather busy.'

She came in fully and closed the door behind her. 'I want to talk to you about James.'

'Ah,' said Moss.

'I don't know what his lordship was thinking, demoting him from valet to footman.'

'He refused to go to Egypt with his lordship,' Moss said, with deep disapproval. 'A shocking impertinence, and a dereliction of duty.'

'I know all that,' Mrs Webster said impatiently. 'But why on earth didn't he just dismiss him? Now *Mister* Hook has gone back to being merely James, at half the wages. He's like a festering sore in the servants' hall. You've surely noticed his attitude?'

'He always was sharp-tongued,' Moss agreed, 'but he's worse now.'

'He criticises everything you do. Pretending it's in a spirit of helpfulness, but he's really just trying to diminish you in the eyes of the other servants.'

'I'm sure your authority is sound, Mrs Webster,' Moss said, bewildered.

She gave an exasperated sigh. 'When I say "you", in this context, I mean *you*, Mr Moss.'

'Oh!' said Moss.

'He's after your job. It's unacceptable that he talks behind your back. Quite apart from *your* welfare, it unsettles the other servants. What are you going to do about him?'

'You know it's not in my gift to sack him,' Moss said unhappily.

'I think it is. He's not a valet any more. The male servants apart from the valets come under your authority.'

'But with his lordship away . . . If he'd wanted him gone, he'd have sacked him himself. Perhaps there is some reason . . . Say his lordship *wanted* him to stay, it would upset him

13

to come back and find . . . Perhaps you could speak to her ladyship. Or Mr Richard.'

Mrs Webster made an impatient sound. Moss looked away, let his eyes rove about the closed cupboards in search of escape. All this unpleasantness . . . It tired him out. He wished Mrs Webster would go away. He had always disliked James, even before his elevation, disliked the way he looked at the maids. He thought about Ada, the new little housemaid, white as a lily, delicate as a butterfly. He longed to escape this unpleasant conversation and seek her out, find some excuse to talk to her and have her look up at him in the respectful, admiring way that swelled his heart. The thought of James *looking* at her, still less touching her . . . ! He wanted to protect her against the whole world. Little Ada, with her long neck like the stem of a flower . . .

'If you're not going to dismiss him,' Mrs Webster said sharply, recalling him to the present, 'at least speak to him, put him in his place. He's already talking about valeting any gentleman who comes to stay without his own man. He's fourth footman now. It's not for him to put himself forward.'

'Well, he *is* experienced,' Moss began.

'You know he's only interested in the tips. To allow him to valet a guest would be tantamount to rewarding him for refusing to accompany his lordship. And I don't think that's what his lordship had in mind – do you?'

Moss drew himself up. 'If any gentleman needs a valet, *I* shall decide who it is to be. I will speak to James. He takes too much upon himself.'

'You should dismiss him,' Mrs Webster said.

'I will deal with the situation. Leave it to me,' Moss said loftily, and she gave him a hard look, and went away. Moss waited until her footsteps had died away, and went back to his own room, where he could close the door. There was almost a quarter of a bottle of claret in his cupboard, left in the decanter last night, which he had poured back into the bottle before the decanter was washed. Obviously you couldn't send up a small amount like that again, and it was a sin to waste it. It was the butler's perquisite, a reward for a lifetime's devotion to the study of wine in his master's service.

He would never, of course, touch the spirits.

CHAPTER TWO

The climate in Egypt was reckoned to be perfect in December for digging, still hot by English standards, but not uncomfortably so; a little rain on the coast but none inland. Nevertheless, there was a general inclination to stop for a day or two at Christmas. Most of the archaeology community was taking the train into Cairo to stay at hotels or with friends and enjoy the delights of civilisation. Giles, having been on site only for a few weeks, was already impatient at the idea of suspending work, but an invitation from Lord Cromer, the consul general, to a ball on Christmas Eve could not be lightly dismissed.

'Why me?' he complained, showing the invitation to his friends Talbot and Mary Arthur. 'He hasn't asked you or Max.'

'You're an earl,' Mary Arthur said. 'I expect he has to impress Egyptian officials. And the French diplomatic circle. Perhaps even merchants.'

'Well, I didn't come all the way out here to start this nonsense again – balls and dinners, indeed!'

The letter from Lord Cromer's aide, Guy Bellamy, which accompanied the invitation, explained that as the consulate-general building was only leased and not very commodious, the ball and its preceding dinner were to be held in a private mansion, lent for the occasion by a Mr Walton Antrobus. A handwritten letter had come for Giles by the same delivery, from Mr Antrobus inviting him to stay with him and his wife at Ismailia House for as long as he cared to.

'And who is this Antrobus person?' Giles continued, showing them the letter. 'I don't know him.'

'He's an American, what vulgarians these days call a millionaire,' said Talbot. 'Cotton and timber, I believe. Inherited the business from his papa, and now spreads joy around the world by spending his fortune wherever the whim takes him.'

'All true,' said Mary, 'but Tal's being whimsical. He doesn't mention that Antrobus and his wife are cultured people and keen Egyptologists. They're coming to join the dig some time in the new year.'

'Well, I'm damned if I'm going,' Giles grumbled. 'It's bad enough getting into evening clothes in England.'

'You did bring them?' Talbot said suspiciously.

Mary laughed. 'See his face! Of course he did!'

'I thought I might need them on the ship, that's all.'

Talbot patted his hand. 'Don't be a fool, old chap. There'll be a decent dinner, clean sheets and hot water. Take the opportunity to get the sand out of your hair. And look, how thoughtful – he suggests you come as early as you can on Christmas Eve, so that you can get ready at leisure.'

'That *is* kind,' Giles acknowledged reluctantly. 'But I don't have a man.'

'There's bound to be a footman who can help you dress.'

'Besides,' Mary added, 'everyone's going to Cairo, and you can hardly stay here and dig all by yourself.'

Giles took the sleeper train: it was more comfortable to travel at night when it was cooler, and the monotonous scenery along the bank of the canal was not something one would mind missing. He shared the compartment with a portly Frenchman, who seemed eager for conversation, so Giles feigned ignorance of the language and then feigned sleep.

With the moving air coming in through the open vent, and the slow rhythm of the wheels, sleep soon became a reality, and he woke only in the morning when the train passed joltingly over several sets of points outside the city.

When he stepped down with his bag to look for a taxi, he was accosted by a chubby-faced young man, who introduced himself as Wrexham J. Antrobus and said his father had sent him to conduct Giles to the house.

'How did you recognise me?' Giles said in surprise.

'Oh, Dad cut a picture of you out of the *Egyptian Gazette*. We get it sent up from Alexandria. They snapped you getting off the ship, sir. They always report when important people come out from England. This way, if you please. We have a car waiting.'

Giles was impressed. Motor-cars were rare in Cairo, where the over-burdened donkey and the skinny, depressed horse were the usual modes of transport. It was large and gleaming, and had attracted a huge crowd of barefoot boys, who were being waved off, like troublesome flies, by the uniformed attendant, only to regather as soon as he turned another way.

Antrobus junior followed Giles into the back seat, having seen his bag stowed. 'Is that all your luggage? Very well, Nobbs, straight home. I understand you haven't brought your man with you, my lord. My father's valet Afton will take care of you while you're here. Have you breakfasted? Do you know Cairo well? Would you care for me to point out places of interest as we go by?'

Giles gathered the young man was nervous, and that nerves made him loquacious. He let the talk wash over him and enjoyed the sensation of being wafted through the early-morning streets, with the shadows of the trees still long across the road and a freshness still in the air, in a comfortable conveyance that scattered the equine traffic and carved itself a passage by its novelty and importance.

Ismailia House turned out to be very large and grand, built

18

in the ponderous French boulevard style. Curved steps up led to vast wooden double doors, standing open on a lobby, with glass doors beyond to keep out the flies. Then came an enormous entrance hall that made Giles think of a very superior hotel, with its marble floors and pillars, a decided prevalence of crimson and gilt, potted palms and mirrors everywhere.

Young Antrobus ushered Giles in. 'Here he is, Dad. Lord Stainton, may I introduce my father, Mr Walton P. Antrobus?'

Antrobus turned out to be a tall man, brisk-looking in a smart suit, with a fair face, receding hair and gold-rimmed eye-glasses. He beamed, shook Giles's hand heartily and said how honoured he was to welcome him to his house. 'Now you must please consider the place as your own, make yourself comfortable, and anything you want, anything at all, you just say the word, and it's yours.'

'You're very kind, Mr Antrobus,' Giles murmured, feeling overwhelmed and wondering if flight was a possibility.

'Walt, please! It's Walt. And the boy here is Wrex. At your service – entirely. We couldn't be happier to have you here. And you must let me present my wife – the real brains of the outfit! It was she who first got me interested in archaeology. Minnie, my dear. Lord Stainton, my wife Minnie.'

A very pleasant-looking, well-dressed lady with a distinct likeness to her son was shaking his hand and he was struggling to keep his eyes on her and respond to her kind welcome, because he was desperate to stare over her shoulder to where a young woman stood: a slim young woman in midnight blue, with large dark eyes and a rather uncertain smile, under a mass of dark hair, coarse and vigorous as a pony's mane.

He had said something proper, he couldn't be sure what, and now at last might legitimately move his gaze. Mrs Antrobus gestured the young woman forward and said, 'I believe you are already acquainted with Miss Lombardi? Giulia, my dear? Giulia is my companion and assistant. We

19

are going out to the Valley of the Kings as soon as the festive season is over, and it wouldn't be proper or pleasant for me to go without another female for support.'

'Yes,' said Giles, in a daze. 'I know Giulia very well.' Her warm hand was in his, and she was looking at him with that same slightly hesitant smile. 'I studied under her father.'

'Oh, yes, Professor Lombardi and I have an acquaintance in common,' Antrobus was saying. 'Dear old Doctor Belzoni. Have you read his *Temples and Tombs of Egypt and Nubia*? A seminal work. It was the first book Minnie recommended to me on ancient Egypt. It got me so hooked that when I discovered Dr Belzoni had moved from Italy to our fine country, to a chair at our local university, I couldn't wait to meet him. And meet him I did! Wealth has its privileges, you see. Then when Minnie and I were first coming to Europe the doctor gave us a letter of introduction to Professor Lombardi. He and his family couldn't have been kinder to us both. We've all become good friends since.'

'Yes,' said Giles, releasing Giulia's hand at last. 'I am well acquainted with the Lombardis' kindness.'

'I haven't a doubt of it! Well, Giulia's quite accustomed to taking notes for her father – and I'm pretty sure she knows more about antiquities than me and Minnie put together – so when she offered to accompany us as Minnie's companion and secretary, we couldn't have been more pleased.'

'I second every word of that, and more,' said Mrs Antrobus. 'Giulia's a treasure, and quite like a daughter to us. But, Walt, dear, why are we keeping his lordship standing in the hall?'

'Oh, good Lord, what a pumpkin head I am! You must want coffee after that long train ride. And breakfast! Won't you come on through? Or would you sooner go to your room and have a bath first? But you must be starving. See here, there's a closet just off the lobby, where you could wash your hands and splash your face, and then have breakfast right away, and go up to your room afterwards. By then my man

Afton, who is going to attend you, will have got everything unpacked and have a bath ready for you. How does that seem?'

Just out of Antrobus's line of sight, Giulia had a teasing smile, obviously accustomed to their host's power of organisation. Giles smiled back, and surrendered to it. He felt, actually, very hungry, and not terribly dirty. Soon he was sitting down to good coffee, in the German rather than the Turkish style, and soft bread, and honey, and eggs, and fruit, and yoghourt, which he'd encountered before on his travels and rather enjoyed. The breakfast-room had long lace curtains at the open French windows, which filtered the sunlight pleasantly, and allowed in gentle airs from the shady garden beyond. The servants were soft-footed and attentive, the Antrobuses easy company, and Giulia was lovely and familiar. Giles found himself relaxing; and, despite the prospect of a consular dinner and ball that evening, was glad he had come.

His room was of a piece with the rest of the house – large, high-ceilinged, lavishly appointed, and with more mirrors than an English gentleman would consider quite *done*. It was pleasantly cool, with French windows open onto a balcony, and a slowly turning ceiling fan.

It was also furnished with a small, thin, tough-looking individual in valet's clothes, who gave him a bow that was counterbalanced by a cheerful grin.

'Afton, isn't it?' Giles said, dredging up the name from memory.

'That's right, my lord. I'm to take care of you. I've unpacked your bag and I'll get your evening dress brushed and pressed ready for later.'

'I'm afraid you'll have found a lot of sand in everything.'

'You don't need to apologise, my lord. It's my business to worry about sand so's you don't have to.'

'A refreshing attitude. My previous valet refused to come

21

to Egypt because he said he couldn't attend me properly in a tent.'

Afton looked stern. 'That's not the ticket at all! A gentleman's gentleman follows his gentleman wherever his gentleman goes, no questions asked, and does his job notwithstanding conditions. If you'll excuse me, my lord, it sounds as if your man was getting a mite above himself.'

Giles was amused. 'I think you're right.'

'It happens now and then,' Afton said wisely, 'that a fellow gets to think he's bigger than his position. I hope you sacked him good and hard, my lord.'

'I sacked him all right,' Giles said, 'but perhaps not as hard as I should have.'

Afton gave him a quick appraisal, and said, 'Now I dare say you'd like a good, long bath, my lord, after that journey, and I've sent for plenty of hot water, which'll be up in a jiffy, but I've got enough here to shave you first, my lord, and by the time that's done—'

'I always shave myself,' Giles interrupted.

Afton was not at all put out. 'I quite understand, my lord, but if you'll forgive me, it's a mistake. I can do a better job than ever you can, my lord, on account of being able to see into all the tricky places. If you'll just let me show you, my lord, you'll see the difference right away.'

'I don't like to be shaved,' Giles said stubbornly.

'I've known many a gentleman a bit nervous – or,' he added, as Giles frowned, 'maybe squeamish is the word. But, bless you, I'm as good with a razor as anyone you'll find on this earth. I had my own barber's shop and all the top gentlemen came to me. Never so much as a graze did one of 'em suffer. Admiral Lord Jellyby – do you know him, my lord?'

'My father did,' Giles said.

'Course he did! Well, my lord, the admiral used to say to me, "Afton," he'd say, "I'd trust you to shave me on board ship in a force-nine gale during a broadside battle." Just let me show you, my lord. The water's nice and hot, and I've warm towels here too.'

'Just this once, then,' Giles said, worn down by the little man's energy.

He found himself ushered into a chair. Afton placed towels with the deft movements of a magician and guided his head back onto a pillow.

'There now, my lord. If you just give in to it, you'll find it very relaxing. Some of my gentlemen used to go to sleep.'

'Don't expect me to,' Giles said defiantly.

Afton chuckled. 'That's right, my lord. Don't give up the bridge till you see the whites of the Etruscans' eyes.'

'You're an educated man,' Giles commented in surprise.

'Oh, you get a lot of time for reading when you're waiting up for your gentleman, my lord.'

'And that's a London accent, if I don't mistake,' Giles said, as the soap was applied. 'What brought you here?'

'Born in Whitechapel, my lord, started as a barber, went into service, got itchy feet, ended up in New York. Did a lot of jobs, learned a lot of things, got my own barber's shop in Manhattan, like I said. Mr Antrobus was one of my customers there. One day he says to me, "Afton," he says, "do you think you could valet?" "Done it before, sir," I says. "Then come and valet for me," he says. It's been a good life, Mr Antrobus is a good master, and he likes to travel so I've got about quite a bit. But I get a queer sort of longing now and then for old England. Seeing the world is good sport, but I wouldn't like to think I'd never go home again. However much you run, there's a kind of tug.'

'Yes,' said Giles, struck with the thought. Never see England again? No, he wouldn't care for that.

'Just relax the jaw now, my lord. That's right.'

Afton's hands were strong but gentle, and there was something sensually pleasant about having his face turned this way

23

and that as the razor glided like silk across his skin. To his own complete surprise, he did find himself drifting off, and when Afton wrapped a soft, warm towel round his face he could definitely have fallen asleep.

Too soon, it seemed, the towel was removed, a little astringent cologne was applied, and Afton whipped off the protective coverings with a movement that was pure barber's shop showmanship, and not a bit gentleman's gentleman. 'All done, my lord.'

Giles heaved himself up and went to the looking-glass, inspected his face and ran a hand over it. He met Afton's expectant eyes in the reflection. He couldn't be churlish with the man. 'Yes, you have done a good job,' he said. 'And a better one than I could have,' he admitted generously.

Afton looked pleased. 'Nice of you to say so, my lord. Now, I've heard the water arrive next door, so your bath is ready, and I'll lay out some clean clothes for you for after.'

Giles turned and made a stand. 'I dress myself, Afton.'

Afton's smile was as innocent as a child's. 'Course you do, my lord.'

Giles went into the bathroom, smiling to himself and shaking his head.

Horatius at the bridge, indeed!

Richard was in London on Christmas Eve, and after an interview with Vogel, the family banker, he turned from duty to pleasure and went to visit Molly Sands. The landlady, Mrs Gateshill, showed him upstairs in person, with the politeness of one who hopes the festive season will encourage a nice tip from a gentleman whose visits were, to say the least, a bit suspicious, given he was a young single man and Mrs Sands was— Well, what, indeed?

Not wanting to foment trouble for Molly, Richard found two half-crowns he couldn't afford, and he was more sorry to see them leave his hand than she seemed happy to have them land in hers. Perhaps she'd been hoping for a sovereign. He wished her a merry Christmas, and she bobbed dutifully but gave him a look as she departed that said as clearly as words, 'Won't get very merry on five bob, will I?'

'Chloë not here?' Richard asked, as he stepped into the small living-room – the only room, apart from the bedchamber beyond.

'She's at the Academy, practising,' said Molly, coming forward to shake his hand. He bent to kiss her, but she turned her face and gave him only her cheek.

'I'm sorry to miss her,' he said. 'I've brought a Christmas present for each of you, and since I can't see you on Christmas Day, I thought we could do as the Germans do and have them today.'

'I haven't anything for you,' Molly said.

'You've given me a reason to live. I couldn't expect anything more.'

She was distressed. 'Oh, my dear – don't! It's too much.'

'By contrast my presents are very small beer, but I'd like to have given Chloë hers in person.'

'I'm sure it will give her just as much pleasure tomorrow,' Molly said.

'But it won't give *me* as much. Present-giving is the ultimate selfishness, you know.'

'How can you be so foolish!'

'I'm quite serious. The giver has all the enjoyment of choosing, spending and anticipating, then seeing the recipient's delight – or a facsimile thereof. He feels noble, generous, a better person. All the recipient gets is the obligation to be grateful. It's a very one-sided transaction.'

'So you agree with the Bible: it is more blessed to give than to receive?'

'Yes, but receiving ought to get far more credit than it does. There's a skill to receiving gracefully and allowing the giver to bask in his own glory.'

Now she was laughing. 'It's not fair. Whenever I want to be stern with you, you make me laugh. Will you have some tea? The kettle's almost boiled.' She pushed it, on its trivet, back over the fire.

'While we wait, open your present,' he said.

It was neatly wrapped in brown paper and tied with string; inside, a small box, lined with jeweller's cotton, on which nestled a cameo brooch. He watched her face anxiously. She didn't speak. 'The image is Proserpina, bringing the spring – the flowers falling from her fingers and coming up where she treads.'

'It's beautiful,' she said softly. 'The carving is exquisite.'

'You are Proserpina to me,' he said. 'When I go away from you, the world plunges into winter.'

She looked up. 'It must have cost you a great deal.'

'No,' he said, 'because it's quite old, though it really *is* Italian. I wish I could buy you more expensive things, but you know how wretchedly I'm situated. I'd like to smother you with diamonds—'

She looked stern. 'Now stop it! You're not to talk like that. And how could you think I would prefer a vulgar mass of diamonds to this lovely, delicate thing?'

'At least you could sell the vulgar diamonds and use the money to move to a better place,' he said. His saving grace was that he never took himself too seriously.

'Well, I shall never sell this,' she said, fastening the brooch on her dress. 'Thank you, Richard.' She moved to kiss his cheek in thanks but this time he captured her lips with his. The kiss deepened, until she pulled away, her cheeks flushed. 'The kettle's boiling,' she said, and turned her back on him to make tea.

While she bustled about, he told her about the ball, which had been a triumph, and seemed to have put new heart into Kitty. He saw that she liked hearing about the high life, and went into detail about the arrangements, the ball itself, who had been there, what everyone had been wearing, exactly what there had been for supper, and how the shoot had gone.

'It must all seem very empty and dull when the guests have gone and it's just the family again,' she said.

'Empty, perhaps. Hardly dull, with so much to do about the estate. Giles ought to be the one to be bothered with it, but now they keep coming to me with, "Excuse me, Mr Richard, but have you considered . . ." And, of course, I never, ever have.' She laughed. 'What will you do tomorrow?' he asked, as she came to sit at the table.

'Chloë and I will go to church in the morning. Then after dinner we'll go for a walk. It's nice to walk round the streets just as it's getting dark, and see the rooms inside lit up, and the Christmas trees all decorated. And in the evening, we'll sing carols together. And perhaps play a game of cards.'

'I wish I could be with you,' Richard said.

She hefted the teapot, poured his cup, and placed it, with the milk jug, before him. 'You'll have a much better time with your family,' she said firmly.

'If only you knew my family! Mama and Linda are furious with Giles for not coming home, and Kitty and the girls will be in tears for the same reason. Uncle Stuffy and Uncle Sebastian will fall asleep by the fire, Linda will complain about everything, and there will be a distinct lack of good cheer all round. The only bright spot will be the Boxing Day hunt.' He had picked up the milk jug, and now peered into it. 'What on earth is this?'

She took it from him and looked. 'I have no idea,' she admitted.

'Milk is supposed to be white, not grey-blue, and I'm pretty sure there shouldn't be black bits floating in it.'

'It's probably only soot – a flake of soot,' she said doubtfully.

Richard got out a handkerchief and with a corner of it removed the offending object. 'I sincerely hope so,' he said.

'I wish we could get decent milk, but it seems impossible in London. When I was a girl, every neighbourhood had its dairyman, who kept a few cows, and brought round the fresh milk in the morning. But all the fields have been built over since then. I don't know where the milk comes from now, but it's never much better than this.'

Richard ran his fingers through his hair. 'I want to take you away from all this!' he wailed. 'Perhaps I should leave Ashmore, get myself a job of some sort, so that I could support you. But, then, what on earth could I do? I'm not trained for anything but soldiering, and I can't even soldier any more with my queer arm.'

'All this anguish for a jug of London milk?' she laughed. 'Have your tea without.'

'I intend to.'

'And tell me what you bought for Chloë for Christmas.'

He called on his aunt Caroline in Berkeley Square before heading for the station to go home. He found her in the drawing-room presiding over the full glory of a proper after-noon tea, in the company of his grandmother and – somewhat of a surprise – Mr Joseph Cowling, the industrialist who had married Kitty's best friend Nina.

Kitty's fortune came from jam – Harvey's Jam, sold all over the country in glass jars. Lately, Mr Cowling had provided some of the capital for expanding the business into exporting jam in tin cans. That he had so readily entered into the scheme had been a good sign, for he was a canny and successful businessman in his own field of boots and shoes, and also now art-silk stockings.

'Hullo, sir!' Richard said, shaking his hand heartily. 'I understand from Vogel that our joint business is about to bear fruit – if I may put it that way.'

'Fruit! That's a good one! Ha!' Cowling said, with a bark that served as laughter. 'Aye, the building alterations are finished, the machinery's been delivered, and they'll be installing it in January. We ought to be producing by the end of the month.' He rubbed his dry hands together with a whispery sound. 'I'm very excited about this venture, I can tell you. The export market is limitless, to all intents. We should make a fortune, lad – a fortune each for me and you.'

'Not me personally, of course,' Richard said, wishing it were otherwise. 'Will Mrs Cowling be joining us,' he went on, 'or are you in London *en garçon?*'

'No, on business,' Cowling said. 'Of a sort. I came up to look at houses. Nina's very fond of Market Harborough, but we ought to have a London house so's we can come up whenever we want, for the Season, and shopping and suchlike. I've always been happy enough staying at Brown's, but I don't like for her to stay at an hotel – without it's just the one night on the way to somewhere.'

'You are quite right, sir,' Grandmère said approvingly. 'Hotels are not *comme il faut* for ladies. There is not enough attention paid, these days, to matters of nicety. Come and kiss me, *petit,*' she addressed Richard. He crossed the room to kiss her cheek, and as he straightened she looked sharply at him and tapped his wrist. 'You have been up to something. You smell of mischief.'

'I smell of coal fires, like everyone else at this time of year,' he said. 'Aunt Caroline . . .' He went and kissed her too.

'Sit down and have some tea, dear,' she said.

Richard took a muffin from the dish and sat down with it, while she dealt with the teapot. 'So, did you find anything suitable, sir?' he asked Mr Cowling.

'In fact, I did,' he said, 'and it's just across the other side of this very square. Lady Sotherton's house. It's not big, but it's handsome, and it has a nice double drawing-room for entertaining. I took a fancy to it, so being as I was in the neighbourhood, I took the liberty of popping in on Lady Manningtree to ask her opinion.'

'And I said it would be very nice to have Mr Cowling and dear Nina as neighbours,' Aunt Caroline said, 'and that I'd never heard any bad of the house. I've never been inside – Lady Sotherton's quite old and hasn't entertained for years, as I understand. I think she lives mostly in the country now. But I know one or two houses on that side.'

'Of course, Nina will have to have her say,' Mr Cowling added. 'She has to like it too. She's more fixed ideas about houses and that sort of thing than me. And she likes old places,' he added, half boasting, half apologetic. 'Me, I'd always sooner have everything new, but I know she's not the only one to see the good in old buildings and old furniture – Sheraton and Chippendale and suchlike.'

Richard had stopped listening. He was staring into the milk jug. 'Where does this milk come from, Aunty?' he asked.

'I haven't the least idea,' Aunt Caroline replied. 'Really, Richard, what a very odd question!'

'*Cherchez la femme*,' Grandmère said, her dark eyes bright with amusement. 'When Richard does something *outré*, there is always a woman at the back of it.'

'Is there something wrong with the milk?' Aunt Caroline pursued.

'No,' said Richard. 'That's rather the point.'

'What point?'

'The point that someone somewhere is making good milk available, but not everywhere, and not enough of it.'

Cowling was looking at him with interest. 'There's a lot of folk in London,' he said, 'and I dare say a lot of milk wanted. You've got cows on your estate at Ashmore Castle, I suppose?'

'Yes. I wonder what it would take to marry the two ends,' Richard said.

'Business sense, for one thing,' said Mr Cowling.

'And that's something *you* haven't got,' Aunt Caroline said to Richard, with an air of finality. She wasn't being unkind to him, Richard knew. It was that she did not believe business sense was something a gentleman needed to have, or perhaps even *ought* to have.

'No more I have.' Richard smiled reassuringly at her, and turned the conversation to the prospects of the coming Season and what plans were forming for Rachel's debut. But a glance at Mr Cowling drew a little affirmatory nod from him, a nod that said, *If you've got a business idea, lad, I'm always ready to hear it.*

I'm a long way from that point, Richard thought. But it was good to know there was someone he could go to, if the idea ever matured.

The snow that had been skirting around them for a week finally arrived on Christmas Day. The first flakes fell as the family drove back from church in the morning, and by the time the carriage reached the top of the drive, it was falling thickly. Alice lowered the window, leaned out, and cried excitedly, 'I can't see the horses!'

'Close the window,' the dowager snapped.

'It's like being in fog. If I can't see them, John Manley won't be able to. Suppose we go into the ditch?'

'Behave yourself. Sit down. Manley knows his business.'

The carriage slowed to a crawl. Joe Green, the second coachman, got down and went to lead the horses, to give them courage. Within moments he was as thickly plastered as they were. By the time they reached the Castle and the family scurried to the great door, the whole of the air had been displaced by snow. Glancing upwards briefly, Alice saw the flakes whirling down in multitude, black against the grey, silent and intent. It was exhilarating, but a little frightening.

It didn't make much difference to Christmas Day – an indoor festival once they were back from church. But on Boxing Day they woke to a world transformed, a bumpy blanket of uniform white obscuring every feature of the landscape, and it was clear there would be no hunting that day. The snow had stopped, but the sky was leaden.

'It's a pity about the meet at Lord Shacklock's,' Kitty said, to comfort Alice, 'but I expect it will be gone in a day or two, and there's the whole of the rest of the season to come.'

But by midday the snow had started again.

Giles couldn't say he actually enjoyed the dinner or the ball. At table, he was placed between a French diplomat's wife and an Egyptian diplomat's wife, both of whom spoke nothing but a heavily accented French, and at the ball he had to dance with a series of middle-aged ladies brought to him by his host. The evening had dragged by. It was hot, the music was loud, and there didn't seem to be anything but a very strange champagne to drink. By the time he'd got to bed, he was thirsty, footsore, and his head was splitting.

The rest of his stay, however, was pleasanter. There were a number of parties, but they were smaller and more agreeable and held among the large English-speaking community, and in between he was able to walk and have quiet talks with Giulia. In fact, so comfortable did he find himself that, far from rushing back to the diggings at the earliest opportunity, he saw no reason to leave Cairo until the Antrobuses did, though that placed a strain on his wardrobe. He was obliged to invest in a few changes. Luckily there was a very discreet second-hand clothes shop in a quiet corner of Zamalek, which dealt only in the unwanted clothes of the affluent European, where he was able to get a couple of lightweight suits. Shirts, of course, could be made to measure within hours by a shirt-maker, who attended at Ismailia House at a moment's notice.

Now he was back in the Valley, and as the days passed he felt this was the happiest time of his life. The work was hard but absorbing, there was a constant air of anticipation, which was most stimulating, he had agreeable companions – and he had Giulia.

He had been a lonely child – estranged from his family, of solitary pursuits that did not attract friends – and he had grown up into a lonely man. Now, it was as if he had been given a second chance at a happy childhood. Giulia was the sister he had never had. Linda had always been too difficult, resentful of his privilege as eldest son and disapproving of a nature so different from hers. Rachel and Alice had been too young to be companions, and by the time they were old enough, he was away at school and then university.

Working alongside Giulia by day, sitting by her in the cool of the evening, talking and laughing, he felt a simple content. They shared tastes, activities and ambitions; they had acquaintances in common and shared memories. He never had to explain his meaning, or apologise for his interests. With her, he felt he could just be himself. She liked in him the things he liked in himself – things of the intellect. She was clever and amusing. And she was beautiful, and he liked to look at beautiful things.

Life could not have been better. The work was progressing and interesting finds were being made. They lived a simple life, which suited him better than the formality and luxury expected of an English earl at home. He was quite happy sleeping in a tent, eating plain food, wearing loose, comfortable clothes. And, as a final fillip, the good-natured Antrobus insisted that he continue to share the attentions of Afton. Giles was accustomed to looking after himself when on digs, but a sensible and wily attendant made the difference between just managing and being comfortable. Clothes cleaned, the ever-encroaching sand swept out of the tent and shaken out of the bedding, water for washing brought, snakes and scorpions ejected. And then there were the little luxuries procured: decent smokes, fresh fruit, coffee, an occasional glass of spirits. There were always, of course, locals hanging around the camp trying to sell their wares to the mad Englishmen, but now he had someone to haggle for him.

He did occasionally spare a thought for England, the Castle, his wife and child, and he knew he would eventually have to go back – the dig would naturally be suspended once the weather got too hot. But all that seemed far away when he sat under the luscious stars that spangled the black velvet sky, and chatted so comfortably with his companions and with Giulia. Max Wolsky had a Syrian oud that he played, and sometimes they would sing. Giulia had a sweet voice.

He was utterly content. If only this could go on for ever.

CHAPTER THREE

People get set in their ways, and when Sebastian was staying at Ashmore Castle – which was more often than he was at his own house in Henley – you usually knew where to find him. If he wasn't where the family had gathered, he was generally in the small drawing-room, where he liked to play the piano and think. He rarely went up to the second floor. But on the 2nd of January it was there that he found Dory, the sewing-maid, sitting in the upper linen room repairing a counterpane.

He watched her from the doorway for a moment, before she registered his presence and stood up in a hurry, dropping two skeins of embroidery silk that had been in her lap. Sebastian stooped to retrieve them, she tried to forestall him, and in the flurry dropped her darning mushroom too. Then she desisted, and let him perform the small service for her.

'Thank you,' she said, receiving her own again. She spoke almost without moving her lips, and without looking at him.

'You'll ruin your eyes, sewing in here. The light isn't good enough,' he said.

'It's the snow,' she replied. 'It makes it dark everywhere.' The snow had fallen for two days over Christmas, ceased for a day, then begun again. It had stopped halfway through New Year's Day, and now it was freezing hard. Frozen snow stuck to the outside surface of the panes of the small linen-room window, creating an artificial twilight.

Sebastian regarded her bent head with tenderness and pity. 'You've been avoiding me,' he said.

'No, sir,' she said, still looking down.

'You don't need to do that,' he said. More silence. 'Dory, please look at me.'

Reluctantly she raised her eyes. 'You don't need to avoid me,' he said again. 'I miss you. I miss having you listen to me play. I miss our conversations.'

Her heart was aching. He had refurbished his whole house to her taste, making a nest for her, and then asked her most honourably to occupy it – to marry him. He had offered her permanent security of a sort a servant could rarely dream of. And love as well, and cherishing. But it was the making of the nest that had touched her unbearably. 'It's different now,' she said woodenly.

'Not for me,' he said, and moved a step nearer, put out a hand to touch her cheek. She saw the hurt in his eyes as she moved out of reach. 'Don't shy away from me,' he said. 'I would never force you to do anything you thought was wrong. If you can't marry me, we can still be friends, can't we?'

'No,' she said miserably. 'It can't be like it was.'

'But we're the same two people. With the same feelings.'

'That's why we can't be friends. I have to stay away from you – or I'll have to give my notice, and go away.'

His hand was back by his side. He looked defeated, and suddenly older. 'I never meant to hurt you,' he said.

'You've been nothing but kind, and good, and – and I wish with all my heart . . .' She didn't finish the sentence.

'Could you tell me about it?' he said, after a moment. 'That day, in Henley, you just dropped a bombshell and went away, and you've been avoiding me ever since. Don't you think . . . ?'

She knew he had been going to say, 'Don't you think I deserve an explanation?' She also knew he had not finished the sentence because at the last minute he didn't think he *did* deserve it. He was a man of astonishing modesty. And his modesty laid the onus on her.

'I'll tell you about it,' she said, with a sigh, 'but you must promise never to tell anyone else. If it ever got out – there are those who would use it against me. That James, for instance, if he should ever find out, he would try . . . You'll understand better when I tell you. But my life could be in danger. Please promise me.'

'I promise. I don't understand – but you have my word nothing you say to me will go any further. Please – go on.' He leaned against the door jamb, folding his arms, to let her know she could take her time, that he would listen patiently for as long as she wanted.

She put her sewing things down on the chair, and stood before him with hands clasped, like a good servant waiting for orders. 'I got married when I was very young,' she began at last. 'I was only sixteen. He was handsome and charming – people always liked him straight off. But underneath . . .' she paused a moment, then finished, with a small gesture of the hand '. . . he was bad all through. Like an apple that looks good on the outside, but when you split it, it's full of worms.'

She paused again, for so long this time he felt she needed encouragement to go on. 'Your parents, did they not . . . ?'

'My mother died when I was ten,' she said. 'My father – he was a sick man. I didn't know, of course. He'd brought me up since my mother died but . . . You see, he had a little draper's shop in Cheyne Walk. It was hard work. I took Mother's place and helped him in the shop, but even so . . . He was so tired at the end of the day, too tired to talk. I was just a child still. I didn't know he was dying. I think, now, that he wanted to be sure I was settled before he went, with someone to take care of me. Otherwise, perhaps he'd have seen through Jack.'

'He forced you to marry?' Sebastian asked in concern.

'He would never have done that. I *wanted* to marry – I was mad in love, the way only a girl of sixteen can be. But if Dad hadn't been dying, I think he'd have made me wait, got to know Jack better. And he'd have seen through him in the end. He was a shrewd man, my father, in his health. But he was sick and weary, and afraid for me, and Jack . . . he seemed so plausible.' She was staring at her hands, as her fingers pleated a fold of her apron over and over. Now she looked up. 'I had a dowry, you see. Dad had saved five hundred pounds. That's what Jack was after. Two months after the wedding, Dad was dead, and I was a prisoner.'

She seemed not to want to go on. But she looked past Sebastian, at nothing, frowning, her lips tight, her fingers moving, pleating the fabric with the rhythm of her thoughts. He waited, and at last said, 'Tell me about him. This – Jack.'

'To the customers, he was the gay, handsome man I'd fallen in love with. He could charm the birds out of the trees. Carriage folk came to us, and they loved him. He was respectful and jolly with the gentlemen, and just a little flirty with the ladies. He was a tailor by trade, and he knew his work. He took over the shop next door, and expanded the drapery business into tailoring and repairs. I learned to do the fine work on ladies' garments. I worked in the back – he didn't want me serving in the shop. He hired girls to serve.'

He was beginning to see where this was going. 'These girls?' he began.

She looked up. 'Oh, yes,' she said bitterly. 'A succession of them. They were all mad for him, of course. They were used, cast off and replaced. And I was the prisoner in the back, stitching away, never to be seen, never allowed out, never—' She stopped.

'Did he – hurt you?'

'Not – like that. Not at first. But he paraded his women in front of me, insulted me. He let me know I was not as important to him as they were. I was just the skivvy. Later,

38

when I was a bit older and tried to stand up for myself, that was when I got the back of his hand.'

Sebastian drew a sharp breath, but she went on as if she hadn't heard. 'It was the humiliation as much as the pain. I'd never been struck in my life, never. My father didn't believe in it. Now I was helpless before a man who despised me and showed it. I had no friends, no family. No-one to turn to. I wasn't allowed to speak to anyone. I never left the house. We lived in the rooms behind the shop, and at night, the doors were locked and he kept the key in his pocket. One time I tried to escape out of an upstairs window, and he caught me and beat me. He said if I tried it again he would kill me. He said if I managed to get out, he would hunt me down and kill me. I believed him. If you'd known him – there was no end to his malice.'

'You could have gone to the police?' Sebastian said uncertainly.

She looked at him bitterly. 'You don't know, do you? You don't know policemen. If a man beats his wife, he's just keeping her in order, the way a man ought to do. Women are like dogs – useful, as long as you keep them under control. They would *never* side with a woman against her husband. If I'd gone to the police they'd have delivered me straight back to him with a grin and a wink, and told him to teach me a lesson.'

'Oh, God,' he said softly.

She hunched her shoulders a little, in something that was almost but not quite a shrug. 'I was young, and life is strong in the young, and I survived. But men like him don't stay the same, they get worse, and he did. I think he'd have killed me in the end. But he started to drink more and more, and that was my hope. When he was drunk, he beat me, but eventually he would fall heavily asleep. One night he fell into such a stupor I was able to get the key out of his pocket without waking him.'

39

'You got out?'

'I ran. I was terrified. I didn't know where to go or what to do. I dared not get picked up by the police. I couldn't go to the workhouse for relief because they'd report me to the peelers. I had to hide myself away. I knew he'd come after me, so I hid by day and moved about by night.'

'What did you do? How did you live?'

'I had no money, just the clothes I stood up in. After three days I was starving. Then I had a piece of luck. I met some prostitutes who took pity on me. They bought me a pie and a mug of coffee from a night stall, and told me about a philanthropist lady who was always "bothering them", as they put it, trying to reform them. I think they didn't want me competing with them for customers, but perhaps they were also taking pity on me, being so young. I looked younger than I was. I went to this lady – I was terrified she'd take me back to Jack, but I was desperate. But she was good to me. She believed my story. She gave me a bed for the night, and food, and some clean clothes. In a day or two she got me a position as a between-maid in a big house. There was a group of philanthropist ladies who took on lost girls in that way, rescued them from the street, helped them to start a new life, mostly as servants. And I've been in service ever since.'

She stopped again, and seemed exhausted by her own tale. He didn't want to press her to go on, but at last he said, 'Yet you seem so normal – cheerful, even. How can you be, after such a start?'

'It was hard at first. I had to move often in those early years. I knew he'd come after me. I'd get a hint that he was sniffing around, and move on. Luckily servants in London rarely stay beyond their six months. But the housework was exhausting. Then one day I was on the stairs when my mistress came past. I flattened myself against the wall, as one does, and as she went by, her skirt caught on a loose nail on a banister and tore. She cried out in vexation because it was a favourite gown. She was a good mistress, and without thinking, I said, "Don't worry, madam, I can mend it for you." So then, of course, I had to explain I was experienced in fine work, and she took a chance on me and let me mend it. After that, things took a turn for the better. When I left her service, it was with a reference.' For the first time the frown relaxed a little. She didn't exactly smile, but her voice reflected the improvement in her fortunes. 'I moved up to better positions. Good sewing-maids are valued. Best of all, I got away from London. I was able to choose between opportunities, and I chose country families.'

'You could have been a lady's maid,' Sebastian suggested.

'I could have. But ladies' maids are obliged to travel with their mistresses, and often it's to London. I never wanted to go back there. I knew he would never stop looking for me. And I like my life now. Apart from the constant dread in the back of my mind that he'll find me, I'm happy – yes, in spite of everything. I live in a nice house, I have enough to eat and I can save a little of my wages for a rainy day. I enjoy the work, and I prefer to stay in the background. You see more that way. It's amusing to study humanity. Sometimes you discover interesting people with interesting stories.' She paused, staring musingly at nothing. Then her eyes refocused on him, and she gave a painful small smile. 'I was content with my lot. To be bitter about things would have been to let him win. So I made a life for myself, as best I could. Then I came here to the Castle, and I met you.'

'I never meant to make you unhappy,' he said awkwardly.

'*You* haven't. I shall always be grateful to you, sir—'

'You mustn't call me "sir"!'

'But I must, you see,' she said. 'From now on I must be nothing but a servant. There's no reason our paths should ever cross. I'm never called to the public rooms, and I always use the back stairs. You won't know I'm in the house. We will never speak to each other again.' She forestalled his protest.

41

'That's the only way I can stay here. Otherwise, I shall have to go away and find another position.' She put out an impulsive hand, but pulled it back before it reached him. 'Don't you see? It's too painful otherwise.'

He shook his head, unable to find words to persuade her.

She went on, in a softened voice, 'You gave me something I never thought to have in my life – the admiration of a good man. And I shall cherish that for as long as I live. I shall never forget you, sir, and I'll never stop praying for your happiness. You haven't made me unhappy, never think that. Quite the opposite. I am proud to have been the object of your affection. It's that man who ruined our chances. He blights everything he touches.'

Sebastian thought of making one more plea, but then reflected – plea for what? Things had gone too far for them to return to what there was before. By reaching for more, he had destroyed what he had. Now all he could do was refrain from making her less comfortable.

He bowed his head to her in submission, and said, 'Goodbye, then.' And took himself away, to a life from which the sunshine had gone.

In mid-February the final flight of steps in KV20, one of the tombs at the east end of the Valley of the Kings, was cleared, giving access to the burial chamber. It had been slow work – the infill was so hard that at times it had been impossible to tell if it was rubble or living rock. In this last corridor they had been finding funerary items, mostly stone vases bearing royal cartouches. It had long been believed and hoped that KV20 was the burial place of Hatshepsut, the illustrious female pharaoh, so it was very exciting to discover that some of the cartouches were those of Hatshepsut and her father, Thutmose I.

'I'm so glad we were here to see this,' said Mr Antrobus. 'It would have been dreadful to miss it, but we really have to leave by the end of the month. I have business commitments back home—'

'And I really must spend a few days in Paris on the way, to look at the new fashions,' said Mrs Antrobus.

'But what will you do?' Giles asked Giulia. 'Will you go home? How will you travel?'

Giulia really did not want to leave before the excavation was finished. Mary Arthur, who was listening to the conversation, offered to chaperone her after the Antrobuses left. 'It's no hardship to me to have a female companion,' she said. 'Not to mention the best secretary in Egypt! You can stay with me as long as you like, my dear. And, here's a thought. When we leave, why not come back with us to England for a visit? The London Season will have started, and though I know you're a serious-minded young woman, I'm sure you won't be wholly against a little dancing and a few parties.'

Giulia laughed. 'Not in the least – though I *have* always wanted to spend time in the British Museum. The collection there!'

'You shall – as much time as you like.'

'I'll cable my father, then, but I'm sure he'll agree. He'll be glad such a chance has come my way. You are very kind, madame.'

'Not at all. And tell him, if you please, that we will find some respectable family to escort you when you go back to Italy. There are always people of our acquaintance travelling to Florence. He will want to know that you will be properly looked after. You are, after all, still a very young woman.'

Giles never thought of Giulia in terms of a young woman, but he was too absorbed in the new findings and the prospect of breaking through into the burial chamber to give the statement much thought.

He was forced to think about it a few evenings later, however, when he found himself alone for a moment with Minnie Antrobus, who laid a restraining hand on his arm and said, 'Now, my lord, I really must talk to you, and I hope you will not mind if I am rather frank.'

'I shan't mind, as long as you don't keep calling me "my lord",' said Giles, smiling.

There was no answering smile from Mrs Antrobus. She looked quite grave. 'As you please,' she said. 'Now, I don't want you to be offended, and you might say it's none of my business, but I took that young lady under my wing when I removed her from her home, and I feel responsible for her. I know if it was a daughter of mine, I should want her chaperone to give a hint, no matter who the gentleman in question was.'

Giles looked baffled. 'I'm afraid I haven't the least idea what you're talking about, except that I'm guessing it concerns Giulia. But what have I to do with it?'

She looked stern. 'Surely you must know she's in love with you.'

Giles was taken aback. 'Oh, nonsense!' he said robustly. 'She's just a—'

'She's not a child, she's a grown woman, with a woman's feelings.'

'But I've *known* her since she was a child. She's like a little sister to me,' he protested.

She softened a little. 'Now, I don't accuse you of any wrong-doing, my lord –'

'I'm glad to hear it!'

'– but harm can be done all the same, without intention. You treat her with a friendliness and a lack of formality that can only encourage her. The way you sit and talk with her late into the night, your heads together and your voices lowered: it gives an impression of intimacy that . . . Well, I was quite shocked in the beginning, knowing you to be a married man. Now, I've watched you, and I do you the justice to believe you *don't* mean anything by it. But, land's sakes, man, she's a warm-blooded young female, and she's far from home, and if I don't miss my guess she's had a crush on you for years! A handsome man – and a British lord at that – and he all but makes love to her night after night under the stars! What on earth did you think was going to happen?'

Giles stared at her in dismay. 'Are you entirely serious about this?'

'I'm warning you for her sake, but also for your own good. You're a married man, and you surely don't want to stir up a hornet's nest, besides breaking that little girl's heart.'

'I have no wish to do that,' he agreed helplessly. 'But what must I do?'

'Step back a little. Don't be so friendly. Act a little more formal around her. Stop the night-time tête-à-têtes. Talk to other people more, and her less.' Giles was silent, thinking how much sooner he would always talk to Giulia than anyone else. As if she read his thought, Mrs Antrobus said, 'Yes, I know, it'll be a sacrifice on your part. But you need to untangle yourself from her. I wish to God I could take her with me when I leave, but she is determined otherwise, and she's over age, so I can hardly insist without telling her why. Now, I can't *make* you behave a different way, but I think you're a good man, and I hope you *will*, for her sake. And I hope you're not offended that I spoke up, but it was with the best intentions.'

Giles got to the end of a train of thought, and said, 'I'm not offended. I honour your motives. But I think you're wrong about Giulia. I'm sure she sees me as a brother, just as I see her as a sister, and you probably mistake our fraternal manner towards each other for something else. But I promise you I will be on my guard, and if I detect any . . . *undue* fondness, I shall take steps.'

She looked at him for a long moment, then said, 'I suppose that's the best I can hope for. Thank you, at any rate, for taking it well.' And she went away.

They broke through into the burial chamber the next day. The ceiling had collapsed in one place and there was considerable debris to clear, but thanks to three large supporting columns along the length of the room, it was in fairly good shape. And there was great excitement on discovering *two* sarcophagi, and a canopic chest. Both sarcophagi were open – the lids were lying separately at a distance – and both were empty, which was a disappointment. But one sarcophagus was inscribed for Thutmose I, and the other for Hatshepsut, as was the canopic chest. So wherever the remains might now lie, this was where they had been interred.

There was intense discussion, as to whether one of the female mummies discovered the previous year in KV60 might be Hatshepsut's, perhaps moved to a different burial site by a descendant – it was known that Thutmose III had tried to write her out of history. Or, of course, the mummies might have been victims of ordinary grave-robbers.

There were dozens of vases, bowls, jars, boxes and figurines among the debris, as well as fifteen limestone slabs, designed to line the chamber walls, with inscriptions that needed to be deciphered. At this point the Antrobuses had to take their leave, having at least had the satisfaction of seeing Hatshepsut's sarcophagus. Howard Carter, the leader of the dig, presented them with a faience bowl from the chamber for their local museum as thanks for their contribution.

There was one more surprising conversation for Giles before they left. Mr Antrobus's valet, Afton, came to Giles and begged, with a mixture of embarrassment and determination, to be allowed to stay and enter his service.

'Mr Antrobus is a good master, my lord, but he's going back to America, and I've got such a longing in my bones to go home. You did tell me you were without a man at present. I promise you wouldn't be disappointed, my lord, if you was to give me a chance.'

'And I suppose as soon as you land in England you'll be off like a hare and I'll be without a man again,' Giles said.

Afton looked hurt. 'Is that what you think, my lord? That

I'm just using you for a ticket home? I'm a valet, my lord, that's my job and my calling, and if I can't work for you I'll work for someone else. But I'd sooner it was you, my lord. I think I know how to make you comfortable, and I'm a sticker, my lord, I'd never leave until you made me. But I can't *make* you believe me, my lord – only ask you to.'

Giles was rather touched by his passion. He thought how much his comfort would be enhanced by having this lively little man as his attendant instead of weepy old Crooks or sour, slit-eyed Hook. 'But what about Mr Antrobus? It would be dastardly to steal his servant, especially when he's been so kind to me. And if you're a sticker, why aren't you sticking with him?'

'I discussed it with him, my lord, of course I did, before I came to you, as was only fair and right. And I told him some time ago that I wanted to go home and he said he understood and would let me go as soon as I made arrangements. So there'll be no hard feelings, my lord, I promise you, or I would never have presumed to mention it.'

'Very well. I'll talk to him myself, and if he really doesn't mind, I'd be happy to give you a position.'

Afton grinned. 'Thank you, my lord. You won't regret it, I swear.'

'Just one thing,' Giles said. Afton turned back enquiringly. 'Your name isn't *really* Afton, is it? I keep thinking about "Sweet Afton", which my nanny used to sing to me.'

'It's all the name I've got, my lord. I was left in a box, as a baby, outside Whitechapel Workhouse, and since nobody ever claimed me the workhouse superintendent give me my names. Stanley, after the explorer, because he was her hero, and Afton, because it was her favourite song. She was a Scottish lady by birth, my lord. Thought the world of Rabbie Burns. I'm surprised she didn't call me Robert Burns, really, but Stanley Afton it was.'

'Very good names they are, too,' Giles said, and thought

that one day, he must hear the rest of the story. From Whitechapel Workhouse to New York gentleman's gentleman was quite a step.

In England, some said it was the hardest winter they remembered. Snow and freezing temperatures kept the family trapped in the house. All Kitty's plans for entertainment were scuppered, and there was no hunting. By dint of hard labour, a circuit was dug out and kept clear in the nearest paddock and straw was laid down, to give the horses walking exercise. It was laborious and time-consuming, and Alice gave many daytime hours to helping the grooms by leading a bored and restless horse round and round in the icy air. For her, it was better than frowsting indoors all day. She missed riding, and probably felt the curtailment of her freedom more than anyone else in the house.

When the grooms were not exercising the horses, they were 'volunteered' to help the tenants with their stock. Having the cattle inside meant extra work with feeding and mucking out. The sheep stayed out, but had to have fodder taken to them, and sometimes after a snowfall they needed to be dug out.

At the end of February and into March, all hands were required to help with the lambing, building shelters with hurdles and straw bales and assisting with difficult births. Richard threw himself into these tasks and found a satisfaction he had not expected, which kept his mind occupied and won him respect with the tenants and labourers.

In mid-February, when the snowfalls ceased for a time and it froze hard, the sun came out, glittering on the cruel white world from a sky of acid blue. The dowager, Maud, seized the opportunity to escape to London, taking Rachel with her. The Season had not yet started, but there were plans to devise and clothes to have made. It required a great deal of labour on the part of a large number of men to clear the route down the hill to the village, but she never gave a thought to work when she was paying for it – or, in this case, Kitty was paying for it.

Linda joined the escaping party – uninvited, but if she had waited to be invited she would never have gone anywhere – and Cordwell, with the air of a scolded dog, started the long journey back to Dorset. Their children they left behind. Sebastian departed the next day, saying he would call on a friend in London before going back to his own house.

With numbers so depleted, and no entertaining in prospect – hunting was still impossible and travel between villages difficult – the house slumped into a semi-doze. Kitty discussed future refurbishments with Mrs Webster, drew up ambitious plans for the gardens she wanted to create, and dreamed about Giles coming home.

Alice, feeling sorry for them, spent some of her time with Arabella and Arthur. She had never had much instruction herself, and regretted it, so she tried to lighten their ignorance a little bit every day, with old schoolbooks of her own, and whatever she could find in the library that was at all suitable. They were grateful for the attention, if not the requirement to concentrate, and Aunt Alice became their favourite person. She didn't exactly enjoy their company, but she felt she was being useful; though it did occur to her that if she didn't eventually marry anyone, she might really end up as a governess. It was not a prospect to entice; it almost made her feel that marriage would be preferable.

The unhappiest person at the Castle was the former valet Hook, now footman James again. With no entertaining, he hadn't enough to do to take his mind off his wrongs. He had been demoted, and not even to *first* footman, which was his right by seniority and training, but fourth, below even Cyril, whom he himself had trained. It was humiliating. He would have believed Mr Moss was punishing him, if it weren't that Moss was an old fool incapable of doing anything but doddering from one routine task to another.

He wanted to lash out – he wanted to hurt someone. He

49

needed a scheme to occupy him. He needed to get one over on somebody to restore his faith in himself. He started up a card school in the hayloft, through which he could fleece the grooms and some other local idiots of their pay, but that was not enough. He tried to seduce the new maids, but they didn't respond to him. The only maid who would 'let him' was Mabel, and he'd had her long ago. It took care of his carnal needs, but it wasn't a challenge.

'I'm going to break out,' he warned his reflection, as he shaved in the morning. 'Something's coming. I can feel it.' His reflection looked back through slitted eyes, darkly glittering and dangerous. *Pretty good*, he thought admiringly. *Sinister, even.*

Nobody got the better of Sid Hook for long.

Moss was standing on a painted and gilded royal barge floating down the Nile. The little housemaid, Ada, was gazing up at him in adoration as he pointed out the wonders of the scenery and explained everything to her. The flooding of the Nile, the building of the Pyramids, the making of papyrus, the working of the Archimedes Screw – words flowed from him in a stream of dazzling eloquence, and the more he spoke, the more she adored him. Her face turned up to him like a flower on the delicate stem of her long, white neck, and he stooped, slowly, slowly, to place a kiss upon the sweet rosebud of her lips—

His forehead gently struck the open book on his table, and he straightened up hastily, to hear the unwelcome voice of James saying sarcastically, 'Your eyes hurting, Mr Moss? You don't need to look at the book that close, do you? P'raps you need a magnifying-glass.'

James was lounging in the doorway surveying him with a sneering smile. The *A to Z of Universal Knowledge* lay open at Cleopatra, one of Moss's favourite topics, and he had evidently dozed off while reading. Little Ada was not in the room with him, alas. She had only been part of the dream.

He pulled on dignity like a mantle. 'I was just resting my eyes for a moment,' he said sternly. 'I wasn't asleep.'

'Course not,' James said, with what sounded like a snigger.

Moss drew towards him the other open book on the table, which happened to be the cellar book – pulled it over the top of the *A to Z* and pored over it with a magisterial forefinger. 'What is it you want?' he demanded, not looking at James. 'I'm busy. Some of these older vintages need drinking up and new laid in. I wish his lordship would come back. What do you *want*?' he concluded irritably, as James seemed to be whistling under his breath.

'I was thinking I could help you, Mr Moss,' James said. 'Seeing as there's not much on at the moment, till the snow clears and we start entertaining again.'

'Help me with what?'

'Well, rearrange the cellar, and check everything against the cellar book, maybe,' said James. 'You just said some old stuff needs drinking up. And there'll be gaps that need filling. Do a thorough check. Make lists. You could have it all ready for his lordship when he gets here.'

Moss was indignant. 'What do you think I do all the time, every day? Keeping the cellar book is one of the butler's most important responsibilities. In fact, the word "butler" comes from—'

'Oh, give it a rest!' James muttered.

Moss turned red. '*What* did you say?'

'I said, maybe I could give you a rest. If you give me the keys I could do it for you.' If he had the keys, he could rearrange things so as to liberate some bottles, which he could then sell, and alter the cellar book to cover the disappearances. Or, better still, make it look as though Moss hadn't kept the book properly. 'You're looking tired these days, Mr Moss, if you don't mind my saying so.'

'I *do* mind, thank you very much! I am *not* tired, and no-one but me will touch the cellar. The cellar keys never leave my person.'

James shifted his weight to the other side. 'Well, the silver, then. It's a long time since there was an inventory took, and I noticed last time that some pieces were in the wrong place. Those new young boys put things away careless. Now, we could take everything out, make an inventory, clean it all, and put it all back in a better order, so the things that are used a lot are easy to get at.'

And if he didn't manage to snaffle something pocket-sized and valuable in the process, his name wasn't Sid Hook. And the best of it would be, if he did the writing down as well (and trust him for that! "You call it out, Mr Moss, and I'll write it down – you're the one who knows what everything is!"), he could miss it off the list so it would never be officially missing.

He smiled ingratiatingly at Moss. 'That'd be a good use of our time, wouldn't it? Better than having me standing around doing nothing.'

Moss found James's smile unnerving. It was probably only because he had just been dreaming about the Nile, but it put him in mind of a crocodile. But Moss did love turning out cupboards and taking inventories. It was a way of imposing order on an imperfect world.

'Very well,' he said. 'We'll start tomorrow. You can get young Wilfrid to help.'

That wouldn't suit James's plans. 'Oh, I don't think so, do you, Mr Moss? Those greasy fingers all over everything? And he's a real dropper. Dropped the sugar bowl only yesterday, sugar all over everywhere, and you know how that attracts the ants. He'd drop some fine bit of plate and put a dent in it. Much better it's just you and me, men who are trained to handling good stuff.'

'Yes, you're right,' Moss said. 'Some of the older pieces

are worn quite thin. They're delicate. Very well, we'll do it ourselves. Thank you, James.'

He said it as a dismissal, but James chose to interpret it otherwise. 'No, thank *you*, Mr Moss,' he said, with a bow that was not entirely ironic.

CHAPTER FOUR

There was very little snow in Market Harborough that winter, and the hunting season had gone ahead without let. It also went ahead without Nina, whose husband had forbidden her until the shocking episode of her riding astride had been forgotten.

'Come the summer . . .' Mr Cowling had hinted, half apologetically.

Nina was quick to pin him down. 'You'll let me ride in the summer?'

'If the gossip dies down, I'll buy you a horse and you can go on quiet hacks like a proper genteel lady.'

'And hunting next winter?'

'We'll see.'

It was the best she could hope for. It was galling to see her friend Bobby dressed for the hunt, mounted on one of her fine animals, going off from meets. Bobby had not yet got up the courage to hunt astride. Her husband, the mild and gentle Aubrey, had had reservations. 'I fear the world is not yet ready for the sight of Lady Wharfedale leading the field in trousers,' he had drawled. Bobby told Nina that Aubrey so rarely put his foot down one was bound to obey when he did. She declared herself disappointed, but in truth, she was quite glad of the excuse not to expose herself all alone. *Next* winter, she thought, *with* Nina, and perhaps Lady Clemmie . . . There was safety in numbers – and effective protest, too.

Despite not hunting, Nina had enjoyed the season. There were parties, dances and dinners every week, and though Mr Cowling had often been absent on business, he had always encouraged her to accept a solo invitation if it came. Her wardrobe had kept up with her social engagements: Mr Cowling was always eager for her to order new dresses – in truth, more often than she really wanted them. He loved her to be decked out in finery, and never came back from a business absence without a present for her: a fine pair of gloves or new silk stockings at the very least. More often it was a bolt of silk to have made up, or a fur piece, or jewellery. He had a good eye for jewellery, and loved to see her sparkle. Her collection grew to the point where Mrs Deering, her housekeeper, urged her to ask the master to have a safe installed. Mr Cowling saw the wisdom of it, and it was done.

Nina's new friendship with Lady Clemmie Leacock was flourishing. Clemmie was educated and amusing, and had a keen interest in the advancement of women's rights. She held several meetings during the winter, with an invited speaker, often down from London, to talk about the franchise or another current preoccupation. Mr Cowling encouraged her friendship with Clemmie, whom he saw as a very proper, genteel lady of the old school, just the sort of friend he wanted for his wife, rather than that harum-scarum Bobby Wharfedale. He never attended Clemmie's meetings and Nina never mentioned specifically what was discussed. She suspected he wouldn't be comfortable with her being exposed to yet more revolutionary ideas.

Still, Nina did feel a little wistful one fine sharp morning when she stood in the market square to watch the Fernie meet. Her terrier, Trump, strained at the leash, his whole body aquiver with excitement at the smells and sounds and movement.

'I know how you feel,' Nina told him, giving him a tug, 'but if I have to behave myself, so must you.'

'They say talking to oneself is the first sign of madness,' said a voice just beside her. She turned to see Bobby's brother, Adam Denbigh, smiling at her wryly. 'Though I've always thought,' he went on, 'that it merely shows superior taste.'

'Adam?' she exclaimed.

'Nina?' he exclaimed back, in the identical tone.

'I'm surprised to see you,' she explained hastily. 'I thought you were hunting. Bobby said you were going out with her.'

'So I was,' he said. 'But my first horse has an overreach, my second horse has a cough, my groom has a cold in the head and is, frankly, quite a disgusting sight, and my valet has discovered a split in the seam of my favourite breeches, which he ought to have noticed when I last took them off, but didn't. I am pondering whether or not to dismiss him – but he does have a way with boots. So, all in all, it became simply too much effort, and Mr Denbigh will *not* be hunting this morning. You will see a notice pinned to the gates of Welland Hall, as they do it at Buckingham Palace when the King is unwell.'

'I'm sure you could have managed somehow,' Nina said reproachfully, for it seemed an awful waste when she would have loved to go. 'Your second-best breeches and a borrowed horse?'

'Perhaps it was a trifle *se couper le nez pour vexer le visage*,' he said languidly, 'but, though I fear it will shock you to learn it, Mrs Cowling, even I am not perfect.'

'Yes, I am shocked,' Nina said, enjoying Adam's nonsense (and he was not the harder to talk to for being extremely handsome). 'But it shows a nobility in you, to come to the meet when you can't hunt.'

'I could say the same of you.'

'I was walking Trump anyway, so I thought I might as well come this way as another.'

The hunt was moving off now, and they were silent a moment, watching, until the last horses and the foot-followers

56

had disappeared down the street. Then Adam said, 'It's a cold day to be standing about. May I escort you to the Copper Kettle for a restorative cup of cocoa?'

Cocoa became instantly the thing Nina wanted most in the world; but she hesitated. Adam smiled knowingly, watching her expression. 'You are wondering whether it's quite proper for a married lady to visit a café with a single gentleman, even if he is the acme of respectability and the brother of her best friend to boot. Or – wait! – perhaps you just don't like me enough?' He buried his head in his hands. 'The humiliation! Oh, my wounded feelings!'

She knew he was joking, but still she hastened to reassure him. 'Of course I like you! But I *was* wondering if Mr Cowling . . . You see, he *is* very careful about appearances.'

'"And he *does* disapprove of you, Mr Denbigh,"' he supplied, imitating her tone.

It was true: her husband thought Adam Denbigh rackety. She blushed. 'Not at all,' she muttered.

'My dear child, a married man is suspicious of any unmarried man who comes within twenty feet of his wife, no matter how honourable his intentions. Be he as chaste as ice, as pure as snow, he shall not escape calumny.'

'I'm sure you are all those things, but isn't it wrong to disobey your husband?' she said.

'It depends on whether his orders are wrong in the first place.'

It was a shocking thing to hear said aloud, even if Nina had thought it about the ban on her riding. There had been hints in Lady Clemmie's meetings of something along the same lines: what right did men have to dictate to women what they might or might not do? It had not been said in so many words, but there had been an unspoken undercurrent. And the answer, of course, seemed to be that since women could not earn their own living, but were dependent on the man who kept them, they must obey. However much they sometimes disliked it.

'You mustn't say such things to me, Mr Denbigh,' she said.

He repented. 'No, I mustn't. I apologise.' He sounded sincere, though she still looked at him doubtfully. 'Well, let us stand out here in the cold and talk. No-one can suspect any wrong-doing when we are subjecting ourselves to this cutting wind. They will see how unattractive I look with a red nose and you will be quite safe from gossip.'

She laughed unwillingly. 'Your nose isn't red. But it is too cold to stand still. I shall walk home, and you can accompany me to the gate if you like.'

He fell in beside her. 'You are still coming to our ball this evening? Bobby says Mr Cowling is away but you will come alone.'

'He's had to go to Leicester to visit his factories, and won't be back for a few days, but he did tell me I should go. He doesn't want me to miss all the fun.'

'And you dine there first,' he said. 'I think Bobby has paired us for dinner – oh, the inestimable value of the unattached man! I could dine out every day of the week, you know, just for the purpose of making numbers even.'

'I don't believe for a moment that Bobby cares about even numbers.'

'Well, on the whole, you're right, she doesn't. But every now and then an impulse comes over her to be elegant. At all events, I shall take you in to dinner, and talk to you agreeably – though not *too* agreeably, given that all eyes will be upon us—'

'Fool! Of course they won't!'

'That's better. I prefer "fool" to "Mr Denbigh". But "Adam" is best of all. Makes it sound as if we were in the nursery together, and nothing could be more innocent than that.'

'If we'd been in the nursery together I should call you "Kipper".'

'Only Bobby calls me that. My other sisters call me "Oh,

Adam!" in tones of disapproval and despair. But to resume – I shall take you in to dinner, and may I hope for the honour of the first dance?'

'With pleasure,' Nina said. 'I don't suppose anyone else will ask me.'

He sighed. 'You do know how to wound a man's vanity, don't you?'

'What have I said? What should I have said?'

'That although you will be besieged by requests from every man in the room, you will spurn them all to dance with me.'

'Fool!' she said again, laughing.

Nina had had a new evening gown at Christmas, a present from Mr Cowling, which she had worn only once. Having been poor most of her life, she still had a mental reservation about wearing her 'best' things unless the occasion was exceptional, something she tried to laugh herself out of, now she was married to an immensely rich man. *What are you saving it for, silly girl?* she asked herself, and told Tina to put it out. It was of celadon-green silk tulle, with a three-quarter overdress of black lace, the scalloped hem edged with black net and weighted with jet beads. The sleeves were full to the elbow, with tight-fitting black lace cuffs from elbow to wrist. The contrast of pale green and black was striking, she thought – almost daring. Mr Cowling had said she looked radiant in it. With it she wore her emerald necklace and spray.

Bobby, in her usual blue, greeted Nina with a kiss and moaned, 'You look far too good for our humble ball. We don't even have any royalty coming! The best I can put up is the lord lieutenant.'

Nina's eyes widened. 'But he's a duke!'

'Are you impressed?' Bobby laughed. 'You, whose husband knows the King?'

'Well, I'm glad I wore my new gown,' Nina said. 'Mr

Cowling will be sorry to have missed meeting the lord lieutenant.'

'I expect he knows him too. He knows everyone,' Bobby sighed. 'You're so lucky.'

'How do *you* know him?'

'He and Aubrey were at school together.'

Nina laughed. 'You're such a humbug!'

Bobby grinned. 'Well, Rutland *is* rather a poppet. And much more fun than his predecessor. Now, promise me you'll dance every dance!'

'That rather depends on my being asked, doesn't it?' Nina said.

But she was in no danger of sitting out. She danced the first with Adam, then was immediately claimed by Lord Foxton who, despite being over sixty, was a determined flirt and an amusing companion. She was then asked by the duke, who was very agreeable, and then there was a sort of scuffle for her hand between Lord Belton and Johnny Faversham, who were both cut out by Sir Bradley Graham, the local MP, while they were arguing.

'You seem to be setting the room by the ears, my dear,' Sir Bradley said. 'I must say I'm not surprised.'

'*I* am. It's very silly,' she said firmly. 'I think it must be the Wharfedales' wine going to their heads. There's nothing special about me.'

He smiled. 'A sentiment a gentleman is bound by honour to disagree with – but in this case I am happy to be able to do it with sincerity. You are a very lovely young woman, and that gown sets you off to perfection.'

'I'm sure you're flattering me, but thank you.'

'Mr Cowling is away on business, I gather?'

'Yes, it does call him away a good deal.'

'Hm,' said Sir Bradley. 'If an old man might presume to offer advice, beware of Mr Faversham. He has a reputation as a rake. And Lord Belton, though married, is not much better. Forgive me, but you are still very young. They make themselves agreeable, but they will not enhance your standing.'

'Surely they must be respectable, if the Wharfedales invited them?' she said uncertainly.

'Indeed. But there are degrees of respectability. However, I am being impertinent in thrusting my advice upon you. Please pay no attention.'

But she did, and perhaps laughed a little less and romped a great deal less than she otherwise might have, being surrounded all evening by flirts determined to flatter and charm her. She was still only nineteen, and though education had perhaps made her older than her years, she had not had a great deal of fun since she married, and had been left alone a good deal. It was only natural that she should want to enjoy herself, and should respond to the attentions of amusing men.

Still, it was a relief when Adam claimed her for the last dance before supper, and she could relax, as with a brother.

He seemed more serious than usual. 'You are extremely popular this evening,' he remarked.

She looked up at him. 'Have I done wrong? I was trying to be seemly, but they try so hard to make me laugh. And they are all so ridiculous when they flirt.'

'You find flirts ridiculous? Well, that's reassuring, at least. And saves me from having to.'

'I didn't know you did,' she said, wide-eyed.

'Oh, cruel! Have I wasted all my best ploys on you?'

'It seems you have. Now you will have to talk to me sensibly instead.'

So he did, discussing impressionism and the difference between Manet and Monet, and she relaxed further. By the time the music stopped, she was quite comfortable. He was to take her down to supper, so she unhooked her train and tucked her hand under his arm. He said, 'Let's wait a moment for the crush to ease,' and stepped back from the doorway with her. When the crowd was almost gone, he said, 'Before we go down, let me show you that Monet I was telling you about. It's on the next landing upstairs – one of his paintings of his garden. You will see what I meant about the brush-strokes.'

She thought nothing of it, and allowed him to conduct her up the stairs, but when they turned the corner of the landing he suddenly took her into his arms and kissed her.

He was a young, handsome man and she liked him, and it was perhaps understandable that for an instant she did not struggle. Her body was starved of affection, and responded automatically; her lips softened for his. It was when his own kiss became more urgent that she came to her senses. She pulled back, and struggled out of his embrace. 'No,' she cried.

'No?' he repeated, with a wry lift of the eyebrow.

She blushed. 'How could you? You – you took advantage of me!'

'Nina, my dear, your lips say "no" now, but a moment ago they spoke a different message.'

'It's wrong. You know it's wrong.'

'But you want to.'

She began to say *no*, but stopped, then shook her head, staring at the floor. She knew she should flounce away from him, but she felt confused and unhappy.

Sensing it, he spoke gently. 'I'm what you need, Nina. And I can give it to you safely. It would be our secret. No-one would ever know. You cannot believe I would ever allow harm to come to you. In the time I've known you, you have become very dear to me. If you weren't married, I would—'

She looked up sharply, and he stopped. 'But I *am* married,' she said.

He took her hands. 'When an old man marries a beautiful young girl, what does he expect?'

She pulled her hands away. 'Don't *say* that! You don't know him. He's kind, and good, and—'

'Does he make your heart race? Does he fill your thoughts? Does he haunt your dreams? Does he make you feel like this?' He raised his hand and cupped her cheek, then trailed his fingers softly over her lips.

She caught his hand, pushed it back against his chest. 'Stop it,' she said. Her body might react to him, but she had a defence he did not know about. There *had* been someone who made her heart race. He had filled her thoughts and, despite anything she could do, he still haunted her dreams. She tried to sound wryly matter-of-fact. 'You're just amusing yourself. You know you don't really love me.'

'But I could,' he said seriously. 'I so easily could. And I hate to see you wasted, Nina. You should be loved and caressed and made to sing like a happy bird. Your life should bloom with happiness and satisfaction. You should walk about with a little secret smile on your lips, remembering the night just past and looking forward to the night to come. Let me do that for you. Let me make you happy.'

'We must go down,' she said. 'We'll be missed.'

'Think about it,' he said. 'Just consider it. I will wait for you.'

She was angry now at his lack of repentance. 'What would Bobby say if she heard you?'

'She would be in full agreement,' he said.

'Then she would be as wrong as you.' She turned away.

He fell in beside her, still unshaken. 'Just remember I am here whenever you want me. And take my arm on the stairs. It would be held much against me if you were to stumble.'

She took his arm – it was difficult to descend a staircase in a long gown – but said, 'No more of this, please. You must stop.'

'Consider me stopped,' he said; but added quietly, 'For now.'

And at the bottom of the staircase, she almost walked into Decius Blake. Her husband's secretary and right hand. She met his eyes with a startled look, and blushed deeply.

He regarded her with an expression so neutral it was as good as a rebuke. 'Mrs Cowling,' he said.

She was angry with herself for blushing; she felt dishevelled, though she knew she was not. *One kiss, and that not even wanted by her!* But what must Decius be thinking, seeing her come down the stairs with Adam when she should have been in the supper room?

'What are you doing here?' she asked, pulling her hand away from Adam's arm.

Adam responded to Decius's glance with a slight nod, but he said nothing.

'Mr Cowling asked me to come back. He felt guilty about your having to come to the ball alone. He thought that if I could get here in time, I could at least take you in to supper, and look after you for the rest of the ball.'

'Mrs Cowling has had no shortage of partners so far,' Adam said. 'I'm sure she will not need to fall back on your services after supper.'

Decius did not look at him. 'And I'll escort you home afterwards,' he went on, as though there had been no interruption.

'You are – he is very kind,' Nina faltered.

'He thinks about you all the time,' Decius said, and for the first time there was a hint of reproach in his voice. He offered his arm. 'If I may?'

'*I* am taking Mrs Cowling in to supper,' Adam said.

'Don't you think you've done enough?' Decius said quietly. He looked at Nina, his arm insistently crooked. 'Mrs Cowling?'

She took it obediently and, without looking at Adam, allowed herself to be walked away. At the next landing she stopped and said earnestly, 'Decius, nothing happened. I promise you.'

'Didn't it?' He looked at her sadly. 'Life is full of pitfalls. Every journey is beset by highwaymen. You have to be on your guard.'

'You think Adam Denbigh is a highwayman?' She wanted to laugh at the idea, but felt much closer to crying.

'It's easy to think a person like him is incapable of deep feelings,' Decius said. She knew he didn't mean Adam. 'Perhaps it seems almost a comic idea. But he has a heart that could so easily be broken by you. He loves you, more than he can possibly express.'

Nina took a deep, trembling breath, and said the thing she had never meant to say out loud. 'But I don't love *him*.'

There was a silence in which the words seemed to circle like black, deathly birds, looking for somewhere to settle. Where they landed, leaves would wither, grass would die, darkness would fall. She felt release, relief, and a deep sorrow. There was no going back from here.

Decius looked at her steadily, and in his eyes were understanding, and pity. 'But you married him.'

'Yes,' she said. That was the contract. There was no getting out of it.

Richard entered the library, and found Adeane, the bailiff, and Markham, the agent, waiting for him. Tiger and Isaac, Giles's dogs, pushed past him and went to do the honours, tails swinging. When Giles was away they usually followed Alice, but she had gone out that morning, so they'd attached themselves to Richard as the next best thing.

'You're looking unusually grave this morning, gentlemen,' Richard said.

'Bad news, sir,' said Markham. 'Ezra Bunce is dead. He passed away last night.'

'Bunce? That's Hundon Farm, isn't it? What did he die of?'

'Pneumonia, sir. He'd been ailing some time. Got soaked through going out in the snow to see to his cattle, caught a cold and went downhill from there.'

'Well, I'm sorry to hear it. Do we send something to the widow?'

'Taken care of, sir,' said Markham. 'A note of condolence and a ham will be sent over today. And if you should feel able to attend the funeral, it will be well taken.'

'Let me know when it is. And I must remember to call in next time I'm passing. What happens to the tenancy? Do I remember a son?'

'His younger son John, sir,' Adeane said. 'The older boy, Tom, and his wife both died of a fever a few years back. They left a little daughter. Bunce and his wife have been bringing her up.'

'Yes, I remember seeing a little child when we visited the house. What a sad thing.'

'Yes, sir. It was a tragedy for the Bunces, because Tom was a natural-born farmer and keen to take over, but John – well, his heart's never been in it. Now he wants to quit and go and get a job in Aylesbury. They're taking on men at the brewery, and it's good money.'

'Shorter hours, too, I imagine,' Richard said. 'No getting up at dawn to milk the cows, eh? So who takes over? Mrs Bunce – the widow?'

The men exchanged a glance, and it was Markham who answered. 'I doubt she'd be able to manage, even if she wanted to. But when I spoke to John this morning he said his mother was to go with him to Aylesbury – and the little girl – and he'd get a place for them all together.'

'He's always been a mother's boy, has John Bunce,' said Adeane, 'and he's very fond of the child. Never wanted to get married himself, so I dare say it makes him a kind of family that he wouldn't have otherwise.'

'But it leaves us with a problem,' Richard said. 'Or does it? Can you find another tenant?'

Another exchanged look, and Markham said, 'The difficulty is, sir, that the farm's in poor shape. Good tenants are hard enough to find at the best of times, but for Hundon's . . . I'm afraid we shall have to take it back in hand, and improve it before we can let it again.'

Richard's gaze sharpened. 'But it *is* capable of improvement?'

'Oh, yes, sir,' said Adeane. 'It's good enough land at heart, but it'll take money. And then it's a problem of making enough profit from it to be worthwhile. A lot of farms,' he added gloomily, 'are being left unworked for that very reason.'

Richard grinned. 'Well, it seems as though the gods are smiling on me.'

'Beg pardon, sir?'

'This comes just at the right time. I have an idea I'd like to try, and now Fate has presented me with a farm on which to try it.'

'And what idea's that, sir?' Adeane asked indulgently.

'Milk,' said Richard. 'No, hear me out! I've been in London, and seen how hard it is to get good fresh milk. In some parts, the stuff is hardly drinkable – thin and grey and full of bits. Bits of what I don't like to know! Now, London is barely an hour away by train. If we can get the milk promptly from farm to station and arrange the distribution at the other end we could make a fortune. Everyone wants good milk, and no-one's providing it. The market is wide open.'

'Interesting idea,' Markham said. 'But could you produce enough from Hundon's to make it worth while?'

'Not from poor old Bunce's twelve bony cows,' Richard said. 'My idea is to clear the pastures, expand and improve the herd, raise the quality of the milk, and then, once we've got the thing established, bring in all the other farmers along the valley. They would keep the cows, produce the milk, then we'd collect it along with our own and send it up to London for the capital's breakfast tables. "Ash Valley Milk – the Londoner's Choice!" What do you think?'

'You're talking about a very long-term project,' Markham said. 'This can't happen in months – it will take years. And you'd have to have a standard quality of milk.'

'I don't see that as a problem,' Richard said. 'At the

67

moment, each farmer just keeps a couple of cows for the house, but if you told him he could make a profit out of milk if he increased his stock and followed some rules, well, he'd jump at the chance, wouldn't he?'

'I know some as would,' Adeane said. 'But there's others that'd want some convincing. Farmers don't like change. They want to do things the way their fathers and grandfathers did.'

'But farmers have sons who will be taking over from them one day,' Markham said. 'And they'll want to take over something that has a future.'

'Exactly. This *is* the future.' Richard smiled engagingly at them. 'I'm thinking – Dairy Shorthorns. I've looked into it, and they're hardy, productive, and they give high-quality milk. We encourage our farmers to buy more cows, and we keep a top-quality bull to serve them. We oversee conditions and practices, and build up a sort of co-operative herd. London will clamour for our fresh, clean, creamy milk. No fine lady will brook anything else on her tea-table.'

Adeane was shaking his head. 'They'll never go for it, sir. It's not farming the way they know it. It more like . . . manufacturing. They won't like it.'

'I think the younger ones might take to the idea,' said Markham. 'But it'll need a lot of investment – on their part as well as on ours.'

'But think of the returns! For them as well as us.'

'And there's the business side of it. Collecting the milk and getting it to the station – well, that's just a matter of organisation, I suppose, but it'll need some thinking about. And then the distribution in London – that's not an area of commerce we know anything about.'

'Fortunately, I know a very canny businessman . . .'

'Someone in the dairy trade?' Markham said hopefully.

'No, but business is business, and what he doesn't know, he'll know how to find out. After all, jam wasn't his area of expertise, but he jumped on board our expansion there.'

Markham's brow cleared. 'You're thinking of Mr Cowling?'

'Indeed. He's my sister-in-law's best friend's husband, which makes him practically my brother-in-law, and one should always make use of family connections.'

'What's in it for him, sir, giving away all this advice?' Adeane asked suspiciously.

'Well, if he thinks the idea has possibilities – which I'm convinced it has – he'll probably want to come in with us as a partner.'

'It wouldn't be a bad thing to have someone with some business experience involved,' said Markham. 'But first we need to talk through the whole scheme, work out some details, and put something down on paper.'

'You're in favour, then?' Richard said hopefully.

'It's worth looking into,' Markham said cautiously.

'I'm not. It'd be throwing good money after bad,' said Adeane.

'If we've got to take the farm back in hand anyway, we might as well be bold and try to make something of it,' Richard said. 'And it won't be your money that's thrown at it, Adeane, my good fellow, so you needn't look so glum.' He strode to the desk, pulled out a sheet of paper, and headed it in big capitals, ASH VALLEY DAIRY COMPANY. He looked up at the other two men and grinned. 'It's rather fun being in at the birth of something, isn't it?'

The thaw came. Slowly at first, but increasingly rapidly, the white blanket retreated, revealing a world almost forgotten, a world of greens and browns, grateful to the eye starved of colour for so many weeks. The grim silence that had gripped the land relaxed, and suddenly there was sound and movement: drips and trickles, little spurts and forces, gurglings and chucklings, as the great mass of water held up in the snow came back to life and rushed gladly on its way. The two little brooks, the Shel and the Wade, that ran down the hillside swelled into streams and chattered self-importantly as they bounded down to join the Ash at Watersmeet. The ditches filled and overflowed; the tracks flooded and became rivers; leaves and twigs and other debris were borne along, spinning. The Ash swelled and ran fast, crowding under the arches of the stone bridge, tugging impatiently at tethered boats and tree roots as if suddenly realising it was late for its appointment with the sea. The level in the Carr rose, and its normally still water ran and flowed. There was water everywhere, vast sheets reflecting the sky. Life was starting up again, for water is life, and spring could not be delayed for ever.

Kitty stood at the window for hours, watching the countryside change. There was still no going out – even the tops were too muddy and slippery now, and it would be a few more days until the floods went down and the wind dried the earth. But then, she thought, nothing would keep her in. There was her garden to walk round and inspect; there were still a few more weeks of hunting; and there was a pent-up backlog of visits to be received and made, before country families went to London for the Season.

She thought about Giles. There had been no further letter from him, but she hadn't expected one. What would he have to say, anyway? Every day she had wondered when he would come back. Now, she began fearfully to wonder if he would return at all. It was so easy for a man to be elsewhere – for any man, but most of all for a wealthy lord for whom there were, effectively, no limits. She had brought him her fortune, which had freed him to leave her and roam the wide world. In return, she had got a home, a position, and her adored son. It was a reasonable exchange. That didn't mean she liked it.

If Giles didn't come back, what would she do? She would have to make a life for herself without him, just as she would if she were a widow. Well, there were plenty of materials to hand. The house, her gardens, the raising of her son. She wondered if management of the estate would fall to her.

She imagined interviewing agents and bankers, talking about crop rotation and investments, making decisions. The manufacture and sale of jam had made her a considerable heiress and the profits were supporting Ashmore and its revival, but she had never had to understand how it all worked. Still, if necessary, she would learn. She was not a clever person, but she'd had a good education at school under Miss Thornton, and she believed she could understand things as well as anyone if they were explained carefully. Mr Cowling, who had taken so gladly to the jam trade on their behalf, would help. He was clever about business, and though she had been rather afraid of him when she first met him, she felt now that she could face him and ask for help.

She felt quite stimulated by the thought of taking charge. She had been tired lately, and rather out of sorts, but a new wave of energy went through her as she stared out at the rapidly emerging world. If Giles did not come back, she would manage the jam business and the estate. She would show them, she thought – without a clear idea of who 'they' were. She would do it for Louis, so that he would inherit a thriving estate, and never have to marry someone he didn't love for their money.

And she would run the house as well. She would be a great lady, like her mother-in-law, and a noted hostess. She would be the true Mistress of Ashmore Castle, and no-one would ever compare her scathingly with her predecessors, or shake their heads and call her middle-class.

For a moment Kitty viewed with satisfaction the future she had mapped out, but then she sighed, and her shoulders sank. It was all very well if she were a widow, but she wasn't. She was still in love with Giles. She would always wait for him to come back, and hope that when he did, he would stay, and that they would be happy. She was too young to give up her dream of 'happy ever after'.

She was jerked from her reverie by her maid, Hatto, coming in. 'May I speak to you, my lady?'

She pulled herself together. 'Of course. What is it?'

Hatto seemed embarrassed. 'Well, my lady, it seems to me that – er – we haven't seen a certain visitor lately.'

'We haven't had any visitors,' Kitty said, puzzled. 'We've been snowed in. But I do mean to start entertaining again as soon as possible.'

'No, my lady, you misunderstand. I didn't mean that sort of visitor.' Kitty stared impatiently. Hatto tried again. 'I meant that it seems to me something hasn't happened that should have happened.'

Still Kitty stared. 'What? What hasn't happened?'

'That time of the month, my lady, hasn't been that time of the month,' Hatto said desperately. 'Not for ages, not since before Christmas, if I don't mistake.'

'Oh,' said Kitty, enlightened at last. She thought back. 'I think you're right,' she said slowly. Her cheeks were a little pink. It was an embarrassing thing to talk about, even with one's maid, who helped one into and out of the bath.

Hatto met her eyes. 'Is it possible, my lady, that you could be . . .' a long pause '. . . with child?'

Kitty's thoughts rushed to that night, a week before Giles had left, when he had come to her room. He had come only to tell her he was going away, but she had kept him there, played the wanton and drawn him to her bed, and they had made love with a fire and a passion that had taken her back to their early days together. But it had not been enough to keep him. 'I'm suffocating!' he'd cried. And a week later he'd been gone.

She thought of the absence of the 'little visitor'. A lady's maid had to prepare the bindings, so it was something she would notice. She thought, too, of her recent tiredness and of feeling out of sorts. Yes, it all fitted. She was pregnant. There was a moment of elation and excitement at the thought. And then her spirits sagged. So she would not be going hunting this season after all. She would spend another year

72

tied to the house by her expanding body. And when she finally had the baby, would Giles even be here?

All these thoughts tumbled through her mind in the fraction of a second. To the waiting Hatto, she said only, 'Yes. I think I am.'

Hatto waited for more, unsure how her mistress felt about it. She alone had witnessed her tears after the master left. Probably only she knew that the mistress feared he wasn't coming back.

'It's good news, isn't it, my lady?' she ventured at last, to break the silence. 'A brother for little Lord Ayton?'

Kitty pulled herself together. 'Yes, it's good news,' she said. She thought about how much she adored Louis, and imagined holding a second child in her arms in that magical moment just after birth, when you finally met the intimate stranger you had carried unseen for so many months. It *was* good news, and this child must never have a shadow cast over its life. It must never think it was less than wholeheartedly wanted.

'It's very good news. But don't tell anyone else for the moment.'

'Oh, of course not, my lady. Not until you say.'

'I need to think about it a little first. Just for a day or two.'

'His lordship will be so happy, my lady, he's—' She almost said, 'He's bound to come back when he knows.' Better sense stopped her making such an error. But Kitty knew what the unsaid words would have been, and Hatto knew she knew.

CHAPTER FIVE

The unlocked water rushed down the hill, scouring under hedges and tangles of bramble, pounding through ditches, teasing out debris that had been hidden and held all winter and carrying it away.

Moss was agitated to receive another visit from PC Holyoak. It wasn't that he had anything against the young man – who was very polite – or against the police in general: as an upright citizen he supported His Majesty's Constabulary in their necessary work. But he felt it reflected badly on the house for a constable to be seen there more than once in a decade.

The reason for the official visit, it emerged, was more upsetting even than he had feared. It was not that one of the servants was in trouble for petty theft or drunkenness in the village. 'We have discovered a body,' said Holyoak.

Moss's trembling fingers reached behind him to locate his chair and he sat down rather hard. 'A *dead* body?'

Holyoak was patient. He was accustomed to dealing with the public, their slowness and their ridiculous questions. 'Indeed, sir, quite dead and much decomposed.' Moss flinched at the word, but Holyoak carried on with no variation in tone. 'It was discovered lying under water in Ashmore Carr, but we have reason to believe that it had not been there long. From the position in which it was lying and the recent movement of floodwater, we think it was washed down from higher up the hill.'

'But – but why are you telling me this?' Moss said, bewildered.

'Because it seems likely that the body is that of your absent footman, Mr Edgar Speen, who went missing last November and has not been seen since. We require you, or someone else from the house who knew him, to come and inspect the body with a view to identifying it.'

Moss's lips moved in an appalled *why?* that he could not articulate.

Holyoak explained. 'Deceased has nothing about him to identify him, but he's dressed like an upper servant, and the fact is, Mr Moss, that no-one else is unaccounted for – no-one else, that is, of the right age, sex, height and build. So we should be glad of your assistance in this matter.'

'Oh, I couldn't – I couldn't—' Moss stammered. Even thinking about a dead body made him feel quite ill. He had barely got over the finding of the cook, Mrs Oxlea, who had hanged herself in her room. Such things were so irregular, *not* what was expected of a nobleman's household, where all should be order and harmony. What was happening to them? Was there a curse on the house? Was it his fault? As butler, he was ultimately responsible for the smooth running of the household. His self-belief wavered for a terrifying moment. He felt old and shaky and not up to coping with these violent matters. It was not reasonable to expect him to go and look at a corpse. He wouldn't do it. He couldn't.

'How – did he die?' he managed to ask.

'He took a crack on the head,' Holyoak said, 'that might or might not have been done deliberate. We'll come to that later. For the moment, let's concentrate on identifying the body. I'm afraid it's not a pretty sight,' he added. 'The freezing weather preserved it to an extent, but it looks as though the stoats and weasels had a go at it before the snow came down.'

Moss fell back in his chair, white and gasping. One of his hands waved like a random branch in the breeze, but

Holyoak deciphered a general direction, tried a cupboard, and came back with a bottle and a glass. He administered a stiff brandy, and while Moss was dealing with that, holding the glass in both shaking hands, Holyoak went to the door and beckoned a boy who was loitering not far off with ears akimbo.

'Here, you, what's your name? Eddie, isn't it? I know you, Eddie Bracken – you live down Mop End. Your dad's a hedger.'

''S right, sir,' Eddie said nervously.

'Who's second in command here, under Mr Moss?' Holyoak demanded. The boy didn't understand the question, so he changed it. 'Who's the under-butler? Or first footman?'

'I dunno about no under-butler, sir,' he stammered. 'First footman is William.'

'No, not him,' Holyoak said, frowning. 'Better fetch the housekeeper.'

'Yessir!'

But before Eddie could obey, James came in from the yard, where he had been having a smoke, stopped short at the sight of the law, then collected himself and came rapidly forward. 'What's up, Constable?' He smiled ingratiatingly – not a pretty sight. 'Anything I can help with?'

'Mr Moss has had a funny turn,' Holyoak said; and to Eddie, 'Go and fetch Mrs Webster, quick, and tell her to bring smelling-salts.' Eddie scuttled off, and Holyoak explained to James what had happened. 'I presume you knew this fellow Speen?'

'Valet to Mr Richard. Yes, I knew him. We worked side by side often enough.'

'Then I'll ask you to come with me and see if you can identify the body. I don't reckon Mr Moss is up to it.'

James agreed to come, studying for an air of solid citizenship. If you had anything to hide from the police, he reckoned, the best thing was to disarm their suspicions by being as helpful as possible – and there was the little matter of a pair of Georgian silver sugar casters to which he didn't want attention to be drawn.

There really wasn't much face to speak of – not enough to recognise anyone by. James had a strong stomach, but it took all his composure to do the job properly. The body seemed shorter than Speen had been in life, but Holyoak told him corpses always looked shorter. His calm indifference steadied James, and he tried to emulate it. The build was right, he said, and from what he could see of the clothes and boots, they were the sort of things Speen wore. The hair, what was left of it, was of the right colour and curl.

'Did he have any distinguishing marks?' Holyoak asked. 'Any scars or moles or deformities that you can remember?'

James thought about it. 'He had a mole on his cheek,' he said. Holyoak's silence was enough to remind him. He thought again. 'Oh, the forefinger on his left hand was crooked – the tip of it bent to the side.'

'The fingers have been nibbled as well,' said Holyoak. He uncovered the left hand and they both looked. Hard to say. 'Anything else?'

James thought back. 'I saw him in the bathroom once. He had a lot of freckles on his shoulders.'

Again, hard to tell, the skin being discoloured.

'Can you identify this body as that of Edgar Speen?' Holyoak asked formally.

'I think it's him,' James said. 'I get the feeling it *is* him.' *And who else could it be?* he added, inside his mind. The clothes were too good for it to be a vagrant or tramp, and no-one else was missing. 'How did he meet his end?'

Holyoak turned the head a little, to reveal a massive wound on the back of the skull. 'The critters will have made it bigger, nibbling around it. The blood would have attracted them. But either he fell backwards and hit his head on something, hard enough to kill him, which seems unlikely, or someone hit him a mighty blow with a heavy object, like a rock.'

'Murder, then?' James said, with interest.

'Hit from behind,' Holyoak commented. 'A cowardly blow. Not done in a fair fight.'

James arranged his face into a serious, reluctant expression. 'I expect you know that one of our chaps, William – William Sweeting, he's a footman – went out after Speen that night. Dashed out after him in a temper.' Holyoak's face was expressionless, his eyes steady. 'I don't want to peach on a chap, but it *is* murder after all – and a cowardly one at that, like you say. He came back with scratches on his face, William did, and a black eye, as if he'd been fighting.'

'Yes, I know,' Holyoak said. 'Did he say anything to you afterwards about it? About how he got the scratches? Did he ever admit meeting Mr Speen?'

James looked at the floor, the picture of reluctance. 'No, he never talked about it. But – I have to tell you – he was angry with Speen, because he'd just found out Speen'd been diddling his girlfriend. Mad as fire he was. He rushed out of the house, though it wasn't his evening off, shouting, "I'll see to him!" or "I'll sort him out!" Something like that. I couldn't swear to the exact words.'

Holyoak nodded impassively. 'I did speak to Mr Sweeting at the time. But I think I had better have another talk with him.'

'He's been very quiet since Speen disappeared,' James said earnestly. 'As if he's got something on his mind. Not his usual self at all.'

Moss went with William to the police station. William was sweating heavily and in a debilitating panic, and it was doubtful he would have made it down the hill without Moss's steadying support. 'I didn't do anything, Mr Moss, I swear it,' he kept saying. 'I never saw Mr Speen that night.'

All Moss could say was, 'If you're innocent, you've got nothing to fear. The scales of justice weigh true.'

'I'd never murder anyone,' William cried. 'My ma'd kill me if I did.'

'You just tell the truth, my lad, and all will be well. The truth shall set you free.'

That didn't seem to comfort William as much as it should have done, but it did shut him up. They completed the journey in silence. By the time Moss handed him over to the police sergeant, he was quivering with terror.

'Now, Mr Sweeting,' said Holyoak, leafing through his notebook to find the previous interview. William's eyes followed the movement of every page as it flipped, like the prisoner in Poe's story watching the pendulum.

'You've told me the truth about that night, have you?' Holyoak said, not looking up.

William nodded eagerly, then said, 'Yes.'

'You're sure about that?' Now he looked up. William's Adam's apple bobbed as he swallowed nervously. 'You see,' said Holyoak expansively, almost kindly, 'there are some anomalies in your story.' William looked blank. 'Inconsistencies,' Holyoak tried. Still blank. 'Things that don't make sense – don't add up.'

'It's the truth,' William whispered.

Holyoak gave a pitying sort of sigh. 'You've just told me you slipped going down the hill and fell into a ditch.'

'That's right.'

'But here in my notes from November, which I wrote down as you were speaking to me, you said you fell into the ditch going *up* the hill.'

William stared, his mouth open. Holyoak resisted the impulse to feel sorry for him. You needed a certain level of intellect to be a successful liar, and William Sweeting didn't have it. 'So which was it? Going up, or going down?'

'I don't remember,' William said helplessly.

'You *will* remember. Either here, or in the Crown Court in front of the judge.'

'Up,' said William, desperately. 'I was going up the hill.'

'You're sure?'

'Yes. Up. It was dark, very dark, I couldn't see where I was going. I tripped over something. A stone or something. Fell into the ditch in the dark.'

'Hm.' Holyoak appeared to consult another page. 'Would it surprise you to know that on the night in question, Wednesday, the fourth of November, the moon was just one day past the full. The sky was clear. It was a very bright, moonlit night. Almost as bright as day, according to some witnesses who were out that night.'

William licked his lips. 'Maybe – it'd gone down by then.'

'No, you were back at the Castle before moonset.' He paused and let William sweat. Then, 'How did you get the scratches on your face and hands?'

It took William a moment to adjust to the new direction of questioning. 'I – it was— The ditch. It was full of brambles. I got all scratched, trying to get out.'

'And the black eye?'

'When I fell in the ditch. I must've banged it on something. On a stone.'

'You banged your *eye* on a stone?' Holyoak said disbelievingly. 'How on earth did you manage that?'

William's voice rose a pitch. 'Look, I didn't kill him! I went out after him – I – I wanted to talk to him – but I never saw him. I never saw anybody!'

Holyoak consulted his notes again. William was beginning to hate that notebook. He wanted to grab it, tear it to shreds and stamp the bits into the ground. 'You told me, when I spoke to you before, that you didn't see anyone that evening, not man, woman or child.'

The fatal hesitation, before William answered. 'That's right.'

'Yet someone gave you a black eye.'

'I told you, I fell into a ditch.'

'No doubt you could take me to that ditch and show me exactly where you fell in?'

'I don't – it was— I can't remember. It was dark. I mean, it was just a ditch. I don't know what one.'

Holyoak put down the book. 'Here's what I think happened. You'd just found out that Mr Speen had been seeing your girl. You were very angry, as a man would be. You ran out after him. You caught up with him on the way down the hill, and accused him. You tried to hit him, and there was a scuffle, but he was a better fighter than you, and he blacked your eye. Then he turned away and walked on – perhaps he laughed at you. He wasn't afraid of you, Mr Sweeting, and that made you madder than ever. So you grabbed a rock from the ground, and you hit him on the back of the head. Perhaps you didn't mean to kill him. Probably you didn't – I don't think you're a murderer at heart. But kill him you did. You were horrified when you found what you'd done – and terrified. You rolled his body into the ditch and pulled some bramble sprays over it to conceal it. That was when you got the scratches on your hands and face. And then you went back to the Castle, hoping he would never be found.' He looked straight into William's eyes. 'That's what happened, isn't it?'

'No! It's not. I never— I didn't! I never saw him!'

'Then how did you get the scratches and the black eye?'

'It was nothing like that!'

'So what was it like? *Some*body gave you those injuries. If not Mr Speen, who?' William was silent. 'Don't be stupid, boy. If it was someone else, they can vouch for you.' Silence. 'But there wasn't anyone else, was there? You lost a fight with Edgar Speen and hit him on the head as he walked away. That's what happened, isn't it?'

William turned sullen. 'I'm not saying any more. You don't

believe me anyway, so what's the point? I didn't kill him, that's all.'

Holyoak looked at him for a long time, while William stared at the floor. Then he said, 'I'm afraid I shall have to keep you here.'

'Lock me up?'

'Lock you up. William Sweeting, I arrest you for the murder of Edgar Speen on the night of the fourth of November 1903, which is against the King's Peace.'

William put his face in his hands and sobbed.

Sergeant Mayhew was disconcerted to receive a visit from Richard. In all the years the police station had existed, no member of the Stainton family had ever entered it. The gentry way was to send for the police if they wanted them. The old lord had once stopped in front in his carriage, and sent the footman to fetch the sergeant out, and had spoken to him through the carriage window, but that was the closest they'd been.

Mayhew was happy for it to be that way. The distinctions of rank ought to be maintained. That way, everybody knew where they stood. It made for an orderly world. Excess friendliness between people of different stations in life led to impertinence, erosion of manners, lax behaviour, and eventually to unrest and revolution. You only had to look at France.

Mr Richard Tallant should not be standing in the station room, looking around with interest, and smiling. It was laudable he should be concerned about his footman, but there were ways, and there were ways, of showing that concern.

'I'm sure there must be some mistake somewhere,' Richard said. 'I've known William for years, and he's a quiet, meek, blameless sort of chap. Not the sort to go doing violent murders.'

'Every man has his snapping point, sir,' Mayhew said. 'And it's often the quiet ones that surprise us.'

Richard shook his head, smiling. 'I can't believe it. Not William.'

'We're doing our job, sir,' Mayhew said stiffly, 'and I'd be obliged if you'd let us get on with it.' Just because a member of the Family smiled and unbent and twinkled at him, he wasn't going to deviate one inch from his duty, which he carried out without fear or favour, no matter who. If it was Lady Stainton herself – the dowager, he meant – standing before him, he'd say the same thing. Though her ladyship would *never* have lowered herself for to do such a thing. She was a proper lady of the old school. *She*'d have sent for him, not turned up in person like this.

Richard read the grim expression, and said, 'Oh, I would never stand in the way of your duty, Sergeant, but perhaps you could tell me what makes you think William is guilty. I mean, I know he went out of the house that evening, but—'

'There are serious inconsistencies in his account of himself, sir,' said Mayhew, and recounted them. 'He's lied, sir, and gone on lying. And he had a serious beef with deceased. We have one or two things still to check, but we feel we'll have a strong case against him, to present to the magistrate.'

'Well, can I take him home until you've finished your investigations?'

'No, sir,' Mayhew said sternly. 'He has to stay in custody. This *is* a capital matter. And there's always the chance that he'll cut – hook it – run away.'

Richard saw it would be no use to argue with this monolith of the law. 'May I at least see him, Sergeant?' he asked politely. 'I feel a responsibility for his welfare. In the absence of my brother.'

'That you may, sir,' said Mayhew, and unbent enough to say, 'If you have any influence with him, sir, perhaps you can persuade him to come across – tell the truth. It'd be in his best interests.'

'I will certainly do what I can,' said Richard.

★ ★ ★

William had gone downhill fast. It would not have been possible for a man to look more miserable. He raised his eyes in hope when Richard was shown into the cell, but his face drooped again when it became clear he had not come to free him.

'It's kind of you to come and see me, sir,' he said, seeming on the brink of tears.

'Look, old chap,' Richard said gently, 'why don't you just tell the truth? You said you went to see your mother that evening, because she was ill, but they know you didn't. They've talked to the neighbours, and none of them sent for you or saw you. They've even talked to your mother, and she said the same. She also said she didn't have a nasty turn that night.' William said nothing. 'And then there's this stuff about falling into a ditch in the dark. It was a bright, moonlit night – I remember it myself. So what *did* happen?'

'I didn't kill him, sir. You've got to believe me,' William said desperately.

'I want to believe you,' Richard said. 'I don't think you're a violent man. But if you tell lies, what are they to think? If you won't say where you were—'

'I can't say,' William said, looking at the floor.

'Why not?' No answer. 'If there's someone else involved, who can vouch for your whereabouts, why not say? Are you protecting someone, is that it?' Silence. 'Is it something you're ashamed of?' William stared at the floor, but the tips of his ears reddened a little. 'Whatever it was you were up to, it can't be as bad as what you're accused of. Don't you under-stand, old chap? This is murder. They could hang you.'

William looked up, and his lips whitened. He had evidently not got as far as this in his thoughts. 'Hang me?' he whispered. 'No, sir! No, sir! They can't! Not the rope! Not that! I didn't do it, I swear!'

'Then tell the truth. Where did you go that night?'

'I can't say,' William said desperately. 'But they can't hang me. I'm innocent. If I didn't do it, they can't prove I did, can they?'

'I'm afraid it doesn't always work that way,' Richard said.

'Yes, yes, the scales of justice,' William said eagerly. 'The might of the law, like Mr Moss says. It's the glory of England. They wouldn't hang an innocent man. I didn't kill him, so I've got nothing to fear. They can't prove I did it when I didn't.'

Richard left him, feeling thoughtful and rather depressed. He was quite sure now – where before he'd only been largely sure – that William didn't kill Speen. But he didn't have the footman's complete trust in the workings of the law. The blind goddess with the scales and the sword might be perfect in justice, but man was imperfect, and it was men who would judge the case. It would be a horrible thing – horrible! – if William were to hang. He could only hope that thinking about the noose in the solitude of the cell, he would come to the conclusion that the truth must be told.

Below stairs, the atmosphere was a mixture of horror and excitement. The excitement was forgivable – nobody actively wanted William to hang, but day-to-day life was very dull, and anything that broke the routine was welcome, more especially when it was something sensational.

Those girls to whom William had attached himself romantically over the years attested to his gentleness – though often they had called it something less complimentary. It gave an extra frisson to the thought of the hood, the rope and the trapdoor. They enjoyed a sort of celebrity, and set themselves up as experts on his character and proclivities. They could never have believed it of William. 'Now, if it had been that *James*,' they said, with knowing wags of the head.

James didn't mind being regarded as tough enough to be capable of murder. He had never sought to be popular, but he liked to stand out from the herd. And while everyone's mind was fully occupied with the fate of William and the prospect of hanging for one who had so lately walked among them, they were not watching him, which gave him a welcome latitude. Mr Moss was completely overset by the whole business. He had palpitations, and his hands shook so much he could not properly perform his duties. For the first time in his life he relinquished his keys: he put them into James's hands, grateful to him for being so sympathetic and helpful. Well, William was *hors de combat*, and though Sam and Cyril technically outranked him, James was experienced as they were not. To Mr Moss, James played the grave, honest and helpful underling, stepping competently into the breach. Privately, he was making hay. This was the best chance he was ever likely to have.

Everyone was stoutly loyal to William in theory, and maintained his innocence; but there were tense, whispered conversations in corners about each person's memories of that night, whether they knew anything or not. Stories passed from mouth to mouth and accreted ever more spurious detail: William had gone out in a fury . . . His face had been white and his eyes wild . . . He had vowed to kill Mr Speen . . . He had carried a stout ashplant . . . had said he would bash his head in . . . had come back with his clothes torn to shreds . . . the ashplant covered with blood . . .

Mrs Webster, Rose and Dory did their best to quell the more outrageous of the stories, but it made little difference, only further muddying the field, so that few of the servants any longer knew what was fact and what fiction. If the police ever came to question them, it would be a poor look-out for William.

In all the talk, Speen was hardly mentioned. He had never been one of them; no-one had much liked him; he was not missed. His part in the current drama was confined to playing the 'orrible corpus: word had got about that the stoats and weasels had been at it, and the younger boys whispered highly imaginary and increasingly fevered descriptions to each other of what it had looked like, until the youngest stable boy went home in tears and told his mother. She came up to the Castle to complain shrilly to Mr Giddins, the head man, who boxed a few ears and put a stop to it.

Josh, the groom who attended the young ladies, had finally decreed that the ground was dry enough for Alice to go out on Pharaoh. It was not just a matter of horses coming back muddy and giving him extra work: they lived on a hill, and when the slopes were greasy with mud it was easy for a horse to come down, with dangerous consequences for rider and, in his view more particularly, horse. But today with his sanction she had gone out for an early ride, and then had Biscuit put-to in the trap and said she was going out sketching. She had established with Giles before he went away that, while she had to be attended by a groom when she rode, she could drive alone, as long as she stayed on the estate. Josh might disagree – he *did* disagree – but he couldn't go against his lordship's decision, however much he grumbled about it.

So Alice flew, like a bird to its nest, to Castle Cottage in Motte Woods. Biscuit knew the way by now, and trotted along, ears pricked, enjoying being out, requiring no rein to tell him when to turn off the main track. It was a chilly day, rather grey, but the catkins were dancing in the breeze, the blackthorn was showing green tips, and the birds were singing again, unseen in the thickets.

Axe came out of his cottage to greet her with his usual quiet, steady look, as though assessing the situation before committing himself to anything. Dolly, his terrier, was less reserved, bustling past him with the vibrating tail and motherly tongue that were Alice's due. Alice made much of her, to avoid immediately looking at Axe. She felt suddenly shy. The last time she had seen him, she had thought for a moment that he was going to kiss her. She had brooded over it so much during the long absence of the snowy months that she was no longer sure what was true and what was only her imagination.

He had come over to take hold of Biscuit's rein – purely a courtesy, as Biscuit had no intention of going anywhere now he was here – and she could no longer crouch there petting the dog on a level with his boots. She had to stand up and look at him. The first glance made a little gasp inside her chest. She had forgotten how beautiful he was; how very blue his eyes were; how he had such *presence*. He had a sort of innate, unstated power that seemed the essence of being a man.

'Hullo,' she said at last, fiddling with the cuff of her glove as an excuse to look down again.

'Hullo,' he said. A pause. 'Haven't seen you for a long while.'

'Well, there was Christmas. And then the snow,' she said. She looked up again, and had a mad impulse to ask, *Did you miss me?* He was smiling – that small upward curve of the mouth corners that made him look like a big golden cat. 'How's Della? And Cobnut?'

'They're all right. How's Pharaoh?'

'I had him out this morning. He was very fresh, after so long with just paddock exercise. Josh thought he'd have me off, but he's not unseating. I expect he could get me off if he really tried, but he never does.'

'Josh has to worry about you. It's his job.'

'I know. It's annoying, though. I brought you something.' She reached back into the trap. 'It's not a present, I'm afraid, just to borrow. A book.'

He wiped his hands down the back of his trousers before taking it carefully, almost reverently, and read out the title and author from the cover. '*The War of the Worlds.* H. G. Wells.' He looked up, an inscrutable flash of blue. 'I read his book *The Time Machine*. It was grand – exciting.'

'This is too – about invaders from another planet.'

'Well, now. I shall enjoy that. Thank you.'

There was an embarrassing silence as they each found it hard to meet the other's eyes. Alice broke it by asking, 'Have you got any new animals?'

He seemed glad of the change of subject. 'Got some rabbit kittens. Found 'em in a hollow 'mong some tree roots. They were hungry. I reckon a fox must've got the mother.'

'What will you do with them?'

'Feed 'em till they're bigger, then eat 'em.'

'Oh, no! Not really?'

'That's what rabbits are for. Not much on a wild rabbit, but they make a nice stew.'

She examined his face and the little enigmatic smile at his mouth corners. 'You're teasing me. You won't really eat them, will you? You didn't mean it?'

He had meant it, but he knew how tender-hearted she was about animals. 'Maybe I won't, then,' he said. 'Though if I let 'em go, a fox'll get 'em anyway.'

'If I give them names, you won't be able to eat them,' Alice said. 'Like the Red Queen said, it isn't etiquette to *cut* anyone you've been introduced to.'

'Which queen is that, then?'

'It's in a book, called *Through the Looking-Glass*.'

'Not come across that one.'

'We have it in the library. Anyway, it's a joke, really, but it's true all the same. You wouldn't eat an animal with a name. Like Dolly – you wouldn't eat Dolly.'

'Dogs aren't good eating. D'you want to see the rabbits, then?'

'Yes, please.'

'I got a barn owl, too. Young one. Hurt its wing. Been feeding it on mice.' He smiled at her. 'Never gave *them* names, so you don't need to worry.'

She fell in beside him. 'You think I'm silly.'

'No. I think you're female. Females think differently about things. That's all right. That's the way the world wags.'

After the rabbits and the owl, she went to see Della and Cobnut, and was entranced to find one of the cats, the tortoiseshell, couched on Della's broad rump, white paw tips folded in, dozing.

'She doesn't mind,' Alice marvelled.

'Horses like cats. They know they keep the mice away,' Axe said. 'Always have a few cats around stables. Same as spiders. Never clear away spider webs from stables.'

'Because they catch the flies that would bother the horses?'

He nodded. ''Sides, if you cut yourself, you c'n clap a handful of spider web on it, and it won't go bad.'

'Is that true?'

He nodded again. 'Got something in it, spider web, that kills off germs.'

'I never knew that.' She was straightening Della's forelock between her ears and combing it flat with her fingers. Della's eyes were closed, her lip trembling with her half-asleep breathing. 'It's very fair, her mane. If she were a human, she'd be a beautiful blonde lady.'

He was amused by her fantasy. 'What'd Biscuit be, then?'

She considered. 'A grocer's assistant. A little stout man in an overall coat, with a pencil behind his ear.'

He laughed. 'You do say some things, Lady Alice! Want a cup of tea? I was just going to brew up.'

'Yes, please. But not "Lady Alice". Not here.'

'It's what you are,' he said, meeting her eyes. The enigmatic smile was there, but it didn't touch his eyes. She felt a little thrill of something, like danger.

'I don't want to be.'

'Can't escape from what you are,' he said, and turned away. She followed him. What did he mean? Was it a warning? She wasn't sure she liked it.

In the cottage, she sat at the table and watched him while

he moved about making the tea, laying the table, fetching down the biscuit tin, filling the milk jug. She loved to watch him – whatever he was doing, his every movement was spare and perfect, no fuss or bustle, just things getting done as smoothly and without effort as a fish swims.

'Heard there's trouble up at the Castle,' he said, bringing the teapot to the table and sitting down opposite her.

'Oh, you mean William – our footman?'

''S right. You can be mother.' She wrinkled her nose at the expression. 'Let it mash a bit first.'

'I know. There's biscuits?'

'Shortbread. Our Esther made it for me.'

'I love shortbread. How do you know about William?'

'Everybody's talking about it.' He looked at her seriously. 'Murder's a hanging matter, you know.'

'Oh, but he didn't do it. And the law would never hang an innocent man.'

'Don't you be so sure.'

She was perplexed. 'Richard was talking about it. William's so silly – he won't say where he really went. And because he was out that night, and won't say, the police think it must have been him that killed Speen. Why won't he say? Richard says, whatever he was doing, it can't be worth hanging for.'

'You just said the law won't hang an innocent man.'

But she was worried now. 'I know, but – well, *you* think it might.'

'Tea's fit to pour now.' While she was thus occupied, he said, 'There's a female, lives down Warner's Rents.'

'Those cottages in Ashmore Carr?'

'Name of Tabby Mattock. Used to be barmaid at the Dog and Gun.'

'What about her?'

'She had a baby, back in Feb'ry. A boy. Her ma talked to rector last Sunday, asking about baptism. That's how I heard about it. She's living with her ma.'

'Oh, is her husband dead?'

'She's not married.'

Alice looked up at that, and blushed slightly. 'Oh.'

'Was supposed to be marrying your footman, William, but he called it off.'

Now she looked indignant. 'Did he? After getting her in the family way? How horrid! I would never have thought it of him. Perhaps he's not as nice as he seems.'

'"Twasn't him as got her that way.' He looked at her steadily. 'I wouldn't normally talk about this sort of thing to a lady, it's not seemly. But a man's life's at stake. So you should tell your brother, like – Mr Richard – to talk to Tabby Mattock. Cos according to what I heard, it was her as William went to see that night. That was the very night he broke it off. And that's all I'm saying. Have a bit of shortbread.'

She took a piece absently and nibbled it, thinking. At last she said, 'But why wouldn't *she* tell the police that? She must know he's been arrested.'

'I can't answer for other folk. Maybe she's got her reasons.'

'Then why don't *you* tell the police?'

'They wouldn't listen to me. No, it'd come better from your brother. If there's anything in it.'

She shook her head. 'It all seems very rum to me.'

'People are rum,' he said. 'There's nothing queerer than folk. Unless it's cows.'

'Cows?' She was startled out of her thoughts.

'Mysterious animals, cows. Horses, now, they're straightforward, you always know what a horse is thinking. But cows . . . They live in another world.'

She stared a moment, then laughed. 'You're teasing me again.'

'Not a bit,' he said, smiling. 'Maybe they come from another planet. Think Mr Wells'd like to write a story about cows?'

'Animals all do strange things in *Through the Looking-Glass*. I think you'd like it. I'll bring it next time I come.'

'So there'll be a next time, then?' he said, offhand, looking at the level in the teapot.

'If that's all right,' she said politely.

He didn't answer directly, but he smiled as he topped up her cup. 'When you've finished your tea, d'you want to come up the top end with me and Della? We've got a tree to fetch out.'

'I'd love to,' she said.

Richard frowned. 'Who told you all this?'

'Axe Brandom,' said Alice.

'The blacksmith?'

'He's our woodsman now.'

'Oh, yes, I'd forgotten.'

'You know him – you know he wouldn't make it up.'

'How did you come to be speaking to him?'

'I met him when I was out driving,' Alice said. Well, that was the truth, wasn't it?

'And where did he hear it?'

'He heard Tabby's mother talking about her at church.' Well, that was also the truth, if not all of it. Alice surveyed her brother's face anxiously. 'What will you do? Will you tell the police?'

'It could just be gossip,' Richard said. 'I don't know this Tabby woman. I don't want to stir up trouble for her if she's respectable – though everyone must know by now that William's been arrested, so why wouldn't she come forward to clear him, if she could? Hmm. I think I'd better talk to her first, before saying anything to the police. And *you* won't say anything either,' he added sternly to Alice. 'Not to anyone.'

'Of course not. But you do think William's innocent, don't you?'

'I really hope he is.'

CHAPTER SIX

The cottage smelt of babies and damp, and an underlying dirtiness Richard recognised from occasional visits to the poorer villagers. The smell wafted out when the door was opened to his knock. A short, blowsy woman, her hair scraped back in a bun, stood there, looking at him sullenly. In the background, a baby began to wail. Over her shoulder he saw a number of discoloured napkins drying in front of the fire.

'What do you want?' she asked sourly.

'Are you Tabby Mattock? I'm Richard Tallant,' he began politely.

'I know who you are. Half your servants come drinking at the Dog. Not that I work there any more.'

From her expression, you would think she blamed him for that. She obviously wasn't going to ask him in – for which he was grateful – so he leaned against the doorpost and said, 'I believe you were walking out with William Sweeting, who's a footman up at the Castle.'

'Maybe I was. What's it to you?'

'You know that he's been arrested for murder?'

She turned her head away, and picked at a back tooth with her little-finger nail. 'Heard something about it.'

'I have it on reliable evidence that he visited you on that particular evening, the evening Mr Speen disappeared. You are in a position to give him an alibi.'

She turned her face back to him, her eyes flat and hostile.

'Why don't you mind your own business? I don't work for you, Mr Richard Tallant, so you can't scare me.'

'I have no wish to scare you, Miss Mattock. And it *is* my business, because William *does* work for me. I'm responsible for his welfare.'

'My baby's calling,' she said, stepping back and trying to close the door.

Richard inserted a boot in the door's path. 'You can't let an innocent man hang.'

'Who says he's innocent?'

'You have evidence that would clear him. You must go to the police.'

She looked at him derisively. 'Oh, yeah? What's in it for me?'

'You want paying for doing your duty?'

Suddenly she was spitting like a cat. 'Don't you talk to me about duty! You men are all the same! You want your buttered bun, oh, yes, but you're not so quick to pay for it, are you? Your precious William promised to marry me, then he called off. Now I've got a baby to bring up. Where's *his* duty? Where's yours, if it comes to that? *You* ought to be paying for this baby. It was *your* precious footman as put me up the pole. Now he thinks I'm going to get him off, does he?' She gave a bark of derisive laughter. 'Well, he can think again!'

'Actually, William has stayed loyal to you. It wasn't him who told me about you. He's still refusing to say where he was that night.'

'More fool him,' she muttered.

'He did visit you that night, didn't he?'

'Came to tell me he was calling it off, the dirty dog. Came to tell me he was chucking me and the baby on the rubbish heap. *That*'s your sainted footman!'

'I don't say he's a saint, Miss Mattock, any more than any of us,' Richard said, giving her a sharp look, 'and I don't say he did right by you. But this is more serious. You can't let him hang because he let you down.'

'I can do as I please, *Mister* Tallant. Go away now. You're letting the draught in.' She tried again to close the door.

He caught the edge of it, to add to the resistance of his foot. 'Look here,' he said. 'I can't pay you money to go to the police, because that would taint the evidence. But I can promise you this. You do the right thing by William, and I'll see to it that your baby is supported.'

She gave him a very long, calculating look. 'How much?' she asked at last.

'A shilling a week. Until he leaves school.'

'Pigs might fly! I can guess how much of that I'd see once I'd been and told my story and got William off.'

'I am a gentleman, and I keep my word,' Richard said, holding his temper.

'You can keep your word – I'll keep the money. Five pun' in me hand. Two years in advance. That's my terms. Or they can stretch his neck for all I care. I'll come and watch.'

An older woman appeared behind her, coming in from the scullery at the back. 'Whatcher doin', Tab? Whoyer talkin' to?'

'It's him from up the Castle. Wants me to tell police William was with me that night.'

Mrs Mattock evidently knew which night was in question. She came up close behind her daughter and squinted up at Richard's face. Then she smiled at him ingratiatingly, showing the stubs of her discoloured teeth. 'She's a respectable girl, my Tabitha. Respectable girls don't like to have nothing to do with the police. Doesn't look good. Girl like my Tabitha goes inside a police station, everyone knows about it. There's talk. She was supposed to be prop'ly married by now, but that wicked man jilted her at the altar. What's she supposed to do now, with no job and no money? And she'll never *get* another job if she's seen going in a police station.'

'She won't have to,' Richard said. 'I'll speak to the police, and they'll send someone here to take her statement. I just need you to promise to tell them the truth, Miss Mattock. About seeing William that evening.'

The old woman laughed. 'She can tell 'em about seeing William all right!'

'Stow it, Ma,' Tabby growled. To Richard she said again, 'Five pun'. That's my terms.'

'I haven't got that much on me,' Richard said.

'Then you'll have to come back,' she said flatly. '*Before* the pleece come. If it's not in me hand before they turn up, I'm saying nothing.'

'And what's to say you'll speak up once you've got the money?' Richard said. 'Two before, and three when I hear from them you've done it right.'

'You're not as green as you look, Mister Richard Tallant,' she said, with an unpleasant laugh. 'All right, but I better get it, or it's back to the police I'll go and tell 'em you bribed me to lie to save William's neck. Then you'll be in trouble and he'll get stretched.'

'Agreed,' Richard said. 'I'll be back.'

'You better,' Tabby said, and shut the door.

Inside, mother and daughter exchanged a look. Mrs Mattock said, 'A fiver?'

'He said he'd support the baby, a shillin' a week. I said two years in advance or it's no go.'

'But I thought you was going to that Miss Eddowes and givin' the baby away?'

'Well, he don't have to know that, does he? Why d'yer think I want the money in advance?'

'I dunno, Tab. Talking to the pleece – it's dangerous. What if they finds out about the other chap and what you did—'

Tabby could move like a cat, too. She had her mother by the throat. 'You shut your mouth, old woman. Nobody never knows about that, d'you hear?' She let her go. 'You talk too much.'

'Sorry, Tab.' She was frightened of her daughter when she got in a mood. Years of pulling beer pumps had given her mighty strong arms and hands. And if she lost her temper . . . She'd lost it with that other chap, the skinny one. Two of 'em giving her the brush-off in one night. It was no wonder she'd gone a bit crazy-like. That soft William was lucky she'd bashed him first, before she really got her rile up . . .

'Anyway, once I got that fiver and the baby's out the way, I'm off out of here. They'll never find me, even if they look. But if I ever find out you bin talking, I'll come back and kill you, all right? You know I'd do it.'

'I won't talk,' said Mrs Mattock. 'Not about – *that.*'

'Not about anything, you hear?'

Sergeant Mayhew was sternly disapproving. 'I don't say you haven't come by some useful information, but you should have brought it straight to us, sir, and let us investigate, not gone asking questions yourself. Who knows what damage you might have done?'

Richard assumed humility. 'I'm sorry, Sergeant. I didn't think of that. I was just eager to prove William's innocence.'

'We have our job to do, sir, and it doesn't make it any easier to have well-meaning members of the public getting in our way.'

'I have no wish to get in your way, Sergeant, I assure you. And I'm more than happy to leave everything else to you. Can I take him home now?'

'Certainly not, sir. We shall have to check up on it ourselves before we can accept the truth of it. And there's still the question of the scratches and the black eye, and all his lies.'

Richard suppressed a grin. 'I have an idea about that, Sergeant.'

Uncle Sebastian was back, and appeared at dinner that evening. He seemed subdued, but in a thoughtful way rather than sad or depressed. The dowager and Rachel were in London, so it was to the audience of Sebastian, Kitty and Alice that Richard told the day's news.

'He didn't rush out of the house after Speen, as the police assumed. He went straight to see Tabby, to try to sort out the truth. He wanted her to be the innocent maiden of his dreams, but there was the unfortunate difficulty to get over, that she had told him human gestation takes six months, while someone else had told him it was nine months. Which was true? If it *was* nine months, the baby couldn't have been his, and she'd been lying to him.'

Sebastian stirred. 'Should you be talking about this sort of thing in front of Alice?'

'I know about gestation from helping on the farms, Uncle,' Alice said. 'And I was the one who told Richard about Tabby's baby. I promise I won't be corrupted. Richard, please go on.'

'All right, but for the Lord's sake never repeat any of this to our mother or she'll slay me,' Richard said. 'Well, William walked down to Warner's Rents and asked Tabby the awkward question. I imagine the woman knew the game was up, because sooner or later William was going to find out from some irrefutable source that it *was* nine months – and, besides, she might have been banking on his meekness and his besmitten state. At any rate, she admitted the baby wasn't his. But, apparently, William found some backbone, and said in that case the wedding was off. What else was said between them I can't tell you, though I wish I'd been a fly on the wall – and, by the by, one more fly would not have been noticed in that cottage, I can tell you!'

'Get on with it, boy,' Sebastian said.

'At all events, words were had, and Miss Tabby lost her temper and flew at William, making a very nasty scratch down his cheek. He got other scratches on his hands trying to defend himself, though it speaks well for him that he wouldn't use any force on her, just tried to keep her away from him.

Well, he grappled with her, and when she desisted he dropped his guard, and that was when she punched him, hard, right in the eye, and gave him that shiner. At that juncture he decided there was no point in continuing the conversation and legged it. He went the long way home, round Mop End, instead of straight up the hill, because he was still very upset about the whole thing – apparently he had really loved Miss Tabby, and to his disillusionment was added a broken heart – and he didn't want to face anyone straight away.'

'So if anyone in Mop End saw him, that will clear him completely, won't it?' Alice said eagerly.

'You have an unnerving grasp of criminal procedure,' Richard said.

She shrugged. 'It's just common sense.'

'But why didn't he tell the police all this in the first place?' Kitty asked.

'Because he was ashamed, the big loon. Ashamed of having fallen for her wiles – his mother, apparently, is very proper and would be horrified at his making the beast with two backs outside the bonds of marriage.'

'He *should* be ashamed,' Sebastian said. 'Even if this Tabby was Helen of Troy herself, there's no excuse.'

'Quite,' Richard said briefly. 'And he was ashamed of his stupidity in being gulled, ashamed of leaving her in the lurch with the baby, even if it wasn't his, and most of all ashamed of being beaten up by her. In all this wallow of shame, all he could think of to do was to make up a story and stick by it. Of course, he was horrified when he discovered he was suspected of murdering Speen but, like a rabbit frozen in front of a stoat, when facing the terror of the law he simply stuck to his story all the harder.'

'So they're letting him go?' Kitty asked.

'After they've checked the story with Tabby Mattock.'

'But will she tell the truth to the police?' Sebastian asked uncertainly.

'I think she will,' said Richard. He didn't mention the five pounds – the fewer people who knew about that, the better. It was a large sum to come out of his allowance, and was William worth it? But he couldn't have let him hang.

'It leaves us with two problems,' Sebastian said, after a pause. 'The first is, what to do with William.'

'We have to take him back,' Richard said, but he looked at Kitty. It really was her decision, as mistress of the house.

Kitty was gratified to be consulted. 'I think we have to, don't we?' she said diffidently. 'Otherwise, it will look as though we don't believe he's innocent.'

'But it will be very awkward below stairs – for him as much as anyone.'

'Oh, well, we shall probably never know anything about that,' Richard said. 'Moss will sort it all out. A great household is like a swan. We upstairs only see the bird gliding along serenely. Downstairs they see the frantically paddling feet under the waterline.'

Alice laughed. 'Clever, Richard!'

Kitty said, 'What was the second problem? You said there were two.'

Sebastian looked down at his plate, where he was removing the last shreds from a mutton cutlet. 'The problem, which I fear will haunt us for a long time, of who really did kill Speen.'

There was an awkward silence. Then Richard said lightly, 'Oh, I expect it was some tramping man just passing through, and long gone now. Tried to rob him of his purse and hit him too hard by mistake.'

Actually, he had a different idea, but it was not one he wanted to share with anyone – or even, really, with himself. He changed the subject. 'Who's hunting on Saturday?'

'I am,' Alice said at once.

'I think I'd like to go out, if there's anything that will carry me,' Sebastian said. 'The fresh air and exercise will do me good. I've been feeling a bit jaded lately.'

'I thought you didn't seem in spirits,' Richard said. 'Giles's two should be up to your weight, for half a day each. Archer can take one out, and you can swap over halfway. What about you, Kitty?'

'I don't think I'll go out,' she said, trying to sound casual about it.

But Alice protested, 'Oh, no, you must come! It's the last hunt, and we've missed so much of the season. Do come, Kitty! It won't be nearly as much fun without you. Why would you miss it?'

'I'm out of practice,' Kitty said. 'And Richard rides Apollo so well.'

'I'm looking forward so much to seeing London,' Giulia said, as she and Giles leaned on the taffrail of the after deck, watching the *Queen of the Nile*'s wake turn the water from ultramarine to turquoise. Day by day they were leaving Egypt's heat behind and passing into western Mediterranean spring, but it was still warm enough on deck during the day – even warm enough to venture up after dinner for a little while.

Giles glanced at her. 'Your English has improved so much on this trip. I think it's as good as your mother's now.'

'Do you think I will pass in London for an English lady?'

'No English lady looks quite like you. Even those with dark hair and eyes don't have your particular glow.'

As soon as he'd said it, he wished he hadn't. He had got over his initial awkwardness with her, which had been brought on by Mrs Antrobus's well-meaning intervention. And it had been his habit in former years to compliment her quite openly – as an older brother does a favourite younger sister. But now she met his eyes and he felt the tension rise between them. The silence was uncomfortable.

She broke it. 'Will I see you in London?' she asked lightly.

'I shall have a great deal to do on the estate when I get back,' he said. 'And I don't go to London very often.'

'*Quanto sei serio!*' she teased him. 'But did not you tell me your sister is . . . "coming out"? Is that what you say? Won't you go to London for that?'

'My mother will be bringing her out, yes. It's mostly a female rite. We men have little to do with it. I shall have to be there for her ball, I suppose, in my father's place. And perhaps for one or two other occasions.'

'Then I shall see you, I hope. The ball – it will be *magnifico*, will it not?'

He laughed. '*Maestoso*, perhaps, but also *tedioso* in the extreme.'

'No, you cannot say so!' she protested. 'I know you, Giles. You are not such an old man to hate a ball. I have seen you dance.'

'When?' he demanded disbelievingly.

'Years ago, at the Palazzo Visconti, at the Christmas ball. You were the last to leave the floor. I believe the musicians were falling from their chairs with tiredness but you would still dance.'

'I was younger then,' he protested. 'And not a married man.' Another thing he wished he had not said.

But she rode it out. 'Does she not like to dance, your wife?'

'I'm sure she does, but there have been few opportunities since our wedding.'

'You must dance with her at your sister's ball.'

I would sooner dance with you. He did not say it aloud, but the thought shocked him. He had sent Kitty a cable from Alexandria to say he was on his way home, but apart from that he had not thought of her once. He straightened up and stared at the churning wake, the darkening eastern sky, and wished he were travelling in the other direction. He did not want to go home.

'We should go down,' he said. 'You're getting cold. And we must change for dinner.'

She gave him a thoughtful look, but said nothing, only

turned away obediently. The sunset breeze was getting up. It fluttered the little wisps of hair at the nape of her neck, the ends that always would escape her chignon. As she turned, her stole slipped from one shoulder and he caught it as it descended and put it round her; and had the maddest urge to kiss the back of her neck as he did. This was bad – this was very bad. He cursed Mrs Antrobus for putting ideas into his head.

He went down the companionway in front of her and turned at the bottom politely as she stepped off. Her hand was cold from the air on deck. *Che gelida manina*, he thought. She met his eyes and he knew with certainty that she was thinking the same thing. She, he and her parents had been of a party that went to *La Bohème* at the Teatro della Pergola at Christmas 1900. Giulia had been wearing a gown of deep sea green beaded silk, with an ostrich feather dyed to match curling from her hair. At the end of the first act he had taken her hand to help her up the steps of the box, and he'd said then, *What a cold little hand!* Sung it, in fact – and she'd only laughed. Things were easy between them then.

As she stepped off the companionway, a rogue wave passed under the ship and it rocked suddenly, throwing her against him. She was in his arms. Their eyes met for an instant, and then he was kissing her, crushing her against him. Her lips were warm and eager; he was a man in the prime of life, who had been suppressing all natural urges for a long time. There was no excuse, of course. It was a moment of madness, but it was sweet and wild and glorious, and for that moment he had no thought in his head, just sensation.

Then the ship rocked them apart and he knew himself again. He drew her hands from around him and imprisoned them between them. 'Giulia,' he whispered, 'I'm sorry.'

Her eyes seemed enormous, dark and glistening. *'Non dispiacerti,'* she whispered, *'mio più caro.'*

There were footsteps. Someone was coming along the

passageway. When the steward caught them up, they were walking quite normally side by side, her hand resting on his arm, as he saw her to the door of her cabin.

The stable boy Timmy was brushing the earl's groom Mr Archer's horse, Abelard, and taking his time over it, because he didn't want to wash yards, which was the next job. His brush-strokes were slow and the rhythm was soporific. Both boy and horse were half asleep when the door slammed open, making them both jump, and Giddins, the head man, grabbed Timmy by the collar and yanked him backwards.

'Come with me! No, get Wally and Jim, quick. Everybody into the yard!' he shouted as Timmy scurried off. In moments, everyone except those out exercising had assembled, some still clutching the tools of their trade, one surreptitiously chewing.

Archer appeared from round the corner with the littlest boy, Oscar, who had been sent to fetch him. 'What's up, Mr Giddins?'

'Her ladyship's coming home!' Giddins cried. 'Sent a telegram. She'll have to be met at the station, and the train'll be there in less than an hour. We've got to get the greys ready.'

'Right, then,' Archer began. 'P'raps we should—'

His pace was too leisurely for Giddins. 'They'll all have stable stains. They've got to be washed before they can be groomed. Get them out and tie them up – we'll do it out here in the yard. Two to a horse. I'll do the tails. You, Oscar, go and find John Manley and Joe Green. Tell 'em to drag the carriage out right away, make sure it's clean. They can get the harness ready as well. Then come back here – I'll need you.'

Steven, Wally and George had already started towards the stable where the carriage horses were kept, but Will, who was new, said, 'Can't we just do two, Mr Giddins? If it's just for the station?'

Giddins whirled on him in a movement more like a ballet dancer than one would have expected from a man of his age and condition. '*Four* horses for her ladyship! *Always* four! Now get moving!' He glanced up at the stable clock and moaned. 'We'll never have time to plait.'

'Her ladyship won't expect plaiting,' Archer said, 'not at short notice.'

'There's no knowing what she expects,' Giddins said. 'It's what we can deliver. And what she'll say afterwards. That's the point.'

The dowager Lady Stainton swept into the drawing-room like a flotilla, displacing so much air it made the last petals on a tulip in a vase on a table fall. Her sweeping eye took it in, on the way to inspect Kitty, who came forward to greet her, the dogs at her heels.

'Keep those animals away from me,' was the dowager's greeting. 'Where is Richard?'

'He's out with Adeane, visiting the farms,' Kitty said, trying not to feel flattened. No matter what her resolves when alone, her mother-in-law's sheer presence tended to cast her back to a previous timid self.

'And Alice?'

'She's out riding, exercising Apollo for me. Are you staying long?'

'I shall return to London this evening. I came to make arrangements, that's all. I have rented a house for the Season, in Portman Square. Not my first choice of location, but the house has a ballroom, and they are hard to come by. I've taken it from Lady Pelham, and she keeps a staff there, but I shall need more people. Ring for Moss and Mrs Webster and I'll decide who to take. I shall want Moss, at any rate, and two footmen and perhaps six maids.'

'You'll leave the Castle short-staffed,' Kitty dared to object. Maud stared. 'What can it signify? You will not be entertaining. Richard will be up – I shall need him. And Giles – have you heard from him yet?'

'I had a cable from him yesterday, sent from Alexandria. He's on his way home. He expects to be here towards the end of April.'

'He is cutting it too finely,' she grumbled. 'I hope he has the common sense to call in at Caroline's before leaving London. It would be foolish of him to come all the way down here only to go straight back.'

'Must he go back?'

The dowager looked astonished. 'He must act as host for the ball. As the head of the family he will be in the receiving line with me. However little he likes it,' she added grimly, 'he will do the right thing by his own sister.'

'But he'll want to spend some time here first,' Kitty said, in desperate hope. She wanted to see him again, to have him to herself. 'Catching up with business. And he'll want fresh clothes – Town clothes.'

'Richard can tell him all he needs to know – that's why he was left in charge. And Crooks knows how to pack a trunk. He can accompany it to London and valet Giles while he's there. Sebastian will have to manage without him. Where *is* Sebastian?'

'He's away. He went to London for a few days. He said he'd stay at the club.'

'So you're here all alone,' Maud said, with a snort. 'You seem to have an uncanny knack for driving people away.'

Kitty was hurt, but with an effort did not show it. 'Have you a date for Rachel's ball?'

'The second of May. It will be the ball of the Season. His Majesty has promised to look in – he and my husband were great friends. It's a great pity Giles has not troubled himself to get to know the right people. Money is all very well, but connections matter quite as much.'

This was a dig at Kitty, as she knew. She struck back. 'If

the estate had been in good order, Giles would have been free to marry for connections,' she said. 'However, as his father's mismanagement left him bankrupt, he was forced to marry a nobody with money.'

'You are impertinent,' Maud said frostily.

Kitty refused to be frosted. 'And isn't it lucky he did? Because your plans for Rachel's come-out sound very lavish, and someone will have to pay for them.'

Maud returned the ball hard. 'It would hardly serve the family if Rachel did *not* have the debut appropriate to her position. But I don't expect *you* to understand the nuances of society. Rachel will make a great marriage, and it will reflect well on all of us. Your son will reap the benefit – little Lord Ayton. I must see him before I leave. Have him brought down after luncheon.'

'You could go up and see him now,' Kitty suggested pointedly.

Maud raised an eyebrow. 'Oh, I think not. And now, if you'll ring, please, I'll talk to Moss and Mrs Webster. Oh, and send someone after Alice and have her brought back. I'm having some gowns made for her, but they'll need to be fitted, so she'll have to come up.'

'But she's not out yet,' Kitty said, surprised.

'There are plenty of places a girl not yet out can be shown, and I wish to shape her before her debut next year. She is much too rough about the edges. She won't have a come-out like Rachel's – there'd be no point – but I will not have her make a show of us. Ring the bell, Kitty,' she concluded impatiently.

Kitty turned away to obey, and for a moment was in profile to the dowager. She heard a hiss of indrawn breath, and when she turned back, having pulled the bell, she found herself being closely scrutinised.

'So,' Maud said, in a deadly voice. 'Have you something to tell me?'

Kitty was startled that she had latched on so quickly – none of the others had noticed anything yet; though of course when you saw someone every day you were less likely to see a difference that had come on gradually. But she knew there was no sense in prevaricating. 'Yes, I am expecting another baby,' she admitted.

'Indeed? And how far along are you?'

'Four months, I think.'

Maud's nostrils flared. 'You were proposing to tell me when, exactly? Or was I to be kept in the dark? Upon my word, Kitty, you have some strange ways of going about things. I wonder, indeed, what it was your parents taught you. Perhaps people who live in *Hampstead* have different customs from the rest of us.' She said *Hampstead* as if it were *Borrioboola-Gha*.

'I wanted Giles to be the first to know,' Kitty said stiffly. 'My own parents don't know yet. We *Hampstead* people believe the baby's father is the most important person.'

Maud was gathering her forces to retort, but the door opened and Moss came in. When the dowager rang, the butler himself answered the drawing-room bell.

'Ah, Moss,' Maud began. 'I sent for you to—'

But Kitty couldn't allow that. She spoke over Maud, with determined authority. 'I should like to speak to you and Mrs Webster together, Moss. Please bring her here to the drawing-room, right away.'

It was only a small triumph. But with the dowager, that was all Kitty could hope for.

Rose, going past the door, saw Dory in the ironing-room and paused to watch her. 'What's that, then?' she asked, after a moment.

Dory lifted the garment by the shoulders and shook it out for Rose to see. 'A dress for Miss Arabella. I made it out of an old thing of Lady Alice's.'

'You've done a nice job,' Rose remarked.

'I can't help feeling sorry for those poor children – nobody seems to want them. I'm going to make something for Master Arthur next. Knickers and a Russian blouse, I thought, for him to play in.'

Rose nodded, examining Dory as she put the dress back on the table and applied the iron again. 'You've been spending a lot of time in the nursery lately,' she said.

Dory didn't look up. 'I take my sewing up there sometimes, instead of the sewing-room. It's nice to have company while I work.'

'Hmm,' said Rose. 'You do seem to have been a bit glum lately. Since Christmas, really. Is everything all right?'

'Of course,' Dory said. Now she looked up. 'Winter gets everybody down, doesn't it?'

'And working in the sewing-room, I suppose you'd notice that Mr Sebastian doesn't play his piano so much, these days. I think you used to enjoy his playing, didn't you?'

'Yes. You can really do with something to listen to while you sew. Now I can listen to Jessie and Nanny chatting. And children always liven up the place.'

Rose snorted, and pushed away from the door jamb. 'Most people wouldn't agree with you there. Children should be seen and not heard.'

'Poor things! Sometimes, when Jessie's busy, I tell them a story to keep them from under her feet, and they sit and listen, so quiet and good.'

'Well, don't let Mrs Webster catch you up there,' said Rose, moving away. 'You know she likes people to be in their place.'

The man waiting for Sebastian at the Blue Posts in Rupert Street was as nondescript as it was possible for a person to be. He was dressed like a member of the clerking fraternity, his clothes old but well-kept, his boots decent and polished, but not to a high shine. His face was clean-shaven, his hair neatly cut, and his features were so unremarkable that if you turned away from him it was hard to remember what he looked like. If you had to describe him to a third party, 'medium' and 'ordinary' would be the words you reached for. His name – or the name he chose to give – was, appropriately, Mr Bland.

It was not a place in which to appear too wealthy and fashionable. Rupert Street itself might be respectable in a small-trader way, but it connected with a couple of narrow courts which teemed with lower forms of life. The area in general was shabby and run down, and the many pubs were of the sort that tended to be described as 'haunts', whose customers 'frequented' them.

They sat at a table in a corner on the far side, facing the door. It occurred to Sebastian that this had been a deliberate choice. With the oak panelling on two sides of them they were in the shadow and no-one could get close enough to overhear them without being seen, while they could watch everyone who came in and out. Sebastian would never have thought of any of that, but Mr Bland had somehow sharpened his wits.

'Now, sir,' said Mr Bland, 'I have made some progress. There *was* a draper's shop in Cheyne Walk, a family business called Spencer's.'

Dory had given her surname as Spicer, but it was close enough, thought Sebastian.

'A neighbour I spoke to remembered that it was well thought-of, but began to go downhill a bit when Mrs Spencer died and Mr Spencer had to run the business alone.'

'And the daughter?'

'The neighbour didn't remember a daughter, though there was a young woman who served in the shop sometimes.'

'I suppose that was her.'

'Could be, sir. Well, now, when we come to the tailoring business, that's much better remembered. The proprietor was

111

a Mr Percy Hubert, known as "Jack", and he was apparently quite a live wire. Always full of jokes and chat, but he was said to be a good tailor. They undertook fine repairs to ladies' clothes as well.'

'You seem to be talking in the past tense. Is the shop no longer there?'

'No, sir. It was a double premises, and the larger part is now a hardware shop. The smaller part is a second-hand-clothes shop, selling men's and boys' suits. It's called Smithson's now, but under the shop sign, which is painted over the window, you can still just about make out the outline of "Hubert Tailoring". So there's no mistake. It's the place, all right.'

'And this fellow, Jack Hubert?'

Bland shook his head. 'Gone, sir. So far I haven't managed to find out anything but that he supposedly took to drink and the business suffered. It will take more work – and more time – to track him down.'

'But you believe you can?'

'Oh, yes, sir. There are lots more people to talk to, and threads to follow. And all the other resources – the police, hospitals, poor-houses. If he drank enough to lose his business, he almost certainly came to the attention of one or another. The question is, Mr Tallant, how far you want me to go. It will probably take many months, and you know my fee.'

'I want him found. I don't care what it costs. Are you willing to go on?'

'Yes, sir, if that's what you want.' He cocked his head. 'When I *do* find him, what do you want me to do?'

'Nothing to alarm him. Nothing to reveal who is paying you. That's crucial.'

'Of course.' He sounded just slightly wounded. 'Discretion is my watch word.'

'Just send to me straight away, by telegram, that you've found him, and where. And you must keep an eye on him until I decide what to do, in case he moves again.'

Bland nodded. 'May I ask what's he done, this cove?'

'You may not.'

'As you please. Just tell me, does he know you're looking for him? And is he likely to be armed? I have my own safety to think about.'

'No, he doesn't know. And I don't suppose he will be armed, but I couldn't say for sure.'

'Very well,' said Bland. 'And now, to the delicate question of my fee.'

'Yes, indeed,' Sebastian said, reaching for his pocket-book.

'Not so obvious, Mr Tallant, if you please,' Bland said quickly. 'Under the table, and try not to show it. Two guineas for what I've discovered so far, and another three on account for the next stage – I'll have expenses, you see, hotel bills and suchlike.'

'Five guineas, then.'

'Make it sovereigns for a gentleman such as yourself. Thank you, sir. It's a pleasure to do business with you.'

'Find him,' Sebastian said, with quiet emphasis.

'I will, sir. You can count on it.'

CHAPTER SEVEN

Thanks to some diligent work on the part of Constable Holyoak, a woman had been found in Mop End who remembered looking out of her kitchen window on the evening of the 4th of November and seeing a man go past who sufficiently matched William's description. She had been looking out for her husband to come back from the Red Lion, and seeing the dark human shape had thought at first it was him, till he went right past the gate and was lit for a moment by the bright moonlight. Holyoak knew her husband, who frequently got drunk at the Red Lion – a very low sort of beer house – and when in his cups liked to bash his wife a bit. So it made sense to him that she would have been looking out of the window, and that she would remember the approaching shape that turned out not to be the man whose return she dreaded. He believed her, therefore, and it was the final scruple to add to the scales on the side of William's innocence.

Sergeant Mayhew did not set much store by Mrs Porrit's evidence, or indeed by that of Tabby Mattock, who, he opined, was a baggage who would say anything. In fact, he regarded women in general as unreliable and most of them inveterate liars. But he was inclined to believe William's account, now he was willing to give one, because he did not think a man would admit to something as embarrassing as being beaten up by a woman unless it was true. So the charge against William was dropped, and word sent to the Castle. Richard came himself and collected the footman, so that he could be sure Tabby had kept her end of the bargain before he paid her the second instalment.

'So William is definitely in the clear?' he asked the sergeant.

'Free to go, sir,' said Mayhew.

'Without a stain on his character?'

Mayhew writhed a little at that. 'You might tell him to steer clear of females like that Mattock piece,' he said uncharitably. 'Consorting with them won't do his character no good.'

'Consorting,' Richard said, savouring the word. 'No, I dare say "consorting" is never a good idea. I shall have the butler give him a good, fatherly talking-to.'

'A proper thrashing is what I'da got from my old man,' Mayhew said sternly, 'and the better for it. Course, he's got no father, and Mrs Sweeting may be a God-fearing woman and a church-goer, but she's a quarter that William's size and couldn't raise a welt on him if she stood on a chair. Spare the rod, Mr Tallant, and spoil the child. That's what I always say.'

'I'll try to see William is put on the right track,' Richard promised him. 'And what will happen now to the, er, case – is that the word? – of Edgar Speen?'

'Put aside, Mr Tallant,' Holyoak said, 'pending further information.' Mayhew only sniffed disapprovingly, so he continued, 'I don't suppose we'll ever know who killed him. My betting is it was a tramping man, passing through, and long gone now. We do get 'em, making their way to London – out-of-work labourers, or ruined men, hoping to make a new start in the capital. It's a main route, along the valley, from a number of places.'

'What happens to the body, by the way?' Richard asked.

'Buried on the parish,' Mayhew said. 'Deceased had no family that we could discover.'

'My family will make a donation, seeing he was in our employ,' Richard said. 'And a simple headstone, perhaps.' He

115

felt bad about Speen, who had been his valet, and would never have come to Ashmore to get himself killed if he hadn't engaged him.

'That's as you please, Mr Tallant,' said Mayhew. 'You'd better talk to Rector.'

'I think my brother would expect it done,' Richard said.

Richard chose a quiet moment to walk down to Warner's Rents. It was a fine breezy day after several showery ones. All the way down the hill he was passing washing laid out on hedges to dry, and at the rents themselves many had washing pegged out in the long front gardens. No washing blew at the Mattock house. He saw the door was open, which again was a common thing – all these cottages were desperately damp, and on a day like this the door would often be left open so that the breeze could dry the floor and walls inside.

He walked down the path, paused politely at the door and rapped on the frame, calling 'Hulloo, the house! Anybody home?' but it was all quiet within. Then he noticed that there were no napkins or baby clothes drying in front of the fire. He took a step inside and looked round. The cottage consisted of one room, with a lean-to scullery behind, so he could see the whole thing from the door. A bed in one corner where presumably Tabby, her mother and the baby all slept, a wooden table, two wooden chairs and an open-fronted cupboard in which a few items of crockery and the heel-end of a loaf of bread were all that could be seen on the shelves. No human being of any size.

Suspicion slipped into his mind. He stepped back out, thought a moment, and walked away to where a chestnut tree gave him a large trunk to stand behind while he watched the house. After a few minutes, Mrs Mattock came along, bent sideways under the weight of a bucket: the cottages shared a privy and a water pump at the end of the row. She went into the cottage with it. He waited. It was ten or fifteen minutes later that he saw Tabby approaching, with a covered basket on her arm. He waited until she turned down her own path before he came out, swiftly covered the ground between them, and caught her arm.

It was almost the undoing of him. She whipped round at amazing speed and flung a fist at him. Only his own quick reaction saved his face. It grazed his ear in passing as he jumped back and cried, 'Steady! It's only me!'

Her face shut down into a secretive blankness, enigmatic as a cat. 'You frit me! Creeping up on a person like that,' she complained. 'What's the idea?'

'I thought you'd be expecting me,' he said. 'William's been released. He's back at the Castle. There's no charge against him.'

'Oh,' she said, surveying his face carefully. 'Well, good. So you know I told the pleece the story, like I promised.'

'Yes, they told me all about it,' Richard said. 'Where's the baby?'

'Beg pardon?' It was a strategic deafness, he saw, to give her time to think.

'The baby. The one I'm going to help support.' He gestured to the basket on her arm. 'You're not carrying it about in there, are you?'

'Don't be daft,' she said shortly. The basket was nowhere near big enough to hold a baby. 'It's just a bit of stuff for our supper.' Her eyes narrowed. 'So where's my three pound? Hand it over.'

'Where's the baby, Miss Tabby?'

'In the house,' she said, not meeting his eye. 'Ma's minding it.'

He shook his head. 'I've seen inside,' he said. 'No baby in there. No baby napkins or clothes, either, drying by the fire or outside.'

'I dunno what you're talking about. Gimme my money.'

He caught her upper arm again, to stop her escaping. 'What have you done with it?'

Mrs Mattock, hearing voices, came to the cottage door, saw them together, and scuttled back inside in an action redolent of guilt. Tabby wriggled, testing his grip, and knew the game was up. She blew out an angry gust. 'It's gone, all right? I give it to that lady in the village, that do-good, to put with a fambly, and that's the end of it. Did you think I was going to saddle meself with a brat for the rest of me life? You try it, Mr Richard Tallant, with your fancy clothes and your big house. *You* didn't want it, did you? So why should I? It's gone and that's that. Now gimme my three pound.'

He released her arm, saddened, but not surprised. 'You've had two pounds already.'

'Yeah, and I had to give it to that Miss Whassername to take the baby. I need the rest.'

'No,' he said. 'The money was to support the baby, and there's no baby to support any more.'

She lowered her voice to a hiss. 'The money was for me to get your precious William off the hook, and I done it. So don't you come the high-and-mighty with me! If I want a sermon I'll go to Rector. Five pound for talking to the pleece, that was the bargain, and don't you dare go back on it.'

He stared at her without speaking, and she took a half-step closer to him. 'You give me the other, or you know what I'll do. I warned you! I'll go to the pleece and tell 'em you bribed me to lie.'

'That'll get you into trouble.'

'Won't do you no good either – and you've got further to fall. What'd your brother say, what'd your *ma* say, if you was put on a charge?'

Richard knew she was right. He felt a little sick. 'If I pay you, what will you do?'

'Get to hell out of this place,' she said promptly. 'Go to

London and disappear. You'll never see me again, you can bet on that.'

'How do I know you'll keep your word?'

She laughed coarsely. 'You don't! That's the joke, ain't it? But I don't wanter be here any more'n you want me here. I'll clear all right. I've only been waiting for the money.'

He really had no choice. He could only hope that self-preservation would make her go away and stay away. Reluctantly he reached into his pocket and handed her the money. She made it disappear into her bodice so quickly it was a blur. 'All right,' she said. She looked once into his face, then turned away. 'Better clear off, Mr Tallant, 'fore anyone wonders what you're doing here.' She sniggered. 'They might think you're paying me for a—' She used a coarse word, and he flinched. She laughed. 'You look as if you could use one all right. But you won't get it from me!'

She went on down the path, and he hurried away, feeling unaccountably as though he needed a bath.

When giving a ball for a debutante, one of the most important things for a hostess was to secure enough unmarried men. Nothing, as Maud knew, was more deadly to the success of a ball than an excess of girls over men, and the consequent sight of rows of girls in their finery sitting out, wilting slightly like cut flowers for which there was no vase.

It was in her mind as she read the letter from Cecily Tullamore (who was actually her aunt, but as they were of an age and had grown up together, they always called each other cousin). It was a letter of courtesy, informing Maud that the whole Tullamore family was coming up to London for the Season, and would be taking a house in Russell Square – which was a little too far east for fashion, but though the Tullamores were wealthy (Cecily's husband owned a good deal of land and several coal mines) they were not of the first consequence.

All the same, among the Tullamore children there were two grown sons, Angus who was twenty-four and Fritz who was eighteen, both nice, well-behaved boys. She considered long and hard, tapping the end of her pen against her lips. Angus and Fritz would do to dance with some of the less important girls, who might otherwise find themselves without partners. But if she invited them, Cecily and Gordon might also want her to invite the eldest girl, Beata.

Perhaps, she thought, she had better write a completely frank letter to Cecily, who as a mother would understand the issue at hand and send her two eldest sons on their own. Maud could always dine her and Gordon later in the Season as a way of saying thank you.

And another happy thought came to her. There were among the Tullamore brood two very young children, Mannox and Mary, who, if she remembered correctly, were about ten and eight respectively. Would it not be *very* convenient if Cecily were to invite Linda's children to stay while everyone was in London? They could play with the youngest Tullamores, and the Tullamore nanny could take charge of them all.

Otherwise, since it was obvious that Linda did not mean to go back to Dorset, but was clinging on to Portman Square like a barnacle, Maud might end up with Arabella and Arthur under her roof, which would *not* be convenient.

Yes, a letter to Cecily, framed in just the right language, with the hint of a dinner and perhaps a longer stay at Ashmore Castle at some point in the summer . . .

She drew paper towards her, and as she dipped her pen, her eye fell on a card that had been left earlier by Prince Paul Usingen, just arrived in London. He was considerably older than Rachel, but very eligible, and he had shown interest in her during their stay in Germany. Probably he had come to London looking for a bride. Yes, she must make sure he got an invitation – with 'Do come!' written across it in her own hand. People could never resist the

120

personal touch. She'd do it straight after the tricky letter to Cecily.

Crooks found William in the plate-room lethargically sorting out the silver for dinner. He had always been a well-fed young man with a high colour, but since his ordeal in the police cell he had changed. He was gaunt and pale now, and drooped moodily. He avoided the other servants as much as possible, and could often be found hunched in an obscure corner of the yards, smoking and staring at nothing. Some of the maids tried to be kind to him, but there was an undertone of no-smoke-without-fire suspicion about him, and Sam, who had shared a room with him until his arrest, had asked to be moved. No-one else wanted to share, and there were no single rooms. But when William listlessly seconded the request, Mr Moss had allowed him to move his bed into a tiny room among the rafters that had been used for storage. It was probably not helping his mood.

Crooks felt sorry for him. There must always be an element of doubt while the killer of Speen went unidentified, but he knew the adage of the law, that a man was innocent until proved guilty, and felt that as Englishmen they should put that into practice. Of course, he thought, being a gentleman's gentleman, he naturally had more refined sensibilities than some of the lower servants. Still, William was one of their own and ought to have their loyalty.

So he paused in the doorway and, after watching for a moment, said in a kindly way, 'Separate salt cellar for each place, don't forget.'

'I know,' William said, not looking at him.

Crooks stepped in. 'Come, now,' he said, 'you've got to try and buck up.'

'Easy for you to say, Mr Crooks,' William muttered gloomily.

'Life brings challenges to everyone,' said Crooks. 'You were tested, but you came through. You were found innocent. Now you must put it behind you, and use the experience to make you a better person. The refiner's fire, d'you see?'

William didn't see. There was nothing fine about it, as far as he could see. 'But my ma's done with me, because of Tabby, and everybody here thinks I did it. I can't go home and I can't stay. Even if I left, I'd never get another job with that hanging over me. Word gets about, you know.'

'Nobody here thinks you did it,' Crooks said, not quite truthfully.

'James is telling everybody I did.'

'James is a bad person. He says bad things about everybody. You mustn't pay him any attention.'

'But if everyone believes him . . .'

'I'm sure they don't. It's just gossip. And if I hear anyone saying anything of that sort, I shall speak out, firmly.'

'But what am I supposed to do?' William said miserably.

'You must rise above it. Show everybody by your own actions that you are a good man. Bear witness in your everyday life to the Christian virtues, and people will soon forget all this nastiness. You must rise, William. Rise!'

William gave him the downtrodden but faintly hopeful look of a dog that believes the scolding might be over. 'What've I to do, exactly?'

Crooks examined him. 'Smarten yourself up, to begin with. If a man is clean and shaven and his clothes are pressed and worn properly, he feels better about himself right away. Don't slouch. Walk briskly. Hold up your head and look people in the eye. Do your work with energy and take pride in doing it well. Do all that, and people will take you at your own estimation.'

It sounded daunting to William, but Mr Crooks was waiting, so he made an effort to stand up straighter. 'You're very kind, Mr Crooks,' he muttered.

Crooks laid a hand on his arm. 'I'll stand by you, William.

And if you have any difficulties, come to me. Or to Mr Moss,'
he added, but it was a dutiful rather than a heartfelt
addendum.

Giles was not alone with Giulia again. He made sure it
didn't happen. Usually she was in the company of the
Arthurs, or at least of Mary, but he even grew wary of
joining their party at all, making excuses to stay in his cabin
alone. He no longer went up on deck after dinner, for fear
Mary and Talbot should wander off together and leave him
alone with Giulia.

He felt hideously guilty. It was a betrayal of all his affection
for the Lombardi family, his gratitude towards Flavio and
Lucia, his duty of care towards their daughter. Very well, it
had been only one kiss, but she had called him *her dearest*
– what emotions had he stirred up? He was a married man.
And even if a married man took a mistress – which was not
something he countenanced – it would never be the innocent
unmarried daughter of a decent family. Such a thing was
unthinkable.

After the toils and hardships of the Valley, the luxury of
the ship wearied him but did not tire him out. There was
not enough to do. The only physical exercise available was
walking round the decks. His rested body began to feel
different wants, and he could not sufficiently distract
himself from its clamour. He began to have erotic dreams,
in which, aching with desire, he pursued some woman
along endless corridors, while she kept teasingly just out
of reach, laughing and beckoning him on. In the dreams
he never saw the woman clearly. He told himself one could
not be responsible for one's dreams, but it did not assuage
his guilt.

He had always preferred to shave himself, and even after
the demonstration in Cairo of Afton's superior skills, he had
insisted on wielding his own razor. But now, in his state of

irritable languor, he began to allow Afton to shave him. Afton was an excellent servant, silent unless encouraged to speak, but ready to chat if required. Spending more time lying back looking up into Afton's face, he could not but become aware that he was a handsome fellow, with a lean, firm-featured face and very blue eyes. He must, Giles thought, have been attractive to females. One morning, to distract himself, he spoke the thought aloud.

'You must be quite a devil with the ladies. Have you ever been married?'

'No, my lord,' Afton answered easily. 'Been close to it a few times.' He glanced to see if conversation was wanted, and went on, 'When I was younger, I didn't have the time or money. Then I was in service – where, of course, you *can't* marry. Then, with my own shop, I was too occupied with business to look for a wife. It's a time-consuming thing if you're going to do it right.'

'And you would always want to do it right,' Giles said.

'No point otherwise, my lord. Whatever I'm doing, I want to do it as well as it can be done. And females, well, you can live without them, if you put your mind to it. But they're so soft and pretty and beguiling, my lord, I can quite see that once you'd started you'd never be able to stop. So I don't start. But perhaps one day, when I've got a bit saved and can settle down . . .'

'You're a wise man, Afton.'

'Turn a little to the left, my lord, if you please.'

'But don't you . . . ?' Giles hesitated.

'Yes, my lord?' Afton encouraged him.

'There are – um . . . A man feels . . . certain – er – wants. Urges, perhaps. Don't you find?'

'Oh, yes. The body has a mind of its own, my lord, if I may put it that way.' He pushed Giles's face gently further to the left, to shave below his right ear, and went on, 'The dreams, my lord – they can be insistent.'

How did he know? Giles thought. The man was a wizard. Or was it just coincidence?

'But a man has no control over his dreams, my lord,' Afton went on. 'In my opinion, one should just, as it were, lie back and enjoy them.'

'I find them troubling.'

'Yes, my lord,' Afton said. No more than that. Then he said, 'You must be looking forward to getting back to London, my lord. There'll be lots to do there.'

'Yes. And you, Afton – have you friends to catch up with?'

'No friends any more, my lord. But lots to see and do during my time off.'

'I shall try not to encroach on it.'

'Thank you, my lord. But my duty comes first, always. As I know it does with you.'

Now, Giles thought, relapsing into silence, *was that a compliment? Or a warning?*

That night the dream came again, but it was different. The woman was not running away, but waiting for him at the end of the corridor, and this time he could see her clearly. It was not Giulia. There were dark eyes, yes, but a whiter skin, and hair the colour of a wheatfield at harvest time. He remembered a voice, a presence, a mind that seemed to match his; a spirit that fitted his as the curve of a bird fits its nest. In the dream, he knew that if he could reach her, all the longings of his life would be resolved: in her he would find his home. But walking towards her was like struggling through thick mud; and no matter how he strove, he never got any nearer. She seemed even to be drawing further away, fading, like a ghost. He cried out to her, and woke himself up: in the dream he had shouted, but in reality it had been a feeble whimper.

On the last day, as they were coming into Trieste, he found himself on deck, at the taffrail with Talbot and Giulia, watching the cranes and warehouses and bustle of the dockside grow nearer. It was a breezy day, with clouds bowling across a pale spring sky, shadows running over the restless dark sea, gulls wheeling and crying above the ship. Mary was below, supervising some problem that had occurred with her maid and the packing. And then the thing he had been dreading happened – a steward came and took Talbot away with a question about a packing case, leaving Giles alone with Giulia.

She turned to him at once. 'You have been avoiding me,' she said. It was an accusation, but her tone was tender. '*So che devi essere discreto*—'

He hardly heard her in his rush to apologise. 'Giulia, I am so sorry!' he said. 'What I did was unforgivable. I am not that sort of man. It was a deplorable lapse on my part, and I have been racked with guilt ever since. Please believe, it will never happen again.'

He saw he had offended her. Her nostrils flared. 'Do you suppose,' she said tautly, 'that I am some mindless doll, a child's toy to be moved this way and that?'

'No – I—' he began, startled. 'I don't think of you like that.'

'You don't think of me at all!'

'That's not true. I have always been very fond of you.'

'Fond!' She almost spat it. '*Una parola veramente inglese!* You toss me a scrap from your plate, because you are *fond* of me, like a dog. And then the idea of it hurts your pride, so you are *sorry!*'

'No, Giulia – no!'

'You kissed me. And you think, by that, that I am just waiting for your kisses! That if you shall happen to want it, I shall let you kiss me again and be grateful!' She dropped into Italian, too angry and rapid for him to catch it all, though the word *stupido* seemed to feature more than once. Then she flicked a glance away from him and interrupted herself. 'Hush, Mary comes.' She closed her lips tight and drew herself up with dignity.

126

'Oh, my troublesome maid!' Mary exclaimed, laughing, as she reached them. 'She was in a panic because she thought she'd mislaid my passport and pocket-book, and then it turned out she'd packed them in the trunk and we had to turn everything out! I'm so looking forward to London and being in one place! Are you staying in London at all, Giles, or will you go straight down to the country?'

His mind was sore from Giulia's words, but he roused himself to answer. 'No, I shall have to stay in London for the moment. My sister's come-out, you know.' An idea occurred to him. 'You must come to her ball,' he said, a look gathering Giulia into the invitation. 'If I know my mother, it will be the event of the Season, something not to be missed.'

Mary smiled. 'I'm sure we would love to come, but won't she already have sent out the invitations?'

'That cannot signify. I shall be paying for the whole thing, therefore I shall invite anyone I want – and I want you and Tal and Giulia. Please say you'll come. I must have some friends of my own, as counterweight to my mother's "significant people".'

'Oh, so we're not significant people?' Mary laughed. 'No, my dear, I'm just teasing you! We'd love to come, wouldn't we, Giulia? And, in return, you must promise to dine with us at least once before you go down.'

'It would be my pleasure,' Giles said. By a heroic effort, he didn't look at Giulia as he said it.

Going to Pelham House was a new lease of life for Moss. He had been feeling tired and lethargic lately, but coming to London and preparing for an important event was like a return to the grand old days of his late lordship. He became the Moss of yore, the major-domo who controlled the establishment with a lift of his eyebrow, and received the cream of society, and royalty both British and foreign, as though it were an everyday thing. In the old days, dukes, margraves, highnesses (both royal and serene), all had known his name, had pressed grateful guineas into his palm. 'You're a marvel, Moss,' they had said, when he solved some delicate problem for them. Many of them had told his lordship they envied him Moss; some had even tried to entice him away.

Her ladyship (it was a relief, in Pelham House, that the dowager was again simply 'her ladyship') had chosen James and Sam as the footmen he should bring. And with regard to maids she had said, 'Rose and three others. You may decide.' So he had been able to sidestep Mrs Webster with apparent lordly indifference, and choose Ada along with Doris and Ellen.

Mrs Webster had not been entirely quiescent. 'Ada is not very experienced. And rather small. There may be heavy work in the preparation stage. Why not take Mabel instead? Or Tilda – she's strong.'

Moss had had to think quickly. 'Her ladyship may require them in the public areas. Taking coats and escorting ladies to the dressing-room and such. Mabel and Tilda may be good workers but they won't do as parlour-maids.'

Mrs Webster looked at him sharply. 'Did her ladyship ask you to pick pretty ones?'

Moss couldn't quite lie. 'I believe it was implied,' he said loftily.

Ellen was excited about the trip. 'You never know but what there may be an opportunity for me,' she said to Rose. 'Some lady needing her hair put up or a gown pinned or something. I could show what I can do, and if, say, they were looking for a lady's maid . . .'

Rose snorted. 'You go on thinking like that,' she said. 'As if anyone at the ball of the Season is going to notice a maid!'

'Still,' Ellen said defiantly, 'there's all these girls going to get married soon, and they'll be needing a maid for the first time—'

'They won't remember you by the time they get married.

Anyway, what about your Tom?' Ellen was walking out with Tom Trapper, the chimney-sweep's son. 'If you get a lady's maid job you'll be moving away and that'll be that.'

'Oh, Tom . . .' Ellen said consideringly. She was fond of him, and she liked the distinction of having a steady walk-out, unlike the other maids. On the other hand . . . 'Tom's nice, but he always smells a bit of soot, no matter how much he washes. And I'd get to meet lots of smart London valets.'

'Oh, yes. Like Mr Speen,' Rose said. 'He was smart all right.'

'Ooh, Rose, you mustn't speak ill of the dead! Anyway, I bet *you* wouldn't say no to a nice valet, if you was asked.'

Rose snorted. 'I've had enough of men to last me a lifetime, thank you very much. We'd all be better off without them. London's going to be hard work, and don't you forget it.'

There was always the chance of nice tips, though Rose didn't mention that. But when the time came, she didn't go at all. She woke on the morning of departure coughing, sneezing, and streaming at the eyes, and was obviously not fit to be taken. Moss was quite put out, having expected her to keep a firm hand on the maids when they were in London. Mrs Webster, however, put an end to his dithering. 'Of course she can't go. You'd have your entire staff down with it. You had better take Dory.'

'But she's not a housemaid,' Moss objected, his brow furrowed.

'She's done most things in her time, and she's older and sensible and will keep the younger ones in order.' And seeing he was still doubtful, she added, 'Having a skilled needle-woman in the house can only be an advantage, given all the new gowns that will be coming through the door. Her lady-ship will think you've shown initiative.'

So Dory was told to pack her bag. She was not sorry to get away for a bit, for the sense of Sebastian's brooding sadness haunted the house for her. And though she had avoided London ever since she ran away, surely there was no chance of bumping into Jack as long as she stayed inside the house.

In Portman Square, Moss discovered, to his pleasure, that her ladyship was sparing no expense. A large number of extra local staff had already been employed, and were busy cleaning – though not busy enough, to his mind. He strode in and chivvied them up. Everything had to be cleaned to the highest standard: floors, woodwork and furniture waxed and rubbed to a glow, carpets, curtains and upholstery beaten, windows and mirrors polished, ornaments and chandeliers washed. After inspecting the house on the first day, Moss opined to her ladyship that some of the paintwork was not up to standard. He was relieved and proud that she accepted his suggestion and instructed him to hire decorators to repaint anything he thought needed it – an instruction he decided included a little bit of re-gilding.

There were all sorts of arrangements to be made for the ball itself. Carpenters had to build a dais for the orchestra. Rout-chairs had to be hired for the ballroom, and an expert had to come and inspect the floor for springing, and to chalk it on the day. There would be tubs of flowers for the entrance, the reception hall and the ballroom. A huge number of candles to order. A card-room had to be set up: tables and chairs hired, new packs of cards, pencils and ashtrays purchased. The police would be needed to keep the crowds back from the entrance and to direct the traffic. The supper was entirely in the hands of the caterers, but suitable rooms had to be prepared.

A room had to be cleared just off the reception hall for coats – Moss told James he would be in charge of that on the night. It needed an experienced hand to make sure the right mantle went to the right person, and James was very happy to accept the responsibility, with its opportunity for tips and possibly the odd bit of 'lost property'. And ladies' and gentlemen's dressing-rooms had to be prepared upstairs. He would have put Rose in charge of the ladies' on the night, but he saw now that Mrs Webster had been right and that Dory would do even better. Evening gowns with trains, combined with heat, excitement, flirting and dancing, were a recipe for sartorial mishaps, and a skilled sewing-maid in the dressing-room would be regarded as a thoughtful addition to the ball.

Moss bestrode the house like a Colossus, directing, controlling, anticipating, answering questions and solving problems. He felt ten years younger and a foot taller, and though her ladyship would not demean herself to comment, he thought he saw a look of approval when she happened to pass him. More importantly, he saw Ada's eyes fixed on him in what he decided was deep admiration – almost awe.

The presence of Lady Linda was something of a drawback, as she had always had a tendency to meddle, but Moss found he could keep her out of his way by asking her to deal with the outsiders who were not in his remit, like the caterers, the florist, and the commissioner of police.

Lady Rachel he barely saw, except as she passed through the hall on her way to or from an engagement. She seemed in fine looks, and buoyed up with excitement, which was as it should be. When he contemplated what all this must be costing, it was just as well, he thought, that she was so very pretty. She sometimes threw him a distracted smile in passing, and just once she addressed him, as he happened to be in the hall when she was leaving for a party, and held the door open for her. 'I'm glad you're here, Moss,' she said. 'It makes me feel everything will go off all right.'

'I'm sure everything will, my lady,' he said.

'I'm frightfully nervous,' she confided, glancing up at him with a shy smile that took him back to her schoolroom days.

He became human, and his smile was fatherly. 'There's no

need, my lady. You will be the belle of the ball. All will be well.'

'Thank you, Moss,' she said, with a look that was as good as a kiss on the cheek, and whisked herself away.

CHAPTER EIGHT

Vogel, the family's banker, approved Richard's dairy plan, as far as it went. 'The estate needs investment, and with agricultural prices as low as they are, it's good to think about moving in a new direction. We can't go on in the same ancestral way.'

'I'm glad you agree,' said Richard. 'When I say the same thing to the tenants they shake their heads and give me the look that says, "Impetuous young devil. You'll learn!"'

Vogel laughed. 'I know that look well.'

'It's the silent resistance. They think I'll just talk myself into exhaustion, and then they can go back to what they were doing before I lost my mind.'

'That's human nature, sir – we all cling to what we know. But, to be fair, your plan is a significant departure from the past, and it needs thinking out carefully.'

'Yes, I know. And I know just who to turn to for the thinking.'

It was convenient that the Cowlings had taken a house just on the other side of the square to Aunt Caroline, where Richard stayed when in London.

Cowling received him with a hearty handshake, and said, 'Now, this is right civil of you to call on me. Mrs Cowling will be sorry to have missed you. She's not here at present.'

'Oh, is she still in the country?'

'No, she came up with me, but we brought her friend with us – Lady Clementine Leacock.' He said the name with obvious pride, and Richard smiled and nodded, though he didn't know the lady. 'It's nice for Nina to have a companion while I'm busy, and Lady Clemmie was eager for a trip to London. They're out somewhere together, I don't know where.'

'It was you I wanted to talk to, sir – on a matter of business.'

'Business, eh? Well, you'd better come into my study.' He led the way, saying, 'Something about the jam factory, is it? I was there last week and it's all going splendidly. Had another idea for expansion, have you? I'm not sure what else we can do with jam that we're not doing, but I'm all ears.'

'No, it's not jam, sir. Something probably even more ambitious, but I'd like to know your opinion of the scheme, and ask your advice, if that's not too presumptuous.'

Cowling conducted him into his business-room and gestured to a chair. 'Well, well, sit thee down, lad, and let's hear it. I never mind being asked my opinion by those who'll listen. But I'll speak plainly, you know that. If it's nonsense, I'll say so.'

'I'm depending on that, sir,' Richard said. He seated himself, and described the plan – with the advantage that, as he'd already had to outline it to Vogel, he had got his words in order.

Cowling listened gravely, sitting back in his chair, staring at nothing and not moving, except to tap the pen he had taken up once or twice on the desk, as if in punctuation. When Richard had finished, there was a silence, which he had enough self-control not to break. If Cowling didn't think the scheme workable, pleading wouldn't help.

Finally, Cowling spoke. 'This is a long-term plan you've taken a mind to. We're talking years rather than months before you see a reasonable return.'

'I know, sir. But that's usually the way with the land. We've farmed that valley for three hundred and fifty years, so what's a few more, if we get it right? We can't go on in the same old way, that's certain. Farming as we knew it just doesn't pay.'

'Aye, you're right. The world's a different place now. Corn from the American prairies, meat from the wilds of Australia – stuff from the four corners, all brought in by steam-ships that don't need the wind at their backs to get here. We have to think different. And,' he looked at Richard now, 'I like to hear a young man think big, beyond what's in front of his face. But what d'you want me to do? If it's my money you're after, I have to tell you agriculture's not one of my interests.'

'I know, sir, but I mean to turn milk into a business, and business is business whatever the end product.'

Cowling nodded approvingly. 'You're right there!'

'But it's just advice I want for now.'

'Fair enough. Well, now, it seems to me that it's going to take a while before you have your product – the milk – ready for market; so that gives you time to get the other end, the distribution, set up.'

'That's the part I really know nothing about,' Richard said. 'I hoped you might have an idea of whom I could go to.'

'What I don't know, I can always find out. I think the best way would be to discover a London delivery dairy that's willing to expand. They'll have the expertise with customers, which'll cut some corners. I'll get my people on to it. As to the transportation, I happen to know Sam Fay of the Great Central Railway – he's a grand chap, worked his way up from junior clerk to general manager. He'll know how it's to be done. But you'll have to arrange to get the milk from the farms to the station at your end. That'll need thinking about. It's got to be done fast, so the milk is fresh, and I know what country roads are like.'

'Yes. I realised we'd have to invest in road repairs, along

with the improvements to the farm buildings. I was thinking that if each farm gets its churns down to the road by a certain time each day, we could have wagons going past from farm gate to farm gate, picking them up. That would save going up to each farmhouse separately.'

'Aye, good notion,' Cowling said absently, looking thoughtful.

'Sir? You've had an idea?'

He shook himself. 'Nay, it's something for further down the line, and you've got enough on your plate to be going on with. But I will say, if you get this right, it could be the saving of all your farm tenants. The old kind of farming – a few hens, half a dozen cows, a pig and six acres of wheat – that's going out, and it'll soon be gone. We're in a new century. You want industrial thinking, my lad, and I reckon you might have hit on it.'

'Thank you, sir.'

'I'll have a word with Sam Fay, and ask around about a local dairy, and I'll let you know how I get on. You've got the bigger part – getting those herds up to scratch.' Richard gave a rueful smile. He knew it. 'What does your brother say, his lordship?'

'I haven't talked to him about it yet. As soon as he's home from Egypt . . .'

'Aye, that was a rum do,' Cowling said reflectively. 'Hopping off to the Pyramids with a new wife at home and plenty to be done about the estate. But,' he corrected himself, 'it's not for me to comment, and no doubt he can feel confident, with you back here to catch the ball.'

There were not many times in Richard's life that anyone had suggested he was competent to catch the ball, and it was rather gratifying. It went some way to proving the old adage, that virtue was its own reward.

Giles left the Arthurs and Giulia at the station and took a cab to Berkeley Square. He took a four-wheel growler rather than a hansom so there would be room for the luggage, and Afton sat perched on the forward seat, pretending to be a statue as a valet should, and heroically not looking out of the window, though he must have wanted to.

When they reached Aunt Caroline's house Giles was not surprised to see it lit up, and messenger boys going up and down the steps with deliveries and notes. The ball was on the day after next, and excitement and activity would be growing. He grinned at his manservant. 'You can stare if you like, Afton. I won't tell anyone you displayed human curiosity.'

'Thank you, my lord,' Afton said imperturbably.

'But most of the action will be happening in Portman Square. We shall have only the ripples and after-shocks here.'

'I'm sure you will enjoy the tranquillity, my lord.'

'Shall I? But what about you?'

'I shall be glad of the opportunity to look over your dress clothes, my lord. I'm afraid there may still be sand in them.'

'It'll be knee breeches and stockings for the ball,' Giles said sadly. 'I hope my brother had the sense to have mine brought up from the country.'

'We'll manage, my lord.'

'I dare say *you* will,' Giles said. 'Who knows what purgatory awaits me?'

'My dear child, why didn't you tell us what train you'd be on? I'd have sent to meet you,' Aunt Caroline said.

'I wouldn't put you to the trouble,' Giles said, kissing her soft, scented cheek. He got the worst question over first: 'Is Mama here?'

'No, I've hardly seen her this week. She's at Pelham House with Rachel. Linda too – and Stuffy will be staying there when he comes up. My servants have enough to do with Richard, Alice and Kitty staying. And now you, of course – not that you're not very welcome, my dear,' she added hastily.

'Where is Kitty?'

'She's upstairs with Alice. She'll be down soon, I expect. Shall I ring for some tea, dear, or will you bathe first?'

It might have been a pointed question, but he was very thirsty. 'Tea, please, if you don't mind.'

Caroline surveyed him as she walked to the bell-pull. 'You look as though you need a good tea. I expect the heat out there was very wearing. I know I found Paris extremely tiresome on my honeymoon. I could hardly eat a thing – though of course I was very much in love, and French food was *not* what it was cracked up to be. My dear Sir James always said it was because all the best French cooks came to England to work, which may be true. I do remember that the meat was *very* tough, and there was quite a horrifying amount of gristle when you looked closely.'

Giles laughed. 'Dear Auntie! You must never go to Egypt.'

'I certainly shall never do that,' she promised him solemnly.

At that moment the door opened and Kitty and Alice came in. Kitty's eyes flew to his face; but Alice dashed past her and flung her arms round her brother impetuously. '*Darling* Giles! You're back! I was afraid you were going to miss the ball, and Mama said it would look terribly bad if you weren't here, though Uncle Stuffy could always do the honours, but it wouldn't be the same, and apart from putting Mama in a temper, *I*'d have hated it if you weren't there. Have you had a dreadful journey? You do smell rather oily and sooty. But it's *lovely* to see you.'

He embraced her absently and said, 'The journey was long rather than dreadful. I see you haven't grown up yet.' He was looking past her at Kitty.

'Heaven forbid!' Alice said. 'I mean to make the most of my last year.'

He put her gently aside and went to Kitty, who had remained just inside the door as if halted there by some invisible force. He took her hands, which were folded at her waist, and held them away from her. He felt a shock, but kept it, he hoped, out of his face. Instead, he said teasingly, 'What have you been up to, Lady Stainton?'

She was not able, in this first moment of seeing him, to accept a joke, even one so mild. What she wanted, what she needed, was a wholehearted delight in her condition. She said, rather stiffly, 'How are you, Giles? You look very thin. Didn't they feed you in Egypt?'

He waved that away. 'My dear, are you . . . You're expecting a child?' She nodded, waiting for his reaction. But his expression didn't change from the slightly quizzical. 'When?' he asked.

'In July or August.'

He hardly needed to ask, really. There had been just one occasion, shortly before he left. She had clung to him, and he had been carried away by the moment, and by memories of previous times. That must have been when it happened. He felt shocked by the randomness of Fate – that a life could be begun with so little thought or intention. And she had been carrying his child for five months, all the time he had been in Egypt and in ignorance. He couldn't decide how he felt about it, apart from surprised. 'I didn't know,' he said blankly.

She searched his face. What was he thinking? His expression gave nothing away. At last she had to say, 'Are you pleased?'

It brought him back to himself, to his duty. 'Of course I'm pleased,' he said automatically. But as soon as he heard the words, he discovered that he really *was*. 'How could I not be?'

Another child to love as he loved Louis. His feelings for his son were so blissfully uncomplicated, free of history, of the anxieties and tangles, misunderstandings, hurt, nuances, apprehensions, huffs and cold shoulders that made adults so hard to keep loving. Louis beamed at the mere sight of his father's face. He chuckled in delight when his father lifted him up. To grab Giles's nose and have him honk with pretended shock was for Louis the pinnacle of fun, a moment of sheer, unshadowed pleasure. He knew that it could not be like that for ever, that Louis would grow up and change, but that made it even more precious. And a second child – the other son they needed for dynastic reasons – could only be more of the same delight.

He came back from his thoughts to see that Kitty was still waiting, the smile she had managed to summon drooping at the corners with the effort of maintaining it. His recent guilt over Giulia streaked across his mind. This was his chance to atone. Poor Kitty had been alone with this knowledge for months. She was his wife: he must make her happy. He lifted her hands to his lips and kissed them, and smiled. 'It's wonderful news!' he said. 'But how are you? Are you well? Are you comfortable? You're looking well – blooming and beautiful.'

Her grateful look was his reward. He tucked her hand under his arm and turned to the room to say, 'I'm going to be a father again!'

'Yes, we know, dear,' said Aunt Caroline. 'It's very good news.'

'Especially as it means you can't go off travelling again,' Alice added.

'I'm glad to be home,' Giles said, and squeezed Kitty's hand against his ribs.

Kitty felt the comfort of his presence, the strength of his arm under her hand and the warmth of his hand over hers. Yes, she thought, for the moment his longing to wander was satisfied. He would throw himself into home matters, and he would be good to her, kind, attentive. And perhaps by the time the baby came it would have become enough of a habit. Perhaps with two children in the nursery he would settle down, cease to see his home and family as chains, the Castle as a prison.

★　★　★

'Vogel is cautiously in favour,' Richard said, as he and Giles walked about Aunt Caroline's rather gloomy, laurel-shaded garden, enjoying a cigar and the chance to get away from come-out talk. 'Mr Cowling believes it can work—'

'You've spoken to Cowling?'

'I wanted to get as much done as I could before you came home. And, frankly, not knowing *when* you would come home, if you came at all, I saw no point in delaying. Why? Do you think I've gone beyond my remit?'

Giles hesitated. 'I thought you were just keeping things going. This innovation . . . It would involve a considerable outlay of funds, and when would we see a return on the investment?'

'Will, not would,' Richard insisted. '*You*'ve talked about it before – the idea of going in for milk—'

'Talked about it, but only in the vaguest terms.'

'Well, it's time to stop being vague. Bunce's death gives us an opening and a spur. Adeane and Markham agree that we won't get a decent tenant for Hundon's as it is, so if we have to improve it, we might as well do it for ourselves: create a modern dairy farm and show the others the way.'

Giles shook his head. 'The milk from one farm will hardly—'

'Oh, I've got Shelloes and High Ashmore on board already. The Bottoms will come in, I'm pretty sure, when they see others jump. Topheath is mostly sheep, and Hillbrow may be too far from the road, but I think you should go and talk to Lord Shacklock. He has a fine herd, and plenty of money, too. Talk to him nicely and you might get him to invest in the scheme, as well as join it. And that opens the way to other farms further up the valley. This could be a very large scheme indeed.'

Giles frowned. 'Why must I talk to him? If you've included him in your incontinent planning, you might as well do it yourself. I'm sure you're more eloquent than me.'

'Yes, and much prettier, too,' Richard said, with a grin. 'But you're the earl. He'd expect any approach to come from the boss.'

'Hmm. And what has Cowling to do with it?' Giles asked half resentfully. 'He's already got a finger in our jam.'

'Disturbing image! I didn't ask him to invest at this stage, but he's finding things out for us, regarding the transportation and the distribution.'

'And why would he do that?' Giles said.

'Because he's a businessman and likes to encourage enterprise. And because he's a good old boy and loves his wife, so he wants to help his wife's bosom friend's family.'

That was what Giles was afraid of. It was bad enough having Cowling as an investor in the family fortune. He didn't want to be beholden to him for disinterested kindness – not the man who had married Nina.

It was a warm evening on the night of the ball, and the multitude of candles made it even warmer inside Pelham House. That was very well for the women with their décolletage and bare shoulders, but for the male half, trussed up like turkeys in breeches and tight stockings, serge jackets, stocks and high collars, it was far less pleasant. Giles stood as still as possible and suffered in silence.

The house was dazzling, everything sparkling clean, with fresh paintwork and gilding, and flowers everywhere. Now London Society was making its way up the stairs to the reception line, to where the dowager glittered formidably in silver and purple with crystal beading, a pearl and diamond choker borrowed from Caroline, and a tiara hired from Garrard's.

Giles stood beside his mother as the official host; Kitty was excused the line because of her condition. Rachel, next to his mother, did not seem, he noted, at all nervous. She had taken to it like a fish to water. When he told her that

142

she looked beautiful, she had accepted the compliment calmly, almost as her due. She was in white, as a debutante should be, but it was ivory-white tulle over a pale pink silk under-dress, which better became her fairness. Her hair was dressed with pink and ivory rosebuds and she wore only chaste pearls, but everything about her toilette was of the first quality, the most elegant taste.

Moss was plainly enjoying himself. His chest well out, his back rigid, his head up, eyelids grandly lowered, he announced the arrivals in sonorous tones, the emphasis finely graded to rank and importance. He did not stumble over a single name or title, even when trickily foreign. It was, Giles thought, his finest performance. He might never top this moment; he would certainly never forget it.

Up the stairs they came, the beaded evening gowns, the black-and-white breeches and stockings, the pastel, hopeful girls, the young men eager or supercilious; names, titles, medals, jewels, faces. A watered ribbon of order here; a coloured jacket of a foreign army there. A bow of the head and a word of welcome from him and they were passed on. Giles slipped into a sort of dream, until his mother jolted him out of it with a hiss of outrage.

'Giles! Who *are* those people?'

He jerked back to the present. The Arthurs were coming up the stairs with Giulia. They were appropriately dressed, but evidently not people of wealth or distinction. Giulia was in a beaded garnet-red dress, with dark red silk flowers in her hair. Not at all debutante-ish. She looked striking, even exotic.

'Friends of mine,' he muttered to his mother.

She leaned back to address him behind Rachel's head. 'You invited your *university* friends to my ball?' She made *university* sound like *music hall* with a hint of *seraglio*.

Giles gave way for once to irritation. 'I'm paying for this ball – I'll invite who I damn well please,' he whispered, and saw his mother flinch. Her nostrils flared and *how dare you?* was in every line of her visage, but she couldn't quarrel with him now. She greeted the Arthurs with icy propriety. Rachel, who had no idea who they were, gave them a formal smile and looked over Giulia with quick assessment as she might any rival young lady. Giles tried to compensate with a hearty handshake and welcome; Mary Arthur raised an eyebrow and gave him an amused look.

He said, 'I'm *very* glad to see you here, and I hope you will enjoy yourselves,' which was as near as he could get to saying, 'Don't pay any attention to my mother.'

Mary said, 'I'm sure you do,' which was as near she could get to saying, 'I'm not troubled by her; I expected nothing more.'

Talbot said, 'Tremendous affair, Stainton.'

Giulia said nothing, gave Giles a blank look as if she had never met him before, and passed on to Uncle Stuffy, next in line and happy not to have to be hosting in Giles's absence.

When they had moved away, Stuffy grasped Giles's arm in a vice-like grip, leaned close and whispered hotly into his ear, 'My God, Giles! Who is that transcendent creature?'

Giles blinked. 'Which one?'

'Who do you think I mean? That glorious vision in red,' Stuffy said impatiently. 'I've never seen such a beauty in all my life! She's like – she's like a Russian tsarina. Or an Egyptian princess. She walks like a queen. And those eyes!'

Amused, Giles said, 'She is the daughter of an Italian professor who was my mentor. Her name is Giulia Lombardi.'

'Giulia Lombardi.' He seemed to taste the words. 'It's like poetry. It suits her. She could never have been a Dorothy or a Susan. Please tell me she's not married. Or betrothed.'

'What an odd question. As far as I know, she is quite unattached.'

'Good,' Stuffy said decidedly. 'Glorious, glorious creature!'

Giles, a little startled, would have asked a question, but

the next dignitary had arrived at the line, and he had his duty to do.

After the receiving line, Rachel had enjoyed a flattering rush of candidates for dances with her. Her mother, of course, had overseen her acceptances, at least for everything up to the supper interval. There was an order of precedence, her grim expression told Rachel, even for dancing.

In the brief moment of hiatus before the first dance, her cousin Angus came up to her, looking so handsome in breeches and stockings (he had *very* good calves, as she knew already from having seen him at home in Scotland in the kilt) that her heart had given an unruly jump.

She gave him her hand and said formally, 'Mr Tullamore, how nice to see you.'

He was not at all formal. 'I suppose, with all these terrible foreign dukes clustering round you, you don't have a dance to spare for a mere mister?'

'Why terrible?' she asked, rather enjoying his hint of grumpiness after all the flowery politeness.

'They have blue chins and they smell of mothballs!'

She laughed. 'Oh, they do not!'

'Some of them do. But that's better – you sound like Rachel again. I was afraid they'd spoiled you with all this.' He waved a hand around the magnificent room and the glittering throng. 'However, you do look very, *very* pretty tonight. If I'm allowed to say so?'

'You can say what you like to me,' she said, with a naughty smile. 'Cousin's privilege.'

'Give me a dance, then – cousin.'

'I've nothing left before supper. Ask me again after that.'

'I can't wait until then – you'll fill up your card with blue-chins. Write me in now, so I know.'

'All right – the second after supper.'

'Why not the first?'

'Mama will be bound to buttonhole me at supper and ask me who has the first.'

'And you'd be ashamed to say it was me?'

'Don't go red in the face. It's not me, it's her. She'd just cross your name out and write something else in. You don't know what she's like.'

'Oh, I do. She's a dragon.'

'Ssh! Here she is with my first partner.'

'A blue-chin! I knew it!'

'Hush, she'll hear you. That's Prince Ludwig of Fürstenstein. He *is* a bit blue, now you mention it. I didn't notice before. I'll see you later. I must go.'

Alice caught Rachel during a brief moment between dances, standing at the end of the room and fanning herself. 'Here, let me,' Alice said, and plied the fan while Rachel turned her face and neck this way and that in the breeze.

'Oh, thank you! You're so good at it. Am I very red?'

'No,' Alice said. 'Just a hint of pink in the cheeks where it should be.'

'Thanks,' Rachel said. She put a hand up to her head. 'Is my—'

'Perfect. Everything's perfect. Don't fuss.'

'Are you having a nice time?' Rachel asked, straightening her skirt. Alice, not being out, was sitting with the chaperones, and she felt a little guilty.

'Oh, yes. I like watching people making fools of themselves.'

'That's not very kind.'

'Making fools of themselves over you is what I meant. All the men want to dance with you. They all seem to be in love with you. And you are flirting so madly I can't tell if you favour any of them.'

'I'm not flirting,' Rachel said indignantly. 'I'm just – being pleasant.'

'Of course you are,' said Alice. '*Do* you favour any of them?'

'Oh, I don't want to get serious about anybody yet,' Rachel said. 'I'm having too much fun. As soon as you accept someone, it's all over. I want to have them all running after me for as long as possible.'

Alice nodded. 'Well, you do it very nicely, I must say. And you look lovely.'

Rachel pressed her arm, touched. 'Thanks. You're very sweet. And your turn will come. Next year, this will all be for you.'

Alice laughed. 'Mother won't do it for me – and I wouldn't want it. Don't worry about me. Just enjoy yourself.'

'I will – except for the next dance. Mother made me accept Paul Usingen, and I hate him. He creaks when he bends, and he has breath like deathly coffins.'

'Hide,' said Alice. 'Look, if you stand behind this flower tub when the music starts, he might not find you.'

Giles had danced, as he was bidden by his mother, with various girls who, for one reason or another, found themselves without a partner. After circling with a very young debutante who answered every attempt he made at conversation in a terrified whisper, he determined to have a break from them. He saw Giulia not far off, unpartnered at the side of the room. He had invited her, and it was his responsibility to see that she did not feel left out. He went up to her, bowed, smiled, and said, 'I should count it a great honour if you would dance the next with me.' The thought came to him that she was like a wild rose, though with her dark eyes and mass of dark hair he could not quite determine why that was. 'Will you?' he urged.

The tint of red in her cheeks deepened, and her eyes were bright. She looked at him scaldingly. 'No,' she said.

He was taken aback. 'I beg your pardon?'

'I do not wish to dance with you, my lord. You will excuse me.' And she walked away.

Someone chuckled behind him, and he turned to find Richard there. 'Oh, Lord!' he said. 'What a set-back! Thank God no-one's ever refused me like that! What on earth did you do to make her so angry with you?'

'Nothing!' Giles said vehemently.

'It must have been something. Come on, you can tell me. I swear I won't repeat it.'

Giles hesitated, but Richard understood women much better than him, and he knew he was to be trusted with a secret. He lowered his voice. 'I kissed her,' he said, feeling his face grow hot.

'Oh, you dog!'

'Don't look like that! I didn't mean it to happen. It was on the spur of the moment. And I apologised,' he went on quickly. 'Over and over. I told her it was a terrible aberration on my part and I was heartily ashamed, and I promised it would never happen again.'

Richard struggled not to laugh. 'Oh, my God, you really *don't* know anything about women, do you?'

'You needn't laugh,' Giles said angrily.

'When you kissed her, did she try to stop you? Did she struggle?'

'No – in fact, she seemed to like it. But what has that to do with it? I should never have done it.'

'Agreed. But then you compounded the error by apologising.'

'How is an apology wrong?'

'A woman can forgive a man for sinning, but not for hurting her pride.'

'What are you *talking* about?' Giles said in exasperation.

'Try to see it from her point of view. You kissed her, and perhaps she'd been hoping you would – you are *quite* a handsome chap, after all. Not in the same class as me, but I can see how some women might fancy you. But then you told her it was the worst mistake of your life, and you would never repeat it for any consideration. Are you surprised she's furious with you?'

'Then – what was I supposed to say?'

'You should have said you'd been overcome with uncontrollable passion. That not to kiss her again would be a titanic struggle against your most powerful urges. That the memory of the kiss would illuminate even your deathbed. Instead you gave her to understand she was a deplorable lapse of taste on your part and that you felt only shame and loathing.'

'For myself, not her.'

Richard patted his shoulder comfortingly. 'It's a good job Kitty was willing to marry you, because it would give me deep pain to have to watch you courting again, inept as you are.'

Giles shook away the hand. 'What should I do? Should I talk to her, explain—'

'God, no! You'd only make it worse. No, I'm afraid you've lost that one. If you ever have to speak to her again, I should go with the fatherly approach. Be extremely married, out-of-the-running, boring. Talk about the weather and how the crops are doing. Don't worry, a girl like that won't regret you for long. She'll have plenty of suitors to wash away the memory of your unique approach to gallantry.'

'I'm glad you think it's funny,' Giles said crossly.

'Oh, I do, I do,' said Richard.

The King had arrived with a party, had walked about a little being pleasant and retired for a few hands of cards, before going on to another supper engagement. It was as much as was expected, or needed. He did not dance any more, and his brief appearance and kind words to Rachel would secure the cachet.

While Giles was circling with an ingénue and trying not to seem bored, he was surprised to see Uncle Stuffy dancing, on his face an expression of bliss that would have suited a schoolboy unexpectedly in possession of a whole jar of jam.

Giles could not see who he was dancing with – his partner was hidden by the crowd. But then an intervening couple moved aside, and Giles saw that it was Giulia.

He was astonished. He had never seen his uncle dance in public. Stuffy was only just forty, but his ways made him seem older, and as far as Giles was aware he had never shown any interest in women before. Giles had been surprised enough at his reaction to Giulia, but that he had asked her to dance! That she had accepted!

He manoeuvred his partner to keep them in sight, and Giulia, turning her head, saw him watching. She gave him a cold look, then said something to her partner, who gazed down at her and smiled rapturously.

The crowd came between them again, and Giles circled moodily with his current partner almost forgotten in his arms. He felt extremely hard-done-by. Yes, it was wrong to have kissed Giulia, but he had apologised, and it was unreasonable of her to be so very upset by it. Richard said he had hurt her pride. But they had been friends for a long time. Surely friends gave each other a little leeway when they made mistakes. He didn't understand. He trundled his partner to the end of the dance, and went back to Kitty.

It was the supper break, and he offered his arm. 'Shall I take you down?'

'Aren't you engaged to someone else?' she said.

She looked tired, and he thought it could not have been much fun for her, sitting out. He must be nice to her. 'Who would I be engaged to but my own wife?' he said, with a smile.

For a moment she seemed pleased; but then her eyes focused on someone behind him, and her expression changed. He looked. Uncle Stuffy was walking by with Giulia on his arm, heading, like everyone else, for the door to go down to supper.

He turned back to Kitty. 'Is that . . . ?' she asked.

'Yes,' he admitted. 'It's Giulia.'

'How on earth did she get here?' They had spent part of their honeymoon with the Lombardis, and she had been bitterly jealous of his closeness to Giulia.

He was forced to explain. 'She was at the dig, and when it was ended, some friends of mine, the Arthurs – you remember them – invited her to come and stay with them in London. So I – invited them to the ball.'

'She was at the dig?'

'Yes. She'd come as secretary to one of the archaeologists.'

'She was there the whole time? Why didn't you tell me?'

'Well, it didn't come up,' he said awkwardly. 'I haven't really spoken to you about the dig at all. I didn't think you were interested.'

'You've spent the last five months hobnobbing with her daily but you didn't think to mention it? And plainly even that wasn't enough – you had to invite her to Rachel's ball as well!'

'Oh, Kitty, don't—'

'And now she's staying in London, so I suppose you'll find lots of excuses not to go down to Ashmore. Perhaps she'll never go back to Italy. Wouldn't that be convenient?'

He bent over her, gave her a little shake, and said in a low voice, 'Kitty, behave yourself! Don't make a scene. Think of Rachel.'

'*You* think of Rachel! You didn't think of her before inviting your mistress to her come-out.'

Giles was shocked. 'She's not my mistress! How can you think such a thing? She's just the daughter of my old professor. She means nothing to me—' Kitty's look made him rephrase. 'Not like that, anyway. How can you think for a moment that I would—?' He stopped, felt himself colouring. Kitty looked away with an almost inaudible sigh. He spoke again, quietly, firmly. 'She's not my mistress, and I'm not in love with her. You must believe me.'

'It doesn't matter,' Kitty said, and he didn't know what she meant by that. 'We had better go to supper. People will notice.'

Richard arrived beside them, with Alice. 'Supper time,' he said brightly. 'Pusscat, let me offer you my arm. I've been watching Giles dance and he has two left feet. You're not safe on the stairs with him.' Kitty transferred her hand to his arm without comment.

'Oh, Richard, you're too unkind,' Alice said, falling in behind with Giles. 'He can dance nicely if he has the right partner, but Mama's made him dance with all the leftovers.'

'That's no excuse,' Richard said. 'I've been dancing with leftovers, as you call them, but I'm never less than exquisitely gazelle-like.'

CHAPTER NINE

The next morning, the dowager was still dressing when Miss Taylor was called to the bedroom door to receive a message from Moss. She returned to the dressing-table and continued imperturbably pushing pins into her mistress's coiffure as she said, 'Prince Usingen has called, my lady, requesting a private interview with you.'

'So early?' Maud said, and frowned. 'It appears to suggest a lack of regard for the conventions.'

'Perhaps it suggests an over-full heart, my lady.'

'Don't be impertinent,' Maud said automatically. She stared unseeing at her reflection as she put in her earrings. He would not, perhaps, have been her first choice, but his rank and fortune deserved to be considered. Certainly it was early days to be crossing anyone off the list. 'I will see him,' she pronounced.

'Yes, my lady,' said Miss Taylor, who had already told Moss to ask the prince to wait. Her ladyship would not hurry down to him. Half an hour, she thought, would be the correct amount of time.

Dismissed by her mistress, Miss Taylor went down to the servants' hall, where she found the household canvassing the visit. Everyone assumed a proposal was in the offing.

'Poor Lady Rachel!' Ellen was saying, with a shudder. 'I shouldn't care to have to marry him. He's so old!'

'An older husband is not always bad thing,' Dory said, 'as long as he's kind.'

153

'Well, I wouldn't want some dried-up old stick pawing me about,' Doris said, tossing her head. 'When I get married, I want a nice, well-set-up *young* man I can cuddle up to in bed.'

'It's different for the nobs,' said Aggie, one of the hired maids. 'They marry for the money, and do their cuddling elsewhere.'

'That's enough,' Miss Taylor snapped, catching them all by surprise. 'It's not for the likes of you to comment on upstairs matters.'

Dory lifted her head from something she was stitching. 'Does her ladyship favour the prince, Miss Taylor?'

'He's in the running,' Miss Taylor allowed, in concession to Dory's greater age and sense. 'She'll see him, at least.'

'And Lady Rachel?'

'She's not up yet,' said Miss Taylor.

'And not likely to be,' said Maureen, another hired maid. 'After dancing the soles out of her shoes last night, the precious! She won't be awake for hours yet.'

'She wouldn't be required to see the prince at this stage, in any case,' said Miss Taylor, quellingly. 'It's for her ladyship to receive all the offers and consider them before putting the final choice before Lady Rachel.'

'All the offers?' said Doris. 'Has there been more, then?'

'There will be,' said Miss Taylor, shortly.

'This prince is getting his word in early,' said Aggie. 'He must really want her. Has she got a big dowry, Miss Taylor?'

'None of your business,' Miss Taylor snapped. 'Have none of you got anything to do? I thought you were in charge of the maids,' she added, with a glare at Dory.

Dory only gave her a sympathetic look in return. She knew, as the outside maids didn't, that Rachel had next to no dowry, and that it was a sore point with Miss Taylor. 'Everyone's a bit tired after the exertions yesterday,' she said.

'What has that to do with it? There's all the clearing up to do.'

Dory distracted her. 'By the way, there was a velvet opera cloak left in the ladies' retiring room last night. Pale blue chiffon velvet with a black silk lining. Very expensive. You wouldn't happen to know which lady left it?'

'No doubt someone will send round for it,' Miss Taylor said. 'I must speak to Mr Moss about the luncheon arrangements,' she added, and stalked out.

In the yellow drawing-room, Maud found the prince standing by the window staring out at Portman Square gardens. He turned as she came in, bowed, and gave her a nervous smile. '*Gnädige Gräfin!* Thank you for seeing me,' he said. 'I fear I am rather early – the butler seemed surprised. Have I offended?'

'It is perhaps a little before the conventional hour. But I took it to mean you had something urgent to say to me,' said Maud, graciously, and extended a hand towards a settle. 'Won't you sit down?'

She took the settle opposite, but he put his hands behind his back and said, 'Forgive me, I feel I must stand. What I have to say is—' He cleared his throat, fidgeted, and slipped into German. '*Es ist aus dem Herzen—*'

'No, no, in English, please,' Maud interrupted calmly. 'I cannot hear you in anything but English.'

'I am not so fluent in English,' the prince said, 'and I would wish to do justice to the feelings that bring me here, but it shall be as you wish, *gnädige Gräfin*. I – er – let me first assemble my words.' He walked away a few steps, paused, and then came back to stand before her, like a supplicant, but still seemed unable to speak.

She liked his uncertainty – it spoke of a proper appreciation of Rachel's rank and position in society. He should not be too confident that he deserved her. 'Please,' she said, with a gracious gesture, 'open your mind to me. I am listening.'

'You are so kind! I think it cannot have escaped your notice

155

that since your visit to the Wachturm last year, I have been stricken – overmanned – I have experienced some deep feelings, of a kind that . . .' He coughed and started again. 'I am a bachelor, dear lady, though that is not in accordance with my nature, which is, I believe, a domestic one. Yet I have never had the fortune to meet the lady I could give my whole heart to. Until now. You know of my circumstances. It is perhaps not *höflich* to speak of money—'

'In the circumstances, it is permissible,' Maud murmured.

'You are most kind. Very well, I am a rich man, if I may say so. Of land and money and all that is desirable I have good store. Houses. Furnishings. Stables. I am in a position to support a wife in comfort. In the first of style. I am well connected and can offer the *Eintritt* to the courts of Europe. My wife would lack for nothing. And she would most assuredly not lack for the whole love of my heart, my complete devotion.'

'That is pleasant to hear, Prince, and I think I may say that you *are* on the list. Naturally I cannot make a decision immediately, before hearing the other offers I confidently expect to receive in the near future, but—'

She stopped because he was looking surprised – no, shocked. He felt behind him for the settle, and sat down rather hard. 'The list?' he said, in a ghost of a voice. 'You are expecting many other offers?'

She was offended. 'Naturally. What can you be thinking? After last night's ball, which was a triumph – the King himself was present – you surely cannot believe that you, however eligible you may be, are the only person who will be making an offer for my daughter.'

Now he was quite white. 'Your daughter? *Was bedeutet das?* Dear madam! Please, how can you so misunderstand me? *Sie is ganz Lieblichkeit* – all loveliness – but I do not offer for her. It is not – *das ist nicht*—' His half-and-half stammering disintegrated into rapid German and she held up a hand to stop him.

'In English, sir, in English. What are you saying? I have been aware from the first of your interest. You have taken pains to ingratiate yourself, you have been pointedly attentive, you have come hurrying here at the earliest hour on the day after her debut ball, and now you say, just because I do not close immediately with your offer, that you are withdrawing it? That is not the behaviour of a gentleman, sir.'

'No, no,' he moaned. '*Bitte verstehe* – I did not offer for Lady Rachel! She is perfection, but a child, a mere child. How did you not see it? It is you I have loved from the start, only you I have tried to please!'

Now Maud was as astonished as he had been. 'But— You have been most attentive to Rachel. Every time we were in company—'

'To get to know your daughter, I have taken pains, yes, to show you I am good person.' In his agitation, his English deteriorated. 'To love you I must love your family. That is correct thing, all understood. But it is *you* I make offer for! Last night, at the ball, you were so gracious to me, I think you favour me, not? Then this morning, to receive me so kindly as you do, I am all hope. *Ich glaubte . . . Sie haben gesagt—*'

Maud stopped him again with a raised hand and said coolly, 'Let me understand you plainly. Do you tell me you have come here to propose marriage to *me*?'

He seemed restored to equilibrium by the clarity. He slipped from the settle to his knees and captured her hand. 'Oh, *yes*!' he cried, in relieved tones. 'I wish you to marry me, *gnädige Gräfin*! I offer you hand, heart and fortune, all I have, all I am. Be my wife. Say you will be Princess of Usingen, and I will be the happiest man in the earth.'

Maud pulled back her hand. 'Please rise, sir, from that ridiculous posture.' She felt ruffled, unsettled. She felt as if someone had made a fool of her, though she could not in fairness blame this awkward man, who seemed to be suffering even more than her. But really – who would have thought *she*, a widow of mature years, could be the object of his attentions? It was almost absurd. She felt uneasily that it *would* be thought absurd if it were known about, and she hated to be laughed at far more than to be disliked. She would choose loathing over ridicule every time.

'You have taken me aback,' she said, since something had to be said.

He had resumed his seat on the edge of the settle, and was looking at her with a mixture of hope and apprehension. 'But you will – you may – you do *like* me? You said I was suitable?'

'For my daughter.'

'If for her, then so much more for you, dearest countess!'

'I am recently widowed.'

'Not so recent,' he said, with growing confidence. 'I have waited, to give you time, to make all decent. At first, yes, it would have been too soon, but I am patient man, I can wait for what I want, and now I believe it is good time.'

'I have no thought of marriage.'

'But you will think of it now.'

'It is impossible.' She stood up, so he had to. 'I must ask you to leave, Prince. I am quite—' She was unsettled, so much so that she could not think of the correct word. The only one that came to her was *decomposed*. It annoyed her to be at a loss for vocabulary. 'Please go,' she said irritably.

He bowed, with a hint of clicked heels. 'I go,' he said. 'But I do not give up. I will return. Good morning, *gnädige Gräfin*.'

The Arthurs lived in a large house on Clapham Common, a place Stuffy had vaguely heard of, though he could not have placed it. It turned out to be on the south side of the river. He could not remember ever having crossed the river, except by train when heading for Dover and Abroad. And, of course, one did not look out of the windows in the early part of the journey as the train rattled through those grim suburbs with their rows and rows of identical, close-packed houses. One was always busy settling oneself in one's corner, with reading-matter, spectacles, handkerchief, foot-muff, barley-sugar twists and all the other little necessary comforts disposed to hand.

His manservant McGregor, on whom he relied for information, told him that Clapham Common could be reached easily by Underground, being the terminus of the recent extension of the City and South London electric railway. Stuffy shuddered at the thought of going underground and waved him to continue. Or, said McGregor, a journey of twenty minutes from Victoria on the London Brighton and South Coast railway would bring him to Clapham Junction, from which a cab could be taken, Clapham Common lying only a mile or so distant. Now Stuffy remembered why the name had been faintly familiar – he must have travelled many times through Clapham Junction on the way to the south coast, though without particularly remarking it.

'Am I to understand, my lord, that ye're considering undertaking such a journey?' McGregor enquired forbiddingly.

'Oh, perhaps – or perhaps not. Mere idle curiosity,' Stuffy said, avoiding his eyes.

'The Common is, I believe, an agreeable green space, with level paths, fine trees and a bandstand,' said McGregor, his grey eyes boring into his master. 'Although Hyde Park is considerably closer, if it was a walk ye were wanting.' He said this straight-faced, though the earl had never yet been known to regard walking as a recreational activity.

'Um – hmm,' Stuffy said, staring at the ceiling.

'If it was fishing ye were after, my lord, I believe the ponds on Clapham Common are stocked with carp, roach, tench and bream,' said McGregor, to a man who owned one of the finest salmon and trout stretches of the Spey but rarely took out a rod.

'I'm not going fishing, damn it!' Stuffy said.

'Howsoever, I am sure Lady Manningtree would not object to ordering her carriage out for you, my lord, to go as far as Clapham Common. 'Twould be but a journey of five miles or so, not too far for her horses.'

Stuffy looked at him with narrowed eyes, wondering whether McGregor had guessed what allure Clapham Common suddenly held for him. 'I do not wish to ask my sister for her carriage,' he said. 'It is – a private matter.'

'Then may I suggest, my lord, that I walk down to the rank on the corner and select the most respectable jarvey to drive you all the way and wait to bring you back.'

Stuffy considered. A hansom cab was not the most comfortable conveyance for a journey of that length, but he would have to take a cab in any case to Victoria station, so he might as well stay in it and save the tiresome changes from cab to station and station back to cab. 'That's probably best,' he said, not noticing that the enquiry had now passed from the putative to the actual.

'And I shall accompany you, my lord,' said McGregor.

'Indeed, no!' Stuffy exclaimed.

'Indeed so, if you will forgive me,' McGregor said, in the steely voice that Stuffy knew meant he would not back down. 'It is not a part of the metropolis known to you, my lord. If something were to happen . . . And I shall remain with the cab, my lord, until you have concluded your business. Otherwise, the jarvey will require to be paid for the outward journey on arrival in Clapham, and once he has his money, there is no assurance that he will wait.'

'Oh, very well,' Stuffy said weakly. McGregor made it seem as though he was penetrating the dark continent, instead of driving a few miles across London. That McGregor feared harm to him if he went alone was obvious, but exactly *what* harm was less so. He probably, Stuffy reflected, when he had left the room, just wanted to know what his master was up

to. These old-established servants could be annoyingly posses-
sive.

Mr Cowling's business-room in the Berkeley Square house
was suddenly crowded, with Cowling himself, Giles and
Richard assembled there to meet a Mr Elthorne and his two
sons.

Giles had wanted the meeting to take place at Aunt
Caroline's house, or at the Elthornes'. Much as he longed to
see Nina, he knew it was better for his peace of mind to keep
contact with her to a minimum. Particularly given the delicate
state of affairs between him and Kitty. But Richard, who had
been talking to Cowling, had let slip that Nina would be
visiting Kitty at the same time, so Cowling's house seemed
like the safest place to be.

Elthorne senior was a thin, slightly stooped, grey-haired
man, who seemed in his fifties. His sons both towered over
him, tall, beefy young men, who looked more like country
folk than town dwellers. It would be easy to imagine them
heaving a straw bale up onto a shoulder or deftly hauling a
struggling ewe into the shearing pen. The sons let their father
do all the talking, but they followed the conversation with
bright, intelligent eyes.

Cowling introduced Elthorne, who did not seem over-
powered by Giles's title, gave him and Richard a civil nod,
and said, 'My sons, Rob and Tom. I understand you've a
proposal to put to me.'

'We haven't got as far as that yet,' Giles said. 'The scheme
is still in embryo.'

Cowling stepped in. 'Elthorne delivers milk daily to Lisson
Grove and a bit of Paddington. And he'd like to expand his
business.'

'I've two sons, as you see, with me in the company,' said
Elthorne, 'and the time will soon come when they'll want to
start families. We've got to expand if they're to stay with me.

Now, if we could start delivering milk into Marylebone, there's a mass of houses there, and wealthy folk, too. There's big money to be made. But we need good-quality milk. I'm getting my milk from two local farms, and between you and me, the quality is not what the carriage trade would pay for. But if you could provide me with fresh country milk every day, well, I reckon we could all do ourselves a bit of good.'

'That's what we're hoping to do,' Giles said.

'We're planning on a large scale,' Richard said. 'Eventually bringing in all the farmers in our valley.'

'And how many gallons a day are you producing?'

Richard and Giles exchanged an awkward glance, and Cowling again took over. 'Now, Elthorne, I explained to you that they're just at the beginning. We're simply trying to find out if such a trade is feasible.'

Elthorne said impatiently, 'I can tell you if it's feasible if you tell me what quantity of milk we're talking about.'

Richard smiled ruefully. 'It seems as if we can't set up a business until after we've set it up. We can't sell the milk until we've got milk to sell, but we can't produce the milk if there's no-one to sell to.'

Elthorne shook his head, but with a gleam of sympathy. 'Aye, well, I've been at that end of things. When I was a lad I started with a handcart and one churn I had to fetch myself from the farm up at Grove End. I pushed that barrow round the streets, and when the churn was empty that was that. So I borrowed a bit from my uncle who had a butcher's shop, and bought a pony and cart. But the farm couldn't give me more than two churns – it's gone now, the farm, all built over with houses – so I had to find another that could let me have two more. Then I had the milk and had to find the customers. So I understand. Aye, it's an awkward thing, starting up. What's your herd?'

Giles was about to say, 'We haven't got one yet,' but Richard stopped him with a glance. 'We're going in for Shorthorns –

twenty head to begin with. That should produce thirty to forty gallons a day by the end of the year, but it'll be a gradual process. Quantities should double the following year when our other farms have got going, and further into the future – well, there's no limit.'

'But you've got it all still to set up, transport and everything; and nothing to sell me yet,' Elthorne said thoughtfully. 'And when you do have milk it'll be coming through in dribs and drabs.'

'Aye, you're right. We're just feeling our way forward,' Cowling said. 'But once that good rich milk is available in quantity, everyone'll want it. Anyone who was helpful along the way would get first dibs.'

'Well, I tell you what, gentlemen: I want to help you out, and help myself at the same time. With a guaranteed supply of, say, a hundred gallons a day, it'd be worth our while investing in more carts to expand our milk round. We could match future expansion to your future increased production, do it in step, so to speak. I'd like to get my boys delivering right through Mayfair.'

'But until we have milk available in those quantities?' Richard said.

'We can take smaller amounts to begin with.' He glanced at his sons who nodded agreement. 'But it seems to me you've got a lot to do before you get even to that point.'

'We have,' said Cowling. 'But it's good to know you're ready at this end. The other end,' he looked at Richard and Giles, 'is like to be the more difficult.'

When the Elthornes had gone, Richard turned to Cowling and said, 'I notice you were saying "we" all through. Was that just a diplomatic plural?'

Cowling gave him a fatherly smile. 'Ah, well, as you said to me, business is business, and I can't help getting interested in new ideas, when they're good ones. I'll go along with you and hold your hand as far as that goes. But I won't part with any brass at this point. I'd like to hear what you propose about collecting the milk and getting it to the station.'

'Well,' said Richard, with relish, 'this is what I'm thinking so far.'

Giles listened, watching his brother's face and marvelling at his enthusiasm. It was good that languid, sophisticated Richard had at last found something he could be interested in. Giles would never have expected it to be related to farming. For himself, he was still not mentally back in England. When he closed his eyes, it was the Valley of the Kings he saw, not Berkeley Square.

'How was the ball?' Nina asked. 'Was it very splendid?'

She and Kitty were sitting on a bench in Berkeley Square gardens, with Trump lying at their feet, quivering with suppressed excitement. Nina had him on a leash, because he was passionate about chasing pigeons, of which there were multitudes in the gardens.

When she had called on Kitty, she had proposed going out somewhere, but Kitty looked tired, and further said she didn't like to be seen in public now that her pregnancy was obvious. So a stroll in the gardens was suggested, and they had walked a little; but when an empty bench in a secluded spot presented itself, Kitty sat down.

Nina's question seemed to rouse Kitty from absorbing thoughts. 'Oh – yes, very,' she said. 'Everybody important was there – or so my mother-in-law tells me. The King called in, and there were lots of the nobility and foreign royalty. Rachel looked very lovely and of course she danced every dance.' She sighed a little. 'She really enjoyed herself: she loves all the attention. I wish I could have felt like her when I came out.' She glanced at Nina. 'If you hadn't been there to encourage me, I should never have got through it.'

'You were braver than you gave yourself credit for,' Nina said. 'And look at you now! You've changed so much – don't you think so?'

'I'm not sure. Do we ever really change inside? I know how to face up to things now, that's the difference. I do enjoy parties at home, when I know everyone – but I still feel frightened when I have to meet very high-up people.'

'Dearest Kitty, you *are* high-up people!' Nina laughed.

Kitty smiled unwillingly. 'Well, I don't feel it.'

'You don't see what I see,' Nina said, waving a hand over her. 'A very smart, fashionable lady, a society lady in a killing hat – a countess, no less. And a mother, too. Are you *very* thrilled to have another baby coming?'

'Oh, yes,' Kitty said, her face lighting for a moment. 'I adore Louis, and the thought of having another . . . It ought to be another boy, for the family's sake, but I can't help feeling it would be nice to have a daughter, too. I often think how it would have been if my mother had lived, how close we might have been.' She shook her head. 'I can never understand how little my mother-in-law seems to care for her daughters. Alice is such a dear girl, and a good companion.' Nina was listening sympathetically, her warm dark eyes fixed attentively on Kitty's face, and Kitty suddenly felt guilty. 'But you – no sign of a child yet for you?'

'No,' Nina said. She hesitated, but not even with Kitty could she discuss such an intimate problem. Girls went into marriage in absolute ignorance, and talking about it was tabu. She did not know, of course, how other people's marriages went, or what was 'normal', but she was sure things were not right between her and Mr Cowling in the bedroom. There had been one time when, in retrospect, she believed the expected thing had taken place, but there had been nothing like it before or since. Now, on the occasions when he was at home, he rarely came to her bed; and, when there, did nothing more than put his arms round her and fall asleep. He *was* always very tired, of course, she reasoned, working so hard and for such long hours; but he loved her – she believed that honestly – and from all that literature had taught

165

her, when a man loved a woman, the physical side followed naturally. She wished she had an older married friend with whom she could have a frank discussion. But she certainly could not talk about it with Kitty.

'No, no sign of that,' she said. 'Never mind me, though – tell me about you. Are you feeling well?'

'Yes, very well. I was a little out of sorts in the early months, but that's passed now.'

'I thought you were looking tired.'

'Oh, that's . . .' Kitty hesitated. But this was Nina, who had been there from the beginning. 'I've something on my mind.'

'Tell me, then,' Nina said.

Kitty hesitated again, then plunged in. 'It's Giles,' she said. 'I suppose I'm being foolish – I hope I am – but I can't seem to help it.' In stilted sentences that gradually became more fluent, she told Nina about Giulia Lombardi – how on their honeymoon he had paid her more attention than he paid Kitty, how he delighted in her company, how they talked together for hours in a mixture of English and Italian. 'And – well – in the end I shouted at him—'

'You?' Nina said in astonishment. 'At *Giles*?'

'It wasn't like me,' Kitty admitted 'But I was jealous. In the end I couldn't bear it any longer.'

'My brave Kitty! But what did he say?'

'That he didn't care for her that way. That she was like a sister to him. That *I* was his wife and I had no reason to be jealous. And I believed him. But now she's back.'

'Back?'

'I've discovered that she was in Egypt on the dig with him the whole time. Four months out there, working together, living in the same camp. I keep imagining them eating supper under the stars, talking deep into the night, looking into each other's eyes . . . She's very beautiful, you know.'

'But, Kitty, *you* are beautiful!'

'Not really,' she said.

'But you *are*! How can you say that?' Kitty shook her head. 'Anyway, Giles is back home now—'

'But she came to London,' Kitty said. 'She's in London now. And he invited her to the ball.'

Nina was silent a moment. Then, 'What does Giles say?'

'The same, that she's like a sister to him.'

'Don't you believe him?'

'I want to. I do with my mind but – my heart is burning! I'm so jealous. Am I stupid to be jealous? But I feel so unattractive now, like this.' She gestured towards her burgeoning figure. 'And she's not only beautiful, she's clever, and you know how he's always loved clever women.'

Nina could only be grateful that Kitty was staring down at herself so didn't see her momentary expression. Oh, yes, Giles loved clever women. He had loved her. Guilt seared her. She had married Mr Cowling in part to be safe from her unconquerable feelings for Kitty's husband, feelings that must be for ever suppressed, hidden and abhorred.

The irony was not lost on her, of Kitty being jealous of Giulia Lombardi, while she, Nina, was envious of everything Kitty had. But she must answer, reassure, support Kitty, who above all must not suffer.

'I don't think you have any reason to be jealous,' she said, and found, as she said it, that she believed it. Was she, Nina, jealous of Giulia? No. And how did that come about? She knew him at a deep level. He was not a man to run after another woman. He was not a man to be distracted by a trivial passing fancy. 'He has twice told you she is like a sister to him,' she said, 'and I really don't think he would lie about something like that.'

'He might not understand his own feelings,' Kitty said, in a small voice.

'He's known her since she was a child, according to what you've told me,' Nina said. 'It would be natural for him to feel about her as he does about Rachel, say, or Alice.'

'He *is* very fond of Alice,' Kitty said, with faint hope.

'I think he's old enough to know his own mind. If he had fallen in love, he'd know it,' Nina said, holding back her sadness.

Kitty sighed. 'But I still feel . . . Oh, if you could see her, Nina! She's everything I'd like to be: confident, bold, clever, well-read, full of words. She can talk for hours about learned subjects, where I only have the weather and household matters. How can I compete with her?'

'You don't have to,' Nina said, laying a hand over hers. 'You're his wife, and the mother of his children. Nothing can change that.' Nothing, indeed!

In the silence that followed, they both pursued their own thoughts, idly watching the sparrows dust-bathing in a patch of sunshine a little way off. Trump had gone to sleep, and was making little puffing noises through his lips as he chased pigeons in his dreams. The trees were coming into full leaf, and as the breeze disturbed them the light dappled and fluttered over the people strolling by, nursemaids pushing prams, elderly gentlemen taking a constitutional, busy folk making a short-cut across the square.

'I'll be going back down to Ashmore soon,' Kitty said at last.

'You're not being driven away by—'

'No, not that. I can't do anything about that. But I'm not comfortable in London in this condition. I want my own house and my own bed, and no strangers to see me. But I shall be sorry not to see more of you. Will you come down to Ashmore for a visit?'

'Of course I will. I'll be in London for a while yet, and I'll have to see what Mr Cowling has planned—'

'Come on your own, if he can't come. Stay a long time,' Kitty urged.

Nina would have liked nothing more than to spend a long time at Ashmore with Kitty. But if Giles was there . . . Was there any worse agony than to be in love with your dearest friend's husband? And there seemed no end in sight.

She needed new ideas, new concerns, new activities to keep her mind away from the forbidden thoughts.

She said, 'Clemmie and I are going to a Fabian meeting tonight in Russell Square – Mrs Billington-Drummond's house. George Bernard Shaw is reading a paper called "Womanliness and Emancipation". Don't you think that sounds interesting? Lepida is coming too. Apparently her father – you remember me talking about Mawes Morris? – knows Mr Shaw quite well. He's drawn him in his cartoons several times. He'd like to go to the meeting too, but he's engaged elsewhere so he's told Lepida to take notes. I've heard Mr Shaw talks very fast so she'll have her work cut out!'

To Kitty it sounded like an abrupt change of subject. But the connection was very clear to Nina, as she talked on about the Fabians, and the new society, the Women's Social and Political Union, which had replaced the defunct Women's Franchise League. She and Clemmie had been introduced to it by Clemmie's friend Mrs Albertine Crane, who was also taking them to the Russell Square meeting. Fabianism, socialism, the franchise, women's rights, factory conditions – there was so much to think about.

Nina was young, intelligent, full of energy and, in her present way of life, directionless. Marriage and child-rearing, the traditional occupations for women, had left her stranded on a dry shore. In these new ideas there was the hope of something to fill what seemed otherwise an empty life.

When Miss Taylor left her that night, Maud remained in front of the dressing-table glass, staring at her reflection. The day had been busy, receiving calls of form all morning, luncheon with the Lathams, then taking Rachel to a debutantes' tea, followed by a dinner and a ball. This was the first moment she had had to herself to think.

The face she saw in the glass had never been pretty. You might call it distinguished: it was thin, the nose a beak, the eyes deep-set with hooded lids. Physical looks had never concerned her. A Forrest girl carried her fortune in her name, not her appearance. Her duty had been to marry well and she had done so. But where had it left her? Not only widowed and supplanted by her daughter-in-law, but impoverished too. Her jewels had been sold by her profligate husband and replaced with paste. She'd had to *hire* a tiara for her daughter's come-out. The humiliation burned her. Rachel's Season had returned her to the centre of a social circle that she had always regarded as her rightful place. But when the Season was finished, and Rachel was married, what then? Was she to dwindle into a grandmother? Was there nothing ahead of her but old age, frailty and death? She felt still in the vigour of her life. She was not ready for that.

Her thoughts reverted to Usingen's proposal. She had feared at first she was being made fun of – society, after all, considered a woman of her age as past marrying. But why should he not have fallen in love with her? She was as fit to be admired as any woman in the land; and he was too rich to be courting her for some fortune he imagined her to have. She felt a surge of pride, which she was quick to push away. Emotions clouded the brain, and made for poor decisions. And she had a decision to make.

She could go back to the Castle and be the dowager, watch the new countess change everything to suit herself. There would not be a grand coming-out for Alice next year – it would be wasted on her. Rachel, once she was married, could introduce her sister into her own circle. Maud, left behind, would have to build her life around her grandchildren, and the very thought made her impatient. She had never cared for small babies, and by the time they were old enough to be interesting, her life would have passed her by.

Or she could marry – not at once, of course, but as soon

as Rachel's Season was over – and become the Princess of Usingen. She would have all the houses and jewels she could want. She would be on intimate terms with royalty – foreign royalty, to be sure, but many of them were descended from Queen Victoria. And Paul himself? Well, he was no beauty, but he was kind, and not at all stupid – she had enjoyed many conversations with him. And, after all, how much time did you ever have to spend alone with your husband?

She would even – it was an unworthy thought but she allowed it for a moment – outrank her youngest sister again. It had been galling to the eldest Forrest girl that the youngest, Victoria, had married a prince while she had only married an earl. But Maud had checked in the *Almanach de Gotha* when she thought Usingen was after Rachel, and Usingen had eight more quarterings than Wittenstein-Glücksberg.

Yes, she had a decision to make. But – and unusually for someone who was always so decisive – she was glad she need not make it quite yet. She would tell Usingen that she would consider his offer, and keep him at her heel until the Season was over. By then she ought to know her own mind.

When they got home from the meeting, Clemmie went straight up to her room, but seeing the light still on in the business-room, Nina went to say goodnight to her husband.

Cowling looked up and smiled as she appeared in the doorway. 'Interesting time?'

'Yes, very,' she said. 'Mr Shaw read a paper – you know, the playwright, George Bernard Shaw?'

'Oh, yes, the Irishman. I've met him,' Cowling said. 'Never knew a man who could talk so much. They say women are wild for him, but I can't see why. Tall, skinny feller with a long face like a corpse. Terrible beard. Messy clothes. Met him at a dinner party once and he was wearing *tweeds*. But the hostess acted like she was blessed to have him. Who was your hostess this evening?'

171

'Mrs Billington-Drummond. Her husband is an MP.'

'Oh, aye – Liberal Party. I think I may have met him. Got some bee in his bonnet about putting all the clocks forward an hour in the summer to make the evenings longer. Feller doesn't realise you get the same length of day. What you gain in the evening you lose in the morning.'

Nina smiled and nodded, glad he had got on to personalities and away from the subject of the meeting. She had not directly discussed the question of votes for women with him, but she suspected he would not be in favour. 'Mrs Billington-Drummond seems a nice enough woman, and very well dressed,' she said.

Cowling asked the question she didn't want to answer. 'So what was this paper about, that this Shaw feller gave?'

Nina cast around for some safe way to phrase it. 'Oh, it was about the nature of womanliness,' she said vaguely. 'How women have a duty to their husbands, their children and society at large. And there was a long discussion afterwards.' She ostentatiously stifled a yawn. 'I think I shall go up. It was all quite tiring.'

'Aye, aye, off you go,' he said indulgently, and she turned away, glad not to have to relay the import of Shaw's lecture – that unless woman repudiated all those duties, she would never be emancipated. A man's path to freedom, he had said, was strewn with the wreckage of the duties and ideals he had trampled on, and so must a woman's be. Nina was not sure she agreed with that, but it wasn't something she wanted to discuss with her husband.

'No, wait!' As she reached the door, he called her, and her heart jumped guiltily. She turned back. He didn't seem displeased. He had picked up a piece of paper from the desk and waved it at her gently. 'I've some news for you,' he said. 'We've been invited to dinner with the Cassels next week.'

'Both of us? I thought he gave gentlemen's dinners.'

'This one will be for ladies as well. His sister will be hostess for him. I'm particularly pleased to be taking you, because the King is invited, so you'll be presented to him, which I've wanted for quite a while. The Keppels will be there too, so you'll meet a monstrous beautiful woman. Clever, too, full of spirit, gets on with everyone. She has influence in all sorts of places. It's how I see you, my dear, in future years. I should like you to be a great hostess, like Mrs Keppel.'

Nina felt a thrill of excitement. What could she do with such influence? She thought of the meeting she had just been to, and the arguments about the emancipation of women. Could she be the person who brought it about – Nina Sanderton who'd shared Kitty's come-out because she had no money and no position? She gave a shiver at the thought.

He saw it, and said, 'Don't be scared. You're well able to go into top society. And I've never known you at a loss for words. You must see tomorrow about a new gown – can't be presented to His Majesty in something you've worn before. You might pop over to Lady Manningtree and ask her advice – she'll set you right.'

'Yes, I'll do that,' Nina said, glad to think it would not be her taste alone that guided her on such an important occasion.

'And the best thing is,' Cowling went on, full of smiles now, 'that we'll be bound to give a dinner in return. We'll have the King here, in our house – what d'you think of that?'

Nina, whatever her husband said, was lost for words.

CHAPTER TEN

When it took place a few days later, the journey to Clapham was one of consummate embarrassment. A hansom cab had room for just two passengers. It was not that McGregor took up a lot of room – he was a very thin man – but to have him sit so close, arms rigidly folded and face grim, as the cab jolted and rumbled over London streets first familiar and then unfamiliar, made Stuffy feel horribly self-conscious. He was sure people were staring at him: a wealthy man in silk hat and an overcoat with a fur collar (it was May, and a fine day, but he was always afraid of feeling the cold) crammed into a common cab with his manservant sitting beside him! It was not long before he wished he had asked Caroline for her carriage after all.

After they crossed the river – on a bridge he had not known existed – they passed some very mean streets and he began to wish fervently that he had not come at all. But then things got better: the streets got wider, though they still had an alien, south-of-the-river look, and the houses larger, and then they came to an open space with green grass and fine mature plane trees, and eventually pulled up in front of a handsome white-stuccoed house, with a mansard roof and an in-and-out sweep round a clump of shrubs and small trees. Obviously the dwelling of a man of taste and means.

The jarvey opened the hatch. 'This is it, guv'nor,' he said.

Stuffy was glad to discover the Arthurs were so prosperous.

It was a house he would not be ashamed to see any of his friends living in. The door was opened by a footman, who took his card and invited him into a large, grand entrance hall. He relieved him of his hat and coat, which were received seamlessly by a trim maid who was standing by, then showed him into a spacious and well-furnished drawing-room. There were some unusual objects displayed here and there about the room, which he supposed were relics dug up from archaeological sites. They did not seem particularly decorative to him, but then neither were many of the family heirlooms he saw scattered around the drawing-rooms of his friends and relatives. He himself had some hideous *famille noire* vases that had belonged to his grandmother and which had stood on the same console for so long he barely registered their presence.

The door opened and Mary Arthur came in, crossed the room with a welcoming smile, shook his hand, and said, 'Lord Leake, what a pleasant surprise. What brings you to this part of the world?'

He realised that this was a difficult question to answer. He had been carried away by the determination to see the glorious creature again, but could hardly offer that as a reason for calling. 'Oh, er – passing, dear lady, passing, you know,' he said vaguely. And then, suddenly afraid she might not know who he was, he added, 'Lady Rachel's uncle, you know – we met at the ball the other night.'

'Of course I remember,' Mary Arthur said. 'Won't you please sit down? May I offer you a glass of wine?'

While he was arranging himself on a sofa, she rang the bell, and the footman came in so immediately he must have been waiting outside in the hall. 'Sherry, please, Thomas. And would you ask Miss Lombardi to come down.'

Stuffy's heart jumped at the last words. He had been wondering how to introduce her to the conversation. 'I hope Miss Lombardi was not tired after the exertions of the ball?' he said.

'Not at all,' said Mary, smiling. 'The young, I think, can never be tired out by dancing. My husband is not at home at present. He will be sorry to have missed you. He is spending the day, as he so often does, at the British Museum. The Egyptian rooms. Are you interested in antiquities, sir?'

Stuffy felt he probably ought to be. 'You have some – er – interesting objects in this room, I couldn't help noticing. That – er – manikin, for instance.' He gestured at random at a figurine, which appeared to be missing an arm and most of its face, and was wearing a very peculiar sort of nightcap, which was standing upright instead of flopping over.

'Oh, the god Horus,' she said. 'Yes, we were very pleased to find that. Quite rare in that condition.'

'What a pity it got broken,' he said kindly.

'It is over two thousand years old,' Mary said gently. 'Some damage is inevitable, especially when something has been buried all that time.'

'Ah. Quite,' said Stuffy. He cast around in vain for another topic.

Mary said, 'Do you make much stay in London? Giles – Lord Stainton – has mentioned you to us on occasion. I believe you live in Northumberland?'

'Oh, that's the family seat. I have a place in Perthshire, too, and another in Norfolk, but I don't spend much time at any of 'em. You travel a lot, I believe? Abroad, and so on? Spend much time here?'

'This is our home,' she said, faintly amused, 'but we go on digs whenever we can.'

Stuffy thought for a moment she'd said 'in digs' and was puzzled why they would live in digs when they had a perfectly decent house, but then he made the connection with archae- ology and said, 'Ah!'

At that moment, the door opened to admit Giulia, closely followed by the footman with the sherry tray. Stuffy rose to his feet, his eyes flying to her face and the blood to his own.

Giulia exchanged an enigmatic glance with Mary Arthur, then extended a cool hand to the visitor. 'Lord Leake,' she said, without inflection. 'How nice to see you again.'

At the touch of her fingers, Stuffy went to pieces. Only a lifetime of urbanity allowed him to speak at all. 'Just passing, you know – felt I had to check – no ill effects from the ball – late night – overheated rooms – your magnificent exertions—'

She released him and sat down, and said calmly, 'I am perfectly well, thank you. It was a very fine occasion, was it not? It was agreeable to me to see Giles's family *in pieno splendore*. It has been hard sometimes to remember that he is an English lord, when I see him mostly in shirtsleeves and streaked with mud.'

'You have known Giles a long time,' Stuffy said.

'More years than I can remember. He is like a big brother to me.'

An apprehension he had not even realised he had left Stuffy's mind. He felt suddenly cheerful. 'Very good fellow, Giles. One of the best. You have no brothers of your own?'

'No, I am the only child – cherished and spoiled. Do you have brothers?'

'Sisters. Three of 'em.' He thought a moment. 'I suppose I was spoiled too. The youngest, doted on. Ah, thank you, ma'am, most kind.' He received a glass of sherry from Mary, sipped, and pronounced it excellent. He wanted, out of politeness, to address some conversation to her, but his eyes and mind were dragged inexorably back to Giulia, who seemed to glow as she sat on another sofa at a little distance in a simple dark green day dress. The colour, he thought, would be his favourite from now on. 'You are from Italy, I believe?' he asked, longing to hear her voice again.

'From Firenze,' she said

'Ah, Florence! *Le atene del rinascimento*,' he said. The Athens of the Renaissance. He seemed to remember someone had once called it that. Or was that Edinburgh? No, that was the Athens of the North.

Giulia's eyebrows had risen. 'You speak Italian?' she said in surprise.

'Oh, a few words,' he said modestly. 'I learned it as a boy, as one does, but one forgets, you know, one forgets. But,' he remembered gladly, 'I have a little place in Italy. In Venice. The Ca' Scozzesi, on the San Benito canal. Bought by my grandfather, and he left it to me. I've visited a few times. Do you know Venice?'

'Yes,' she said. 'I have been there with my parents.'

'Beautiful city,' Mary said. 'Talbot and I had our honeymoon there.'

'Ah! Perfect. Perfect city for a honeymoon,' Stuffy said, unaccountably looking at Giulia as he spoke. 'I should like to go back. Always liked Venice. Shame to leave the house empty. But these old palazzi need a mistress to bring them alive.' He made himself address Mary. 'Where did you stay in Venice?'

A conversation grew up, encompassing Venice and Florence – happily for Stuffy, a three-way conversation. And, happily too, he had done the grand tour with a tutor in his youth and had therefore visited the important sights, the galleries and the museums, so he was able to appear in a good light – not just an idle rich man but a man of education, too. He had not finished one dance with Giulia before realising that intellectual attainments were important to her. As the conversation waxed, she seemed to warm.

At last he asked, 'And what have you been doing, since you came to London – apart from dancing the soles out of your slippers at a grand ball?'

Mary answered for her. 'Giulia has been seeing the sights. It is her first visit to London. We have taken the day off today, but we shall resume tomorrow.'

'Indeed? And what do you see tomorrow?'

'Westminster Abbey,' Mary said, 'and the Houses of Parliament, if we have time.'

Excitement rushed up inside Stuffy as he saw the opportunity. 'Oh, but, my dear ladies, you must allow me to show you around the House. It is rather my *milieu*. And perhaps entertain you to tea on the terrace afterwards.'

Mary consulted Giulia with a glance, but she answered at once, 'That is very kind of you, sir. We shall be very happy.'

'Excellent, excellent. You do me great honour,' said Stuffy. When he took his leave a little later, with the arrangements made, he was treading on air. Even having to get back into the cab under the close scrutiny of McGregor could not dent his euphoria. He barely noticed the drive home, mentally going through his wardrobe, and wishing there were time to have a new suit made. Thoughts of Venice and Florence whirled about his mind in fragments of brilliant light, blue skies, sun dancing on canals and fountains, and buildings of blinding white, ochre, terracotta and deep blue. Why had he wasted his life in England when there were such places to be? He thought of the Ca' Scozzesi – he had called it a little place, but it was in fact quite a large palace, painted pink, just off the Grand Canal – and wondered if it was in a fit condition to visit. He should send a telegram. Ah, Venice! Perfect place for a honeymoon, someone had said. He dreamed as the cab rattled back safely north of the river.

'It is obvious,' Giulia said to Mary, 'that a lord can show us the House of Lords better than a mere attendant. Probably he will have access to special parts that others cannot see.'

'And tea on the terrace is a particular treat, I believe,' said Mary. 'The view over the Thames, Westminster Bridge, Lambeth Palace . . . Exquisite!'

Giulia smiled. 'I love afternoon tea so much, the little sandwiches and cakes, so English. No-one else in the world

does it. I shall have much to tell my parents in my next letter.'
She wrote home every two or three days.

Mary said, 'But has it occurred to you, my dear . . .' She
hesitated, then went on, 'I find it hard to believe Lord Leake
was "just passing". We are a long way from Berkeley Square.'

Giulia looked puzzled. 'What are you saying?'

'I noticed the way he looked at you when you were dancing
with him . . . Does it not occur to you that he may be smitten
with you?'

'What is "smitten"? But, no, I can guess – you think he
has taken a fancy to me. "Smitten". I like this word.' She
shrugged. 'I think he was being polite to Giles's friend. At
home, lecturers who work with Papa are often nice to me at
parties.'

'Hmm,' Mary said, in a reserved manner.

'Is something wrong?' Giulia asked.

She shook herself. 'Of course not. I was being foolish. Pay
no attention.' Mary knew it was not usual for English earls
to exert themselves to be kind to obscure penniless girls. But
Giles had always been unusually accessible, and perhaps his
uncle was the same. The attention was a favour to Giles. Lord
Leake would show them round the House of Lords, and that
would be that. She changed the subject. 'I thought that on
the day after tomorrow we might visit the Wallace Collection.'

'What is there?'

'Some very fine statuary and paintings. Nothing *very* old,
but I think you'll enjoy it.'

'You were wonderful at the ball, Mr Moss,' said Doris at
breakfast. 'We was watching from up the stairs when all the
people arrived, and you announcing them, all those funny
names, and Lord This and Lady That. How'd you ever know
how to pronounce 'em?'

'Oh, it comes with experience,' Moss said, lofty but pleased.

'And your voice, it sounded so – sort of rich. You could

hear every word,' Doris went on, gazing up at him admiringly.

Moss glanced at Ada, two places further down the table. She was not looking at him, but at her plate where she was cutting into a sausage, but he was sure she was listening. 'Ah, the penetrating voice has to be developed,' he said. 'When I was younger, I used to go out into the fields where I would disturb nobody, and practise projecting my voice at the distant trees. I believe famous actors do the same.'

Between Doris and Ada, Ellen was choking into her apron, and under the table Doris gave her a helpful pinch to sober her up. Dory gave both of them a savage glance and raised a question about the day's duties to distract him.

A little while later they left the table, and Ellen, hustling Doris along with arms linked, muttered into her ear, 'Why d'you suck up to Mr Moss like that? I nearly died laughing.'

'I wasn't sucking up,' Doris said indignantly. 'I was just being respectful, and – well, you never know how it might help. If he likes you he could put in a good word for you. *You* could do with being nicer to him, if you want to get on. You've not got so far with your lady's-maiding, have you?'

Ellen looked gloomy. So far, being at Pelham House had done her no good at all. No grand lady had said to her, 'You are exactly what I'm looking for for my daughter's personal servant.' No-one had had a crisis of hair or fastenings right in front of her.

'I don't see him favouring *you*, anyway,' she retorted. 'It's that Ada he talks nice to, for all she never says a word back, far as I can tell.'

'Early days,' said Doris. 'I'll keep working on him.'

'Good luck to it!' Ellen said sniffily. But then she giggled too. 'It was funny, though, wasn't it, about him shouting at the trees?' And they walked off, heads together, sniggering.

Moss, meanwhile, detained Ada on her way out. He had been feeling tired recently, though he put it down to his exertions

181

at the ball. The memory of his performance there had sustained him during the anti-climax that had followed. He would be remembered by all the guests. They might not know his name, but in years to come as they recalled treading up those stairs, they would see in their mind's eye the magnificent figure of the major-domo who controlled and directed everything, the lynch-pin of the evening.

And it was heartening to know that the maids had witnessed and appreciated it. Doris's praise gave him the impetus to put his long-cherished plan into operation. It was the right moment. There was only one more grand dinner party to come, and then the Castle servants would be sent home. And back at the Castle it would be harder for him to get Ada alone. There were always so many people watching you.

He called her to him. As she gazed up at him, his heart fluttered strangely, making his legs feel weak for a moment. It was love, he thought. His affection and desire to protect her had deepened into a powerful love. She was very young, but once he had betrothed her to him, he could wait for marriage. Today he would take that first step. He would make a special day for her, and crown it with his proposal.

It was Sunday, so they would be at leisure after luncheon. And, as if the Almighty favoured his plans, it was a fine day. 'This afternoon I am going to visit the zoological gardens at Regent's Park, and I would like you to accompany me. It will be both educational and amusing. We shall look at the animals, then take tea in the tea-rooms there. We shall leave after luncheon and take the omnibus.'

'Yes, Mr Moss,' said Ada. Her pretty face was always rather inexpressive, so she didn't show her disappointment. She didn't want to go to the zoo with Mr Moss. One of the Pelham House maids had suggested walking in St James's Park to see the pelicans and then to the bandstand where there was bound to be jolly music and interesting young men in uniform with whom to flirt. She had been fancying George, one of the grooms at Ashmore Castle, but so far he hadn't shown any sign of noticing her; and besides, he was there and she was here and there was never any harm in flirting. But it never occurred to her to refuse Mr Moss. He was the butler, and all-powerful. So she just said, 'Yes, Mr Moss,' and thought about her straw hat, to which she had just fixed a new ribbon. She had been going to sew on a bunch of artificial daisies to go to St James's Park, but she wouldn't bother now.

Conveniently, the omnibus went up Gloucester Place, right past Portman Square, so they caught it on the corner. As the horses plodded northwards he told her about the history of the zoo, and some of the astonishing animals that had been housed there in the past, like the quagga and the thylacine. He recounted how it had always been supposed that wild animals from foreign lands would not be able to survive outside in England's climate, but how recently they had tried moving some of them out of doors and found they thrived. 'So it is much easier to view them,' he concluded. 'It will create a richer experience for us, I believe.'

'Yes, Mr Moss,' Ada said obediently.

He wished she would look up at him, but she was staring out of the window, and as he looked down, the brim of her straw hat obscured all but the tip of her nose and the scimitar curve of her eyelashes. He fed on them for the rest of the journey.

When they descended from the omnibus, he escorted her across the road – a rare opportunity to touch her as he cupped her elbow to guide her between the traffic. He paid for their entrance and bought for a penny a folding paper plan that showed where everything was. He had already looked up in his *A to Z of Universal Knowledge* some interesting facts about a few of the animals, and paused now to find their location and devise a route. He had meant to tell her as they walked what they were going to see, but for some reason he found walking and talking at the same time made him rather breathless, so he waited until they stopped by the animal in question before beginning.

He had been sure she would be taken by the giraffes and, sure enough, they astonished her – she had never seen even a picture of one before. Staring up at them revealed her face to Moss, and he was happy to stand there for as long as she wanted, telling her that the pattern on their skin was intended for concealment, and even, when she showed signs of having looked enough, redirecting her gaze by explaining that the horns were not an outgrowth of the skull, but became attached to it in the animal's maturity.

The camel house was a success, and he regaled her with their ability to store water in their humps, and the large feet that stopped them sinking into the sand. She seemed not to care for the orangutan or the kudu, but was entranced by the bright colours of the parrots and seemed in no hurry to leave them. Moss had not prepared anything on parrots, but he was feeling the heat rather – it was a particularly fine, sunny day – and he was glad to stand in silence for a while. Indeed, it was so hot that, after a look at the plan, he directed them next to the Aquarium where they could go inside and cool down.

It proved very soothing, watching the brightly coloured fish cruise aimlessly about, and his spirits began to revive. The tigers and lions were next on his mental list, but though it was early for tea, he found himself consumed with the desire for a cup. He really was very thirsty. Well, he was in charge, and could order them to tea whenever he pleased. Better, in any case, to get in before the inevitable rush. On a sunny Sunday in May, the zoo was well-frequented.

'I think we shall have tea next,' he said, as he guided Ada to the Aquarium exit.

'Yes, Mr Moss,' she said.

As they stepped outside again into the sunshine, he felt his tiredness come down like a weight on his shoulders, and at the same time his forehead broke out in a sweat. He removed his hat and dabbed at it with his handkerchief, not wishing her to see him with moisture running down his face. It was strange, because in the normal way he hardly ever sweated. He thought it common to perspire. He mopped, and the sun beat down and made him squint, and he drew an involuntary great sigh that seemed to do nothing towards inflating his lungs. He felt dizzy and tried to take a deep breath, and it was strangely difficult.

'Are you all right, Mr Moss?' he heard Ada say.

'Yes, of course,' he said. 'Never better.' At least, that was what he meant to say, but not having managed to breathe in properly, he couldn't actually speak at all and only, to his dismay, made a grunting sound. He replaced his hat on his head, looked down at her with a puzzled expression, and fell like a tree.

'*You* will have to deal with it,' the dowager said furiously to Giles. She had taken the trouble to come all the way from Portman Square to Berkeley Square to say it, and said it with the maximum vehemence.

Ada's return to Pelham House in the care of a policeman and a state of collapse had caused such a sensation below stairs that Miss Taylor had felt obliged to disturb her mistress. Maud always rested on her bed at that hour of the day, and insisted that Rachel did the same, a short period of respite between the engagements of the day and of the evening. The debutante round was relentless and exhausting.

Giles, who had been about to go up to dress for an unfashionably early supper with old friends, was not pleased to be interrupted.

'After all,' Maud continued, 'he is *your* butler.'

'Is he, indeed? You managed to forget that when you purloined him from the Castle –'

'*Purloined?*'

'– without consulting anyone's convenience.'

'Rachel is your sister, and you are the head of the family. If you wanted her brought out in less than the finest style you should have told me so.'

'I don't recollect ever being asked,' Giles snapped, even as he realised this was the silliest argument he had ever had.

Maud seemed to realise it at the same moment. She waved it away with one cold white hand. 'Nevertheless, I am *far* too busy chaperoning Rachel to deal with this – *crisis*. We have three engagements this evening alone, and I am already late for dressing. You must go, Giles – and please do not breathe at me in that testy fashion. What is your engagement this evening compared with mine? An informal supper with your university friends can easily be postponed.'

Giles did not want to postpone, but Moss was an old family retainer, and duty was duty. 'Where is he?'

'The St Pancras infirmary, so I'm told,' said Maud, indifferently. 'Wherever that might be.'

'I know it,' Giles said. It had been the infirmary for the local workhouse, a tall, grim building on a dark corner, which he had passed on various occasions when a student, because it was not far from University College, and many of his fellow students had lodged in the streets thereabouts. He supposed Moss had been taken there because it was the closest hospital to the zoo. Actually, it was not too far from the house he had been invited to that evening – John and Mabel Portwine lived in Cartwright Gardens – so he might be able to go on afterwards. They wouldn't mind if he wasn't dressed.

'Very well,' Maud said, as if his knowing the infirmary clinched the argument. 'Then you had better go. Find out what is the matter with him and when he will return to duty. I hope it is nothing long-drawn-out,' she added. 'I shall need him for the dinner party. If he can manage that, he can go down to Ashmore afterwards to recover if necessary.'

'Your compassion astounds me,' Giles said. 'You have a greatness of heart, Mother.'

'Don't be impertinent. And ring the bell – I must leave immediately.'

For the Earl of Stainton, the physician on duty – young, a little shabby, and weary-looking – made himself available. 'It seems to have been a heart attack,' he said. 'Yes, of course you can see him, though he has been given a sedative, so he may be drowsy or even asleep. The most important thing after an episode of this nature is that there should be no strain on the heart – no exertion and no agitation – so if he is able to speak to you, please do not say anything to upset him. My lord,' he added, diplomatically.

'Will he recover?' Giles asked, feeling suddenly discomposed. Moss was a figure from his childhood, an indestructible monument. It should not be possible to knock down an icon.

'That's rather in the lap of the gods,' the physician said. 'He is alive, and that is the first point, but there is no way to tell what permanent damage has been done. Some suffer a lifelong weakness, others recover much of their former strength. Time will tell. He seems to be a man of overall good health, so with luck and good nursing, he has a chance of recovery. He must have absolute rest, both physical and mental – that is the key. No work, no worries or anxieties, no excitement.'

The sister, rather fluttered by the presence of one who was not only an earl but a young and handsome one, conducted Giles to Moss's bed. The long ward, lit only by a window at one end, was stark, with two rows of iron beds, each with an enamel number plate on the bare wall above it. The occupants seemed to be old men, all looking gaunt and sick. Of those propped up, many seemed troubled by a racking cough; those lying down looked as though they hadn't long to go. It was singularly depressing, and made it all the harder to see Moss lying there, so reduced, so helpless.

He tried to struggle up when he saw Giles, and the sister hastened to press him down. 'No, no, you mustn't move. Now then, now then. Rest yourself.'

Giles came closer. 'Yes, Moss, you must rest. Doctor's orders.'

'Oh, my lord, I'm so sorry,' Moss said. He was unexpectedly pale, and Giles only then appreciated how ruddy his face had always been. It looked thinner, too, and the nose sharper, as though the flesh had fallen away from his cheeks.

'There's nothing to apologise for,' Giles said. 'No-one can help being ill. You are not to worry. Everything is being taken care of.'

'It was the heat,' Moss said. He seemed a little confused, and after his first recognition of Giles, he seemed to forget who he was talking to. 'I remember coming out of the Aquarium. Bright sunshine. No shade. So hot. Stopped to mop my brow. Don't remember anything else.' He looked at Giles, puzzled. 'Where am I?'

'The infirmary, at St Pancras.'

Moss seemed to be thinking, groggily. Then suddenly he was alarmed. 'Her ladyship – the dinner party—'

'All will be taken care of.'

'But she needs me!'

'We all need you, Moss – we need you to get well. That's the important thing. And that means rest and quiet. So you are not to worry about anything, do you hear me?'

Moss's eyes filled with tears, which upset Giles even more. It was so far from the stately, unflappable Moss he knew. 'Will I lose my position?' he asked.

'Of course not,' Giles said soothingly. 'The very idea. As if Ashmore Castle could carry on without you. You must concentrate on getting well again.'

'Yes,' Moss whispered, but he looked confused. He rubbed his hand over his mouth in a feeble, absent sort of way. 'There was someone else. Someone—'

At that moment, there was a disturbance further down the ward. A nurse at a bedside, bending over a patient, called, 'Sister! Can you come?' Rapidly screens were drawn round the bed and the sister disappeared inside. After a moment she and the nurse came out and walked off in different directions, but the screens remained. Giles, for some reason, was sure that the occupant of the bed had just died. This was not a good place for Moss, he decided, with the evidence of mortal decay all around.

The sister came back to him to say, 'Forgive me, my lord, but it would be better to leave the patient to sleep now.'

Giles turned to her, away from Moss, and said quietly, 'Can he be moved? Would it be better for him to be taken home?'

'Not at present,' she said regretfully, reluctant to refuse him anything. 'We need to keep him sedated for the first two weeks. An episode of this sort is sometimes followed by a second, more serious. If that happened, it would be better if he were here.'

Giles saw the point. 'After that, then?'

'If all goes well, he could be moved somewhere else to recuperate. But he will need care from a trained nurse. And it is likely to be a long time before he can resume work – if he ever does.'

Giles nodded. 'Very well. I'll just say goodbye.' He turned back to Moss, who seemed to be drifting off to sleep, leaned close and said quietly, 'Goodbye for now, Moss. Don't worry about anything. It will all be taken care of.'

Moss muttered something, and seemed to be drifting deeper. But then his eyes flew open, and he cried in alarm, 'Ada!'

Giles was turning away. 'What is it, old fellow?' he asked, leaning over again.

'Ada was with me. The housemaid. What happened to her? Where is she?'

'She was brought home all safe and sound. Don't worry.'

'She must have been so scared,' Moss said, tears gathering again. 'Tell her – tell her . . .'

'Yes?'

'Tell her I'm all right,' Moss said, with a shuddering sigh. He looked up at Giles drearily, as though all light had gone from the world.

'I will,' Giles said.

A few moments later he was back outside in the sunshine, and found himself breathing deeply and with a strange urge to run, like someone let out of prison. He was suddenly seeing the episode from Moss's point of view, realising how fragile a servant's life was. Illness and old age were an existential threat to someone who had no family, no resources, no financial buffer to fall back on. Work was everything – not an agreeable pastime but the absolute essential for existence. If you couldn't work, there was nowhere to go. All that waited for you was the workhouse, and death.

'Oh, the poor man!' Kitty exclaimed. 'He must be so worried. You did reassure him, Giles? You told him we would take care of him?'

'I told him not to worry,' Giles said. 'But it looks as though he won't be able to work again for some time. And he'll need nursing.'

'We can hire a trained nurse,' Kitty said. 'He'll be better off at home, at any rate. Hospitals are dreadful places.'

Giles shook his head, remembering. 'It was depressing, all right. But it looks like being an expensive business, nursing him back to health. And there's no knowing if he'll ever be fit enough to take up his old position.'

Kitty looked alarmed. 'What are you saying? You can't mean to abandon him, after all these years of service!' Giles didn't answer. 'What about all those old servants who are paid pensions by the estate?'

'A pension is one thing – it's a small sum of money, and they look after themselves. Taking full care of him for month after month will be far more expensive.'

'And what will happen to him if we don't?' she asked.

It was a mild enough question, but her eyes were sparkling and her cheeks were flushed with determination. He was reminded, with a pang, of that moment on their honeymoon when she had turned on him and demanded to be treated with respect. The difference now was that her hands were cupped protectively over her belly as she spoke. Still, he wanted to tell her she was prettier than ever, and that being roused suited her. For a moment he wished she weren't pregnant, because they were alone in her bedroom and he wanted her.

'The workhouse, I suppose. I don't think he has any family.'

'I don't *think* you would actually know, would you?'

He smiled at her, and touched her cheek. She recoiled angrily. 'No, I don't know. But don't bite me, Kitty. I wasn't proposing to abandon the old fellow. I was simply musing aloud that it will be expensive.'

Kitty waved a hand vaguely towards the window. 'You talk about expense, after all *this*?' His comprehension quickened by his awareness of her, he understood she meant Rachel's come-out, the hiring of Pelham House and the extra servants, the ball, the clothes, the carriages, and all the other expenditure of showing her to society.

'The business of the debut and the Season is not something designed by me,' he said mildly, his eyes tracing the curve of her taut lips. 'I don't seek to justify it.'

She took a step closer, looking up, quivering with intensity. 'If you don't take care of Moss, Giles, I shall never speak to you again!'

He laughed, put his arms round her, drew her against him. 'Little firebrand! Moss shall be taken care of. How jealous I am that you care so much about him! Would you fight that way for me, I wonder?' And he kissed her. For an instant she

191

resisted, but then her lips softened and she melted against him, and he felt a surge of sexual desire. Nothing to be done about it, in her condition. After a moment he pushed down his feelings and gently disengaged himself from her. Her face looked flushed and a little dazed.

'Well, would you?' he asked, with tender amusement. 'Fight for me?'

'You know I would.'

'For your information, I always intended taking care of the old boy,' he said. 'Go to bed now. I'll talk to my mother tomorrow.'

He left her and went away to his own room, reflecting that at no point had she mentioned that all the money in discussion came originally from her. Nor had she mentioned her condition. He smiled to himself, thinking that, somehow or other, Kitty had learned a code. She did not use feminine tactics. She seldom fought, but when she did, she fought fair.

He went early to Portman Square to catch his mother before the debutante machine started up, and was admitted to her bedroom, where she was in her dressing-gown, sitting at the table in the window partaking of tea and toast and going through the day's letters and invitations..

Succinctly, he told her about Moss's condition.

'It is a nuisance,' she said. 'I have the dinner on Wednesday. Well, we shall manage. I can hire another man from the agency just for one evening.' She went back to her post. 'Lady Vane – a *soirée*, no less! She seeks to distinguish herself with the use of the French language. If she means a card evening, she should say so.'

Giles smiled to himself, and said, 'You do not ask me what arrangements need to be made for Moss's recuperation. You are not concerned about his future?'

She looked up. 'He is *your* butler. What have I to do with it?'

192

He studied her for a moment, and under his gaze a slight colour came to her cheeks. 'Can it really be that you are detaching yourself from our daily affairs?' he mused. 'That you no longer regard yourself as the mistress of Ashmore Castle?'

'You are a married man, Stainton,' she snapped. 'You are too old for childish games.'

'If that is the case,' he went on, as if she hadn't spoken, 'it would mean that you finally accept the reality of Father's death. Are you planning a new life away from us?'

'Don't be impertinent,' she said, her colour deepening.

He continued to examine her. 'There's something different about you this morning, Mother,' he said. 'I can't decide what.'

'Nonsense,' she said. But she looked away first.

He prepared to leave. 'In case you are interested, in spite of your protestations, I do intend to take care of Moss, though his recovery may be a long one. I was thinking it might be better to move him to a nursing-home. He needs complete rest, the doctor says, and he probably wouldn't relax at the Castle, watching someone else do his job, and thinking how he would do it differently.'

'A nursing-home?' she exclaimed. 'For a servant? You are a fool. But if you wish to throw your money about in that ostentatious and unnecessary manner, it is none of my business. Go away, now,' she added hastily. 'I have to dress.'

He suspected she had been afraid he might be about to mention in counter-argument the throwing about of money over Rachel's debut. He went, reflecting that it was the first time she had called him Stainton, his father's title. *Something* was going on.

In the hall, it was James who brought his hat and cane to him, and fixed his glittering, hungry eyes on him.

'Might I ask, my lord, how Mr Moss is?'

'He had a heart attack, but the doctors think he will recover, though it will be a long process.'

James moved to the door as if to open it for him, but he stood with his hand on the knob, effectively holding Giles prisoner. 'So he won't be able to return to his job for a long time, my lord – if ever?'

Giles was not going to have this argument for a third time, least of all with a servant. 'Thank you, James,' he said pointedly.

'My lord, I can do the job. I've done it all at various times. I'm the senior footman, I'm the most experienced. You don't want a stranger coming in, my lord, who doesn't know the Castle or how we do things. Make me butler, my lord! I'm the right man for it. I won't let you down.'

Giles didn't like James, his cadaverous thinness, his devouring eyes. There was just something about him . . . And he should have dismissed him when he refused to go to Egypt with him. He had only kept him on because he thought the humiliation of demotion would be more of a punishment. But there was something in what he said. Certainly, his manner as a servant to visitors was unimpeachable, and a strange new butler might cause friction below stairs, wanting to change things.

'I'll think about it,' he said shortly.

'Thank you, my lord! But to keep things working smooth, it'd avoid any inconvenience for *you*, my lord, if you were just to appoint me now. You don't want to be having to think about domestic matters, my lord. Let me take all that off your mind, my lord. Make me butler.'

Those were valid points, but Giles wasn't going to be badgered by a servant, least of all one he didn't like. It probably *would* be James in the end, but he wasn't going to satisfy him now. 'The door, James,' he said.

James lowered his eyes, opened the door obsequiously, closed it behind him.

Inwardly, he rejoiced. He felt sure the job was his. If me lord wasn't going to give it to him, he'd have said so. James was under no illusion that Lord Stainton liked him, but everybody knew how disruptive it was to bring in an outside butler. People held on to their butlers, and one who was out of work was likely to be out of work for a reason. He dismissed the idea that Moss might get better and come back – he was an old man, and with compromised health would never be up to it again. Even if they appointed James on a temporary basis, he would make the job so much his own they would never get him out. His ambition was within his reach at last.

As soon as he had time off, he would go round the wine merchants and let them know how the land lay. One of a butler's perks was the commission traders would pay to get the business, and the wine merchant's was the biggest and best. It was a wonderful bit of luck that he was in London just at this moment. And the new Lord Stainton knew nothing about wine – not like the old lord – so he would have power worth paying for.

CHAPTER ELEVEN

'I must say, Mr Crooks, that it's a great pleasure having you back here,' said Mrs May. She was making pastry in the kitchen of Sebastian's little house in Henley. Through the open window from the garden came gentle warm air and the cheerful sound of birds getting on with the pressing business of life.

Crooks, seated to one side of the kitchen by the small table, on which newspaper was decently spread, was cleaning the master's boots.

Before he could answer, Olive came in from the garden with a trug of potatoes, which she dumped in the sink. 'Joe sent 'em up,' she announced. 'First new 'uns.'

'They'll go lovely with that bit of lamb for the master's dinner,' said Mrs May. 'I hope everything's all right with him, Mr Crooks. We were all quite believing that he was going to bring us home a mistress, after all that refurbishment last year. Have you heard any more about it?'

'Nothing at all, Mrs May,' Crooks said, his eyes on the boots.

Mrs May drew breath to speak, then changed her mind. She turned her head towards Olive. 'Be a dear and go down the cellar, and look over the apples for me. Bring me up half a dozen sound ones. I think I'll make this into an apple pie.'

'I was just going to wash the potatoes,' Olive said.

'You can do 'em after. Get the apples first, so I know.'

'I thought you were going to make a mincemeat tart,' Olive objected.

'We might as well use up the apples as let 'em go bad. If there's not enough, it'll have to be apple and mincemeat, won't it, but that's nice too. Don't stand there arguing – go on, do.'

When Olive had departed, Mrs May turned back to Crooks. 'There, she's out of the way. I don't blame you for being discreet with Olive in the room, because there's no doubt that girl does talk. But you can trust me, Mr Crooks – I'm deep as a well. What happened about the marriage plans? I was sure as sure he was doing up the place to bring home a wife.'

'It was never expressed to me in those terms, Mrs May,' Crooks said. 'Nothing was ever said in my presence about a wife.'

'But you thought it too, I know you did.'

'It was the obvious conclusion to draw,' he admitted.

'Why else would he have done out the garden parlour that's never been used in all my time here? And done it so nice and light and – *feminine*, I would call it. I suppose they must have quarrelled. What a shame! And him such a sweet-tempered man. I've been here twenty years and never had a sharp word from him. Do you know who the lady was, Mr Crooks?'

'No, I do not. As to a quarrel, well, he did seem despondent just after Christmas. He stopped playing the piano for a time, and that wasn't at all like him.'

'Ooh dear! That sounds serious. He does love his piano. Is he broken-hearted, d'you think?' Mrs May asked, greedy for sensation.

Crooks frowned. 'A gentleman of mature years and regular temper is never overset by life's vicissitudes.'

'No. I dare say he's not,' Mrs May said blankly, not sure what 'vicissitudes' were.

'But I feel as though things are taking a turn for the better now,' Crooks went on. 'While I can't say he has returned to his former level of cheerfulness, he has an air of purpose about him.'

'So you think they've made it up?'

'I can only say that I don't think he is *really* unhappy.'

'Oh,' said Mrs May, disappointed. While she naturally wished the master no ill, she'd have liked him to be sunk in broken-hearted grief – or exuberant with joy. An air of purpose, whatever that was when it was at home, offered you nothing to get your teeth into. 'So I wonder why he's come down here? It's not his usual time.'

'I couldn't say,' said Crooks. His master, he thought, had an air of waiting for something: news, or an occurrence. But that was the merest speculation. He looked up from the left boot and caught Mrs May's disgruntled expression. 'I *really* can't say,' he said, with more emphasis. 'Because I don't know.'

'Oh,' she said. And then, 'Well, I dare say it will all come out in the wash, one way or the other. And it's very nice to have company. It can be a bit dull here with just Olive and me, and her sleeping out. What would you say, Mr Crooks, to a hand of cards this evening? Cribbage, if you like.'

'That would be most agreeable,' said Crooks.

Molly Sands's last pupil of the day had cancelled, and Richard had taken her for a walk in Green Park. 'You don't get out enough,' he told her sternly. 'Sunlight and fresh air are very important for your health.'

She looked at him with level amusement. 'I'm sure you've shunned daylight for most of your life in favour of frowsting indoors and carousing, like every other young man. Alcohol, cigarettes and games of chance – late evenings in smoky rooms – not waking until noon is long past . . .'

'Now, where did you get that idea?' he asked, with large indignation. 'I was a soldier, don't you remember? Galloping across the veldt under blue South African skies. Sleeping under the stars with my saddle for a pillow. Up with the first grey light of dawn to wash in an icy stream. I could hardly have chosen a healthier life if I'd thought it out for a fortnight.'

'You do talk nonsense,' she said fondly. 'I must say, though, that it is very pleasant to be out while there's still daylight.' She lifted her face to the sun and closed her eyes in pleasure for a moment.

He thought she looked tired, and felt a pang. He longed to snatch her away from her life of toil. 'If only I had a white horse with me, I would catch you up before me and gallop away with you,' he said. 'Take my arm – the path is rough here.'

She took it with a smile of complicity, knowing he just wanted her touch, and they walked on in silence for a while, the silence of people at ease with each other.

After a while she said, 'How was the dinner last night?'

'Large and dull,' he said. 'I would sooner have had a neat supper with you. I was only asked because my mother needed a single man. That's all I am these days – a make-weight at the dinner table.'

'Poor you!' she sad. 'Self-pity is so very painful.'

He pinched her arm in retaliation, and said, 'It was rather strange not to have Moss there, being magnificent in the hall.'

'Any more news of him?'

'No, he's still in the infirmary. Which reminds me, there was a report in the paper the other day about something or other, and they had mis-spelled the word "infirmary" as "infamy". I thought that rather appropriate.'

'Is it very dreadful?'

'Not dreadful, just bleak. But, then, I suppose his bedroom at the Castle is probably not a nest of Oriental luxury. I haven't been in it, you understand – I speak as a matter of general principle.'

'I don't suppose he minds it as you would. One judges from the point of view of what one is used to.'

'Whatever makes you think I'm used to Oriental luxury?' He frowned, thinking. 'The oddest thing about it, you know, is not the heart attack.'

'It isn't?'

'No, he's a large, florid man, and like all butlers I suspect he does rather well for himself on the master's wine, especially the port—'

'Why especially the port?'

'Oh, I don't know. Tradition, probably. My point is that butlers are supposed to be large, florid men, or how can they be imposing? Now, the footman who was standing in for him last night is not at all butlery – a cadaver of a man, all bones and angles. He—'

'You were going to tell me the oddest thing about it,' she reminded him.

'Oh, yes – the oddest thing was that he went to the zoo on his afternoon off, Moss did, and took one of the house-maids with him.'

'Do you find the zoo or the housemaid odd?'

'Both, but the housemaid most of all.'

'Ah, a romance!' she said. 'That's nice. Is she pretty?'

'*I* don't think so. Pale and insipid. But *he* must, or why did he pick her? She was brought back by a large policeman, apparently, and had a fit of hysterics, but the next day she was completely normal and showed not the slightest sign of being upset. Nor has she requested leave to visit him. So if it was a romance, it was one-sided.'

'How do you know all this?' she asked, amused.

'Oh, a footman came over with a message, and Giles's new man Afton got it all out of him. And I got it all out of Afton. Invaluable man, Afton – I like him tremendously. He's valeting me as well as Giles while we're all at Aunt Caroline's.' His smile faded. 'Speaking of being at Aunt Caroline's . . .'

'You're going home,' she guessed. 'To the Castle.'

'Not immediately, but I am leaving the wicked city,' he said, making light because he really didn't want to go. 'I have to go and see a man about a bull.'

'Your dairy scheme?'

'Yes, taking off at last. There's a fellow near Dunstable that has a fine herd of Shorthorns and he has a pedigreed bull for sale. There's a tremendous amount of work to do at home, improving the pastures and getting the buildings up to scratch, but the bull can get on with his side of it in the meanwhile. And the sooner we get the cows in calf to a good bull, the sooner we'll have the new generation of heifers to—' He broke off abruptly. 'It occurs to me that this is a quite improper conversation to have with a lady.'

'Perhaps it's as well then that I'm not a lady.'

'You mustn't say that,' he said seriously. 'You're more a lady than any other female I've ever met. And if only I were not a wretched pauper and helpless pensioner of my brother, I would set you up in the condition in life you deserve.'

'If we all got what we deserved, which of us would escape calumny?' she said lightly. 'When are you leaving?'

'Tomorrow, I'm afraid. Can I take you out to supper tonight?'

'Very well, if you promise not to be sentimental.'

'I'm never sentimental. Passionate, sometimes—'

'No passion, either.'

'Oh, you are a harsh mistress!'

Lady Manningtree, Giles's Aunt Caroline, had taken an unaccountable liking to Mr Cowling, and always welcomed Nina warmly for his sake, as well as on her own account for being Giles's wife's friend.

And having been a debutante long ago, she could, with an effort, remember how nervous she had been at her presentation. 'Of course, I was only seventeen and unmarried. But, still, it is quite a thing. I'm pleased for you, my dear.'

'Mr Cowling knows the King quite well already,' Nina said. 'But it's hard not to feel very small and mouselike. They'll all be much older than me and I won't know any of them. Well, there's Lord and Lady Leven – not that I *know* them, but I went to their summer exhibition when Kitty and I were coming out.'

'Yes, dear, I remember.'

'And Mr Cowling said Lord and Lady Wroughton will be there. It was at their ball that I first met him. But I'm sure they won't remember me.'

'It is rather an elderly company,' Aunt Caroline mused. 'I don't suppose it will be lively. But the Levens are educated people – and I remember you like paintings and all that sort of thing, don't you? You can't go wrong talking about art to either of them.'

'I won't have to talk to the King, will I?'

'He's very nice, my dear, not at all an ogre. And he likes pretty young women. You should work up an amusing story – not too long – about some little thing that has happened to you. Practise it in your head beforehand, so you have it ready if the occasion arises. That will save you the embarrassment of being silent and looking gauche.'

'That's a good idea,' Nina said. 'Is that what you do?'

'It's what I used to do when I was a young girl. I hardly ever meet strangers nowadays. But I expect the other guests will do all the talking anyway, dear, so you'll only need to smile and nod. And then you can save your story for another occasion,' she concluded frugally. 'I presume the Keppels are invited?'

'I believe so.'

'Well, she'll keep everything going. She watches the King like a hawk, and as soon as she sees him grow bored, she intervenes. She's a fascinating woman – always has something amusing to say on every topic.'

'Perhaps she practises at home, too.'

'I shouldn't be surprised. It would be like her to be thorough. Lady Vane says she's like a Christmas tree with a present for everyone. When one is in her company one quite forgets that she's the King's mistress – though, of course, that's not like being a mistress in the general way. One couldn't as a rule condone . . . They live in Portman Square, you know, the Keppels, two doors down from the Pelham house. I don't think Maud realised when she took it. But *he*'s frightfully respectable, she can't complain about that. His father was the Earl of Albemarle, who was a direct descendant of Charles II – though I suppose Maud wouldn't necessarily count *that* as respectable.' She felt she was tying herself in knots and changed the subject quickly. 'What are you going to wear?'

'Mr Cowling wants me to have a new gown.'

'Very proper.'

'But I don't know how grand it ought to be. He likes things with a lot of decoration on them, but . . .' She bit her lip, not wanting to seem to criticise him. 'I have to look *right*,' she concluded.

Aunt Caroline went across to her writing desk, and scribbled a note. 'You must go to Hortense, my dressmaker in Orchard Street. She will know exactly what you should wear, and she'll make it up for you. You can trust her entirely – she has never let me down. This,' she concluded, speaking as she wrote, 'is a note of in-tro-duction to her, explain-ing the sit-u-ation. There!' She signed and folded it and handed it to Nina. 'Because she doesn't often take on new customers.'

'Thank you very much,' Nina said, curbing the urge to go and put her head in her mentor's lap. 'You are so kind. I wish you were *my* aunt,' she added, on impulse.

Aunt Caroline looked pleased and said, 'Bless you, child. And don't worry. It will all go by in a flash, and then you'll wish it wasn't over.'

The gardener's boy, Wilf, was surprised to be waylaid at the entrance to the kitchen yard by one of the grooms, George.

''Ello, mate,' George said, in a friendly manner. 'What you got there?'

'Veggibles for the kitchen. What's it to you?' Wilf said suspiciously.

'I'll take 'em for you,' George said. 'Save you the journey.'

It was only a few more yards. Wilf hugged the basket tighter to his chest. 'What's your game?'

George came clean. 'I want to talk to somebody in the 'ouse. Go on, let me take it.'

'I got to take the basket back,' Wilf objected.

'You wait here and I'll bring it to you. Be a pal. Do the same for you one day.'

Wilf grinned. 'Girl, is it?'

'Might be,' George admitted.

Wilf's grin broadened, but he relinquished the basket. George had wiry fair hair that stood straight up no matter how much oil he put on, and rather round, pale blue eyes that looked startling in his brown face. 'Coo-er! Love's young dream!' he said. 'Go on – but don't hang about. I'll get me ear clipped if I'm not back with that 'ere basket.'

George grabbed it with a muttered 'Thank you,' and walked through the yard up to the back door with what he supposed to be a nonchalant air.

Luckily, one of the younger kitchen maids, Debbie, appeared just then with a mat to shake, and opened her eyes wide at the sight of him. 'What you doing here? Is that our veg? Give it me. Why *you* bringing it, anyway?'

She took hold of one side of the basket, but George hung on to the other. He lowered his voice conspiratorially. 'Want to talk to somebody. Do us a favour, eh? Fetch Ada out here, will you?'

'Why should I?' Debbie said. 'You'll get me into trouble.'

'Oh, go on! I just want to talk to her. Be a pal.'

Debbie sniffed. 'I'll see if I can find her. Stay out there – don't go bringing your dirty boots in. I'm not cleaning up after you.'

George waited, shifting from foot to foot. He suddenly had a thought, licked his hand and pressed his hair down with it, squinted into the dark glass of the pantry window to see if his face was clean. And then Ada was there, dainty as a fairy, pale and golden as a princess, and was looking at him with an expression so blank she might have been a china doll. But she always looked like that, so it didn't put him off. It was her absence in London for several weeks that had made him realise he had feelings for her.

''Ullo,' he said, with an ingratiating smile.

''Ullo,' Ada said. She'd been fancying George for months, and his sudden request to speak to her had set her heart thumping, but she'd never been a great talker. Her prettiness had always meant that other people made the running.

'I'm glad you're back,' he said boldly. 'Did you like London?'

'It was all right.'

'Didn't decide to stay there, then? Big city? Bright lights and everything?'

She shook her head. Then, with a great effort, 'I like it here.'

He was encouraged. 'I like it when you're here. Heard you had a bit of an adventure in London? Is that right, Mr Moss took you to the zoo? What'd he do that for?'

'I dunno,' she said.

'What's his game? Does he fancy you, then? He's old enough to be your dad.'

She actually blushed. He was just being kind. 'He told me all about g'raffes and things.'

205

'What's g'raffes?' George asked suspiciously.

'Animals, sort of. At the zoo. With long necks. And there was – camiles and things. And a lot of fish. But then he was took ill.'

'Yeah, we heard about that. What happened?'

Ada frowned with the effort of composing a narrative. 'We was going to have tea. Then he sort of – went all funny. And he sort of fainted. Only it wasn't a faint, it was a heart tack, or something. They say.'

'What did you do?'

'I didn't do nothing. A lady and gentleman was there that looked after Mr Moss. And somebody fetched a policeman and he sorted it all out. They took Mr Moss away and another policeman took me home.'

'You must've been scared,' George said warmly, stepping closer.

Brigid, the senior kitchen-maid, appeared and said, 'What are you two up to? Ada, get back to your work. And you – you're not supposed to be here.'

'Waiting for the veg basket to take back.'

'That's not your job.'

'Helpin' out,' he said boldly.

She gave him a hard, suspicious look, and said, 'All right, I'll get it. Then you can clear off. Don't you know we've got a new butler, and he doesn't like boys messing about?'

She went inside, and George, realising he had to be quick, actually caught hold of Ada's hand. She recoiled in surprise and looked at him with wide eyes, but he didn't gather she minded too much. 'I'm glad you're back,' he said. 'I been thinking about you a lot since you went to London. Thinking I wouldn't see you again. How about you and me walking out?'

'Don't mind,' she said shyly, looking down.

'When's your afternoon off?'

'Wensdy. When's yours?'

'I'll make it be Wensdy, don't you worry. I'll meet you at the gate and we'll go for a walk. All right?'

She nodded. Then, feeling some encouragement was called for, she added, 'I didn't *want* to go to the zoo with him.' And then, bravely, 'I'd sooner go out with you than him.'

Brigid returned with the basket, which she thrust into George's arms. 'There! Now hook it. And you, Ada, you'd better not let Mrs Webster catch you hanging around the kitchen. She's in enough of a mood with Mr Moss gone and a new butler to cope with.'

Ada scuttled away, her heart singing. No more old Mr Moss learning her about elephants and Egypt and stuff, *and* George wanting to walk out with her! Everything in her garden was rosy.

Hook – formerly James, now *Mister* Hook – was coming along Piccadilly, saw her dash out of the kitchen and away, and was about to shout at her, but then changed his mind. It would be good to have something over Mrs Webster, who was responsible for the maids' behaviour. She had made clear her dislike of his promotion. She had even let him see incredulity, which was insulting, as though it was hard to believe that he could be a butler! They were all going to have to pay attention to him now. That old fool Moss was never coming back – and if he did, Hook would see him off in short time! This was his kingdom now, and no-one was going to take it away from him.

'Home again,' said Alice, eagerly, as the carriage pulled up in front of the great door. In the way that would have scandalised her mother, she did not wait for the groom but opened the door on her side and jumped down, looking round with pleasure and breathing deeply of the fresh country air. From this terrace there was a wonderful view down the hill, across Canons Ashmore and along the Ash valley in all its early summer verdure. Then the doors to the house were opened, there was a grey-brown flash of movement, and she was almost knocked down by the dogs, discovering her again with ever-renewable delight.

Kitty, of course, waited for the steps and allowed herself to be helped down. She looked up at the house and felt glad to be home, too. She pushed to the back of her mind the small shadow that Giles was staying on in London for a few more days. London contained Giulia Lombardi. He had not said anything about her since the ball, but Kitty had no confidence that he would not see her again. She was so beautiful and fascinating, and all the romantic novels spoke about the hot-blooded passion of the Italian race. Could a normal man resist the temptation if it was placed in his way? Well, the romantic novels were pretty clear about that.

She shook away the thought. Mrs Webster and Hook had come out onto the steps to receive her, and the ceremony gave her a little thrill. Giles would have had all the servants lined up for him, but she was satisfied with her share. For perhaps the first time, she really felt like the Countess of Stainton. This place was hers now – and she belonged to it, too.

Mrs Webster got in first. 'Welcome home, my lady,' she said. And she smiled.

Hook did not smile. He was on his dignity.

Kitty had got used to Moss, and had liked the soothing continuity he represented. Hook, now in butler's tailcoat and everyday black waistcoat and tie, looked strange: too thin, his figure not imposing enough, his skeletal face too avid, his eyes too insistent. There was nothing soothing about him. He looked as though he might suddenly do anything, whereas a butler like Moss looked as though he just *was*.

'Welcome home, my lady,' Hook said, a beat behind the housekeeper, but with an emphasis that said *his* welcome was the important one.

'Thank you,' Kitty said, treading carefully up the steps.

'Have you heard anything more about Mr Moss, my lady?' Mrs Webster asked.

'I believe he is a little better,' Kitty said. 'His lordship is arranging for him to be moved from the infirmary to the cottage hospital in Canons Ashmore at the end of the month.'

'That's nice, my lady. It will speed his recovery, being close to home, where his *friends* can visit him.'

Hook glared at her behind Kitty's back. He knew perfectly well she was getting at him, pointing out to him that he was only *temporary* butler. *We'll see about that, you old cat,* his narrowed eyes said.

'I'm sure Mr Moss is very grateful to his lordship,' Mrs Webster concluded.

The brake drew up, bringing the luggage along with Nanny, Jessie and the baby. Alice caught Kitty up, still with the dogs glued to her side, with foolish half-leaps and muzzles pointed adoringly at her face, and they walked in together.

In the hall, there were two tall vases of flowers, one on the table by the door and one at the foot of the stairs. Frilly pale pink paeonies, slender irises, and delphiniums the intense blue of summer skies.

'Oh, the flowers, how lovely!' Kitty exclaimed, shedding her coat into the arms of Miss Hatto, her maid, who walked in behind her.

Mrs Webster answered. 'Peason cut them specially this morning, my lady. As soon as he heard you were coming home.' The dowager Lady Stainton would never have deigned to notice the flowers, she thought, and though icy indifference was the more proper manner for a countess, she had always inspired obedience rather than affection. Peason, the head gardener, had selected and cut each stem with love.

Miss Hatto took Alice's things as well, and she and Kitty walked up the stairs together. 'What's the first thing you're going to do?' Alice asked.

'Nursery, then gardens. What's yours?'

'Stables,' said Alice, and sighed contentedly. 'As soon as I've changed. I feel as if I haven't ridden for months. And I don't care if Josh thinks it isn't ladylike to move out of a walk, I'm going to gallop Pharaoh for miles and miles and miles. He'll just have to keep up with me!'

Kitty laughed. 'I'll see you at luncheon, then.'

Nina walked into her drawing-room. Trump had thrust past her, but halted at the sight of the male silhouette against the window and gave a little growl. Then he recognised Giles, and hurried over to greet him. Nina had already had his card brought to her, but she would have known him anyway by his silhouette. She would know him anywhere, if it was only his back seen through a crowd, or a glimpse of his profile on a passing train. But her voice did not waver as she said, for the benefit of the servant holding the door for her, 'How do you do, Lord Stainton? I hope they told you Mr Cowling is not at home.'

He bowed. 'They did, Mrs Cowling, but I could not go away without paying my compliments to you.'

The door closed, and they were alone together.

'I did actually come to see him,' Giles said, 'but it seemed absurd not to see you, just because . . .'

He didn't finish the sentence, but she knew how it ended. She stared at him hungrily, to feast on him while she could. She couldn't think of anything to say.

He spoke. 'How are you?' he asked gently. 'You look well. You look . . .' he waved a hand to signify her *tout ensemble* '. . . like a lady of fashion.' She was in a dress of fawn silk with maroon piping on the bodice and three bands of maroon satin ribbon around the skirt hem.

'It's hard to *feel* like a lady of fashion, but I'm beginning to get more used to it,' she said. Mr Cowling liked her to look smart, and particularly liked her to spend a lot of money

210

on clothes. He took an interest in everything she wore. Clemmie had told her she was lucky, that from her experience most married men never knew one outfit from another, and that her father, for instance, might have noticed if she or her mother had entered the room naked, but not otherwise. 'It seems strange—' she began, and stopped, unsure if it was wise to go on.

'Yes?' he encouraged.

'It seems strange that we have been staying on opposite sides of the same square for weeks, without ever seeing each other.'

No, it had not been wise.

'It's like a sort of madness,' he said, in a low voice. 'Like those dreams where irrational things happen.' Then words seemed to burst out of him. 'If you only knew how much I need to see you – just to see you!'

'I know,' she said.

'It eases something in me just to be in the same room with you,' he went on. 'To look at you, to know you exist, to breathe the same air. I can't—'

He walked away from her to the window and stood there, staring out. Beyond him, she could see the trees of the square moving in a sharp breeze. His hands were down by his sides, clenching and unclenching. 'I didn't mean to say anything when you came in. Forgive me.'

'You can talk to me,' she said. 'You can tell me anything. I will understand.'

'God, I know that!' he said, between his teeth.

She went over to the window, sat down on the window seat, so that he would sit down beside her. He took her hand, then folded the other over it too, looking at her as she had looked at him, as though to memorise her. His nearness was like the warmth of the sun; to be with him was life. She looked at their linked hands and wondered how it was possible to go on without that.

211

'Tell me,' she said.

It was a few moments before he answered, as though he was pursuing a thread of thought to its end. Then he said, 'I feel all the time like an impostor. People think they're looking at the Earl of Stainton. I wear his clothes, I answer to his name, but I'm not him.' He shook his head, trying to find words. 'Everything seems unreal. I hear myself talking, I watch my hands pick things up, I watch my feet walking, as if they don't belong to me. The whole world is like a photograph, without colour, without depth – an image in shades of grey. Except you.' He looked down at her hand, and rubbed his thumb back and forth across the back of it. 'This hand is real.' He looked up. 'You are the only piece of colour. And I'm not allowed to look at you or touch you.'

She had nothing to say. It all hurt too much.

'I blame my father,' he went on. 'If he'd only lived another ten years, as one was entitled to expect . . . But the whole thing came down on me without warning, like a mountain, burying me, the estate, the debts, the family. Suddenly I was responsible for everything and everyone. Oh, I always knew that sooner or later I would have to take over. If only I'd had time – if I'd come to it in maturity, when I was ready . . . Another ten years of being an ordinary person with no-one expecting anything of me . . . I could have married during that time, married the right person. I could have chosen for myself, for the right reasons, instead of—'

'You mustn't talk to me about Kitty,' she interrupted him gently.

'I know,' he said, with a dreary look. 'The last thing I would want to do is to hurt Kitty. Do me the justice to believe I know how damnable the situation is, for all of us, but especially for her.'

Nina followed her own thought. 'She's jealous of Giulia. She thinks—'

'She doesn't understand, you see. In academic circles, men

and women can be friends, but it doesn't happen in Society. *You* understand – you were brought up in that way. That's why I can talk to you. Oh, God, I have *missed* talking to you. Being with you now, I feel—'

'Do you think I don't feel it too? But we can't – we mustn't—'

'I know. It's impossible. But, Nina, can't we at least be friends? Just that? Must we shut ourselves off entirely from each other? Would it be so wrong just to be friends and sometimes be in the same room, and talk? I think, if I had that, just to know I would see you sometimes, I think I could be what I'm supposed to be. I think I could do my duty.'

She shook her head – not a negative, but at the contemplation of what Fate had done to them. 'It isn't fair,' she said, very low.

'I know.'

'I miss you, all the time. Like a dull ache.'

'Would it be so wrong, to be friends? God will read our hearts, He'll know we mean no harm. Come to the Castle this summer. I swear I won't make it difficult for you.'

Trump, sitting at their feet, sighed and lay down, resting his chin on her instep. She thought suddenly of the evening before. Her gown had come back from Madame Hortense – sea-green twilled silk, a glorious thing of line and elegance and simplicity. Mr Cowling had worried that it was too plain: shouldn't it have more frills, more bows, some beading, some lace, crystal spars perhaps? She had protested she loved it as it was, but only Clemmie's assurance that everyone would recognise the superior quality of the cut and fit had carried him. And he'd said, 'At least your emeralds will go with it.' She had an emerald and diamond necklace and earrings, gifts from him. 'I'll buy you an emerald bracelet tomorrow, to make the set.' That night, he had come to her bed. She had braced herself for one of his onslaughts, but he had only folded her in his arms and fallen asleep. When she was sure

213

he was sleeping, she had gently wriggled free, and lain staring at the ceiling for a long time before she too dropped off. When she woke, he had gone.

She wanted to tell Giles that he had nothing to fear from Mr Cowling, that they did not – do that thing together. But that would have been a betrayal. Above all, Kitty and Mr Cowling must not be hurt. None of this was their fault. She was silent while she assembled her words, and he thought she was going to refuse, and urged her further.

'Come and stay. Kitty would like that. She'll be rather isolated this summer. I won't be a nuisance. I'll be out most of the day in any case, but in the evening you'll be there and I can look at you and talk to you. Let us just be friends. We're owed that.'

Trump sighed again and shifted his heavy head, and Nina thought the sigh could have been hers. Would it be so wrong to be friends? Looking into his dear face, she suddenly felt it was silly and pointless to keep saying they couldn't be, when they were. They could never be more than that, but at least life was sustainable if they had that. She felt she could be happy if she had that.

CHAPTER TWELVE

Nina had doubts about the visit to the factory, even before Mrs Albertine Crane advised them to dress plainly and not to wear any jewellery. But Clemmie and Lepida were both keen to go, and Mrs Crane seemed determined to take them. 'One must see these things for oneself,' she said firmly, and the other two nodded, as if that were an immutable truth. Nina thought she was quite well able to accept things she hadn't seen for herself, if someone reliable vouched for them. Wasn't that what imagination was for?

But Clemmie was so eager for it, she went along with it. The factory, they were told, was on the corner of Grunthorpe Street and Whitechapel Road. Whitechapel was a lot further east in London than ladies were accustomed to venture, though Nina and Lepida had been to Commercial Road several times – that was where Aunt Schofield's Free Library had been set up. Nina and Lepida had visited the library under Aunt's chaperonage. Now it amused her to think that she was in the position of chaperoning Clemmie and Lepida, since she was married and they weren't.

Her misgivings increased when the cab set them down on the corner of Grunthorpe Street and the smell assailed her.

It seemed to worry the cabby, too. 'Are you sure this is where you want to go, ladies?' he asked.

'Quite right, thank you,' said Mrs Crane, briskly, eager as a sheepdog heading up to the hills.

'I don't mind waiting, if you're not too long.' It was Nina he addressed, looking as doubtful as she felt. 'You'd better have me wait, missy. This ain't the sort of street for a lady to wander about.'

'That would be very kind,' Nina said gratefully.

At the same moment, however, Mrs Crane spoke over her. 'Quite unnecessary, thank you. We can take care of ourselves.'

But as she was already walking off, and it fell to Nina to pay the jarvey, she gave him an extra shilling and said, 'Please wait,' and he said, 'Right you are, miss,' and nodded kindly. There was no danger of Mrs Crane hearing the exchange, for there were factories all around making grinding and thumping noises, to say nothing of the traffic going up and down.

'This way,' Mrs Crane called. The other three followed, keeping close together like sheep in wolf country. Nina was glad she hadn't brought Trump. There were a lot of dogs about, but they looked skinny and mean. One dashed past with something purple and wobbly in its jaws, pursued by two others, determined on a share of the feast.

The factory was a grim-looking building of smoke-blackened brick, and what with the soot coating and the paint peeling, the sign across the top of the upper windows was almost illegible. The words Bleaker's Tannery were just discernible. The windows were almost opaque with dirt, and were closed tightly, but despite that, a terrible smell leached out, a mixture of pungent chemicals that made the eyes water, and something horribly organic. The closest Nina had come to smelling anything like it before was when Trump had discovered a very dead fox in a ditch on one of their walks. But this was worse.

Despite 'dressing plainly', they were attracting attention. The drivers of passing drays threw fortunately unintelligible comments, idlers paused in their mooching, smokers leaning against walls turned their heads after them, and women in sacking aprons came to their doors to stare. Mrs Crane, moving briskly, ignored them all. She stopped at last and turned, and the other three crowded up close to her. A boy ran past, and over her shoulder Nina saw him scuttle down a narrow passage at the end of the building.

'About a quarter of the workers are women,' Mrs Crane said. Her eyes were bright and fierce, her expression grim. 'And while they don't carry out the very worst of the tasks, I think you'll find what they do quite unpleasant enough.'

'What is that *smell*?' Nina couldn't help asking.

'The animal skins are put through various processes – boiling and liming, fleshing and bating, and so on. Part of the process involves soaking in dog faeces. Yes,' she said, to their appalled expressions, 'quite true. Oh, and the scraps of the skins that are too small for use are put in a vat of water and left to rot for several weeks, for making into glue.'

Clemmie had turned a little pale. 'It must be dreadful in there. But you're right, we ought to see for ourselves.'

'I'm afraid we won't be welcome,' Mrs Crane said, setting her jaw. 'Understandably, they don't like outsiders to see what goes on. But we must badger our way in. We must be resolute, ladies. It is our duty—'

'Wait,' said Nina. 'You mean they haven't invited us? I thought when you said "visit" it was something you'd arranged.'

'No, no, we must slip in and see all we can before they turn us out,' Mrs Crane said impatiently. 'There is a door round the side that leads into an unfrequented area – storage rooms mostly – and from there we can get onto the main factory floor.'

Lepida and Nina exchanged an alarmed look, but Clemmie had perhaps done this sort of thing before, because she was nodding as if this was understood. She and Mrs Crane went in front, the other two followed reluctantly. But when they reached the narrow passage that went down the side of the

217

factory, they found it blocked by a large man in a leather apron. His face was very dirty, except for white creases radiating out from his eye corners. His hands were black and shiny with whatever he had been handling, and he wore a grimy cap pulled down hard on his head. He glowered at them from under the peak.

'Oh, it's you again, is it?' he said to Mrs Crane. 'Now, then, you know better than this. The guv'nor's said he doesn't want any busybodies spannelling about his fac'try, upsetting his workers.'

Mrs Crane drew herself up. 'Just step aside, my man. We *will* see what we have come to see.' And she flourished the umbrella like a sword.

Whether it was the umbrella, or that he just didn't like being called 'my man', his face darkened. 'You're not coming in, and that's that.'

'Who is to stop me?' she said scornfully.

'The guv'nor put me here to do it, and I'll do it. We knew you was coming.' The boy who'd run past, Nina thought. 'So clear off, or it'll be the worse for you.' He looked at the other three and said, 'I'm surprised at you, nice ladies like you.' Nina felt herself blushing.

Behind the angry man, another appeared, coming out of the factory door: a middle-aged bald-pate in a rather shabby suit.

'What's going on here, Bates?' he demanded.

'It's her again, Mr Bleaker – the do-good. Got her friends with her this time.'

He moved aside to allow Bleaker room, and the factory owner stared contemptuously down his nose at the women. 'What do you want?' he asked coldly.

'We would like to inspect your factory, if you please,' said Mrs Crane, with a smile like a slap.

'Well, I don't please. So just turn around and go about your business, and nobody has to get unpleasant,' said Bleaker.

'This *is* our business,' said Mrs Crane sternly, 'and the business of every decent person. The conditions under which your workers have to toil are a disgrace.'

Bleaker rolled his eyes. 'This is a tannery. Do *you* know how to tan a hide? No, but I do. It's not nice. It's nasty. It smells bad. What are *you* going to do about it? Change the laws of nature?'

Clemmie spoke up at that point, her voice light as a dried leaf on the noisy air, her accent clear as cut crystal. 'We don't mean to make trouble for anyone,' she said. 'We are interested in factory conditions, and just want to look around. We shan't get in anyone's way.'

Bleaker looked at her with irony. 'No, I guarantee you *shan't*,' he mocked. 'Because you're not coming in here. This is my factory, which I own lawfully, and *I* say who comes in and who doesn't. One more step down this alley and it's trespass, and I shall send for a constable and have you taken up. What'd your husbands or your fathers have to say about that, eh? If you have respectable husbands and fathers – which I doubt.'

'Why do you have to be so unpleasant about it?' Lepida asked, quite mildly in the circumstances,.

But he turned on her with a goaded air. '*Unpleasant?* I am going about my lawful concerns, and you – *ladies* – come along here uninvited and stick your damned noses in and try to stop me running my own business! You want to poke about and tut and upset my workers and close down my factory and put my employees out of a job. I'll give you *unpleasant*! If you were a man I'd knock you down!'

'Well, really!' Mrs Crane exclaimed.

Bleaker rounded on her. 'I know your sort,' he said. 'Not enough to do, sitting in your big house all day, fancying yourself better than everyone else, so you've got to go out and interfere with honest folk trying to earn a living. I'll just tell you one last time to clear off. Go back to where you belong. Go on, all of you! Because I don't like getting rough with females, but by God I will if I have to. You young 'uns look like ladies, but it'd be a pleasure to teach this old boiler hen a lesson.'

Two other men had come out of the door down the alley, and a crowd was beginning to gather in the road. Nina, who had been feeling hot with mortification, never having heard angry language like that in her life, now began to feel afraid. The idea of any man rough-handling a lady had never occurred to her as a possibility, but they were far out of their proper sphere, and who knew what the rules were here? She thought longingly of the jarvey, hoped desperately that he had waited. She plucked anxiously at Mrs Crane's sleeve. 'Come away,' she said, low and urgently.

Mrs Crane didn't seem at all put out by the hostility. Indeed, it seemed to have stimulated her. But when Clemmie also took her arm, she allowed herself to be drawn a step back. She waved her umbrella under Bleaker's nose, and said, 'You haven't heard the last of me!' And she turned and strutted away with her head high.

'You'd better hope I have!' Bleaker shouted after her.

The other three clustered round her and they walked away with as much dignity as they could muster. The crowd let them through silently, though there were unpleasant grins on some faces. Nina was trembling inside, wondering how Mrs Crane could endure confrontations like this. He had called her an *old boiler hen*! The impact of the words reverberated inside her head. No-one had ever spoken harshly to her in her life and it was a shock. She wished she'd never come. Much of the crowd had gone about their business, but a ribald remnant was trailing them, hoping for more entertainment, and shouting comments, which, thanks to their accent, she couldn't understand – but could certainly make a guess at. *Don't run*, said a little voice in her head. *You mustn't show fear.* But that was wild animals, wasn't it? Or dangerous dogs . . . If only the cab were still there!

And, thank God, here was the end of the road and, oh, thank God there was the blessed cab and the thrice-blessed jarvey! Seeing they had acquired company he pulled himself up straight, squared his shoulders and cracked his whip in a thoughtful manner. The crowd didn't really mean harm: they were just amusing themselves, and halted at the corner to continue with their commentary, and watch with amusement as the toff ladies climbed in, bested. They transferred their attention to the jarvey, with such well-worn jibes as 'The only way I can tell you from yer 'orse is 'e's better-looking!' The cabby only smiled sardonically as he pulled out into the traffic, performed an audacious 180-degree turn under the nose of a brewer's dray, and headed back towards civilisation.

On the outward journey they had travelled by Underground to Liverpool Street and taken the cab from there. When they were dropped off again at the station, tea seemed to be urgently required, and they retired to the Palm Court of the Great Eastern Hotel. The pleasant hush of civilisation closed over them, and Nina, soothed by it, reflected that, after all, nothing very bad had happened to them, and began to feel more cheerful.

Lepida and Clemmie seemed less upset than disappointed not to have seen inside.

'But you have been in, you say?' Lepida asked.

'It was easier with one,' said Mrs Crane. 'I slipped in and managed very nicely until a foreman spotted me, and fetched the boss, and he asked me to leave. I argued with him for quite a while, which allowed me to go on observing. Perhaps it was unwise of me to try the same thing again with you, ladies. But you see, at least, that they must have something to hide, or they wouldn't have been so determined to keep us out.'

'That's all very well,' Lepida said, 'but we *haven't* seen, so we don't know what they are hiding.'

Mrs Crane reached into her reticule and drew out a note-book. 'Fortunately,' she said, with a smug look, 'I was able to interview a couple of the women when they came off work that evening, and I wrote up these notes straight afterwards. They didn't really want to talk to me at first, but I took them to a pie shop a short distance away and bought them pies and coffee. They talked to me on condition that I never mentioned their names, for fear they'd lose their jobs. But when you hear what they have to endure, you will wonder, as I did, why they want to keep them.'

The tea tray arrived, and Clemmie took charge of it, poured the tea and placed the sandwiches within reach. Then Mrs Crane began to talk.

'Mostly what the women do is carrying, like beasts of burden, but they are also employed in unhairing and scudding – that is, scraping away the dirt, hair, flesh and fat – the smaller hides. The larger hides, I believe, require more muscle, so that is men's work.'

The women worked from six in the morning until six at night, with a fifteen-minute break in the middle of the day to eat whatever food they had brought with them. They worked six days a week, for five shillings – two shillings less than the men doing the same work.

'And they hardly ever *get* the five shillings, either,' said Mrs Crane. 'There's a system of fines, by which the owner claws back much of their wages. If they're caught talking, if they go to the lavatory without permission, if they drop a scrap from the bundle on the floor, if they tear a hide while scudding – all those are all fineable offences. Fines range from threepence to a shilling. If they're late for work in the morning by even five minutes, they're docked half a day's pay.'

'Why don't they leave and get a different job?' Lepida asked.

'I asked the same question. They said it was hard to get

work, and if you left or were dismissed, the word went round the other local factories, and you would not be taken on.'

'Surely some of them must be married.'

'Indeed, but their husband's wages are not enough to keep them and the children. If he *has* work.'

'They have children? Who looks after them?' Nina asked.

'Sometimes an older person, who doesn't work, like a grandparent. Sometimes one of the older children takes care of the younger. One woman,' Mrs Crane tapped the notebook, 'told me her little Annie was a proper mother to the rest. Annie is just seven years old.'

'She should be at school at that age,' Clemmie said.

'She should indeed. But these are not the worst examples. Some of them have to use childminders – very low women, sometimes too old to work, often drunks, who keep anything up to a dozen children in their one room all day. You may imagine the abuses that gives rein to, and the infections that breed. My informant said she would never use a childminder.'

And then, Mrs Crane went on, there were the ill effects of the tanning chemicals. 'They cause sore eyes, they affect the lungs – both of my women had racking coughs. They can develop horrible sores on the skin. And the liver and the kidneys become affected, leading to severe illness and even death. One woman said it was common for tannery women to have yellow skin and eyes – the signs of liver and kidney disease.'

'Something must be done about this,' Clemmie exclaimed.

'Yes – but what?' said Lepida. 'That man Bleaker was right – he's running a lawful business, and I suppose these women work there of their own free will.'

'Yes,' said Mrs Crane, 'but we could at least see that they are paid a fair wage, and that the fines system is abolished.'

'How would we do that?' Clemmie asked.

'First we must interview more of the women, gather more testimonies – two are not enough. Then write articles for the papers, letters to Members of Parliament, rouse up a public revulsion. A petition, perhaps, to take to Downing Street. If necessary, we might have to organise a strike.'

She, Clemmie and Lepida began discussing these and other actions. Nina, too young and inexperienced in the field to contribute, listened to them at first; but then her mind drifted.

She started thinking about the evening before, at the Cassels'. The grand house, every window lit up when they arrived; the liveried footmen who took their coats; the great oil paintings on the walls, the thick carpets underfoot and the glittering chandeliers . . . The contrast with today's setting could not have been more fantastic.

As she had expected, the company was rather elderly – she was the youngest by a good margin – but she was greeted very kindly, and she was glad to find there was no sense that anyone thought Mr Cowling and his young wife were out of their place. Even when the King arrived.

She was nervous when she was presented, and had only a confused impression of him – a big man, blocking out the light. She blessed her education at Miss Thornton's, which had taught her how to curtsey without wobbling. Then the King offered her a very clean, pink hand, and spoke in a warm rumble of a voice, and she had looked up to see a smiling, clean, pink face and very round, pale blue eyes.

Afterwards she had been introduced to Mrs Keppel, who was very kind, and said, 'I'm so glad to meet you, my dear. Mr Cowling has been boasting for ever of his beautiful, clever young wife. I can see you are beautiful, and you *look* clever. Are you clever?'

'I don't *feel* very clever at the moment,' Nina had said.

Mrs Keppel laughed. 'It was a most unfair question, and I withdraw it! Tell me instead what you are interested in. I know all the other guests, and one so longs for something new at these affairs. They can be rather deadly, you know,' she added, in a conspiratorial tone, setting Nina quite at ease.

They had talked about paintings, then, and music, and Nina did not feel she had let herself down too badly.

The conversation round the table was mostly about the Entente Cordiale recently signed with France – 'And isn't it typical of them,' Mrs Keppel laughed, 'that it's named in French, rather than being called the Cordial Alliance?'

There was much to say, not least because the King had been advocating an alliance against Germany ever since 1881 when he was still Prince of Wales. He retold how he had met Léon Gambetta, just about to become prime minister of France, at the Château de Breteuil to discuss it. Britain had been following a policy of 'splendid isolation' for almost a century; France had become isolated after the Napoleonic wars – and was regarded warily because of its perceived liberalism. But Germany was growing in strength. France, still smarting from defeat in the Franco-Prussian war, eyed their expanding navy and army with disfavour; Britain was worried about Germany's industrial might in the Ruhr. And when Germany signed the Triple Alliance with Austria-Hungary and Italy in 1882, it was clear Britain and France needed each other. But it had taken a long time and many diplomatic summits for the old enemies to come together. The ramifications of the Entente occupied a good deal of the conversation. Nina tried to listen intelligently.

There had also been discussion of the death earlier that year of the King's cousin, the Duke of Cambridge. His military career had been dissected among the men, and the women had discussed his private life – he had married an actress, in contravention of the Royal Marriages Act, so his children could not inherit the title – 'Which is a pity,' said Lady Wroughton, 'because there are three very likely sons.'

'I believe he was originally supposed to marry Queen Victoria – they were designed for each other when they were young,' said Mrs Keppel.

'It wouldn't have worked,' said Lady Leven. 'As he said himself, these arranged marriages never do.'

Nina thought of Giles and Kitty, and felt a pang.

Lady Wroughton disagreed. 'Marriage is too important to leave in the hands of the young people themselves. Besides, Queen Victoria's marriage to Prince Albert was arranged, and *that* worked out well enough.'

The two halves of the table reunited in conversation about motor-cars, which had increased in number so much in the past two years that the government had felt required to legislate on them. Now they must be registered and carry an identifying number on a fixed plate at the front and rear. A speed limit of twenty miles per hour had also been enacted. Everyone agreed that the registration was a good idea, but there was a split in opinion about whether twenty miles per hour was too fast, too slow, or just right.

The King, who loved motor-cars, said, 'Cowling, why haven't you got one? You're the man for innovations and new fangles.'

'I've never even kept a carriage, sir,' Mr Cowling answered. 'I've always lived in town, where you can get a cab. Though Mrs Cowling loves horses,' he said, looking down the table at her, 'so she might persuade me to buy a carriage and pair one of these days.'

'Lord, no – get a motor-car!' exclaimed Mr Goldfarb. 'Horses are history, man!'

'But aren't motor-cars always breaking down?' said Lady Leven.

'Not as often as horses,' said Mr Goldfarb. 'I kept a pair once, and between cut fetlocks, twisted hocks, swollen knees, coughs, colic and laminitis, I don't suppose I had thirty days' use of them in a year. Eating their heads off in the stable, and a coachman to be paid for no work, and a groom in league with the feed-merchant and all the time cheating me. No, no, take it from me, it's a motor-car you want. At least you can leave it standing outside when you visit, without it running off or catching cold.'

'And they are much more reliable than they used to be,' the King said. 'The new models hardly break down at all these days.'

'Well, Wroughton and I shall stick to our horses,' said Lady Wroughton. 'I can't abide the smell of motor-cars, or the noise.'

'Ah, but you live in the country, ma'am,' said Cowling. 'Now, I can see that, in a general way, they'd be good for towns. No-one can relish the – er – what the horses leave behind in the street.'

And Nina had suppressed a smile, remembering that when she first saw the King, at the Wroughtons' house, he had shocked Lady Wroughton by saying that in twenty years the streets of New York would be up to the second-floor windows in dung.

After dinner, when coffee was brought, she had found herself sitting near enough to the King for him to notice her. Being obliged to speak, she'd told him the story she had worked up, on Aunt Caroline's advice, about Trump chasing a squirrel up a tree, then being put to the right-about when the goaded squirrel rushed back down and attacked him. 'He had to hide behind me, poor dog, until it ran off. He was quite mortified,' she concluded.

The King had laughed, and told a story of his own, about his little dog Caesar, and she felt she had done all right. Certainly Mr Cowling looked across the room at her with pride.

It was all such a long way from the tanning factory, and the poor women working for five shillings a week. For an instant she felt guilty about being so well-off. But then, she reflected, only the wives of rich men had the leisure and freedom of movement to pursue good works. It was a conundrum.

'I see they've nearly finished clearing Bunce's six acres,' said Axe.

227

'Yes, I saw that as I passed,' said Alice. Axe was fixing the chains to a tree stump while she held Della's head. It wasn't at all necessary to hold Della's head – she knew her job and was controlled entirely by Axe's voice – but it gave her the illusion of being useful. And she liked to think Della enjoyed having her cheeks stroked. 'Though I suppose we oughtn't to call it Bunce's six acres now the Bunces are all gone and Hundon's is back in hand.'

He looked up. 'By rights, then, we shouldn't call it Hundon's. Place names go back to people long forgot.'

'That's true,' Alice said. 'I suppose in centuries to come, people will take a short-cut down Poor's Lane and wonder who Poor was.'

He grunted in response, then said, 'All right, ready now. You can lead her forward.'

Alice clicked to Della and she walked forward until the strain came on her traces; then her ears went back for Axe's voice. It was to his 'Goo-on, gal!' that she threw herself into her collar and heaved. He got his pick into the cavity he'd dug and levered, and between them he and Della dragged the stump out.

'Like drawing a tooth,' Alice called back cheerfully. Della halted with the slackening of the ropes; Axe backed out of the great raw hole, wiping his forehead on the wrist of his shirt. Alice's heart gave a little bump as he stood straight and eased his back, and she saw the cords of his neck stretch and the muscles of his upper arms flex.

He thrust his fingers through his hair to rake it back from his brow, and smiled at her. 'Shouldn't fancy Old Fangs pulling something out o' my jaw like that.'

The dentist in the village was a Mr Fanshawe, who was more generally called Fang-Sure, and referred to as Old Fangs.

'But you have lovely teeth,' Alice said. 'I've often noticed.' She had embarrassed him. His eyes slid away, and he reddened slightly. 'They do the job, I s'pose.' And then, recovering himself, though still not looking at her – he was busying himself rearranging the ropes and chains round the stump for dragging – he said, 'Our dad always said you got to look after your teeth, cos you only get the one lot. "No teeth, no grub," he used to say.'

'Like horsemen say, "No hoof, no horse,"' said Alice.

''S right. He made us all rub 'em with a bit o' cloth every night, and swill round with salt-water. All right, walk on.'

Alice let Della go past her and dropped back so she could walk beside Axe and talk to him. Cobnut, whose panniers she had filled with the small branches and twigs, followed like a dog. 'They're getting on well with the house, too – Hundon's, I mean. The roof's back on and the windows are in. I saw when I came past today. Mr Gale was there and he said it's just the inside walls to patch up and whitewash and it'll be ready.'

'I should think he'll be glad to have it done,' said Axe, 'and have his house to himself again.' The new cowman was lodging with the Gales until his house was ready.

'I don't think he minds. He gets a bit of extra money for putting him up. And Mrs Gale thinks the world of him. Ever such nice manners, she says. If he sees her lifting a bucket he comes and takes it from her.'

'Spoiling her for her old man,' Axe said, but with a twinkle to show he wasn't serious. 'Have you met him? This— What's his name?'

'The cowman? Woodrow. Well, I've seen him, and said hallo in passing, but not to say *met* him.'

With the departure of the Bunces, it was not just the land and the dilapidated buildings that had been taken over but Bunce's twelve cows too. They were in mitigation of the unpaid rent that was owing, and certainly Mrs Bunce, her son and grandchild didn't want them where they were going. That necessitated a new cowman. Richard had said that, since the intention was to start the milk scheme at Hundon's, there was no point in just getting in a labourer to tide them over: they needed a proper high-skilled herdsman who could take the plan forward.

'We want a modern, scientific kind of fellow, who'll have new ideas,' he said, 'not some old chap who'll want to do everything the way his great-grandfather did it.'

Adeane had scowled and growled at the idea that 'the old ways weren't good enough for young folk nowadays', but Markham had agreed with Richard that they had better start as they meant to go on and get the right man in from the beginning. And so, through a mixture of enquiry, advertisement and good luck, they had come upon Michael Woodrow. He was thirty-five – too young for Adeane, but he had plenty of experience, having worked his way up from the age of fourteen to be second-in-command of Lord Denham's herd at Long Ashington. On the way he had studied books and read journals and was itching to be his own master and put some of his ideas into practice.

Richard wanted him in place at once, and so, since the house at Hundon's was barely fit to live in, he was being put up at the house of Gale, the estate carpenter, until it was ready. The house had proved worse, on inspection, than previously thought, and repair had become almost reconstruction.

'That's a big house, Hundon's, for one man,' Axe said. 'He'll rattle about in it, all on his own.'

'His sister's coming to live with him, as soon as it's ready, to keep house for him. And I don't suppose he'll be all on his own for long, anyway. He's very good-looking.'

'Ah,' said Axe. 'And nice manners, too, so you said. He'll cause a stir in the village, then.'

'I think Richard's new ideas will cause a stir all on their own,' Alice said. 'Oh, stop a minute, Della's got hooked up on something.'

''S only a bramble. She'll pull free.'

'It'll scratch her darling face. Let me untangle it. How are you getting on with Jules Verne?' she asked as they resumed walking. She had brought him *Twenty Thousand Leagues Under the Sea*.

'Nearly finished,' he admitted. 'That's an interesting tale. Makes you wonder what there might be down there. How deep is it, do you reckon?'

'I asked Uncle Sebastian and he said a league is about three miles, so that's sixty thousand miles. But he said the circumference of the earth is only about twenty-four thousand miles, so he thinks Jules Verne must have been exaggerating. It can't really be twice as deep as the earth measures right round, can it?'

Axe smiled. 'Asking the wrong person. But he's got an imagination all right, that writer. Living under the sea!'

'If you've nearly finished, I'd better bring another next time,' Alice said. 'You're gobbling them up! Maybe one by Dickens – there's loads in the library.'

'You're very kind, But you don't have to do that for me,' he said shyly.

'It's good for me,' she said. 'It means I have to read them too, so we can talk about them. And Giles always said I didn't read enough. He was shocked when he first came home and found I didn't read a book every day. He called me a little heathen.'

He smiled at her fondly, and it was her turn to feel shy. He noticed, and changed the subject. 'Now, I'm wondering how in the world anyone would know how far the earth was right round the middle. Nobody's got a bit of string that long.'

Alice laughed. 'I've no idea. I'll ask Uncle Sebastian. It's something we ought to know, don't you think?'

She didn't notice she'd said 'we'.

Richard was at that moment down at another of the farms, The Bottoms, talking through the milk scheme again with the Orde brothers, Samuel and Hugh.

'So this fine bull is coming next week? And we gets the use of it? That'll cost a bob or two, I reckon,' said Samuel.

'No, the estate is buying the bull, and if you are in the scheme you'll get his services for nothing. He'll improve your herd, and that will improve your milk yield – and the quality of the milk.'

Richard was amazed to find himself so patient, these days. He had explained all this to the Ordes on two previous occasions, but even so the desire to knock their thick heads together and shout at them was not manifesting itself. It takes time to change the habits of a lifetime, he told himself. Actually, the habits of several lifetimes. The Orde twins had inherited the farm from their father when barely out of school, and had simply carried on doing what he had done, because what else could they do? Their mother had died not many years later, and they had lived alone ever since, with the meagre help of a daily girl, who cooked a meal for them and did their washing. Their lives were hard and empty of anything but work. When it was too dark to see any more, they went back to the farmhouse, and ate whatever the girl had left for them. Richard had gone past the farmhouse one evening after dark – on his way home from a carouse – and had seen through the uncurtained window into the kitchen. A wooden settle stood on either side of the chimney which housed the range and the open fire. Hugh was sitting on one and Samuel on the other, their arms folded, their chins sunk on their chests, their unbooted feet stretched out before them. They were not talking or smoking or playing cards or even dozing: they were just sitting. Not to be working was the most pleasure the day held for them. They would sit like that for an hour or so, and then climb up to their beds. So it was no wonder that it took them a while to grasp a new idea.

'But you must clean up the milking shed, and keep it clean,' he said. 'These walls could do with brushing down and re-whitewashing. And you must sweep it out every day and wash it down, and keep the area around the cows' hindquarters clean. And wash the udders before you milk.'

Samuel shook his head with painful slowness. 'Never done that before. Can't see the reason of it. Cows don't mind their own dirt.'

'No, but this milk will be going to rich town folk, carriage folk, and they want their milk clean.'

Hugh frowned, trying to understand. 'A bit o' muck in the milk never hurt nobody.'

'Nevertheless,' Richard said, 'in this new scheme, there's to be nothing like that in the milk. It'll be our way of selling it, you see – our advertisement. You can imagine it in the newspaper.' He used a hand to block the capitals of the headline on the air. 'Ash Valley Milk – No Bits o' Muck.'

It was wasted on the Ordes, who didn't make jokes, who'd never had to exercise their imaginations, and had rarely seen a newspaper, let alone taken heed of an advertisement. They looked at him with the willing puzzlement of their own milkers.

'Never mind,' Richard said. 'Just do as I say. Clean up the milking shed and keep it clean. And wash the udders. No muck in the milk – understand?'

'Aye, Master Richard, that's clear enough,' Samuel said, with a sigh. 'So, this grand new bull o' yours – he'll service our cows, will he? That'll cost a bob or two, I reckon.'

He was still in the stableyard talking to Giddins when Alice drove through in the governess cart with Biscuit between the shafts.

'Hullo!' he said, going up to her. 'Where have you been?'

'Oh, here and there. Up in the woods. Sketching,' Alice said vaguely.

'Have you indeed? Show me something you've done,' he said indulgently.

She picked up her pad from the seat beside her, and opened

it at a sketch she had done of Della in her harness, standing under an ash tree, dozing while she waited to work.

'That's wonderful,' Richard said, studying it. 'You're really good at this, you know. I don't think I've seen anything better at a London exhibition.'

She looked pleased. 'I ought to practise painting more. I'm not bad at drawing, but I can't seem to get the same effect with paint. I ought to have lessons. I'm sure there are techniques one has to learn.'

'Must be, or there wouldn't be art schools,' Richard said, still looking at the drawing. 'What a pity you didn't have lessons when you were younger. But Mother would have a fit if you tried to be a professional artist.' He handed the pad back. 'Whose horse is it? I don't recognise it.'

'The woodsman's. He was up there working.' She collected her things and jumped down.

'Oh, Josh's brother – what's his name? Axe?' She nodded. 'I haven't seen him since he left off being the blacksmith's assistant. I must ride over there one day and have a word with him. How is he doing?'

She left that question alone and said instead, 'It looks as though Hundon's is about finished – the house. When I went past just now, they were carrying the parts of the old dresser back in, to fix it in place.'

'Yes, I dare say Woodrow will be glad enough to get his feet under his own table at last. He might have things of his own to bring in, but we'll put back the furniture that goes with the house anyway.' Something seemed to strike him. 'You know, he's a nice chap, and I want him to feel comfortable. How would you like to go in and see that everything's ready for him before he moves in? See the furniture's arranged nicely and that there's firewood and the kitchen pump works. Perhaps even take some flowers up – or is that too much? Anyway, if there's anything lacking, you can let me know and I'll see to it.'

She smiled. 'That's such a nice idea of yours, Richard.'

'I'm a nice fellow,' he said modestly.

'You are,' she said, slipping an arm through his. 'And I'd love to do it. It'll be like playing house. Can I take a basket of provisions up, too?'

'Yes, Red Riding Hood,' he said. 'What would you like to take?'

They strolled up to the house together, discussing it.

CHAPTER THIRTEEN

Rose was walking slowly and thoughtfully along the high street. The sun was almost vertical and the shadows sharp. Midday traffic passed briskly, carts and horses running on their own black silhouettes. The Crown had tubs of geraniums to either side of the main entrance, and their scarlet burned like flame against the whitewashed wall. Mr Millet's daughter Polly had just come out to water them, and raised a hand to Rose as she passed on the other pavement. The bar dog, Watch, a big hairy black mongrel, was lying in the meagre strip of shade along the base of the wall, his pink tongue unfurled, and his wolf-yellow eyes followed her incuriously.

She was returning from visiting Mr Moss at the cottage hospital, had taken him a bunch of marigolds, with a message of goodwill from all the servants. Rose had been for taking him lilac, seeing it was still plentiful everywhere and it smelt nice. She reckoned any hospital smelt like a hospital so the relief was to be desired. But there had been a long and tiresome discussion over breakfast about whether it was unlucky to take lilac indoors or not. Some said it was only white lilac that was unlucky, others that it was any colour; someone said it was a funeral flower and foretold death, and someone else said no, that was chrysanthemums. Then Mildred claimed that her gran said when an owl perched on your roof it meant someone was going to die, and Tilda had said stoutly, no, it was three crows on a fence, everyone knew that. The argument

236

had wandered off into obscure ornithological byways, and Rose had decided quietly to take marigolds, because they were cheery and she knew where she could get some. As far as she knew, there were no myths attached to marigolds.

But, as it turned out, she might as well not have bothered, because Mr Moss seemed to clutch the flowers without seeing them. It was a strangely shrunken and diminished Mr Moss, in pyjamas and dressing-gown, no longer the potentate of below-stairs, whose word was law. His voice was no longer orotund; his vocabulary no longer baroque. He thanked her with tears in his eyes for coming to see him, and when she unthinkingly put out her hand to him, he did not haughtily rebuff the touch as he once would have, but clutched it in both his, like a man hanging off a cliff.

She had dredged about for simple items of news to tell him, things that would not precipitate more tears. Her young ladyship was home, and seeming very well; the dowager was still in London with Lady Rachel. Lady Linda was there too. Wilfrid had got bitten by a stray dog and the bite had gone septic. Ida – Mrs Terry as she now was – had made a tray of Bachelor's Buttons and Brigid had upset her by saying they should have had shredded coconut in them. A horseshoe had fallen off the wall in the tack-room and hit Mr Archer on the head – luckily he'd still had his bowler on, so he wasn't hurt, but he'd fetched Oscar such a clout for fiddling with it that he'd got a bad earache and had to go home. There was a new under-gardener called Allsuch that Daisy was making eyes at. Doris had pretended she thought his name was Allsorts, and Daisy had slapped her and accidentally scratched her cheek with a rough fingernail. Miss Taylor—

At which point, Mr Moss had interrupted, and with yearning eyes fixed on her face had asked, 'How is Ada?'

'Oh, she's fine,' Rose said.

'Does she – did she – has she asked after me?'

Rose pushed down the pity she felt and the exasperation

that went with it, and the result was a tone of steady matter-of-factness. 'She hasn't mentioned you at all, not in my presence. She seems to be in good spirits. In fact, she's started sparking with young George from the stables. He's a good lad, and it seems to be going well.' She had hoped her suspicions were unfounded, but she saw Mr Moss's lip tremble, and his hands clasped each other as if for comfort. 'Why did you take her to the zoo?' she asked, quite kindly. Moss sighed and shook his head, unable to answer. 'Was it because you thought she was a bright girl and could get on? You wanted to give her a bit more of an education so she could better herself? Just a fatherly interest?' she suggested helpfully. Moss looked at her with misery, and didn't answer yes or no. Rose leaned forward a little, and fixed him with a commanding eye. 'There *is* a rumour that you were sweet on her, and that's why you took her out that Sunday. But I know that's not true, Mr Moss. As if a man in your position would dally with a housemaid barely half his age! Why, you'd never in a million years contemplate such a shocking thing – that's what I tell them.'

There was a silence while Moss tried to reassemble his thoughts and construct a sentence. 'Who – where does the rumour come from?'

She shrugged. 'I have my suspicions but I won't repeat them. Anyway, I know there's nothing in it. and I stamp on it whenever I hear it. Because you don't want the maids' fathers and brothers coming up to the Castle, thinking their girls aren't safe. What would that do to our reputation?' Tears were seeping from Mr Moss's eyes by that point, and she changed the subject firmly and asked about the hospital day, and was the food all right and were the nurses kind.

Now, on the way home, thinking about all this, she was so preoccupied she didn't notice Miss Eddowes on the other pavement beckoning to her – the shadow was so dense in contrast to the bright sun that, in her customary black, she didn't show up at all. A passing boy was sent across the road to jog Rose's attention. She crossed over between two drays and a one-horse gig, and Miss Eddowes said, 'I'm sorry to break into your reverie, but I heard you had been to see poor Moss in the cottage hospital, and I wondered how he was.'

'He's doing all right,' Rose said, 'but he's not at all like his old self.'

'Oh dear. What's the prognostication?'

'The what, miss?'

'How is he going to be in the long run? What do the doctors say?'

'Oh, I asked him that. Well, he said they told him he's coming along all right, and should be fit to leave hospital very soon.'

'That is good news. Then he'll be going home – back to the Castle? To his old position? Poor man, he must hate the enforced idleness.'

Rose shook her head. 'That's where it is, Miss Eddowes. The doctor doesn't think he should go back. Apparently, when you have an attack of that sort, there's always a chance it'll happen again, and usually worse the second time. He told me the doctor said he shouldn't do a job that causes him strain or worry. Well,' she added, 'it doesn't worry *me* to work at the Castle, but I suppose a butler's job *is* a lot of responsibility. And it would be terrible for everyone if he was to go back and then suddenly drop down dead in the middle of a big dinner, say, with a lot of important people round the table.'

'That would be embarrassing,' Miss Eddowes said. 'And the worry that it might happen would not do him any good – might even bring on the very thing he feared.'

'That's it,' Rose agreed. 'Doctor says he's not to have any worry. But he *wants* to go back. He said to me he was feeling much better. Only tired, a bit, but that would pass, he said. And he can't wait to go home. But he's afraid the doctor will

239

say the same thing to her ladyship – the dowager, I mean – and that she'll decide he can't.'

'The dowager Lady Stainton still decides such things?' Miss Eddowes queried.

'Well, miss, you know how it is,' Rose said circumspectly. 'She's bound to have an influence. Poor Mr Moss,' she went on. 'I don't know what will happen to him if he can't go back. He hasn't got any family. He'd have to get another job, but he'd hate to go down in the world. Even if such a job was to be found. You can't see him a footman, or working in a shop.'

'No, indeed,' said Miss Eddowes, thoughtfully. 'He is quintessentially a butler.'

Rose didn't know what quintessentially meant, but she perceived the sympathy in the voice. 'And if there wasn't a job, it'd be the workhouse. So if you should happen to hear of anything, Miss Eddowes, any position that might suit him . . . ?'

'I shall certainly listen out. I might even be able to make some enquiries.'

'That would be kind, miss.'

'I think I might go in and visit him, see if I can cheer him up.'

'I'm sure he'd like that, miss,' said Rose. Though, in fact, she wondered if he would. He might feel it humiliating to be discovered in such circumstances. It was bad enough Rose seeing him without his uniform, but a member of the gentry, and a lady at that . . .

As Hook walked along Piccadilly with his customary stiff-legged stalk, the maids he passed shrank back against the wall and averted their faces, and the men and boys eyed him warily. He smirked to himself. He had thought being his lordship's valet was tops, but he saw now it was only halfway up the ladder. It was the butler who had it all. The whole house was under his control, and all the servants had to do exactly what he told them. As to the perks . . .

He had already, of course, taken over the butler's room, with its desk and chair, shelves for the ledgers, cupboards and bookcase, nice bit of carpet on the floor. Now that it was obvious, to him at least, that Mr Moss wasn't coming back, he meant to go further: at the back of the room was a door that gave onto the butler's bedroom. It was a small room, with a single iron bedstead, a wardrobe, and a chest of drawers, on top of which was a wash-basin on a crochet-edged runner, with a mirror in a brass frame on the wall above. It wasn't a palace, but it was private, which was the main thing, and he coveted it.

At the next door he looked in, and saw William sitting in an upright chair, waiting to answer bells, chatting to Eddie, the youngest houseboy, who was at a table with newspaper spread on it, cleaning knives. They would do. But first he gave Eddie a rattling.

'Call those clean? Look at the streaks! And what's this – egg? Mustard? You want to poison somebody? You'll have to do better than this, my lad, if you want to keep your job. You do them all again, from scratch. And you, William, you ought to've kept an eye on him, not sat there with your mouth open catching flies. Some first footman you are!' Eddie looked scared, and William looked as though he might cry. Satisfied, Hook said, 'Leave it for now. Come with me. I've a job for the two of you.' He glanced round, picked up a basket of mending, tipped the things out on the table, and thrust it into Eddie's hands.

William dared to protest. 'I'm s'pos'd to be answering bells.'

'You bleat like an old woman! Don't worry, you'll be back in your Bath chair before you're needed – there's nobody in at the moment.'

He led them to the butler's room and through into the bedroom.

'But this is Mr Moss's room,' William said, in a shocked whisper.

As if it was a blessed temple! Hook thought impatiently. 'Not any more,' he said. 'It's mine now. Right, you, William, take Mr Moss's clothes out of the wardrobe and pack 'em in this valise.' He had found it under the bed on his last reconnoitre. 'And you, Eddie, put his bits and pieces in the basket. I'll find somewhere to stick 'em until they can be sent to him.' *If he doesn't die first,* he added to himself. The boys glanced uncertainly at each other, and he shouted, 'Get on with it, then! Sharp, now!' They flinched and obeyed.

There were five books on a short shelf by the bedhead, which also held the night candle in its pewter holder. They had better go, too, Hook thought, and picked them up one by one. The first was old Moss's *A to Z of Universal Knowledge*. The tiresome old bore was always reading bits out of it. The second seemed to be poetry: *The Sonnets of Shakespeare*. Who knew he wrote poetry as well as plays? Then there was a Bible, and something called *The Kings and Queens of England – a Child's Illustrated History*. Hook snorted derision.

The last, a very fat, unruly sort of book bound in red leather, he opened and immediately snapped shut again. *Oho, what's this then?* His back was to the boys, his body blocking what he was doing. He slipped it inside his coat, held it there with his elbow, and turned back.

'Here, take these books as well,' he said to Eddie, passing over the other four, two by two. 'Shove 'em in the basket. And don't be all day about it! Come and find me when you're done.'

He stalked out into the butler's room, stared quickly around, then opened a cupboard and stowed the book behind some bottles and tins. That would do for now. He was pleased with his find. He'd heard that such things could be valuable.

242

He'd take it into the village next time he went and see what Thavey at the pawn shop said.

Giles had stayed on in London only to fulfil his promise to dine with the Arthurs. When the door was opened, he heard the sound of many voices within, and realised there was a party. He felt a moment's trepidation. But the first people he saw in the drawing-room were John and Mabel Portwine, and Quintin and Mary Caldecott – academic acquaintances and therefore comfortable to him.

The Arthurs' son Ptolemy – a very bright young fellow of six – was holding court, and making everyone laugh, though it was for Giulia's sake he seemed to be performing. She was laughing too, looking as vivid as an orchid in a daisy patch in a gown of deep coral silk, with copper-coloured roses in her dark hair.

And then, as Talbot and Mary broke off and came to welcome him, he saw, just beyond Giulia, and to his great astonishment, the elegantly attired figure of Uncle Stuffy.

'I think you know everyone, don't you,' Mary Arthur was saying, 'except I don't think you've met my son, though you've heard me talk about him often enough. Ptolemy, say good evening to Lord Stainton – and then you must go to bed.'

The boy came, made an exaggerated court bow, and said, 'Good evening, my lord. Welcome to our humble abode.' Obviously he was used to being the centre of attention, but his impish grin was infectious and he seemed lively rather than spoiled. Giles returned the bow in kind. The boy immediately appealed to his mother not to be sent to bed, but she was quick to enforce her diktat. He bade a general goodnight to the company, then turned to Giulia and said, in a good accent, '*Buona notte, signorina. A domani. La tua promessa?*'

Giulia answered him, '*Buon riposo.* Yes, I promise to play piquet with you tomorrow after breakfast.'

When he had gone, Mary Arthur said, 'I think someone is rather in love with you, Giulia my dear. I hope you won't break his heart.'

'I do not break hearts,' Giulia said gravely. She gave Giles one cool glance, and walked away to talk to other guests.

General conversation had broken out and, having accepted a glass of sherry from Talbot and exchanged a few words, Giles worked his way round to Stuffy to say, 'What on earth are you doing here?'

Before he could answer, Mary Arthur was beside them, and said, 'Oh, Giles! I must tell you, Lord Leake has been so kind, showing us the sights of London – Giulia and me. Of course, I know many of them from my childhood, but it's good to refresh oneself, and for Giulia it's all new.'

'It has been entirely my pleasure, dear lady,' said Stuffy.

'It makes such a difference, having a male escort,' Mary went on. 'The crowds can be tiresome. And, of course, one cannot extract Talbot from the museum, these days. As well try to remove a winkle from its shell without a pin!'

'We were at the Natural History Museum yesterday,' Stuffy said. 'Don't recall any winkles, though we did see ammonites. Quite interesting. But next time, ma'am, we ought to take a drive out to Hampton Court. While the weather is so good.'

At that moment Quintin Caldecott snagged Mary's attention and she turned away to answer. Giles seized the opportunity to say, 'Showing them the sights? What's come over you?'

'Very educational,' Stuffy said. 'Amazin' how little one knows about one's own city. I believe it's the same everywhere – Romans never going to the Colosseum and so on.' He waved a hand vaguely.

'I know for a fact that Giulia is well acquainted with all the sights of Florence,' Giles said drily. 'But what brought this on?'

Stuffy raised his eyebrows. 'Why so surprised? A fellow can be hospitable in his own town, I suppose?'

'It's a great deal of trouble for you to go to,' said Giles, 'and I've never gathered that you were keen on exerting yourself.'

'I don't know why you're making such a toil of it,' Stuffy said equably. 'Asked Miss L to dance at the ball, followed up the acquaintance – most kindly received by Mrs Arthur. She wanted to show Miss L the sights – made m'self available – invited to dine *en famille* by way of thanks. Everything going along swimmingly. Enjoying myself no end. Mrs Arthur all over gratitude. Everyone happy.'

Surely, Giles wondered, he could not have designs on Mary Arthur. She was a handsome woman, but no-one could suppose she was the kind of married woman who might conduct an affair. And Stuffy had never been that way inclined anyway, as far as Giles was aware. He had never known him show interest in any female.

'What will you do when Giulia goes back to Italy – which she must, sooner or later?' he asked.

Stuffy frowned. 'Not sure I care for your calling her by her first name like that. Not respectful.'

'But you must remember, Uncle, I've known her since she was a child. She's like a little sister to me.'

Stuffy's face cleared. 'Ah, of course! Just so. Well, that's all right, then.'

'You'll be going out of Town soon, won't you? You've never stayed so long before.'

'Helping Maud out with little Rachel. Got to do m'duty. Thought you'd have gone down before now, though – estate to run and so on.'

'I'm going down tomorrow,' said Giles.

'Ah, good! Well, I expect I'll be off too, before long. Just making hay while the sun shines,' Stuffy said, with a twinkle. 'You young fellers mustn't expect to carry all before you!'

'Carry all of what?' Giles asked, puzzled. What on earth

245

was he talking about? But Stuffy just laughed and wandered away.

Alice took Rose with her to Hundon's, and between them they put in the welcoming touches.

'I was never in here before, my lady,' Rose said, as they looked around. 'It's a big old place, isn't it?'

'Used to be even bigger,' Alice said. 'My brother says it was a proper manor house once, but half of it's fallen down over the years, and the wood and stone have been carried away to mend other buildings.'

'I s'pose that's why it's got such big windows,' Rose said. 'Nice in their way, but makes it hard to keep it warm.'

'There are shutters on the outside for the cold weather,' Alice said. 'The Bunces never bothered with curtains.'

'Wasn't anyone to look in at 'em, set back the way the house is,' Rose said. Dory had made red and white gingham curtains for the kitchen windows, and she set about hanging them. 'These'll look cheerful, anyway. Make it more home-like.' She tied the curtains back with a bit of red ribbon, and put a clay pot of thyme on the windowsill in the centre, pinching the leaves to release the scent.

More furniture, belonging to the Woodrows, had arrived by carrier and been installed, but the house still looked rather bare. Alice and Rose moved the pieces around to make the best of them. Richard had had a load of wood and coal sent up, and Rose laid fires ready to light, while Alice arranged flowers in jugs, and dusted around. She primed the kitchen pump and filled a big kettle, Rose lit the kitchen range, and they put the kettle on the slow plate to heat.

The dogs, who had been lying in a patch of sunshine on the kitchen flags, lifted their heads, listening, then jumped up, and a moment later Michael Woodrow came in through the door from the yard, followed by a woman. He stopped abruptly at the sight of them.

246

Alice stepped forward, offering her hand. 'I hope we didn't startle you. I'm Alice Tallant, from up at the Castle. We were just making sure the house was ready for you. I wasn't expecting you quite so soon.'

'I know who you are, my lady. I've seen you from a distance.' Woodrow shook her hand. 'Martha's train was a bit early. My sister Martha, my lady.'

Woodrow was a well set-up, fair young man with a pleasant, open face, somewhat weather-reddened, and unruly mouse-fair hair. His sister stepped forward, very tall, and so thin she seemed gaunt. She looked a good bit older; not much like him in feature, but the same fair hair, going grey and dragged into a strict bun at the back. Her hand was bony and red; she didn't smile.

'We've put the kettle on to boil,' Alice said, 'and there's a basket of provisions my brother sent up from the house – bread and butter, eggs and ham and so on, just a few things to tide you over.'

'It's very kind of you, and his lordship,' Woodrow said, seeming pleased. He was automatically making much of the dogs as he spoke; they had ignored his silent sister and made straight for him.

'And Rose has laid the fires ready for you,' Alice went on. 'This is Rose Hawkins – she's head housemaid at the Castle. I know it's warm outside, but these old houses can be cold inside at night, specially when they've been empty for a while.'

Martha Woodrow gave Rose a glance that might have been thanks, and looked away again. Woodrow looked into Rose's face with frank interest, and shook her hand, too. 'Thank you, Miss Hawkins,' he said. 'You're very kind.' His hand seemed to hold on to hers for longer than was strictly neces-sary. Rose met his eyes, and found herself blushing.

'Well,' said Alice, 'we'd better leave you to get settled in. It was nice to meet you properly at last. And you, Miss Woodrow.'

Woodrow sprang to open the door for her. The dogs shot past, jostling Rose so that she swayed against him, and he steadied her with a touch on her elbow, and smiled at her – the sort of smile that warmed you, like sunshine, or golden butter on hot toast.

Outside, starting off for the Castle again, Alice said, 'That went well. I'm glad we did it. They seem like good people. His sister was a bit shy, I thought.'

'Yes, my lady,' Rose said. 'I expect the house is bigger than she's used to. It'll take some keeping clean.'

'Yes, I suppose she might feel a bit daunted. But he's very nice,' Alice went on. 'He has a nice smile.'

'Yes, my lady,' said Rose.

'It seems ridiculous to keep this great house going,' Linda said to her mother, 'if we aren't going to entertain any more.'

'There will be callers. And I expect we shall have girls and their mothers to tea,' said Maud, leafing through the morning's invitations.

'But now that Uncle Stuffy's moved to his club, there's only the three of us,' said Linda. Her children were still staying with the cousins, who seemed happy enough to keep them. She hoped they could stay with the Tullamores until they went back to Scotland – and then, ideally, go with them for the summer. The savings would be considerable, which made it all the more galling to her frugal spirit that her mother was wasting money on a house with a ballroom after the ball was over.

Maud looked up. 'Where would you expect us to stay?'

'At Aunt Caroline's,' Linda said promptly. 'Richard's left, Kitty and Alice have gone home, and Giles will be leaving tomorrow, so she'll have room. It's such a waste of money.'

Maud did not look up from her letters. She might have said, 'It isn't your money being wasted,' but she didn't. It was vulgar to discuss money – even more vulgar to care about it. In Linda's position, she, Maud, would have done something about it, without ever letting anyone know 'it' existed. She said indifferently, 'The house is taken until the end of July, so it doesn't matter either way.'

Linda thought they would be much more comfortable at Aunt Caroline's, with her well-trained servants and lavish style of living. And in her mother's place, she felt sure she could have negotiated a discount for quitting early. She sought for something else to provoke her with. 'Why is the Prince of Usingen always hanging about us? Are you seriously considering him for Rachel? Because if not, you ought to send him away. I'm sure he's putting off other suitors.'

Maud turned over a letter without answering.

Linda's eyes narrowed. 'Have you *had* any offers for her?'

This was a sore point with Maud. Rachel's ball had been a stunning success, and she was obviously a very popular debutante – she never sat out a dance, and constantly had a group of gallants hanging about her. But the flood of offers Maud had expected had not materialised. There had been the expected approach from Mr Freehampton, but he had no money at all, and he put himself forward for virtually every girl who came out, so it was not a compliment. And there had been some sidelong hints from Lord Lansleigh, but he was a well-known trap, a confirmed bachelor who never came up to scratch. As Maud recalled, he had danced with Linda at *her* come-out. The eligible young men whose offers she would have considered seriously, who had clustered round Rachel like bees around a honey-pot, were not putting their obvious liking into action.

They might, of course, just be taking their time, and there was no absolute *necessity* to get her off in her first Season; but it always smacked somewhat of failure when there had to be a second. Second-season girls might have to make do with younger sons or even the sons of business people. Still, she told herself fairly, the Season was not over yet. Offers would come in. She just wished she had two or three under her belt already, for insurance. Or even *one*.

'It's early days,' she said, still not looking up.

Linda was affronted on the family's behalf, though there was a small, secret and shameful part of her that was pleased, because her own marriage had not been all it should have, and it would have been galling if Rachel, also the daughter of an Earl of Stainton, had done better without a dowry than Linda had done with one.

Maud lifted her head at last. 'What are *you* still doing here?' she asked, irritated. 'Why do you not go home?'

Linda's nostrils flared. 'I am helping *you*, Mama. I know how you dislike having to take Rachel to all these engagements. I could take more of them off your hands if you let me. You are looking tired—'

'I am *not* looking tired,' Maud snapped, 'and I do not dislike escorting Rachel. Indeed, it is a very pleasant way to keep up with my old friends.'

Linda knew her mother didn't have any old friends, but she didn't quite dare say so. 'I thought you might be a *little* more grateful to me,' she said.

'You helped me with the ball, but I don't need you any more,' Maud began, when the door opened and a footman came in.

'The Prince of Usingen has called, my lady,' he said. 'And there is a telegram for Lady Cordwell.'

Linda took the telegram from the tray. 'You can go,' she said to the footman. 'I'll ring if there's an answer.' And when he had departed, she said scathingly to her mother, 'The prince here *again*? If he is going to make an offer for Rachel, I wish he'd get on with it. He's making the place look untidy.'

'It is not for you to decide who calls and who does not call at *my* house. Attend to your own affairs. If Cordwell is so desperate as to send you a telegram, you had better read it.'

With a snort, Linda opened the envelope, began to read, and looked puzzled. 'It's not from Cordwell. It's from Colonel Havering of Frome Abbey, our next neighbour.' Her puzzlement increased. 'It just says, *Terrible accident. Come at once.*' She looked up. 'What does it mean?'

'I cannot imagine,' Maud said impatiently.

'Oh, God, I suppose there's been a flood, or a fire, or something. Or the roof has fallen in. We've been expecting *that* for months.'

But Maud was thinking. If something had happened to the house, Cordwell would have written himself. The message coming from a neighbour suggested he was not able to write. 'You had better go,' she said tersely.

But Linda had no wish to return to Dorset. 'It can't be anything urgent. I'll send a reply and go tomorrow.'

CHAPTER FOURTEEN

The train was crowded, and until Salisbury, where she changed, Linda had to share the compartment with four others: a middle-aged woman with two grown daughters, who chattered without pause, and a dyspeptic elderly man, who looked as though he believed women ought to travel in separate carriages. Luckily, the three females got out at Salisbury, leaving behind a magazine. Linda lingered long enough behind them to seize it before she descended, despite the old man's glaring at her and tutting. There was always half an hour to wait for the branch-line train to Frome Magna, and the latest *Tatler* was a godsend, though she would never actually have spent money on it.

There was no station at Frome Monkton, and it was a long time since she'd had any horses, which meant taking a cab to Holme Manor. When she stepped out into the station yard, however, there was a carriage waiting, with a coachman who touched his hat and a groom who opened the carriage door for her. She recognised them as the servants of her neighbour, Colonel Havering.

The momentary relief was enormous, but as the carriage rattled through the dusty green lanes, she wondered about the reason for such neighbourliness. She was never unnecessarily kind to anyone. Had Cordwell been taken ill? By the time the carriage swung round the sweep in front of the house, she was so concerned she forgot the *Tatler* and left it on the seat.

The house seemed to be more or less intact as she had left it; and here was Colonel Havering, coming towards her. Behind him on the steps were Mrs Clegg, the housekeeper, and her son Job, who wasn't right in the head, but who was biddable enough to act as footman, and for reduced wages.

The colonel reached for her hand, but instead of shaking it he covered it with both his, and looked at her with the melancholy eyes of a scolded dog. 'My dear,' he said, 'you must ready yourself for bad news. Come into the house and sit down.'

She pulled her hand away and stood firm. 'Where is Cordwell? Why did you send for me like that? What is going on?'

'You had really better be sitting down,' the colonel said anxiously.

Linda was afraid, and fear always irritated her temper. 'Tell me this instant, or I shall box your ears!'

Colonel Havering was old enough to have earned respect and politeness from all ages and stations, and it was only his pity for her that restrained him. He drew himself up, 'I'm afraid there has been a dreadful accident,' he said, in a quiet, level voice. 'Lord Cordwell is dead.'

He was shocked when Linda laughed. She was shocked at herself, but for some reason there seemed something irresistibly funny about the whole thing. The old man's solemn face, the servants huddling like sheep in the background, even the rooks, cawing like vulgar laughter in the tall elm trees that kept all the sun out of the rooms on that side of the house – the house that was so cold and damp and was falling gently and relentlessly to bits . . . It was laughable, wasn't it? Like some ridiculous Gothic story by Mrs Radcliffe where the heroine turned out to be the long-lost heiress. Only Linda was heiress to nothing.

'I don't believe you,' she said, and enjoyed the extra degree of shock on the old man's face at the discourtesy. 'He can't be dead. What happened?'

'An accident with his gun, while out shooting,' said the colonel, reluctantly. 'Please, come into the house, my dear.'

He actually got her moving. But she still couldn't see it. A gentleman sometimes got in the way of another gentleman's gun at a shoot, and received a rump full of pellets; occasionally, with an up-swinging gun, there had been a fatal incident. But you couldn't get in the way of your own gun. How was that possible?

'No, there's been some mistake,' she said.

The colonel would not be goaded any further. He tried to take her elbow to guide and support her, but she shook him off, and walked ahead of him into the dark house.

According to the footman, Lord Cordwell had gone out after pigeons, said the colonel. A hedger, Harry Beck, who was working in the lane beside Glebe Wood, had heard the sound of the shot, but had thought nothing of it – gunshot was a normal background sound in the country. It must have been about half an hour later that he had worked his way along to the stile that led into the woods, and found his lordship huddled up on the other side of it. 'It seems as though he must have caught his foot, or otherwise somehow stumbled, and the gun went off, with tragic consequences,' said the colonel.

Linda frowned. 'But—' she began, and then stopped. She was a woman of almost no imagination, and was gloriously lacking in tact; but sometimes self-preservation kicks in, in spite of oneself. She had been going to say, 'Why would he climb a stile with the gun unbroken?' But then it seemed to her a question better not asked at that moment. Instead she said, 'Where is he?'

The colonel looked away. 'At the church,' he said. 'It seemed better. The vicar arrived at the same time as Dr Pinchbeck, and he said . . .' What the vicar had said was that the lean-to shed where the sexton kept his tools was very cold, and as there would have to be an inquest it was better to keep the body as cool as possible. But that seemed more information than was necessary.

'I want to see him,' Linda said at once. Somehow, she couldn't shake the idea that there was a mistake somewhere.

The colonel looked extra kind. 'That would not be a good idea. No, my dear, believe me, it's better not to. Better to remember him the way he was.' There hadn't been a great deal left of Lord Cordwell's head. The housekeeper had produced a white damask tablecloth to wrap it in, and the sexton and his lad had brought up a long box they kept old bell-sallies in, and carried him away in that.

The colonel wanted Linda to come back with him to Frome Abbey to be looked after by his sister, who had kept house for him since his wife had died. He said several times that she should not be alone at such a moment. But Linda wanted to be alone – if nothing else, to think. And the colonel's sister was the sort of female who would weep all over her and offer her sympathy that she would not know what to do with, the most glutinous, sickly sort.

She got rid of him at last, and sat for a long time alone in the parlour, where dusk came early because of the trees. Then she rang.

Mrs Clegg came in, shoulders hunched, like a cold bird, wringing her hands in her apron.

'Job saw him go out, my lady,' she said, under questioning. 'He said he was going to get some pigeons for supper. He just took the one gun and went off on his own towards Glebe Woods. And that's all we knew until Harry Beck came with Colonel Havering and said they was bringing his lordship in. And straight after, four men from Abbey Farm came with him on a hurdle. The colonel was ever so kind, my lady, and did everything. He sent for doctor, though there was nothing to be done, my lady, you could see that.' She looked closely at her mistress as if trying to gauge what she was thinking.

'I don't 'spect he suffered any, my lady. It'd be all over soon as the gun went off.'

'Keep your opinions to yourself,' Linda snapped. The house seemed too quiet; and she remembered her arrival, with no-one but Mrs Clegg and her son at the door. 'Where is everybody?' she asked. 'Where are the other servants?'

Mrs Clegg looked away awkwardly. 'They've all gone, my lady.'

'Gone?'

'Left. Gone home. Give their notice. They've not been paid, you see, not for months, and after his lordship was brought in, they reckoned . . .' They had held an impromptu meeting and decided the chance of *getting* paid had been blown away with the master's head, so there was nothing to stay for.

'You stayed?' Linda said, wondering at such loyalty.

'Yes, my lady,' said Mrs Clegg. She didn't say that she and Job had nowhere else to go. She had lived here all her life, since she came as a housemaid at the age of twelve. She had worked her way up to head parlour-maid, married a footman, and had six months away when she was having Job. Then her husband was killed by a runaway dray in Frome Magna high street when Job was just a few months old and she'd come back as housekeeper with the baby and been here ever since, through thick and thin – mostly thin, since the old master died. Her parents were both dead, as was her only brother. And to get another position with Job in tow would be very hard. So stay she must.

Linda stared at the empty grate, wondering what to do next. 'You'd better light the fire in here,' she said. There weren't many days in the year when it was warm enough inside this house to sit without a fire.

'Yes, my lady.'

'And I suppose I'll have some dinner.'

'There isn't anything in, my lady,' said Mrs Clegg.

Linda looked up, frowning. 'What do you say?'

'There's no food in the house, my lady, bar a bit of rabbit stew left from yesterday that Job and I were going to have.' She swallowed bravely and said, 'You could share that, I suppose.'

'Rabbit stew? No, thank you. There must be something else.'

'Nothing, my lady.'

'What about the kitchen gardens?'

'The gardener was let go before he planted any vegetables, and the fruit's not ripe yet,' said Mrs Clegg. The fact of the matter was that Job had been looking after the garden since the gardener left, and though there wasn't much yet, there were a few new potatoes and early peas. But she didn't feel like sharing those with her ladyship, who wouldn't give you the scrapings from her plate if things were the other way about. She'd have let the master have some if he'd come back with the pigeons. But he was a nice man, who'd always been kind and civil to her, and given Job a position when a lot wouldn't have.

'Some bread and cheese, then,' Linda said, turning away. She wasn't particularly interested in food, but was hungry, not having eaten all day.

'No cheese, my lady. The dairyman's not been paid.'

Linda gave her the bare, furious look of a caged bird of prey. 'Bread then. And tell Job to bring up a bottle of wine from the cellar.'

'Which one, my lady?'

'What the devil does it matter? Any one,' Linda snapped.

She couldn't make it real in her mind. Cordwell dead? And in such a bizarre manner. With a huge effort of imagination she saw him setting off, the broken gun under his arm as she had seen men carrying guns all her life. Why would he lock it again? If he was going after pigeons in the woods, he would

257

have climbed the stile first. Unless he had seen a tempting target while still in the lane. Would he then have climbed over with the gun unbroken? Well, evidently he had. Everyone makes mistakes. She felt a tremor of fury with him, that he had made one with such consequences to other people. A man with a wife and children had no right to be careless. As soon as he came in, she would tell him so, in no uncertain terms . . .

She realised again, with a jolt, that he would not be coming in. She shook her head. It just didn't seem real. She got up restlessly and walked about the room, then from room to room, and finally on an impulse went into his business-room. She hardly ever went in there. It was very much his domain. Perhaps she would find some realisation in it.

It smelt of his cigars and hair oil, just a faint, ghostly aroma against the solid background smell of damp. As soon as she sniffed hard, she lost it. She looked around, but couldn't find him here. She thought, *He's gone. Gerald's gone.* She stared at his smoking-jacket, hanging on a hook on the door, but it was just an old jacket.

Then she thought, *I don't need him. I'm only thirty. I've the rest of my life ahead of me.* She was a widow. Like her mother. But her mother was old. *I should never have married him.* But she hadn't known – none of them had known, not even Gerald – how bad his situation was. Well, he was gone. What now? She shivered. *I hate this house.* There was no need to stay here now. She could go and live at the Castle and be comfortable. Giles would have to support her. She supposed the estate must belong to Arthur now. It would not be her responsibility, thank God. She could leave him to decide what to do with it when he came of age.

I could marry again, she thought. She was young enough. And this time, she could marry someone with a solid fortune.

She had wandered over to Gerald's desk, and now sat down behind it. There were papers on the desk, lots of them, letters and documents spread out untidily, as though he had been reading and been called hurriedly away before tidying them up. Idly she picked up one from the top, a letter with the bank's masthead. Words jumped out at her.

. . . deeply regret . . .

. . . situation of the utmost seriousness . . .

. . . not possible to extend any of the loans any further . . .

. . . see no course but to declare bankruptcy . . .

She read it from the beginning, her knuckles whitening as the letter crumpled under the force of her grip. Then she started to read the other documents, snatching them up and devouring them, her mind now fully awake.

At last she stopped, and stared at empty space, feeling sick. It was too quiet in here. She became aware that she was missing the ticking of the longcase clock that had always stood in the corner, and when she looked, it was not there, just a ghost-shape of slightly lighter wallpaper. The oil painting over the fireplace was gone too, as were the silver cups that had stood along the mantelpiece – cups Gerald had won at school, and in sporting competitions since. She thought about the rooms she had just wandered through. She took little notice of her surroundings, but it came to her they had been even barer than she remembered. Paintings, ornaments, furniture, even some carpets were gone.

Here in the litter on the desk were unpaid bills from tradesmen who declined to offer any more credit. A carpenter's bill. A glazier requiring payment before he would come and replace another broken pane. An assessment from a surveyor about work needed to maintain the building, along with his bill – unpaid. Not just the roof, the gutters and downpipes, but some of the walls crumbling because of damp, window frames rotting, chimneys in danger of tumbling down. Trees too close to the walls, roots damaging the cellars. Bill for estimating cost of tree felling and trimming – unpaid.

Most of the land had long been sold off. She knew the

house and the home park were mortgaged. The home park was let to a local farmer for grazing and timber, the rental just about covering the mortgage payments, but if the house and park were sold, the mortgage would eat up any sale price. And that was it. She gave a snort of laughter. She had thought Arthur could decide what to do with the estate when he came of age, but there *was* no estate, just an empty shell, fragile as burned paper in the grate, which would fall to dust at a touch.

She sat in Gerald's chair behind Gerald's desk and stared at the sea of paper, imagining what his thoughts had been. There was nothing left to sell, no credit to be had, nowhere else to go. Bankruptcy would have freed him from his debts but prevented his ever recovering his position; and the shame would have attached to Linda and the children for ever. She no longer felt like laughing. She really felt rather like crying, but it had been so long since she had allowed a tear to pass her eye, she didn't know how to do it.

Afton had packed and gone to the station with the luggage, and Giles was preparing to say his goodbyes and follow, when the telegram arrived.

Not even in the extreme of her anguish could Linda bring herself to go over the ten words and have to pay extra.

CORDWELL DEAD+MONEY ALL GONE+TELL GILES COME AT ONCE++

'You must go, of course,' said the dowager. 'I wish she had told us a little more. The telegram she received spoke of an accident, but we have no idea what sort.'

'Cordwell dead!' Aunt Caroline exclaimed. 'How can it be?'

'It hardly matters *how*,' Maud said impatiently. 'Perhaps a chimney fell on him. Or the roof collapsed. Linda spoke about the terrible state of repair.'

'Oh dear! I hope it wasn't anything too . . .' She didn't

want to say 'messy'. She was quite pale. 'Poor Linda! What a blessing, as it turns out, that she brought the children to London with her.'

Maud was brisk. 'I must send a note round to the cousins – they will have to break the news. I think it better if the children remain with them for the time being. There is no need for them to attend the funeral, whenever that happens. You will have to arrange it,' she added to Giles.

'Of course,' he said. He was thinking of the sentence *money all gone*. Was that Linda's usual exaggeration, or was it literally true? He had already had to deal with his father's financial delinquency. He didn't want to have to go through it all again with the Cordwell estate.

'The most important consideration,' Maud went on, 'is Rachel. This must not be allowed to spoil her debut.'

Giles came back from financial considerations to say, 'She will have to go into mourning, I suppose?'

'I have been thinking about that,' said Maud, whose mind had been working furiously. 'If he had only waited another month . . . July balls are not important, and out-of-town events can be more easily managed.'

'I don't suppose the timing was in his gift,' Giles said drily.

Maud paid him no attention. Her gaze was fixed on her sister's. 'I don't think,' she said slowly, 'do you, Caro, that in the circumstances . . . ?'

Caroline returned the look, and picked up the thread. 'You mean with the relationship being so remote?' she said intelligently. 'Only a brother-in-law?'

'Merely a sister's husband,' Maud improved. 'Hardly a relationship at all.'

'Complimentary mourning would only require four weeks – perhaps one might make it two? Attending balls, but not actually dancing?'

'But in this case,' Maud pronounced, 'I think slight mourning is all that's required. It's not as if Cordwell was in

261

society. He rarely came to London. No-one knew him. Slight mourning, I think, would amply answer the case.'

'Which means what?' Giles asked.

'Attending balls *and* dancing, but no laughing,' said Caroline. 'Quiet behaviour. And white gowns. With perhaps a purple band around the hem.'

'A mauve band,' Maud corrected. 'And white gloves with a mauve trim.'

'The difference will hardly be noticeable.' Caroline looked up in sudden doubt. 'But do you think—'

'It's what Linda would want,' said Maud, firmly. 'She, of all people, knows the importance of a girl's Season.'

Giles wasn't sure about that. Linda liked to be the centre of attention. He felt she would want to spread her mourning as far in every direction as possible. And there was no reason to think she would feel sympathy towards Rachel rather than resentment.

He had often thought the mourning rules absurd in this modern world, and he saw the sense in not jeopardising Rachel's chances when her relationship with Cordwell had been so tenuous in any case. But he had felt a little uncomfortable as he listened to Cordwell being progressively written out of family history. He couldn't claim to have known the man, though had found him pleasant enough at their occasional meetings; but it seemed hard that anyone should disappear so rapidly, like a pencil drawing being rubbed out – an already *faint* pencil drawing.

A new day had brought Colonel Havering, accompanying Dr Pinchbeck and the constable from Frome Magna (Frome Monkton had no policeman). The constable stood stolidly behind the doctor, who regarded Linda in critical silence as the colonel renewed his condolences. Linda waited in silence for the next blow to fall. She supposed there would be one, though she did not know from which direction.

In the absence of any reaction from Lady Cordwell, the colonel went on.

'I'm afraid, my dear ma'am, that there will have to be an inquest, as there is in every case of sudden death.' Linda looked at him sharply. 'But I do not wish you to worry. As perhaps you know, Dr Pinchbeck is the coroner for this district, so it will be his duty to carry it out.'

Pinchbeck looked eager to please. 'As far as anything can mitigate these tragic circumstances, I am glad to assure you that, given the circumstances, I do not believe there will be any difficulty in my returning a verdict of accidental death.'

He glanced towards the policeman, who took it up. 'I've interviewed Harry Beck, my lady, and I know him to be a sober, respectable sort of man, and a reliable witness. It's clear from what he says that there was no-one else in the immediate vicinity when the accident occurred. And from the position in which he found the body – his lordship, I should say, begging your pardon, my lady – it seems as though he must have stumbled climbing over the stile, causing the gun to go off.'

Pinchbeck went on quickly. 'It's a narrow stile, that one – I know it myself – and it's easy to get a foot caught under the bar as you swing your leg over. I shall take evidence to that effect. I'm sure there is nothing for you to worry about, ma'am.'

Linda glanced at the colonel, who nodded encouragingly. She said, 'I was not worried about anything. Thank you, gentlemen. I should be glad to be left alone, now.'

She sat for a long time staring at nothing, her mind too numb for thought, feeling quite light-headed. Around noon, Mrs Clegg brought in a tray, and laid out a luncheon of cold ham, game pie, fresh bread, and a dish of early cherries.

Linda looked up sharply. 'Where did all this come from?'

'A basket came, my lady. From Miss Havering, the colonel's sister. With con-condolences.' Mrs Clegg looked embarrassed, and avoided Linda's eye. 'There's some other stuff, too. I'll be able to cook you dinner tonight. The girl who brought it said it was to save you the trouble of ordering anything in.'

Linda felt a surge of fury. It would be at the colonel's instigation the basket was sent – his sister never did anything unprompted. How did he know there was nothing to eat in the house? Had Mrs Clegg told him? Had he had the temerity to question her servants? How dare he pity her? Had she come to this – the daughter of the Earl of Stainton?

But on further consideration, she realised she was extremely hungry and that, as no-one else knew about it, she might as well swallow the insult, rather than send it back.

Giles was met at Frome Magna station by the carriage of the Cordwells' neighbour, and before he got in, he slipped the groom a shilling to tell him what had actually happened. Such an excitement did not come often in these remote country societies, and the groom was more than willing to furnish Giles with all the details, so that by the time he descended at Holme Manor he had no need to distress Linda with questions. She came out to meet him, eyes bright and lips tight, and kept silent until she had conducted him to Gerald's study.

For the same length of time he was able to assume her tight lips were holding back tears of grief. Then he discovered it was anger.

'Look!' she cried, as soon as they were alone. 'Look at all this!' She grabbed a handful of papers from the desk and threw them down again. 'Bills, unpaid bills, debts, foreclosures! He was ruined. Cordwell was ruined! The bank wrote three days ago to say they would no longer extend any of the loans. I suppose that was the last straw. But it's the coward's way out. That's what I can't stand! He never thought what it was going to do to us, to me and the children. How could he? How could he?'

Giles was alarmed. 'Linda, be careful! Think what you're saying. Walls have ears, you know.'

She snorted in exasperation. 'Oh, Giles, don't be a fool! As if everyone isn't already thinking it! They brought him in on a hurdle, and God knows how many people saw, and who *they* told. It'll be all over the county by now.'

'It was a tragic accident,' Giles said firmly. 'That's what you must maintain. And you don't know any differently, whatever you may think. I implore you to keep your speculations to yourself. For the children's sake. And,' he forestalled her next outburst, 'because suicide raises many legal and financial problems. However bad things are, they would be worse if that was suspected.'

That made her pause. But then her face darkened. 'It's all your fault!' she cried. 'How do you dare to stand there being pious and proper when it was *you* who drove him to it?'

'Me?' Giles said, taken aback.

'How many times did I ask you to continue the allowance Father paid me?' she demanded furiously. 'You, with your rich heiress and your jam money – tens of thousands a year! – you have no idea what it is to be poor! You never thought what a difference it would have made to us – that poor, paltry allowance that you were too mean and selfish to part with! This is your fault! You drove poor Gerald to despair. I'm a widow and my children are orphans and we're penniless and bound for the workhouse because of you!'

'For heaven's sake, keep your voice down!'

'I'll say what I want! There's no-one to hear. The servants have all run off – there's only the housekeeper and her son, and who cares what they think? I don't suppose they're under any illusion anyway.' Suddenly her anger abandoned her, and her face seemed to crumple. 'What are we to do? There's nothing left, Giles, nothing! What's to become of us?'

He had to comfort her. Theirs had never been a happy relationship, but she was a woman, and his sister, and her face was creased with misery. Instinct took over. 'I'll take care of you,' he heard himself say, even at the same moment as he noticed there were no tears. He had never in his life seen Linda cry.

'But what about the bills, the debts? Who will pay them? He owed a fortune.'

'The personal debts become void on death,' he said. 'But those attached to the estate, any mortgages, for instance—'

'The house was mortgaged, and the land – what there is left of it.'

'Well, they'll have first call on any assets. Everything will have to be sold, up to the value of those debts.'

'What do you mean by "everything"?'

'The contents of the house, livestock and deadstock, and if that's not enough, the house and the land as well.'

'You seem to know all about it,' she said moodily.

'You forget, our father died in dire financial straits. It all fell on my shoulders. I had to learn quickly.'

'Hm,' she said, unwilling to grant him any sympathy. 'Well, they can clear the house, for what it's worth. Gerald had already sold anything of value. The furnishings can't be worth much. And we haven't had any livestock for years. I suppose the bit of land that's left will sell all right, but who in their right mind would buy this house? It's falling to pieces.'

'Gerald didn't have any stocks and shares? Any gilts or reserves? Any other assets?'

She waved a hand at the desk again. 'I've had a whole day to look through all this. He had nothing left but this house. You're welcome to try to find a lost farthing hidden at the back of a drawer if you like.'

Giles rubbed his hands wearily over his face. He foresaw weeks of work ahead for him, assembling papers and dealing with creditors, banks and bailiffs, winding up the affairs of a man who no longer had any affairs. As Linda's next of kin it would fall on him – and Linda and the children, he supposed, would come under his guardianship. He couldn't abandon them. He didn't suppose continuing the allowance would have made any difference – a mere pebble against a mountain of debt – but he could not help feeling an unwelcome prickle of unease about it. They would have to live at the Castle, Linda with her constant complaining. And two children: a boy to set onto a career, a girl to find a husband for. Years of responsibility, chains to tie him down.

But first – 'We'll have to arrange the funeral,' he said, emerging from his hands. 'That had better be done as soon as possible. Is there to be an inquest?'

'Yes,' she said indifferently, 'but the doctor is also the coroner, and he's promised to make it all easy. And there's a family plot in the churchyard. The rector knows all about that.'

'Well, I had better talk to all these people tomorrow,' Giles said, 'while you draw up a list of who should be invited. And there ought to be some kind of reception here afterwards – funeral baked meats. It won't do to skimp the obsequies.'

'You'll need to pay the local tradesmen first if you want them to provide food and drink,' Linda said sourly. 'I hope you brought your cheque-book with you.'

'There's nothing in the house? What are we to eat tonight?' asked Giles, who was starving.

'Colonel Havering's sister sent over a hamper. There's still plenty in that. And Gerald's cellar still has some good bottles. I suppose by rights they belong to the bank, now?'

'I think, in the circumstances, we won't worry about that tonight,' Giles said.

After the dinner party at which Nina was presented to the King, it seemed that the Cowlings were 'in'. Invitations came every day for dinners and evening parties. Sometimes they were from Mr Cowling's set – financiers and business-people – and sometimes from what Nina thought of as 'the King's set', which was more of the same, but with the addition of his personal friends, politicians and members of the armed forces, artists, writers and other interesting people. They never had to have an evening at home if they didn't want.

They were not invited by the other set, the people of fashion and of the high *ton* – the true denizens of the Season. But she didn't mind. She could do without balls now she was married, and there were other activities that were accessible to her: the theatre and the opera, the opening of the Summer Exhibition, the Derby, Ascot, polo at Windsor, the University Match at Lord's. And to occupy her active mind, she went with Lepida to lectures at University College, and with Lady Clemmie to various sorts of meetings.

It was at a dinner at the Keppels' that she encountered Lepida's parents, Mawes and Isabel Morris. Mawes came up to her in the drawing-room, took her hand and examined her from head to foot, and said, 'What a lady of fashion you've become! I can't believe you're the same little girl who used to model for my cartoons.'

Nina laughed, but said, 'I'm the same inside – really I am.'

'I bet you're not! You've grown up, my child, and done it very well. But what's this about a visit to an East End tannery? It's not the thing, you know. I wasn't pleased when Lepida told me what went on. It's too rough, not to say dangerous.'

'I don't think it was dangerous,' Nina said doubtfully, 'only rather unpleasant. I don't think they really would have harmed us.'

'You don't know that,' Mawes said seriously. 'You don't know what these men are capable of. It's bad enough to think of you girls being exposed to their foul language, but it wouldn't take more than a second for it to turn nasty. Suppose someone drew a knife and marred that pretty face of yours? I'm surprised Cowling allowed you to go.' Nina didn't say anything, and he looked at her cannily. 'That is, if he knew about it,' he added gravely.

She couldn't hold his eyes. 'He might not have, I don't remember,' she said. 'He doesn't expect me to ask permission to go anywhere. And sometimes when he gets home he asks me about my day, and sometimes he doesn't.'

'Now, Nina, that's not cricket. You mustn't take advantage of his good nature. Lord knows, I encourage Lepida to take an interest in those less fortunate than herself, but there are more appropriate ways of doing it for a lady in her position – or yours.'

'You allowed her to go,' Nina pointed out.

'I wasn't told it was a tannery. I imagined something like a garment factory, something much less rough. I've told her not to go again.'

'Well, I haven't been back,' Nina said, feeling uncomfortable. 'Mrs Crane said a lot more testimonies were needed and it would be necessary to wait outside the factory in the evening and catch the girls coming out, but I haven't had an evening free, though Lady Clemmie has gone with her once.'

'Look here, I don't mind Lepida going to meetings and writing letters and transcribing the statements and so on. That's perfectly proper. Promise me you'll stick with that, too, and not expose yourself to any more danger.'

He gave her a smile of understanding and irresistible appeal, and she smiled back and said, 'I promise.'

At that moment Mr Cowling came up behind her and said, 'Promise what? Evening, Morris! How's that new horse of yours? What is my wife promising you?'

Seeing Nina's confusion, Mawes came to her rescue. 'She's promising me to come and sit for me again one day.'

'Oh, she should, she should!' Cowling said. 'That portrait you did of her before we married was excellent. Like as life! I should like another to put on my wall – something more formal, in evening dress, mebbe.'

'I'm not sure my poor skill could do justice to her beauty,'

Morris said. 'She is growing into the most handsome woman in London.'

Fortunately for Nina's blushes, Isabel joined them at that moment, and said, 'Mawes, Mrs Keppel says the King loved that cartoon you did about the Entente Cordiale. He wants to know who modelled for the French Trollop.'

'I hope he doesn't want to meet her!' Morris said.

'Who was it, actually?' Cowling asked. 'I was wondering myself.'

'As a matter of fact, it was Lepida,' Morris admitted. 'But I changed the face as much as possible so as not to embarrass the poor girl. My family are very accommodating to me, but there are limits.'

Cowling laughed, and said, 'Well, I don't mind you drawing Nina again, as long as you don't use her for anything at all "off".'

'Perish the thought! And you must come to dinner,' Morris said, in his expansive way. 'When can you come? Tomorrow?'

'I know for a fact we're not free until Tuesday, but we'll make it then, if you like.'

'Excellent. I'll invite some interesting people to amuse you.'

'But *you* always amuse me,' Mr Cowling said comfortably.

Though she was not in the fashionable set, Nina did go across the square from time to time and call on Lady Caroline, who always seemed pleased to see her. On the day she went there to tea, and found Grandmère also present, she learned about the death of Linda's husband.

'And Giles has had to go down to Dorset to deal with the Cordwell finances, which are in something of a muddle. He'll probably be there for several weeks,' Caroline concluded.

'Oh, poor Giles,' Nina said, and was embarrassed as she realised she should have said 'Poor Linda' first.

Grandmère gave her a canny look. 'No, you are right, it is poor Giles. He will hate it very much, and it will remind him of his troubles when his father died. But men have their trials as women have theirs. They must be borne. We cannot help it.'

'What will Lady Cordwell do?' Nina asked. 'I suppose she'll stay in Dorset while she's in mourning.'

'The funeral is next week,' said Caroline, 'and we'll all have to go down, but then I expect Giles will ask her to stay at the Castle. Holme Manor is rather a dreary house, and awfully damp. Very unhealthy. I don't suppose she'll want to stay there in the long term.'

'She cannot come to me,' Grandmère said sharply, 'and you should be careful, Caroline, that you do not get left with her. Once invite her and she will never leave. She is like a leech, that one. She will cling on wherever she can.'

Caroline looked shocked. 'Oh, you mustn't say such things.' Not in front of a stranger, she meant.

Grandmère gave a very Gallic shrug. 'I'm sure this family has no secrets from Nina. Kitty must have told her everything. No, let Linda go to Ashmore if she must go somewhere. That house is big enough for everyone to have their distance.'

'Well, it would be *rather* crowded here,' said Caroline, cautiously, 'especially if she wanted to bring the children. And, besides, I do feel being brought up in a city is not good for children.'

'Nonsense. I was brought up in a city,' said Grandmère. 'It did me no harm.'

'I was, too,' Nina said apologetically.

'And when are you going to present us with a child?' Grandmère demanded. 'We are all waiting.'

Nina was embarrassed. Old ladies had licence not granted to others in polite society, but there were limits. 'I suppose when God sends me one,' she said.

'Hmph! If that is where you believe they come from, you may be waiting a long time,' said Grandmère, sourly, and began rummaging in her reticule.

271

Caroline, rather pink, leaned across to Nina and whispered, 'You must forgive her. She gets crotchety when her digestion is disordered. It's the east wind.'

Grandmère emerged with a small box of cachous, slipped one into her mouth and said, 'The wind is from the south-west today. And I may be old and sour, but I am not deaf.'

CHAPTER FIFTEEN

Dr Pinchbeck was as good as his word. He helped a nervous Job through his evidence that Lord Cordwell had gone out that day after pigeons. He took evidence from Harry Beck and the constable. Colonel Havering gave evidence that his neighbour often went out alone, shooting for the pot; and further that he himself had tripped on occasion going over that particular stile, as it was narrow and one's boot could get caught under the rung as one swung one's leg over.

Dr Pinchbeck concluded that the death was due to a tragic accident, and added that he hoped everyone would respect the feelings of the grieving widow, who now had two young children to bring up alone. The body was therefore released for burial and the funeral could go ahead.

The vicar must have heard loose gossip about Cordwell's death because, when interviewed by Giles, he referred as often as possible to 'this tragic *accident*', mentioned many times what a good and Christian man Cordwell had been, and assured Giles that a full burial service and the family plot awaited the Lord's faithful servant. He went on to say he personally would ensure that the choir and organist were in attendance and that the bell-ringers would do their part. A small honorarium to the organist was usual, likewise to the gravediggers. Beer and pies at the Frome Arms after the service were the traditional thanks to the choir and bell-ringers. Giles, fortunately, had cash with him, and gave the vicar enough to cover everything, plus a donation to the church, which he felt was tacitly expected. The vicar's good will, he gathered, came not from any feeling of sympathy towards Linda, but from a liking for Gerald Cordwell personally – he had been popular in the neighbourhood, the vicar told him, and would be missed.

Giles had paid the wages of Mrs Clegg and her son; had settled with the local grocer, baker and butcher so that funeral baked meats could be ordered; and had hired two local girls as temporary housemaids to clean rooms to a sufficient standard for the funeral reception and to wait on the guests. Colonel Havering and his sister had been immensely kind and placed anything they had, from servants to flowers from the gardens, at Linda's service. Giles had to talk to them and thank them, because Linda had retreated into a surly gloom and would take no part in any planning.

The dowager left Rachel in London to be chaperoned by Caroline, and travelled down to Ashmore, so that Richard could escort her and Alice on the long journey to Dorset. Kitty was excused attendance because of her condition, but to Maud's surprise, Sebastian made himself one of the party.

'There is no need,' she said. 'It is not to be a large affair.' She hesitated, and added in a lower voice, 'It is not a circumstance to which one wishes to draw attention.'

'I'm the nearest thing to a father Linda has left,' Sebastian said. 'And I liked the chap. Poor Cordwell. He had a hard row to hoe.'

Gerald Cordwell, he thought, had been a light, pleasant sort of person who would have done well in easier circumstances. He'd have been a diligent landlord, a popular host, a useful member of the House, and would probably have kept a better check on Linda if he hadn't been worn down by penury. Indeed, Linda would have been a nicer person if there had been enough money. But it took more character than either of them had to make a go of things under such disadvantages.

The day before the funeral, he encountered Dory walking along an upstairs corridor with an armful of linen. Her eyes flew to his face, but then she lowered them, flattened herself against the wall and curtseyed slightly. That was what maids were supposed to do when encountering Upstairs people.

He stopped. 'Dory, don't,' he said gently. 'Don't treat me like that.' She bit her lip, but did not look up. 'Please talk to me,' he said. 'I promise I won't embarrass you, but I miss talking to you so much. Can't we just be – civilised?' At the last moment he did not say 'friends', because he had already had the answer to that question.

He had heard from Mr Bland once, that he was on the trail of Jack Hubert, and hoped to track him down eventually. It reminded him again, forcibly, that he had not decided what to do about Hubert when he was found – for, indeed, what could be done? But he thrust that away to the back of his mind. For the moment, he just ached for the sound of her voice, for one kind look.

She did glance up, briefly and piercingly into his face. Then she looked away, and said, in an almost normal voice, 'Mr Crooks said you were going to the funeral tomorrow. Is that right?'

'Yes. Felt I ought to pay my respects. He didn't have the happiest of lives.'

'Living in a grand house surrounded by his own land, you mean? That *would* be hard.'

'There's more than one sort of hard,' Sebastian said. 'He inherited his father's debts, and had to struggle to keep the bailiffs out of that grand house, while watching it gradually falling to bits. And it couldn't have been easy, being married to my niece,' he added.

A faint quirk of a smile touched her lips. 'You mustn't say such things to me, sir. It's not proper.'

'I know *you* won't repeat it. And must it be "sir"?'

'It's easier for me,' she said bluntly. She sighed. 'At least

275

he *was* married. And had two children. For some, that would be a blessing.'

He wanted to say to her then, 'I'm doing something about it! Just be patient a while longer!' But what, what, *what* could he do? As long as Hubert lived, she could not marry him. If he could somehow ensure Hubert would never come after her, and somehow convince her that he wouldn't, would she consent to live with him unmarried? He could sell the house in Henley and they could go somewhere no-one knew them, and live quietly, out of the public gaze. He had sufficient income to make them comfortable, and to provide for her after he had gone. Would she accept that? Or would she feel lessened even by the suggestion? He didn't know. But at present he couldn't even put it to her. He must confront Jack Hubert first, and he hadn't the least idea how that was to be done, what arguments might work with him. Unlike Christian, he must tackle Apollyon *before* he could rest and refresh himself at the House of the Palace Beautiful.

For now, all he could say was, 'I'm sorry.' He meant it, on so many levels.

'It's not your fault,' she said quickly, putting out a hand as if to touch him, but snatching it back before he could take it. She hesitated, and then said quietly, 'You've given me so much already. More than you know. Don't be unhappy – sir.' And she hurried away along the passage before he could say anything more.

It was a day of heartbreaking beauty, blue and gold, sweetly warm. The trees towered in their summer glory, stirred by soft airs; the gentle rounded hills of Dorset were freckled with browsing sheep; the hedges were busy with birds. It seemed all wrong to Alice to be burying someone on such a day (her father's funeral had taken place in proper January weather, with bare dripping trees and weeping skies.) At the graveside, she looked up at the perfect sky and thought how sad it would be to leave the world in June, the loveliest month. Then she found it was possible after all to weep for her brother-in-law, whom she had known so little.

At the graveside Linda, stiff-backed and unapproachable in her well-worn blacks and heavy veil, was simply enduring, waiting for it to be over. But as the coffin was lowered, she suddenly remembered that Cordwell's father had also died in a shooting accident. Once, early in the marriage, when they had still exchanged intimacies, Gerald had confided to her that he sometimes suspected his father had deliberately shot himself because of his debts. Gerald's mother had still been alive then, and Linda had asked her about it. She had said that it had definitely been an accident. It had been witnessed: he had been out shooting with friends, had stepped backwards to take a shot, tripped, and the shot had gone wild. Linda had never discussed it again with Gerald. Now she was wondering if the suspicion had remained with him all his life, buried at the back of his mind. Had he, at the end, seen it as an example, as the proper thing to do? *Oh, Gerald, you fool!* She had a sudden overwhelming sense of his loneliness, and for the first and last time, tears prickled her eyes.

Afterwards, back at Holme Manor, Cordwell proved to have had many more friends than Linda had suspected, for all his neighbours came, and spoke warmly of him. The Cordwells were an old family and had been at Holme Manor for hundreds of years, and for most of that time it had been a prosperous place. They had done much good locally, opening a village school, building alms houses, and endowing the church. St Mary's, Frome Monkton, was tiny, and of Saxon plainness, but it boasted four very fine stained-glass windows that had been donated by Gerald's grandfather; around the walls there were many marble and alabaster plaques and memorials to Cordwells of former ages, going back to the mediaeval; and two tattered flags hanging from the beams on the decani side reminded the congregation of Cordwells who had given their lives for their country at Sebastopol and Waterloo.

It was good, Alice thought, to remember that Gerald Cordwell was not just Linda's rather beleaguered husband, but the scion of an ancient house. She thought of little Arthur, bumping about in the saddle on Goosebumps' back as she led him in a riding lesson, and wondered what there would be for him when he grew up. She gathered it would not be much.

Uncle Sebastian came over to her and said, 'Very pensive, m'dear?'

'I was just thinking about Arthur, and all this.' She waved a hand.

'Ah yes. It's a sad situation.'

'What will happen to him and Arabella?'

'From what I've heard your mother say, I imagine they'll come and live at the Castle.' He gave her a sympathetic look. 'I know they've rather been left on your hands on past visits.'

'Oh – well – I don't really mind . . . not *too* much,' she said awkwardly. It seemed unkind to express reluctance at a time like this.

'You're a good girl,' Sebastian said. 'But you shouldn't be forced into the role of childminder. I shall talk to Kitty and Giles about it. If the children are to live permanently at Ashmore, they must have a governess. And, in time, Arthur must go to school and be put in the way of a career. It's a serious responsibility. You can't just take in orphans and then ignore them.'

'Like Jane Eyre,' she said, 'and Mrs Reed.'

'Kitty and Giles will do the right thing, I'm sure, however much—' He stopped short.

Alice wondered whether that sentence would have ended *however much they dislike Linda*, or *however much it costs.*

He began again. 'Now, there's a very fine buffet laid out for us over there. I think we ought to go and sample it, don't you?'

'Yes, especially as Giles has had to pay for it all twice over,' said Alice, falling in beside him as they crossed the room. 'I heard Linda telling Richard he'd had to pay the tradesmen's bills before they'd provide anything.'

Some flakes of plaster descended gently onto Sebastian's sleeve, and he brushed them off with a glance upwards. 'I hope the house remains standing until tomorrow, at least.' They were staying the night there.

'But if it does fall down,' Alice said, 'at least it's warm enough outside to sleep in the garden.'

'How practical you are,' Sebastian said admiringly.

'I'm so *glad* to see you!' Kitty cried, embracing Nina. 'We never seemed to have any time together in Town. Now we can talk and talk and talk! You can tell me everything you've been doing in London.'

'Aye, there'll be a lot of telling in that!' said Mr Cowling, genially. 'What with being presented to the King, she's been the mad success of the Season. We've hardly had an evening at home ever since.'

'Rachel was the mad success of the Season,' Nina corrected.

'But you came a close second,' Richard assured her solemnly.

Embarrassed, Nina turned to Kitty. 'You're looking really well.'

'I feel well,' she said. 'I'm glad you've come now, because by next month I shall be too heavy to move around much. Now, you must come up and see my baby.'

'Aye, and I want to see your fancy new bull, Master Richard!' said Cowling.

'Oh, it's a beautiful creature,' Richard said. 'Easily as handsome as little Lord Ayton, though a lot bigger. And my new herdsman is quite as much in love with it as Kitty is with her baby.'

Kitty took Nina's arm up the stairs and, a little breathless, said, 'Why do we shut the children away at the top of the house? Nurseries should be on the ground floor.'

'I don't suppose many people would agree with you,' Nina said.

'But *you*'d want to see your child all the time, wouldn't you?' Nina didn't answer, and she said timidly, 'You would like to have children?'

'I don't think that's going to happen.'

'Oh, but you mustn't give up hope,' Kitty said fervently, and then she stopped, and blushed scarlet. A horrible doubt had entered her mind. Nina had married an old man (Mr Cowling seemed so to her) and perhaps old men couldn't father children. She knew very little about the subject – all her mother had told her before marriage was that her husband would want to do strange things to her in bed, but she must never resist and never, never cry. (As it turned out, she had liked the strange things very much.) Children had duly followed. Did Mr Cowling not—? No, she couldn't even *think* the question, far less ask it. Nina was her dear friend, but it simply was not possible.

She forgot all about it when they entered the nursery, and Louis's face lit with delight at the mere sight of her. 'Mama, Mama!' he exclaimed, and took half a dozen steps towards her before descending to hands and knees. He walked for pride, but crawled for speed.

'Goodness, he's grown!' Nina exclaimed. He was such a handsome child, still fair, with blue eyes and a look of Giles about him, especially when he smiled. She felt a sudden pang in her stomach, like a cramp of hunger. Though Kitty had always wanted babies, Nina hadn't much cared about it; but perhaps, she thought, women were designed to want them at last. And, of course, if they were Giles's babies . . . No, she mustn't think like that.

Louis reached his mother, rose to his feet, and with one hand clinging to her skirt, he patted the maternal bulge with the other hand. 'Baba,' he said. 'Baba dere!'

Kitty laughed, and swooped him into her arms. 'Yes,' she said, 'that's a baba in there. Your little brother.'

Nina smiled. 'You've decided to have another boy, then?'

'It's my duty,' Kitty said. 'Two boys for the family. Then perhaps I might have a daughter for myself. Would you like to hold him?'

'No, that's all right,' Nina said, unconsciously folding her arms in denial. It was hard enough just *seeing* a baby that looked like Giles.

Louis, ensconced on Kitty's hip, wanted to chat. It was mostly babble, interlarded with the words he had mastered. Kitty thought about her little brother Peter, who had been 'her baby' long ago when she was a little girl. She had watched these milestones before – the first wobbling step, the first proper word, the growing intelligence. Peter had died when he was four, and Kitty had known her first heartbreak. She gave Louis a sudden squeeze, making him grunt, and then chuckle. She wished Nina a baby as hard as she could wish.

Richard took Mr Cowling in the large trap, pulled by Dexter. 'You see we've cleared those two fields and we've started grazing them. The Six Acres was rather more work, because of the bracken, which is poisonous. We mowed it, then ploughed it to expose the roots, and put the pigs on it – they eat the rhizomes, you see.'

'Rhizomes, is it?' Cowling said, amused.

'Granted I didn't know the word a year ago, but a man can learn,' said Richard, with dignity. 'When the pigs finished with it, we re-seeded, and we'll take a crop of hay off it and start grazing it in the autumn. Though we'll have to keep an eye on it, in case the bracken creeps back.'

'Aye, I see it's a long business after all,' said Cowling. 'I don't know much about cattle – sheep lore I got from my father – but sheep must be smarter than cows, because they won't touch bracken.'

'They may be smarter, but they don't give near as much milk,' Richard said. He pulled Dexter to a halt. There was a gap where they had a view down the hill towards the road that ran along the near side of the Ash. 'You see down there,' Richard said, 'all that activity? That's one of our gangs of men, mending the road. We'll have to keep it in decent repair from now on, if the milk dray is going to get round all the farms in time. When I first looked at it, there were so many holes we'd have had butter, not milk. '

'Ah,' said Cowling. 'You bought a dray, then, did you?'

'Had one adapted. And bought two good horses. If we expand further up the valley, we'll probably have to invest in another. One won't be able to do the journey in the time between the milk being ready and the train leaving. But we solved the problem of getting the dray up to the farms. The farmers bring the churns down to the road, so the dray just has to go straight along the road from one gate to the next. Farmer Whitcroft had the idea of building a wooden platform by the side of the road to stand the churns on and stop them falling over, and the others are doing the same now. And we've had to make some improvements to the farmers' milking-sheds, particularly the floors. You can't have the cows paddling about in lakes of liquid manure and splashing it into the buckets. And I've never yet met a cow that could resist dipping its tail into the stuff and swishing it about.'

'It sounds as if you've had to lay out a lot of money to get going,' Cowling commented, as they drove on.

'So far it's been all expense. The bull wasn't the half of it. All expense and no income.'

'Aye, well,' Cowling said, 'that's the way of business. I told you as much over the jam affair – you have to lay it out to get it back. Luckily, the jam's doing very well – that smashing new contract with the Indian Army'll bring in a pretty penny!'

'Yes, we're very pleased about that. And several hospitals are interested. I just wish everybody didn't always want strawberry jam. If only we could grow 'em all year round we'd make a fortune. You can't think of a cunning way to make strawberries grow twelve months of the year, I suppose?'

'I'm no magician,' said Cowling. 'But somebody will, some day.'

'That's what I call optimism,' Richard said, with a laugh.

'Oh, you'll never go wrong with jam,' Cowling said. 'That's why I was happy to come in with you. As to your dairy scheme – I think it shows promise, any road.'

'Promise? It promises to eat up the jam profits.'

'But that's how it goes. You take the profits from one enterprise and put it into the next, and so on. Just like I did, putting my profits from boots into art-silk stockings. Always looking for the next thing. Can't stand still in commerce, my lad. Ever onward and upward.'

'Sounds exhausting!'

'But you're happy with this bull of yours?'

'Oh, he's perfectly splendid. You'll see in a moment: we're just coming up to Hundon's. So far he's had rather a motley collection of wives to service, but I've six new heifers coming next week, pedigreed Shorthorns, so he'll feel like a sultan with a harem of lovelies.'

'You've bought six more cows? What did your brother say?'

'Giles doesn't know yet. They were expensive, but they'll be the core of our new herd,' Richard said, unabashed. 'Got to build on firm foundations. Besides, I couldn't resist – you'll understand when you see them. Those big brown eyes . . .'

'Aye, I'm a fool for brown eyes, too!' Cowling was chuckling. 'Anyway, you have to invest before you can take a profit.'

'I hope you can convince Giles of that when he gets back.

Oh, there's Woodrow, waiting for us. He's an excellent man, Cowling, full of ideas. You'll like him.'

Rose paid another visit to Moss, and found him in much better spirits. He was quite agitated, in fact, but in a good way. 'Miss Eddowes of Weldon House has been to see me, Rose – you know Miss Eddowes, of course?'

'Of course,' said Rose, but did not elaborate on how she knew her. The episode that had brought them together, concerning the late earl, was too painful ever to be completely healed.

'A true lady,' Moss enthused. 'Of a very respectable family. She lives quietly, but I hear she's very well-to-do, everything done as it should be.'

'I wouldn't know about that, Mr Moss. I've only been inside her house once.'

'And a kind and charitable person, I believe,' Moss went on.

'Oh, she's that, all right.'

'Involved in many good works.'

You don't want to enquire about them too deeply, Rose thought. *You might not approve.* 'So, did she have anything in particular to say to you, Mr Moss?' she enquired. Miss Eddowes had promised to look out for a position for him – though Rose had thought it unlikely anything would turn up that wouldn't be a big step down for someone who had been butler to an earl in a big house.

Moss's cheeks quivered. 'She had indeed, Rose. I can hardly find words to tell you. You know how worried I've been—'

'She's found you a place?' Rose said, to hurry him along.

'She's *offered* me a place.'

'Good gracious!' Rose said blankly. She hadn't expected that.

'Of course, it's a *very* small household. Just a cook-housekeeper, and one girl who lives out. But Miss Eddowes said she feels very much the lack of a male presence in the

284

house. And she says she would like to entertain more. Sometimes she needs to persuade people to donate to some cause, and she wants to give dinner parties or evening parties for the purpose. So it wouldn't be a negligible position.'

'I can see that,' Rose said kindly.

'I should be butler and footman combined. Ordering the wine. Answering the door. Receiving guests.' He went on, more hesitantly, 'Laying the table. I suppose I would have to clear as well as serve.' His voice faltered. 'Cleaning the silver? The shoes? Filling the lamps? I hope not . . .' He came to a halt, and looked at Rose with all the excitement drained away. 'I'd have to do everything, wouldn't I, with no footmen or boys under me?'

Rose, never self-pitying, had no patience with it in anyone else. 'What's the alternative, Mr Moss? You've been knocked down, now someone's giving you a hand up. You can't go back to a job that will strain your heart, and you're lucky that Miss Eddowes has asked you.'

'Yes, I suppose so.'

'No suppose about it. You'll be a butler still, in a respectable house. And Miss Eddowes will never see you want. Think yourself lucky. Some people end up in the workhouse.'

'His lordship would never have let it come to that!'

'There was no promises made. You don't know what would have happened. Now you've got a settled future to look forward to. I hope you accepted.'

'Of course I did. I—' He swallowed a lump of reality and gathered himself. 'I know I am fortunate.'

'You are. When are you going there?'

'I'm to go the day after tomorrow, as soon as my room's been made ready and my things sent down from the Castle.'

'Your things – yes. They've been packed up already,' Rose said. 'Hook's moved into your room, and cleared your stuff out.' She said it to ginger him up, but was sorry when she saw it was a shock.

285

'Hook? But – but I thought he was only temporary. Surely he isn't trying to step into my shoes?'

'He's trying to. Whether he'll succeed . . .'

'He's not suitable, not at all. He's not a butler. And he's not a good person. Oh dear, oh dear, what will become of the Castle if he's in charge?'

'Well, it's not your worry any more, so put it out of your mind and concentrate on Weldon House. I'll make sure your things are sent down right away.'

'My books,' he said. 'Make sure my books are sent. And my stamp collection. If Hook's in my room, I don't want him pawing over it. He'd put fingermarks all over everything – he wouldn't know you're not supposed to touch the stamps, except with tweezers. He might pick them up. He might—' He couldn't even put into words the horrors that Hook could inflict on a precious collection that had taken him his whole life to assemble. *Suppose he spilled something over them?*

'I'll see they're put in,' Rose said.

'I'll miss you all at the Castle,' he said miserably.

'We'll see you when we come down to the village. It's not as if you're going to Timbuktu. You'll be the big man at Weldon House – everyone will know you. And you'll be more important to Miss Eddowes than you ever could be to his lordship. She'll depend on you for everything.'

She was glad to see Moss straighten his shoulders. 'You're right,' he said solemnly. 'It's a great responsibility. But one I am equal to. *De forti egressa est dulcedo*, as the poet says.'

'What poet's that, Mr Moss?'

'You wouldn't know him,' Moss said, loftiness restored.

The dowager, Linda and Giles travelled back to the Castle together, having closed up the house, leaving Mrs Clegg and Job as caretakers. All the papers had been bundled together and sent off to the family solicitor in Frome Magna, who, with the help of a land agent, would settle the estate.

286

Eventually they would report to Giles, who had no great hopes that there would be anything at all left. Probably the house would have to be sold, but who on earth would buy it? The bailiffs had called on the day after the funeral and, indifferent in the face of Linda's fury, had warned that she could take nothing from the house but her own and the children's clothes and their toys. Mrs Clegg had packed the trunks under the dowager's eye, and they had been sent off to the railway station.

Linda and her mother were to stay a day or two at the Castle before going to London and thence to Scotland, where the children had already been taken by the cousins. Giles tried not to feel relief that his sister would be elsewhere for the summer, but family loyalty only went so far.

He found himself unexpectedly glad to be home. It was the contrast, of course, with Holme Manor, but it did not look nearly so much like a prison as he was driven up the hill from the station. He caught a glimpse of the valley road as they crossed it, looking good after the repair gang's attentions. The milk scheme was really Richard's baby, but he was interested in it, wanted to hear if anything new had happened.

It was startling to see Hook at the door in butler's uniform to greet him. He really ought to do something about that. Hook was only supposed to be standing in, but he seemed to be giving himself the air of permanence, and Giles did not want him to be rewarded by default. He must enquire immediately about Moss's state of health, and if he was not coming back, a permanent replacement must be found. And what, in that case, would he do with Moss? The man had been butler since his boyhood – he couldn't just be turned out like a stray cat.

Kitty was there to greet him in the hall, and he stooped to kiss her cheek and ask if she was well. Behind her stood Uncle Sebastian and, to his surprise, Joseph Cowling. He had forgotten the Cowlings were coming to visit. He thought of Nina and felt a pang. 'How do you do, Cowling?' he said, shaking the hard, dry hand. 'Are you here *en garçon*?'

'How d'ye do, my lord? No, the wife is out riding with Lady Alice. Should have been back here to greet you, but you know what it is when young ladies get a-horseback – time flies out of the window. And Nina doesn't get much riding at home.'

Mr Cowling had gone with her and Alice to the stable yard, and seen her mounted on Kitty's horse, witnessed her delight, and had felt guilty that he had prevented her from riding at home. There had been good reason to begin with, but perhaps he had kept up the embargo too long. When they got home, he'd see about getting her a horse of her own – as long as it was understood she was to ride side-saddle and never any other way. She had looked very fine and elegant, dressed in a habit of Lady Alice's, but she'd look even better in a new habit of her own, and mebbe one of those tall hats with a veil – he could see it all. Lady Alice rode side-saddle, of course, and he was sure it would never cross her mind not to. It was those modern ideas, Fabianism and suffragism, that were corrupting female minds, and he must keep an eye out, when they got home, that Nina didn't get too caught up in them. If only, he thought wistfully, she had a little baby to occupy her mind . . . That was the natural state for females. Lady Kitty, for instance, was as feminine and proper a lady as you could wish to see.

The letter was brought to Giles in the drawing-room. 'Well, this is excellent news,' he said. 'I've been wondering what to do about Moss, and now someone's offered to take him off my hands.' In courtesy, he explained to Mr Cowling. 'Old family retainer, no longer fit to work.'

'Aye, I remember Moss – the butler, wasn't he? Grand old fellow.'

'It must have been worrying you,' Nina said.

'Yes, it's been nagging at my mind. One can't just cast such people off.'

She smiled faintly. 'Part of the boulder?'

'It begins to feel a little less like a boulder, these days,' he answered her.

'Sisyphus was punished for hubris,' she reminded him. 'What was your crime?'

Kitty raised her head from the baby shirt she was embroidering, looked questioningly from his face to Nina's.

'Leaving the Underworld and having to be dragged back, I suppose,' Giles said.

She shook her head. 'You can't really call this place the Underworld.'

The dowager made an impatient sound. 'What on earth are you talking about, Giles?'

He turned his attention to her. Mr Cowling was still staring thoughtfully at Nina. 'Sorry, Mama. It's time for Moss to leave the cottage hospital, and most fortuitously someone has offered him a position. As butler, moreover, which will be a salve to his pride.'

'Oh, that's good,' said Kitty.

'It's a much smaller household, of course,' Giles said, 'but as he couldn't cope with the strain of a larger one, that's just as well. My problem is solved with no effort or expense on my part – and it's not often one can say that.'

'You're right,' said Cowling. 'It must be a relief to you.'

'Well,' the dowager interrupted impatiently, 'who is it that has offered him a place?'

'Miss Eddowes, of Weldon House. I believe Moss will be the only male servant, but she keeps a very small establishment so I don't suppose the work will be arduous.'

'No!' said the dowager.

He looked at her, surprised. '"No" what, Mama?'

She pressed her lips together, realising that she could not say what she wanted to say in front of strangers. 'I should like to speak to you in private, Stainton,' she said, rising. Of course, Giles and Mr Cowling had to rise as well, and since he was on his feet, Giles thought he might as well get her objections over with at once. He followed her out of the room.

Cowling sat down again as the door closed, and said to Nina, 'What was all that about boulders and the Underworld?'

She reached for a piece of work from the common basket to hide her face from him. 'An old Greek legend. It was nothing – just nonsense.'

Cowling left it, and picked up the newspaper, but he didn't read it. He was thinking of that exchange between Nina and the earl, of the sense he'd had of intimacy between them. He looked at her bent head, her beauty, and felt a pang of jealousy. She had looked at Stainton – well, she had never looked at *him* like that: as if they were of the same species, and everyone else somehow came from a different world.

It was not the first time he had noticed that Nina and Stainton talked to each other differently from everybody else, almost in a sort of code, referring to things no-one else knew about. They were a match intellectually. Nina was clever and well-educated – it was one of the things he loved about her. And he knew that her mind didn't always get the exercise it needed. She could say things to Stainton she couldn't say to him.

He had never felt jealous before, but now he stared unseeing at the newspaper, and brooded. Another man was making his wife smile, engaging her attention, stimulating her thoughts – *his* wife! He was angry, confused, and afraid – and because he was a wealthy businessman who had succeeded in commerce and risen to be an adviser to the King of England, all entirely by his own efforts, what he mostly felt was anger.

Giles followed his mother into the hall, and as she stopped and turned to him he said, 'Now, Mama, what was that about?'

'That woman,' Maud said, with suppressed fury. 'She has the audacity to offer a position to *my* butler? It shall not be! You will refuse, Stainton, and in terms that make clear such effrontery is not to be tolerated!'

'I have no idea what you're talking about,' Giles said impatiently. 'It's an offer that's very agreeable to me. I can't keep Moss at the cottage hospital for ever, and he can't come back here. This seems an excellent solution, and no doubt she's made the offer out of the kindness of her heart—'

'Rubbish! She has done it to humiliate me! I will not be provoked in this way.'

'I can't see how it has to do with you at all,' Giles said.

'Of course not. You never see anything, even when it's beneath your nose. You have always been selfish. You were a selfish, selfish boy, and you've grown up to be a selfish man. You abandoned your duty to your home and family to indulge your foolish hobby, and—'

Giles interrupted the tirade, knowing it could go on for minutes. 'You had better tell me exactly what your objection is to this arrangement.'

'I *have* told you. The Eddowes woman is doing it purely to spite *me*.'

'I fail to understand how it can bother you so much. In any case, if it settles Moss comfortably, I can't see that her motive matters.'

'It's the only thing that matters!' Maud's nostrils flared and her face quivered with the effort of containing her rage. 'I will not have it!' she hissed. 'You will write to her at once and refuse your permission. I insist!'

'*You* insist?'

It stopped her, and she reddened as she realised that she really had no power any more. A hollow feeling was in her stomach. She could not *make* Giles do anything. She lowered her voice and tried to speak more reasonably. 'You cannot allow this to happen, Giles. It will shame the family if our butler is reduced to working for one of the villagers. It will look as if we can't afford to take care of our own.'

'She's hardly a villager,' Giles said. He raised one eyebrow coolly. 'Hadn't you better tell me what this is really about?'

She was stymied. Giles did not know about his father's shameful activities, or how Miss Eddowes had become involved in clearing up the mess. And not for anything would she tell him.

She rallied. 'I am your mother! You should do as I say without asking the reason.'

'I'm afraid it doesn't work like that any more.' He looked at her levelly for a moment. 'There is one alternative.'

'Which is?' Maud asked rigidly.

'You can go to the dower house, and take Moss with you as *your* butler. He'll still be employed by the family, but the work will be much lighter.'

She couldn't speak for a moment. 'You are jesting,' she managed at last.

'Not at all. Why should you think it?'

'You know the dower house is not fit to live in.'

'It's not as bad as you think. Ahearn had a look at it back in the spring. Any work that needed doing would of course be carried out, and any alterations you wanted.'

'*I will not live in that house*,' she said, in a deadly hiss.

'Then Moss goes to Miss Eddowes,' Giles said, turning away, 'and I have done with this conversation.'

And to prevent any spying servant seeing her left standing, she had to walk away too, head up, and heels angrily rapping the marble floor.

CHAPTER SIXTEEN

Nina looked up as Giles came back in. He said nothing, but sat down and picked up a book, meeting no eyes. She longed to be able to ask him what was wrong, but with Kitty and Mr Cowling both in the room, she could not.

She had found this visit easier than previous ones. She had got used to being in the same room with Giles in London, and he seemed less tense around her. The danger was that they delighted so much in talking to each other they were sometimes too much at ease. Once or twice, at the table or in the drawing-room, she had found they were the only two talking.

The men were busy during the day with things that took them out of the house and, except when she went riding with Alice, she spent most of her time with Kitty. They sat in her room and sewed as they talked, or walked slowly about the gardens discussing her horticultural plans. 'I know my fortune was meant for restoring the estate, but I would like *something* for myself,' she said once, half apologetically.

'The garden is part of the estate,' Nina pointed out.

'It's not as if I'm extravagant in other ways,' Kitty went on, arguing with herself. 'I noticed your lovely necklace at dinner last night, and your evening gown. I thought how funny it was, that you now have more clothes and jewels than me.'

'Mr Cowling loves to buy me things – especially jewellery,'

Nina said. 'But remember our come-out, when I had to wear the same dress to every party?'

'I would have lent you some of my things,' Kitty said, 'but I was afraid my stepmother would object.'

'She would have.'

'But it didn't matter in the end,' Kitty said, 'because we both married well.'

Dinner that evening was dull, with the dowager projecting an icy atmosphere, Linda still sunk in gloom, and Sebastian for some reason silent and distracted. Richard, who could usually be relied upon to keep things lively, was dining out with friends, and finding Mr Cowling's eyes more often than usual fixed upon her, Nina remembered how he had asked her about the Sisyphus conversation and kept herself in check.

Alice brought up the subject of shearing and asked Giles a question, and since Mr Cowling's father had been a shepherd, a conversation arose which, if not lively, at least was enduring.

Then Giles mentioned the traditional supper that was given when shearing was finished, and Nina reminded him of the shearers' feast in *A Winter's Tale*.

Giles smiled and quoted Tusser:

'Wife, make us a dinner, spare flesh neither corn,
Make wafers and cakes, for our sheep must be shorn.
At sheep-shearing neighbours none other thing crave . . .'

Nina joined in and they said the last line in unison:

'But good cheer and welcome, like neighbours to have.'

Alice was delighted with it, and wanted to know where the verse came from, but the dowager looked sour, and Nina found Mr Cowling staring at her, and realised she'd lapsed again into too much ease.

That night he came to her bed for the first time since the Levens' party. She did her best to welcome him, but there was only a grim struggle as he attempted again and again to engage with her body. There seemed little pleasure in it for him, and she couldn't help remembering how her aunt had told her that gentlemen enjoyed the act and liked to do it often.

In pity for him, she whispered, 'How can I help you?'

She really wanted to help, but it seemed only to put him off. He stopped what he was doing abruptly and rolled away from her, lying on his back with one arm over his face.

'I'm sorry,' she whispered. 'Please, won't you . . . ?' She hardly knew how to phrase it.

He said, 'Oh, Nina!' almost in exasperation, as if she were being slow to understand something. Then he got up, put on his dressing-gown, and went away, leaving her sad.

Given the length of Moss's service with the family, Giles felt he should go and see him in person to make sure he was happy about his new position.

Moss was almost overcome by the honour. He stammered, 'Oh, my lord – too kind – I never presumed—'

'No, you never did,' Giles said heartily, 'and I want to thank you for your long and faithful service to the Staintons and to Ashmore Castle. Your going will be the end of an era.'

He meant to be kind, but it overset Moss, who had to turn his head away and drag out a handkerchief to wipe his eyes. 'It's been an honour and a privilege, my lord. Your late father, her ladyship – oh, my!'

'Cheer up, old fellow,' Giles said awkwardly. 'It's not as if we shall be far away, and you are always welcome to visit.'

'Thank you, my lord. I shall miss everyone very much. If I might . . .' He hesitated.

'Spit it out, man.'

'Might I enquire who is to be my replacement? I heard a

rumour, my lord. Being naturally interested, I did feel, if you'll forgive me, my lord, that . . . well, I have known him for some years and do not feel he has the necessary qualities for the position. In fact—'

'You're speaking of Hook,' Giles divined. 'He is temporarily covering your duties.'

'Temporarily!' Moss exclaimed in relief.

'He was the best placed to do it, in the emergency, but I have my doubts about his suitability in the long term. I suppose I'll have to give him a fair trial, but if it doesn't work out, I'll remove him without regret. We could never replace *you*,' he added, with a smile, 'but we'll have to do our best.'

'Oh, my lord!' Another application of the handkerchief.

'I must be going,' Giles said hastily. 'The carriage will be coming from the Castle in an hour or two to take you to Weldon House. No, no, don't thank me – Miss Eddowes doesn't keep a carriage, I understand, and we couldn't expect you to walk. Now, I just want to make sure you have everything you need.'

'You are too kind, my lord. My valise and a box of my possessions have been brought to me here, but my stamp album was not in either receptacle. I dare say it has been put somewhere for safekeeping, but I should be very glad if you could make sure it is sent down to me. It is bound in red leather – rather old and shabby, but the collection inside is precious to me.'

'I'll look into it,' Giles said. 'And now, goodbye, old fellow, and thank you for all your service.' He shook Moss's hand, and neatly transferred an honorarium to him in the same movement.

Moss's eyes brimmed again, but whether it was from love or the size of the tip, Giles couldn't be sure.

'I've looked everywhere I can think of, my lord. And I've asked, but nobody's seen it,' said Rose.

'You know what you're looking for?' Giles asked.

'Oh, yes, my lord. I've seen Mr Moss poring over it some-times of an evening, in his room. A sort of book with red covers.' She paused, and added, 'I know it wasn't in the box of his things when it was taken over to him because I packed it myself.'

'So it was you who removed his things from his room?' Giles asked, tapping a pencil against the edge of the table impatiently.

'No, my lord, that was Mr Hook. You see, my lord, it was this way – I went looking for the mending basket, because the mending was loose and tumbled all over the place, and Mr Hook said he'd used it to put Mr Moss's things in. So I said I had to have it back, and I found a grocer's box in the kitchen no-one wanted and I put all Mr Moss's things very careful out of the basket into the box.'

'And where was it then?'

'The box, my lord, or the basket?'

'Either. Both.'

'Mr Moss's valise and the basket was in one of the cupboards in the ironing-room, my lord, and when I'd moved the stuff from the basket to the box I put it back in the cupboard, and there it stayed, my lord, as far as I know, until it was taken over to Mr Moss.'

'So it was Hook who initially cleared Mr Moss's room?'

'He supervised, my lord. William and Eddie did the actual packing.'

'We'd better have them all in,' Giles said. He was longing to get out and about his work, instead of being trapped here in the library by this trivial and yet important matter. The minutiae of an earl's life were as tiresome as the larger prob-lems.

They came. William looked miserable, Eddie scared, and Hook his usual cocksure, smirking self. Giles was beginning actively to dislike him.

'No, sir, my lord, I never see no red book,' Eddie said, almost tearful with fear, as Giles got to the bottom of things with patient – impatient – questioning. 'Mr Hook give me four books to put in the basket, but they didn't none of 'em have red covers, my lord.'

William spoke up for the boy. 'He's right, my lord. I was watching.'

Giles looked enquiringly at Hook. 'They were four printed books,' he agreed. 'I just glanced at them. Mr Moss's encyclopaedia was one, and a poetry book, his Bible and a book about kings and queens.'

'And where did you get them from?'

'They were on the shelf by the bed, my lord. I never saw Mr Moss's stamp album at all when we were packing up, and it's certainly not in the room now. If I may suggest, my lord, perhaps Mr Moss took it with him to London, and it was left there after his unfortunate accident. He might not remember that he took it there.'

'It's a possibility, I suppose,' Giles said, in dissatisfied tones. The pencil tapped faster.

'Or, I'm sorry to say, anyone could have taken it,' Hook went on. 'There are no locks on the butler's room door, or the bedroom beyond it. I've long thought those rooms ought to have a lock. May I suggest that it's done, my lord?'

'Are you saying someone stole the stamp collection?' Giles snapped. This was a most unwelcome suggestion.

'Only saying it's possible, my lord. All sorts of people come and go down Piccadilly – tradesmen and so on.'

If an outsider stole it, they would never see it again, Giles thought. But if one of the household stole it, that would present other, and much worse, problems.

'You'd better go and have another look for it,' Giles said. 'Search everywhere.'

They departed meekly. Outside, Rose waited until William and Eddie had gone, then said, in a low, angry tone to Hook,

'You got no right to go saying Mr Moss took it to London and forgot. It was his heart, not his head. He's not gone dippy. In any case, I spoke to Dory and she said she checked everything before they came home, to make sure nobody left anything.'

Hook shrugged. 'Just didn't want to suggest we've got a thief in our midst.'

Rose looked at him bitterly. Once a suspicion of that sort got about, life became a misery below stairs. 'We never had stealing when Mr Moss was in charge.'

'Are you accusing me of something?' Hook said sharply.

'I'm just saying.' She continued to glare at him. 'Poor Mr Moss – losing it'll break his heart.'

'Thought it was already busted,' Hook grinned.

'Don't talk so shocking, James Hook. Don't you have any shame?'

He caught her wrist in one hard, strong hand, his mask of geniality gone. 'You don't talk to me like that, Rosy Posy. Not ever. You just remember I'm in charge now.'

'Not for long,' she said. He started twisting. 'Let me go, you're hurting me!'

'Just as long as you remember, I can hurt you a lot more'n this if I want.'

He released her and she hurried away.

Afton, coming up the stairs, saw her face as she passed, saw her rubbing her wrist, saw Hook's grin as he watched her go, put two and two together, and had to restrain himself from knocking Hook down right there and then. He vowed to get to the bottom of it, and to see that Hook got what he deserved.

The Cowlings had only just got home. They were still standing in the hall, Cowling receiving a bulletin from Mrs Deering, Trump dashing off to inspect every inch of his old kingdom, Nina reading a note from Lady Clemmie – she had sent to say she would be away for several weeks visiting family friends

299

in Scarborough – when Bobby Wharfedale appeared at the front door, which was still standing open for Deering to bring in the luggage.

'Nina! I'm so glad you're home! I can't tell you how much I've missed you!' she cried.

'We've only this instant arrived,' Nina said. 'I've just taken off my hat.'

'I know. I didn't want to waste a moment of seeing you.' She spared a smile for Mr Cowling, who quickly resumed his hat for the purpose of lifting it to her.

'But how did you know we were back?' Nina asked.

Bobby grinned. 'Couldn't be easier. You sent a telegram to warn Mrs Deering – how do you do, Mrs Deering? You're looking well. She told your housemaid, Polly, who is own sister to our housemaid Willa, and she told my maid Sutton, who told me. The most direct line of communication.'

Nina laughed. 'You're right! If the Government had relied on servants instead of the telegraph, they'd have had news of the victory at Waterloo hours earlier.'

Cowling shook his head at the nonsense. 'They do pretty well as it is with the Rothschilds,' he said. 'How are you, Lady Wharfedale? What news from Welland Hall?'

'That's what I've come about. My darling papa has taken a house on the Isle of Wight for three months and we are all going – Aubrey and I and the children and my brothers and sisters – and it's a huge house with lots of room, so he's said we can bring friends, and I want *you* to come.' Her look embraced them both. 'Now, please, you must come – you can't think how perfect it will be. The weather is always wonderful on the island, and there's sea-bathing, and horses, and Kipper's going to borrow a yacht from a friend. I must, *must* have you, darling Nina! Only think how Trump will love it after all those weeks in dusty London!'

'I've too much business to attend to, thank you for asking,' Mr Cowling said. 'But you should go, Nina.'

She looked at him doubtfully. 'Go without you?'

'I shan't be here much anyway, for weeks to come. I've to visit all my factories after being away so long. Things have piled up. I'll be in Northampton, Leicester – I want to see how the jam factory's doing as well.'

'But you'll want me to be here when you come back.'

'I shall only drop in for a change of clothes, then be off again. I'd be no company.'

Since that night at Ashmore, she felt he had been withdrawn, quiet. Perhaps others wouldn't have noticed it – in company he still talked with his usual forcefulness – but she saw he smiled less, and a light seemed to have gone from his eyes. She couldn't bear to think he was unhappy. She was fond of him, for his honest, straightforward character, and for his kindness to her, and she felt obscurely that she had let him down. 'I don't like to think of you being alone,' she said.

He smiled, a tender smile, but with a shadow of sadness in it. 'Bless you, I've been on my own for years, it doesn't bother me. And I shall have Decius with me. And Mrs Deering when I'm here, though that won't be often. You go and have fun. It'll do you good, all that fresh sea air. London's made you pale. Stay as long as you like.' He turned to Bobby for confirmation. 'You'll be staying all summer, you say?'

'We certainly mean to – and Nina's welcome for as long as she wants. And if you find you have a few days to spare, *please* do come too. We'd love to see you. Now, Nina,' she turned to her, 'you see, you must come. For Trump's sake, if not your own.'

'Very well,' Nina said. 'I'd love to. You'll have to tell me what to pack. When do you leave? How do you travel?'

Bobby had plenty to say, and walked upstairs with Nina, chatting volubly. Nina felt a stirring of excitement – she loved the sea, though she had hardly ever been to the seaside, and a summer with Bobby and her brothers and sisters would be

301

wonderful. But she still worried about Mr Cowling. He couldn't have been kinder in urging her to go – but his kindness now made her feel sad.

There was no particular reason why Rose should pass Hundon's on her way to the village – it was rather out of the way, in fact – but on a fine summer day a person bent on exercise might walk in one direction as well as another, mightn't they? And as she passed the entrance to the yard, it was natural for her to take a step in so as to see the house.

She was rewarded by the sight of Michael Woodrow sitting on a kitchen chair, back to the wall of the house, with a mug in his hand, evidently taking a rest from his labours. It was what she had hoped for, but she was all the same suddenly tongue-tied, and stood holding her basket and staring, like a foolish girl.

But he smiled his warm, easy smile at the sight of her and said, 'Well, this is a treat! Martha,' he called over his shoulder, 'here's Miss Hawkins from up the Castle.'

His sister's face appeared at the open kitchen window and disappeared again.

'I just called, as I was passing, to see how you're settling in,' Rose said.

He looked at the basket. 'On your way to the village? Chores to do?'

'No, it's my afternoon off. I thought I'd have a look in Poinings.'

'Oh, yes – the haberdasher's,' said Woodrow. 'I've been here long enough to know everybody goes into Poinings at least once a week.'

'Well, they do seem to have a lot of things one naturally wants,' said Rose.

Martha came out of the house carrying a kitchen chair in one hand and a mug in the other. She put the chair down next to her brother's, thrust the mug at Rose without ever looking at her, and went back inside.

'Tea,' said Woodrow. 'Won't you sit a minute and talk to me?'

Rose sat. 'Your sister doesn't talk much, does she?' she said, a little awkwardly, afraid she had offended in some way.

'No, she never has.'

'Oh?' said Rose. She sipped her tea.

After a moment, he went on. 'She's a lot older than me – my half-sister. She was ten when I was born. Her mother – my father's first wife – died in an accident. Something happened to Martha at the same time, and she went a bit . . . strange. My dad never would tell, and Martha never talked about it, ever. Got upset if it was brought up. So I don't know to this day what happened. But she's all right, really, just not sociable. He's gone now, too, my dad; and my mum, so there's just the two of us.'

'It's good that she's got you to care for her.'

'I look after her, and she looks after me. She's a good housekeeper – none better. She just doesn't warm much to strangers. So don't take it funny if she doesn't speak to you. It doesn't mean anything.'

Rose didn't know what to say to all this; though she felt a thrill of warmth that he would tell her so much so soon. Well, perhaps he was just a talker. Time would tell. In the end, she said, 'How are you liking the bull? Mr Richard raves about it.'

Woodrow's face lit. 'He's a great feller. Would you like to have a look at him? He's in the bull-box just now.'

He obviously meant it as a treat, so she said yes, set aside her mug (it was no hardship, as Martha hadn't put any sugar in it and she liked her tea sweet) and followed him across the yard.

'He's usually out with the cows,' Woodrow explained. 'It helps keep a bull good-tempered, so I've always believed, if he runs with his wives – more natural-like. But he's waiting in for a visitor, a cow from The Bottoms that's bulling just now. Here he is – handsome fellow, isn't he?'

The bull was looking over the high door of the box, between the splayed bars that stopped him getting his horns out. He snorted loudly as the two humans approached, and Rose saw the wet nose poked up and snuffling eagerly. Woodrow spoke crooningly to him and reached in a hand to scratch his poll. 'You can't see him properly from there,' he said to Rose, and courteously pulled across a box for her to stand on. She got up cautiously. 'Go on, you can stroke him if you want. He likes that.'

The bull was an enormous, hot presence, something that was more emphatically itself than seemed quite polite. Its roan coat gleamed in the half-dark; a glint of light caught on the brass ring through its nose. But she didn't see that it could hurt her from behind the bars, so she put a hand in cautiously and scratched between the horns as she had seen Woodrow do. The bull stood quite still, moved its head a little closer to her fingers, and made a soft grunting noise. 'What's his name?' she asked.

'Roderick,' he said. 'Roddy for short. There, he likes you. I knew he would. He's got taste, has this old feller.'

Rose blushed a little at the compliment. Then the bull snorted explosively and she whipped her hand away in alarm.

'Don't be scared,' Woodrow said, smiling. 'He sneezes when he's happy.'

Rose inspected the ropy mucus on her fingers and wished he had a different way of expressing it. Then he stuck his head up and gave a prolonged bellow.

'That must be The Bottoms' cow coming – he smells her,' Woodrow said, looking round.

'I'd better be off,' Rose said, not wanting to get in the way of such earthy activities.

'But it was nice of you to call,' Woodrow said, seeming disappointed. 'You will come again, won't you?'

'Well, I don't know,' Rose began. The bull bellowed, and an answering noise came from the cow just entering the yard, followed by a small scruffy boy urging her along with a stick.

'Please do,' Woodrow urged. 'We'd love to see you.' He was smiling as if he really meant it. No man had ever shown her that sort of attention. She had been a plain and awkward girl, and since she had early got out of the habit of looking in the mirror, she assumed she had grown up into a plain and awkward woman, and had developed a spiky exterior, like a sea-urchin, for defence. He was smiling at her, and she didn't want to be ungracious, but didn't quite know how not to be.

'I don't know,' she said gruffly, from her shyness. 'We'll have to see.'

The boy was grinning cheekily at her from the far end of the cow as though reading more into the situation than she could bear, and she scowled at him and snapped, 'Now then, Sid Parks, who are you looking at? You mind your manners! I've got to go,' she concluded to Woodrow.

But far from understanding that she had to depart as casually as if she had found herself there by accident, he insisted on walking her to the yard entrance and seeing her off with full formality.

Rose walked away briskly, head up so that the breeze could cool her cheeks. Would she call again? One part of her thought she'd like to, and not for the silent sister's sake, either; but another part dreaded making a fool of herself. Or – even worse – someone else making a fool of her.

The whole household was involved in searching for Moss's stamp collection, and theories and suspicions flew around like disturbed bats. Once, Mrs Webster would have spoken to Moss about any awkward situation that arose, but she wouldn't confide in Hook. Crooks had gone for a short visit to Henley with Mr Sebastian, and the only other senior servant on hand was Afton. She didn't know him very well, but something about him invited confidence, and finding herself alone with him in the servants' hall late one evening, she obeyed the tacit invitation of his glance and walked over to sit beside him. He was at the long table, reading.

'Interesting book, Mr Afton?' she asked, to open the channels.

'Very,' said Afton, closing it hospitably. '*The Riddle of the Sands*, it's called. About a man who goes on a yachting holiday in the Baltic, and discovers the Germans are up to something suspicious.'

'Oh,' said Mrs Webster. 'Sort of an adventure story, then?'

'That's right. A bit like Rider Haggard. My previous master was very fond of Rider Haggard. Lots of African adventures in his books.'

'Looks new,' Mrs Webster noted.

'His lordship bought it last year when it came out. We got talking about books one day when I was shaving him, and he suggested I borrow it – thought I'd enjoy it.'

Mrs Webster raised an eyebrow. 'Nice to have that sort of relationship with your master.'

'He's an unusual gentleman,' Afton observed. 'Not a bit high and mighty, not with me, anyway. I wouldn't have been comfortable serving someone who treated me like a member of another species. I've shaved gentlemen who look at you like you're some sort of performing monkey, only not so interesting.'

'You wouldn't have liked his old lordship, then,' Mrs Webster said. 'Very high in the instep, the old lord.'

'You're a bit unusual yourself, Mrs Webster, if I might say. I've watched you, and there's a great deal you don't allow to be seen on the surface.'

'You could say the same of any housekeeper in a great house,' she said, a bit stiffly.

He was not rebuffed. 'For instance, you're worried at the

moment, and I suspect it's about this stamp collection of Mr Moss's.'

'You don't need to be Sherlock Holmes to work that out,' said Mrs Webster.

He smiled. 'You're a reader yourself.'

'I won't deceive you, Mr Afton, books don't often come in my way. I've always felt I could be a reader, and I was fond of a yarn when I was younger, but there's always so much to do, and by the time I've finished my day it's all I can do to fall into bed and sleep. But, of course, I've heard people talk about Sherlock Holmes stories. Very popular, from what I hear, so I suppose they must be good.'

'There is a collection of them in the library here. A book called *The Adventures of Sherlock Holmes*,' Afton said. 'I'm sure his lordship would have no objection to your borrowing it.'

The idea shocked her slightly, but when she thought about it, there was no reason why it should. Books were not for servants, that was what one grew up thinking, and of course some of the really old musty tomes were too precious to be touched, but the newer ones, maybe . . . with permission . . . if one was a trusted senior servant . . . Not, of course, that she would ever ask . . . 'Perhaps one day,' she said dismissively.

'What do *you* think happened to the stamp album?' Afton asked bluntly.

It was as if he had softened her up to get her to blurt out her true thoughts. But she was too canny for that. 'It's not in any of the public spaces, that I do know,' she said.

'The next stage would be to search the bedrooms, I suppose,' Afton suggested.

'And I wouldn't want to have to do that,' she concluded. 'I can't believe anyone carelessly threw it away – everyone must have seen Mr Moss tinkering with it at some time or another. They'd know it wasn't rubbish.'

'Which leaves deliberate theft,' Afton said.

She looked at him sharply. 'All the traders and delivery boys who come in here are well-known and trusted.'

'But the outer doors are not locked during the daytime,' he said, 'so anyone could walk in. Or out.'

She met his eyes for a long, thoughtful moment. 'It's the uncertainty that's the worst part. Suspecting innocent people. Makes for a bad atmosphere. We all live cheek by jowl here, and you have to trust each other.'

'I'll see if I can find anything out for you,' Afton said. 'I've time on my hands – his lordship isn't a demanding master.'

She gave a tight smile. 'Follow the clues, like Sherlock Holmes?'

'Or just follow my suspicions,' said Afton.

'Well, don't tell me your suspicions until you've proof,' she said sharply. 'I have to stay even-handed.'

She got up and walked away. An ally was a useful thing to have, especially for one in her position. For a moment her cautious nature made her wonder what he'd want in return, but as she lit her candle and trudged up the back stairs, she considered that perhaps he just felt the same, and thought she would be useful to have on his side. An alliance offensive and defensive, as the history books said.

Giles had stayed longer than he intended on the hill, helping with the shearing. He didn't take the shears himself, though the men, grinning, sometimes urged him to try his hand. But he helped with moving the hurdles and funnelling the ewes towards the shearers, and he knew he gained respect from the men for 'getting his hands dirty'. His father, who would never have dreamed of helping in that way, had won exactly the same respect from the men by holding himself aloof. It was a mystery.

The shearing process fascinated him, seeing the trim shape of the ewe appearing from inside the thick muffling of the fleece. Released, she would bound off with frantic energy to the far end of the barn to join the other naked ladies. They looked like a completely different species.

The noise was deafening. The half-grown lambs were all waiting outside, yelling 'in fifty different sharps and flats' for their mothers, while the ewes shouted back in desperate bellows. When all were done, there would be the moment, which he loved to see, when the barn doors were opened, the ewes raced out and the lambs rushed forward, and flood met flood, like two mighty rivers converging in boiling chaos. Then, in an astonishingly short time, the families paired off, all agitation ceased, and mothers and young trotted away together in ovine tranquillity, as if nothing had happened. How they found each other so quickly in such a turmoil was one of the miracles of nature.

When he rode back into the stable yard, and handed over Vipsania to Archer, he noticed the carriage waiting to be pushed into the coachhouse. 'Has somebody been out?' he asked.

'No, my lord – it's Lord Leake, not long arrived. Telegram came just after you left, asking for his train to be met.'

Giles hurried in by the side door. Encountering a maid crossing the hall he said, 'I must wash and change quickly. Tell Afton to come up with hot water immediately.'

Afton, as he helped him change, had no more information, but that Lord Leake had appeared in good spirits, not as if there was any emergency going on.

As Giles was about to leave, he said, 'You won't need me again until the dressing-bell, will you, my lord?'

'No,' Giles said, offhand, but paused in the doorway to look back. 'Something wrong? You've never asked me that before.'

'Nothing wrong, my lord – just a little scheme I have in hand.'

Giles examined him. 'You look mischievous. You had better not tell me anything about it.'

'I wasn't planning to, my lord,' Afton said, with a disarming grin.

When Giles entered the drawing-room Uncle Stuffy was standing before the fireplace, chatting pleasantly – about court matters, from the few words he overheard. His mother and Linda were on one sofa, Kitty, Alice and Richard on another. The dogs rushed up to Giles with ecstatic greetings, and Stuffy looked across and said, 'Ah, Giles! There you are.'

'Uncle. I wasn't expecting you. Nothing wrong, I hope?'

'No, no – why should there be? Thought I'd pop down and escort m'sister – she doesn't like travelling alone.'

'Escort her?'

'Back to Town,' the dowager elucidated. 'To collect Rachel.'

'And thence to Scotland. It's time to be heading north. The trout, the trout are calling!' he added whimsically. 'I hope you'll all be coming to Kincraig this summer? It will make a nice family reunion. Long time since we were all together.'

'I shan't be travelling in August,' Giles pointed out patiently, and since his mother and uncle didn't seem to get the reference, he went on, 'My wife is expecting our child in August. Had you forgotten?'

'Oh. Ah. Yes,' Stuffy said, and gave Kitty a shy smile. 'Forgive an old bachelor – not in the habit. Sort of thing that slips one's mind.'

'So has London finally lost its allure?' Giles asked.

'There are no more important engagements,' Maud answered impatiently, 'and it is time Rachel rested. It has been a draining Season for her.'

'Yes, but I was actually asking my uncle,' Giles said.

'Me? Oh – I take your meaning. You are making a jest about Miss Lombardi, I suppose?' He chuckled. 'Yes, the loveliest creature I've beheld in – well, as many years as I can remember. She's gone home, back to Italy.'

310

'Nobody told me,' Giles objected.

'I didn't know you needed tellin',' said Stuffy. 'Bound to go sooner or later, and that couple – your friends, Giles, Mr and Mrs Portwine – were goin' in that direction and undertook to escort her. Couldn't have a fragrant young lady like her travelling all that way alone. They were takin' the train to Venice and said it was no hardship to travel a few miles further and deliver her to the door. Had half a mind to go myself,' he added, 'and see what condition my house is in, but it's too late in the summer for Venice. Can't think what the Portwines will do there, unless they stay on one of the islands. However, London, as you so succinctly put it, has lost its allure, so it's northward-ho for me. Now, Giles, if you ain't comin' for the trout, you'll be down for the grouse, surely?'

'My wife, Uncle? The baby?' he reminded him patiently.

'Of course, of course. Head like a sieve. Well, later on, perhaps, when you're up to the journey,' Stuffy said, with a bow to Kitty. 'Always welcome, you know that. Open house at Kincraig.'

Alice took the opportunity to ask about the cousins and, since Linda didn't seem to have anything to say, about Arabella and Arthur. Giles let the conversation drift away from him, and contemplated Giulia's leaving of London without a word to him, and whether it meant she was still angry with him, and whether, if she was, that was a good thing, or a bad thing. At least, he thought, Uncle Stuffy wasn't exhibiting any unusual signs of grief over her departure, so his fancy had evidently been passing, as fleeting as it had been odd.

He was roused from his thoughts by the realisation that Kitty was looking at him, and he turned his head towards her and raised an enquiring eyebrow. But she looked away, her lips tight and her cheeks pink, and his heart sank a little as he decided he could guess the subject of her thoughts. A good thing, then, that Giulia had gone, if even the mention of her name could upset Kitty. But he felt a little wounded all the same that there had been no goodbye. Theirs had been a long friendship.

CHAPTER SEVENTEEN

Afton had built up a useful reputation below stairs for being chatty and approachable, so when he drifted up beside a servant and asked in general terms about their colleagues, no-one saw anything to suspect, or any reason not to gossip – which was what they liked doing anyway.

The missing stamp album was much talked about, and while most held that Mr Moss had been getting forgetful of late and had probably mislaid it somewhere, the minority view was that if it was in the house it would have been discovered, so Somebody must have taken it. As to who Somebody might be, no-one wanted to say, but there were sidelong looks, and very oblique hints that it would not surprise if a person who was generally disliked turned out to be involved somehow.

As he had already observed, Hook was shunned as bad-tempered and feared as a vindictive bully. He learned that there had recently been disapproval, though no surprise, that Hook had had a lock put on the door to the bedroom behind the butler's room, which he had taken over as his own. Servants were slow to embrace change, and it was obscurely felt that the butler's room and bedroom were still Mr Moss's, and that Hook was taking liberties in his absence. Also, if Mr Moss had not needed a lock, why should he?

Why, indeed, was Afton's unspoken reaction. If he was a thief, he would have to have somewhere to cache things until he could dispose of them, somewhere he could be sure they would not be discovered. And a thief, in Afton's experience, did not stop at one thing. Once they had got away with it, they would do it again.

He was interested to discover that, in Mr Moss's later days, Hook had suggested a thorough inventory of the household silver. Everything had been taken out, catalogued, cleaned and replaced, with the frequently used pieces to the front of the cupboards and the antique, fragile and seldom-seen to the back. William was eloquent on the subject, since he had had to do a lot of the cleaning. Cleaning silver was dirty work, and Hook had kept his hands clean doing the cataloguing, a nice, easy job.

'I'd have thought Mr Moss would be the one to write everything down,' Afton said innocently.

No, he had been in and out, doing other things, and when he was there he had just sat and watched, half asleep most of the time as far as William could see. Hook had bossed the show – which, as he'd only been footman James in those days, and technically *under* William, was a flaming liberty. But that was him all over.

Yes, Afton thought, that was a very good way to cover your tracks. If an obscure piece of silver went missing, who would ever know? And if a question *was* ever asked – there was the inventory to prove it had never existed, or must have gone missing back in historical times. Nothing to do with anyone currently in the house.

If silver had been stolen (and why else would Hook have initiated the inventory? Not for the love of extra work), it could not have been disposed of locally. But there had been the recent stay in London: Hook had been one of those taken up to Pelham House. The stamp album, however, had not been missing at that time. Either it was still here, or had been disposed of locally.

Thus far Afton's Sherlockian logic took him. But he had

no proof against Hook. He wanted it to be him; but being a shifty, unpleasant bully didn't necessarily make you a thief.

And talking of bullying, where did Rose come into it? Afton had witnessed the attack on Rose – the twisted wrist and the threatening words. Was that a case of accomplices falling out? Had she been demanding a better share of the dibs than he was willing to part with? Had he been reminding her that she was as guilty as him?

There was something enigmatic about Rose – he couldn't quite make her out. She had been at the Castle a long time, and was therefore trusted, presumably with good reason. But a person could change: for instance, passing time might bring the realisation that one had nothing saved against old age, a frightening prospect. The chance to lay something by, perhaps by the theft of something no-one would ever miss, might be too much temptation.

Of course, Moss's stamp collection didn't fall into that category – but perhaps that was what the quarrel had been about. Had Rose objected that it was a theft too far, and had Hook reminded her she was all in and had better not think about peaching?

From talking to the other servants, he gathered that Rose had always held herself somewhat aloof, and while she was not disliked, she was not regarded with any great warmth, either. 'Oh, she's all right. She's been here for ever,' was the usual comment about her, and 'She's very strict. You got to do the job properly.'

He hoped she wasn't involved – he rather liked the look of her – but her long service bestowed a lack of scrutiny on her that would be useful in smuggling stolen goods out of the house. The other day, for instance, she had gone out on her afternoon off, carrying a covered basket, without telling anyone where she was going.

Mrs Webster was absolutely right: trust was essential in a

315

big house. You couldn't watch everyone all the time; and suspicion would destroy the lives of all.

So where did Hook go on his days off? From William he learned only that Hook had been accustomed to frequent the Dog and Gun, but that he hadn't been going there lately.

He had to take his investigation slowly: too many questions all at once would provoke suspicion – 'What you want to know that for?' He must just make himself available for comfortable chat, gossip, and the opening of hearts. He wished he could take a peek into Hook's room, but that was not possible.

And he wished he knew about Rose.

Rachel curled in the corner of the first-class carriage pretending to look out of the window in order to avoid having to talk to her mother, who sat opposite her, grimly scrutinising her.

Uncle Stuffy, who had provided them generously at King's Cross with sweets, chocolates and reading matter, had lowered the ear-flaps on his curious travelling-cap against draughts from the window, and had gone to sleep. He was not a great one for reading, conversing or admiring the scenery on journeys. He took train travel very seriously, and as well as the travelling-cap (and, despite the heat, a rug over his knees), he had beside him on the seat a leather-covered case containing everything to counter what Fate might throw at him. Rachel knew it featured a Johnson & Johnson first-aid box, the contents covering everything from war wounds to snake bites. In the lid of the box, in special compartments, were a large silver whistle, a compass, a flask of brandy, and something that looked like a stick of dynamite, which Rachel had worked out must be a flare for summoning help. She had wiled away the first miles of the journey by imagining what else one might need. A pistol, perhaps, in case the train was held up by robbers? A rope ladder, in case it crashed down a ravine? An axe for chopping their way out of the wreckage? She had to stop thinking about accidents, though, because train smashes were not infrequent and everybody knew that thinking about bad things could make them happen.

She thought instead of her Season, the fun she had had, the dancing, the parties, the glorious clothes and, most of all, the young men who had pursued, danced and flirted with her. She had begun the year expecting to fall in love and was half glad and half sorry that she hadn't. Of course, it was always a point of pride to get engaged in your first Season, and she knew her mother was disappointed and saw it as a failure; but lots of girls *didn't*, and it wasn't as though she was *old*. A second Season might not be so grand – she couldn't expect the same sort of money to be spent on it – but she saw no reason why it shouldn't be as much fun.

Or possibly even more because, in fact, it seemed to her that getting engaged meant all the fun must cease: no more dancing and flirting and playing off one suitor against another. She supposed if you were in love, that sort of made up for it, and you didn't mind giving up the fun for married bliss. But she liked all the boys pretty much as well as each other. One or two she *didn't* like, such as the Prince of Usingen with his coffin breath, and Mr Archbold with his sly, pinching hands. But she'd always had plenty of choice. It was a shame that Frittie Landau hadn't made an offer for her – she wasn't in love with him, but he was fun, and she felt they would have got on well together. She *had* had two offers, just enough to salve pride, though she was glad that her mother had refused them, because she hadn't cared for either.

So now they were on their way to Scotland. The Season had been very tiring, and it would be nice to be out of the public eye for a while, to see the cousins, to relax for a few weeks. She was determined not to think about what would happen after that. She was going to enjoy Kincraig. She was going to let down her hair and play games. She was going to pretend to be Alice, and romp.

They arrived at last at Kincraig in the long blue Scottish dusk, which made the lights in the house glow yellow as butter. The cousins must already have been installed, for a crowd spilled out from the main door. Her eyes jumped straight to her cousin Angus, and her heart skipped a beat. He was so very handsome, and he looked so tall and strong and very much in his rightful place, as though he had grown out of the earth and the rock.

He smiled and came straight to her, and took both her hands in his. She felt another pleasant shock – though they were cousins, it seemed a very particular action on his part, and under the gaze of so many eyes.

He had a sprig of heather tucked between his buttons, and in lieu of greeting she said, 'What a colour it is! I've never seen any like that.'

'It's Bird Heath,' he said. 'I picked it for you. It flowers for the longest of all.'

'I didn't know there were different kinds of heather,' she said.

'There are more kinds of heather than you can imagine,' he said. 'I'll take you out one day and show you. Up into the hills.'

'Oh, I should like that,' she said.

That was all there was time for. Arabella and Arthur came running to her with glad cries and outstretched arms and he yielded to them good-naturedly. She petted them absently, passed them on to their mother, and was engulfed by other cousins. The tide of welcome swept her into the house.

Angus kept his promise, and a day or two later he organised a picnic outing up into the hills. Twelve of them went, and they took four ponies, to carry baskets and rugs, and for the

318

less robust to ride on the steep parts. Angus blatantly favoured her and let her ride more often than anyone else. As he led the pony, picking out the smoothest path, she stared at him in a pleasant dream. He had worn the kilt for the expedition. She was charmed by the way the pleats swung with the swing of his walk, then caught herself back, blushing. One was not supposed to think about a man's . . . haunches. She lowered her gaze, and found herself admiring the flex and stretch of his strong legs as they propelled him up the slope – and that was hardly better.

They picnicked on a flat grassy patch above a crag, with a long view of the rose-purple moors, and the distance of indigo hills. There were bees in the thyme flowers, and an eagle rocked on the wind far above them. They ate oat bannocks and cheese and cold game pie – plain fare, but good out of doors when you were hungry – and there was cousinly chat and laughter. Angus was full of jokes and foolery and she forgot her earlier self-consciousness and was comfortable with him. His hair, freed for once from the tyranny of oil, was blown about his face endearingly by the breeze. She told him it was like the ruff on a collie, and he grabbed her bare feet – she had kicked off her shoes – and tickled them until she begged for mercy.

In the evening there was dancing, and Angus picked her first – but that was expected since she was the highest-ranking girl present . . . if such things counted. He was in high spirits, and danced with energy. He was so different from the drawing-room boys of the London Season: so vital, so strong. For a big man he was astonishingly light on his feet – in the leaps, he seemed to hover an instant above the earth. When he concentrated on the steps, his eyelids drooped a little, and his flushed face seemed almost unworldly, like an angel working out celestial sums. But then, when he swung her hands-across, his grin was pure exuberance, and she answered it with an unshadowed beam of her own.

At one point, she noticed his father watching them with a tight mouth and drawn brows, and wondered falteringly if she had done something wrong. But then the dance whirled her away. When next they passed that corner, she saw him talking to her mother, and there seemed something slightly ominous about it – though anything her mother did could always be construed as ominous.

At supper she was part of a boisterous group and didn't see Angus, then spotted him on the other side of the room attending to guests, as was proper. And after supper, he danced with other girls, and that was proper too. She did not lack for partners. She was back in her happy, flirtatious London ways – Lady Rachel Tallant, the most popular girl in the room, dancing every dance.

At breakfast next day, there was no sign of Angus, and in between coping with the clinging attentions of Arabella and Arthur, she asked his youngest brother Mannox where he was.

'He's gone out with the guns,' Mannox said, wolfing toast and marmalade. 'He didn't want to, but Fa made him. There's a big dinner tonight, lot of guests coming, so they're shooting for the pot. Uncle Stuffy's going to take Fritz and Ben and me out later after fish.' Those were his other brothers.

'Oh,' said Rachel. 'What guests are coming?'

'Don't know. I think it's the Alvie Castle lot, and some others,' he said indifferently.

After breakfast, when she was going upstairs to wash her hands, her mother called her aside, and escorted her into one of the small parlours, saying she wanted to talk to her. Her heart sank: being 'talked to' nearly always meant something unpleasant.

Her apprehension was not improved by the multitude of stuffed heads mounted on the walls: sad glassy eyes looking down on her in mute reproach from the background of an oppressive tartan wallpaper. There was a tartan carpet, too – a decorative scheme made popular by Queen Victoria. It was a gloomy room, invested with the stillness of premature death: it felt as though nothing could ever happen there. Even the dust seemed to hang suspended instead of gently falling onto the dark, varnished surfaces. The only thing alive was some blooming heather on the windowsill, and even that had been stuffed into an ugly brass vase.

The heather made her think of Angus again, and she forced herself not to smile. Her mother would not have liked it.

Finally Maud began. 'I have been observing you, Rachel,' she said. 'I hope you are not developing a . . .' She paused, searching for the right word '. . . a *tendre* for your cousin Angus.' She didn't say it as a question, so Rachel didn't answer, though something cold clenched around her heart. 'If there is anything of that sort in your mind, you will thrust it out immediately, because nothing can come of it.'

'Come of it?' Rachel queried falteringly.

'There can be no question of a marriage,' Maud said definitively.

Rachel blushed. 'I hadn't thought . . .' she began.

It was true. She hadn't got as far as thinking about marriage. She had been living in the moment, just enjoying her handsome cousin's attentions. But now the thought was put into her mind, she saw that there would be something delightful about marrying Angus, being his chosen one, seeing him every day. In a little sidelong peep of imagination she thought *And every night as well*, and her blush deepened.

Maud was watching her face. 'No question at all,' she repeated. 'I have been talking to Sir Gordon.' Angus's father had been elevated to a baronetcy earlier that year. 'He would not in any circumstances permit Angus to address you. He has quite other plans. And *I* have other intentions for *you*. You are to marry higher than a *baronet's son*.'

Maud said the words with scorn, and her eyes sparkled as

she remembered the conversation with Sir Gordon. To have a mere baronet warn her that *her* daughter was not to think of *his* son! Tullamore wanted money to expand his interests, and Angus was to marry a Scottish heiress of large fortune. Rachel, while a nice enough girl, had too little to tempt Sir Gordon. It had taken all of Maud's wits to twist the conversation round so as to be the one to reject the idea of a union first. *Lady* Rachel was destined for a titled marriage, and Maud was at pains to let him know that candidates, *multiple* candidates, were already being ranked in order of desirability, and that royalty was not out of the question.

'So if you *are* feeling any slight preference, you must nip it in the bud,' Maud concluded. 'You have come here to rest after your Season, that is all. You will not allow yourself to be attracted to anyone without my permission. Do you understand me?'

'Yes, Mama,' Rachel said, staring at the carpet. Strange how tartan could look so dead and disagreeable laid across the floor, yet when clothing an athletic young man's *haunches* it was a thing of life and beauty . . .

'Don't pout,' Maud said. 'And stand up straight. Everything is in hand. An excellent marriage of high rank will be yours. You need have no doubt about that. That is all I have to say to you. Oh,' she contradicted herself the moment Rachel turned away, 'there are guests coming this evening. The Eassies of Alvie Castle have a house party staying, and they are bringing them over for dinner and a musical evening. The Prince of Usingen is among them. You will take care to be polite to him.'

'I'm always polite to everyone,' Rachel said, a trifle sullenly. *Not Paul Usingen!* she thought. *Please don't let that be the high marriage she's got planned for me.*

The drawing-room was crowded that evening, but the Prince of Usingen made a bee-line for Rachel, and bowed over her hand. His felt slightly disagreeably damp, and she had to force herself not to snatch hers away. With her mother's eyes burning into her, she smiled, but not too much, and said, 'How nice to see you again,' but not too warmly.

'And you, Lady Rachel,' he said. 'You look blooming. "Bonnie" – is that not the correct, Scottish word?'

'Perhaps,' Rachel said cautiously. She didn't want to accept anything from this man, not even a compliment.

'At all events, I am glad to see in you no fatigue from your exertions in London. You are not pale and weary.'

'Not at all, thank you. I'm surprised to see you here,' she went on, managing a touch of hauteur – she had observed for years how her mother crushed pretensions. 'I did not know you ever came to Scotland.'

'Scotland is very like Germany in so many ways. One feels at home. I do not care very much for the shooting of the stag,' he said, letting go her hand at last. She dropped it to her side and tried surreptitiously to wipe it on her skirt. 'But the fishing – that is *ausgezeichnet*. Lord Eassie most kindly made the invitation to come and fish, and I was hasty to accept. But when I heard also that you and your mother were staying close by, ah, then I was to come with much joy, *um Sie besser kennenzulernen.*'

He smiled, a dreadful sight to Rachel, and she gave him a tight and ghastly one in return, murmured an excuse, and slipped away to lose herself in the crowd. It was easy enough to avoid him among so many (easy to miss Angus too, it appeared – was he avoiding her?). The prince was not seated near her at the table, which was a blessing. But when they all gathered after dinner in the baronial hall for the musical performances, she saw him seek out her mother and engage her in private conversation. Their heads were close together, Rachel noted gloomily. She hoped they weren't talking about her – but what else could he have to say to Mama? To be a princess would be agreeable, but not at any price.

Rachel was called to the piano early to play and sing, and knowing her limitations she chose a simple Scottish folk song, well within her range. She had hoped that Angus would come and turn for her, but Henry Eassie rushed into the breach before anyone else could move. She couldn't even see where in the room Angus was standing. At the end of the song she was asked politely for an encore but she declined gracefully.

Among the Eassie party were Sir Philip and Lady Huntley and their daughter Diana, and when she went to the piano, Angus suddenly appeared and took up station beside her. Rachel supposed, a little miffed, that he was to turn for her, but it was worse. He announced that they were to sing a duet, 'The Braes o' Balquhither'. There was a murmur of approval – it was a very popular song.

Diana Huntley was an unusually good-looking girl – masses of dark hair, and dark eyes, and a proud, sculpted sort of face – and she certainly sang well. The tune demanded strong voices, and Angus's fine baritone twined confidently with her accomplished soprano. He looked at Diana as they sang:

Let us go, lassie, go
To the braes o' Balquhither,
Where the blaeberries grow
'Mang the bonnie Highland heather . . .

Rachel felt a pang of something – was it jealousy? The song was about the wild thyme and heather blooming on the hills, and she thought of the picnic, and sitting beside Angus looking out over the view from the crag. It should be to *her* that he made the appeal, *will ye go, lassie?* – not to the undeniably beautiful Diana Huntley.

Did she have a large dowry?

Now the summer is in prime,
Wi' the flowers richly blooming,
And the wild mountain thyme
A' the moorlands perfuming;
To our dear Native scenes
Let us journey together . . .

The song was poignant, longing. Rachel felt the pang again
– something both sweet and painful. And now as he sang,
Angus looked at her. His eyes found her among all the faces,
as though he had known all along exactly where she was. She
felt a delicious shiver that ran from her scalp all the way
down her body, and she remembered with sudden, piercing
clarity how the year before he had kissed her in the orangery
at Alvie Castle, remembered the riot of feelings that had
romped through her. He had asked her to marry him then.
But they had both been children, she hadn't yet had her
Season, and of course it wasn't a proper proposal, not without
going through their parents. It had just been a bit of excitement, an urge of the moment . . .

Did Diana Huntley have a large fortune?

Lady Huntley was wearing a magnificent ruby collar, so
they were probably rich.

The song ended, and there was real, sincere applause.
Angus took Diana's hand to raise her to her feet for them
both to bow; and then he lifted the hand to his lips and kissed
it flamboyantly, raising increased applause and approving
laughter.

There was no more pleasure in the evening for Rachel.

Ashmore Castle had been built halfway up the valley side,
not only for the view but for the fresher air. But now even
the expected breeze had failed, and August hung heavy and
humid over everything, so that breathing seemed an effort,
as if the air had turned to cloth. Kitty wandered from room

325

to room, standing at one open window after another, feeling the truth of the phrase, *heavy with child*. She was all alone. Even the dogs had abandoned her – they were outside somewhere, lying in whatever shade was the deepest. Alice, who had been her most constant companion, had gone out riding – Kitty had insisted she must have a break. 'You're getting quite pale, shut in here with me all day.' And Giles, of course, was somewhere about the estate, probably supervising a harvest – wheat, wasn't it, in August? She was having to learn these things. The heaviness of the weather suggested a storm was brewing, so they would want to get the wheat in before it got wet.

Richard was in London, on business, and Uncle Sebastian had gone to Henley for a few days to meet friends. He had seemed low for months now, and she was glad that he was going to have some society, hoped it would cheer him up.

Hatto found her. 'Beg pardon, my lady, but Nanny was wondering if you'd care to have his little lordship out in the garden for a bit. The sun's off the gravel walk, and it would do him good to get some fresh air.'

Kitty almost smiled. It was a blatant ploy. Nanny would never voluntarily suggest her charge leaving her sight. It must be a kind thought on Hatto's part that, her mistress having been left all alone, a walk with Louis would cheer her up.

It did. In the last few weeks his walking had improved so much he no longer resorted to all fours and, stronger every day, he was showing a marked propensity to climb. The shadow of the house lay over one end of the walk that bordered the parterre, so it was a degree cooler, and she strolled slowly, thinking about how she would make a proper garden here when she was out of confinement. Louis ran about eagerly on his sturdy little legs and climbed on low walls and benches. He was talking much more, too, and his favourite phrase was 'What dat?' accompanied by a pointing forefinger. She was quite well aware that he mostly asked just to hear her talk, but it pleased her to tell him the names of things, and to imagine some of them might stick.

But even in the shade it was stifling. There were roses, in shades of red and pink and coral, their scent heavy on the air, the hot colours jangling on her senses. Their petals were falling fast in the heat, scattered over the walk underfoot. Louis picked up one and presented it to her, with a beaming smile that displayed the kernels of his new teeth. Then he picked up another, deep crimson, and pressed it onto his nose, where it stuck to his damp skin. It looked like blood.

After the baby had come, when she was out and about again, she would send for Sir Reginald Blomfield and begin her pleasure garden, and there would be roses, she decided, but only white ones, cool and refreshing to the eyes against the green of the background. Perhaps she would have nothing but white flowers in the beds nearest the house – roses and lilies and phlox and white delphiniums, and those tall daisies for gaiety, and noble white iris like spears. White paeonies with creamy hearts full of heartbreaking scent. White foxgloves for the bees. Was there such a thing as white lavender?

Louis had reached the end of the walk and came running back. He had stuck petals on his forehead and cheeks, and she had a sudden horrid image of him stumbling and falling and cutting his precious face. 'Be careful! Don't run!' she called – but, of course, he ran, full of the new joy of mastering his body. *White flowers would gleam in the summer dusk, as though they were phosphorescent.* 'Louis!' He stumbled, fell on hands and knees, but was up again instantly, beaming at her. The crimson on his face was not blood. *White roses – they must be white.*

'What dat?' Louis said, pointing at the ground by her feet.

Red. A lot of it. She felt the disagreeable sensation of wetness under her skirts. Then a pain whipped through her, doubling her up.

'Mama?'

She tried to straighten, gasping, and bent over again, then sank to her knees. Despair gripped her heart. *No, no – please no!*

'Louis,' she said. Oh, God, he was so young! If he were even a year older . . . She couldn't get up. Grinding pain. 'Run to the house.' What to tell him? 'The first person you see, say to them, "Help Mama." Can you remember that? Say, "Help Mama".'

He stared at her for an agonising moment, his mouth bowed down, tears threatening like a summer storm.

'Don't cry, Louis. Run to the house. Say "Help Mama." Run!'

And then he ran.

There was plenty to do at Kincraig, and plenty of people to do it with, so Rachel could not claim she was neglected, even though she missed Angus's special attentions. She concluded that he had been warned off by his father as she had been by her mother. When they were in company together, he was pleasant and cousinly. At least he did not single out anyone else in her place. But he was now often absent, and she could not enquire more than casually where he was. On two occasions, when someone said they thought he had ridden over to Alvie, her imagination offered her a picture of the dark hair and dark eyes and swan neck of Diana Huntley, and Angus bowing over her hand. She tried bringing subtle enquiries as to Diana Huntley's dowry into the conversation, but either she was too subtle or no-one knew – or, more likely, no-one cared – because she never got any clear idea on the subject.

She was glad, anyway, to be able to avoid the attentions of the Prince of Usingen, who, though he often came over, seemed content – dull dog that he was – to have drawing-room conversations with her mother, or middle-aged walks along the dry paths with the grown-ups. Twice when there were dances after dinner, he asked her to dance, which was agonising; but she was too popular a partner for him to be able to monopolise her.

In fact, in the absence of Angus, Henry Eassie seemed to be taking over, positioning himself at her side, asking her to dance more often than anyone else, dashing to pick up her fan or catch her slipping shawl, sitting by her at picnics, refilling her glass. She liked him, and enjoyed his attentions: he was handsome, in the same Scottish way as Diana Huntley – very dark hair and very white skin – and was pleasant company, but he elicited no spark from her. Low be it whispered, but she found him a little dull. She often had to think of things to say, whereas with Angus it was he who led the conversation and kept it effortlessly flowing.

It was, perhaps, not quite *romantic* that Angus had relinquished her so easily, and she often found her eyes drifting to him of their own accord across the crowded room or down the dinner table. Often, when she looked, she found his eyes just withdrawing from her. And once, when they passed in a doorway and brushed against each other accidentally, he paused and looked down at her – such an intent look! – and seemed about to say something, and she caught her breath in quivering expectation. But the moment passed and he gave her only a brief, tight smile before passing on.

It would be very bad, and wrong, and pointless, but she secretly wished he would resume his attentions to her. She was completely rested now from her Season, and wanted something new and exciting to think about.

When Louis ran to the house, the first person he encountered was Afton.

The valet was just coming back from a walk and had thought to take a turn in the garden if there was nobody about. He saw the child running towards him, took in the strained expression, the frantic effort of the chubby legs.

Stooping towards him, he said, 'What's the matter, young 'un?' The boy flung himself into his arms, scaled him like a monkey, and clung on, wrapping tiny arms fiercely round his neck.

Louis couldn't remember the words he was supposed to say. He couldn't speak at all.

'What is it? What's the matter?' Afton asked in concern, closing his arms round the trembling body.

The child flung out an arm and one frantic pointing finger in the direction he had come from.

Something was wrong, Afton thought. The child shouldn't be unattended. What had he run from?

Just then a gardener's boy appeared, pushing a wheelbarrow full of trimmings, and gave him a startled look. It was one of the new boys taken on that spring – Cox was his name, Afton thought. He tried loosening the child's arms but they only clung harder. 'You, boy – Cox! Come with me,' he said.

Her ladyship was lying on the ground, and there was a lot of blood. Louis moaned and pushed his face into Afton's neck. He held the boy closer and said to Cox, 'Run to the stables, tell them to send a man on horseback to the village for the doctor, and another to fetch his lordship back. Then run to the house and send anyone you can find here to help me. Quick as you can. Run!'

Luckily the boy seemed to have kept his wits. He did not stare or ask questions, but whirled on the spot and was gone, showing a good turn of speed. Afton, hampered by the child, could not go to her ladyship. There was a stone bench nearby. He unfastened the boy's legs and set his feet on the bench, then tried to release the clinging arms. 'You must let me go, Louis, so I can help Mama. Will you be a good boy and stand here? That's right. Don't look, my dear – look over there, look at that tree. Can you see any birds in it? Stay there. Good boy.'

He had thought for a moment that there was blood on the

child's face too, but it turned out only to be a rose petal, stuck to his forehead.

A ball at Invereshie House – quite a grand ball. Henry Eassie had been flirting with Rachel all evening, but it had developed an edge, and she thought she knew what it was. She escaped to the conservatory – not as grand a one as at Alvie Castle, but densely planted with greenery and quite as good for hiding – to think.

Henry was handsome, and obviously smitten with her. He was an eldest son, and the Alvie estate was a good one (at least, it was a large one – she had no knowledge of their financial standing) but Lord Eassie was only a baron. What would her mother think about that? She had said she had everything in hand and that a fine marriage would happen, but was she thinking about Paul Usingen? Would she even consider a baron's heir, if a prince, albeit a German prince, was hovering?

And suddenly she tired of the whole business. 'I don't want to marry anybody,' she announced petulantly to a fronded palm that was brushing her shoulder. It wasn't true, of course: she wanted to marry, but why did it have to be so complicated? Last year, she had thought it would be simple – dance, fall in love, marry. She hadn't imagined anything might disrupt the process.

There were footsteps on the tiled floor, a rustling of foliage, and Henry was there, a little flushed in the face, though that could be from dancing – it was a very warm evening.

'Rachel,' he said, in a husky, insinuating voice. He came up close to her, and she could smell his heat through the velvet jacket, the frilled shirt and stock. A hint of sweat, which for some reason came across to her as pink and childish. Sticky – she thought he would be sticky.

Without a further word, he put his arms round her waist and kissed her. His mouth was soft and hot and damp, and she didn't like the pink, childish smell of him. His body pushing against her seemed too soft – like marshmallow. She struggled against the kiss, but his mouth only pressed harder, and his teeth hurt her lips. Finally he raised his face and she gasped, 'No!'

'No?' he queried, with half a smirk.

'I don't want you to kiss me.'

'Oh, come on! You've been flirting with me all evening, and then you slipped in here. What was I to think?' His big face loomed closer again.

'Stop it! Leave me alone,' Rachel said, shoving him hard in the chest.

'Oh, come on, Rachel. I've been longing to kiss you for days. You gave me every reason to think—'

She shoved him again and he released her, but was still standing close, and looking at her with an honest perplexity that made her want to hit him.

'But I want to marry you,' he said, as though she ought to have realised that. 'I really do. It's not just . . . you know. I was going to ask you, honestly I was.'

'Well, I don't want to marry you,' Rachel said. Why did she feel so cross about it? It was a nice thing, to receive a proposal, and he was a nice boy. 'In any case,' she went on, trying to sound reasonable, 'our parents would never allow it.'

'Don't say that. I'm sure my pa wouldn't mind.'

'Well, my mother would. She wants me to marry a duke, or a prince, or something.'

'But what do *you* want?' Henry said. His arms went round her again. 'I bet I know. I bet your mother would allow it if you made a fuss. Will this change your mind?'

He was going to kiss her again. She struggled against him. 'Let me go! Leave me alone!'

And then someone else was there, and Henry was plucked away as easily as if he had been a twig caught in her hair.

332

'You heard what she said,' came Angus's voice. 'Step away. This is not the way to carry on a courtship.'

'Oh blast and damn you, Tullamore! What's it to do with you? You think you can just—'

'Go back in the ballroom, Eassie, and stop making a fool of yourself.'

A glance at Rachel told him she wanted him to go. 'All right, I'm going. Keep your hair on,' he said crossly. And he was gone.

Then there was just her and Angus. The air seemed suddenly cooler and fresher. At all events, a little shiver ran down her spine.

'Did he hurt you?' Angus asked neutrally.

'No. He was just annoying,' Rachel said.

'I'm afraid that's what happens when you encourage the wrong people,' Angus said, in a flat voice.

She peeped up at him uncertainly. 'Are you angry with me?'

He sighed. 'No, of course not. Not with you.' He looked down at her with a faint, wry smile. 'I'm always rescuing you from cads, aren't I? Last time it was Johnny Etteridge. In the orangery at Alvie.'

'I didn't think you remembered that,' she said, in a small voice.

'Didn't remember that I kissed you?' Angus said. 'Didn't remember the best moment of my whole life so far?'

'You—' She began to remind him of what had happened next, and stopped.

'I asked you to marry me.'

'Yes,' she said. There was a silence. She was very conscious of his breathing. She had a wild urge to lay her hands on his chest – under his jacket, against his shirt – so she could feel his breath going in and out. She thought she would feel his heartbeat, too.

'Rachel,' he said, in quite a different voice.

She looked up into his face, feeling on the edge of something momentous, as though she might actually go up in flames, like a piece of paper. 'Yes?'

'You really have got to get this flirting under control,' he said, smiling. And then he was kissing her.

It was entirely different. It was heavenly. His lips were firm and warm and dry and his breath was sweet and the smell of his skin was like something she had always known, and filled her with longing. Her arms crept up round his neck, and his were round her waist, and the kiss went on and on and she wanted it never to end.

When it did, he drew her close, folding his arms round her, and she pressed herself against him, feeling safe and loved. He rested his chin on the top of her head and she rested her cheek against his chest, and she could hear his heart beating, strong and steady. She was so happy she could hardly bear it.

Several years later and much too soon, he loosened his grip enough to be able to look down at her and speak.

'You know they'll never let us marry,' he said, and it was hardly a question.

'Why does it have to be so complicated?' She asked the question she had thought earlier.

'I'm going to ask,' he said. 'I'll ask my father and your mother, but I know what they'll say.' He paused a moment. 'Fa wants me to marry Diana Huntley. She's an important heiress. She'll have coal mines.'

'My mother wants me to marry a prince.'

'So I imagine. But I love you.'

'I love you, too,' said Rachel, and when she said it, she knew it was true. There was release in saying the words out loud, as though she'd been holding back a great weight of water against a door. For a moment she felt the rush of joy, of loving and being loved. Then she remembered. 'It's hopeless, isn't it?' she said – willing him, hopelessly, to say no, it wasn't.

He said fiercely, 'We have to *think*. There must be a way. There must be! I don't want to marry anyone but you, Rachel. You're like the other half of me.'

'I – I feel the same.' Suddenly, the idea of marrying anyone else but Angus was horrible. Even kissing anyone but him. As to the Thing that an over-zealous German maid had told her about – the Thing that married people did . . . *Oh, my Lord, not with anyone but him!*

'We must just hold out,' he said, pulling her close again. 'Hold out and wait and see what happens. There must be a way.'

But what if Mama finds someone else for me? The idea of defying her mother filled her with tremulous dread.

He divined her thought. 'Remember, they can't *make* you marry against your will. That's the law of the land.'

But could she be brave enough to hold out against everything that would be urged against her, forced on her? Her mother's dominance, her personality . . . 'Do you really love me?' she asked, in the smallest voice yet.

He smiled down at her. 'Oh, Rachel, my dearie dear! Do you doubt it?'

And then in his lips and arms and warm, strong body and steady beating heart, and the sheer *thereness* of him, she found all the proof she needed.

Kitty felt she had been away for a long time. There had been vague perceptions: she had known at one time that Dr Arbogast was leaning over her; and at another there had been a nurse in white veil. Once, Alice had been sitting by the bed, weeping. She didn't feel she had actually *seen* them: she just knew they had been there.

Now she was drifting. It was like being under water: sometimes deep down, sometimes rising close to the surface, where she could hear voices, though not the words they said. She didn't want to break through into the air – not yet. She couldn't remember what had happened. She didn't want to know . . . She let herself drift down deeper.

Sir Gordon was not wholly unsympathetic, but he was firm. 'It's out of the question.'

'Father—'

'When I told you to pay attention to Miss Huntley, when I told you not to favour your cousin, did you think I was not serious?'

Angus stood before him in formal pose, hands clasped behind his back. By chance it was the same parlour where Rachel had been warned – a small, little-used parlour off the entrance hall, convenient for private conversations. Standing like a soldier, Angus didn't see the sad beast eyes or the dreary tartan. He fixed his gaze over his father's shoulder on the sky beyond the window.

'I did try, sir,' he said. 'But I don't care for Miss Huntley and she doesn't care for me. My feelings for Rachel are – not easily brushed aside.'

'I don't entirely blame you,' his father responded. 'She's a fetching little thing, and if matters had been otherwise . . . But I'm afraid it's common knowledge that the late Lord Stainton only cheated bankruptcy through death. He left nothing for his younger girls. I gave a hint to Lady Stainton on the subject, though it went against the grain, and she gave me to understand that she would by no means welcome an offer from our side, even if it were to be forthcoming. And it is *not*. You must make your mind up to that.'

'But, Father—'

'No, no. This is not a subject for discussion. You and the girl must allow your elders to know better in this case. Marriage for people of our station – it is not a simple matter of four bare legs in a bed.'

Angus winced at his father's attempt at unbending. He

336

fixed his own expression on the graver side of solemnity. 'Father, I feel my honour is engaged.'

But Sir Gordon was not impressed. 'Whatever you may have said to the girl, it is not binding, not without the permission of your parents and hers. You have taken a fancy to her, I can see that, but these feelings are not uncommon, and they fade, my boy. Trust me, they always fade. Marriage is too important to be concluded on the basis of a passing whim. Now, Sir Philip Huntley and I have discussed the matter fully, carefully, soberly, and we have decided that the match will be beneficial to all parties. And she's a handsome girl, Angus – it's not as though I was hitching you to a gargoyle. Handsome and well-bred and, as far as I can tell, good-humoured. You'll thank me one day.'

'Have you decided between you on a wedding day? And how many children we're to have?'

Sir Gordon gave his son a close look, noted the flared nostrils, and decided to ignore the near-impertinence, rather than risk provoking an uproar. 'We see no reason for a long engagement. Miss Huntley is not a girl just out of the school-room.'

Angus's heart sank. Were they going to try to hurry him into a marriage – to leave him no room for manoeuvre? 'Father,' Angus said desperately, 'I can't do this. I love Rachel.'

Sir Gordon only raised an eyebrow. 'I'm sorry to hear you say so, but your fancy for Lady Rachel does not come into it. All this has been agreed. You *will* marry Diana Huntley.'

'You can't make me,' Angus said. Oh, how childish it sounded! He wanted to be magnificently defiant, but beside his father's monumental assurance he was like a baby throwing a toy in petulance.

'As a matter of fact, I can. You are financially dependent on me. But I would prefer you complied with my wishes with a good grace. You ought to be grateful, in fact, that such a golden future is being planned for you. Now leave me, Angus, and do not speak in this foolish manner ever again. I have always thought well of you: I don't wish to alter my opinion, especially over something so trivial.'

Trivial? Angus's spirit rose. 'I tell you now, Father, that much as I respect you, I cannot do as you wish. My honour and faith are given. You had better tell Sir Philip there will be no wedding.'

Sir Gordon merely waved a hand. 'Enough, now. Go away. I won't hear any more.' Angus tried to speak, and his father said sharply, '*Go!*'

Trained to obedience, he went.

Kitty opened her eyes. The room was dim, blinds drawn, but sunlight pressed hard against them from outside, so it must be day. How long had passed? She felt utterly flattened, as though everything had been drained out of her, leaving only an empty sleeve of a body. She breathed slowly and lightly, the minimum necessary. She was capable of nothing more.

Giles was lying back in a chair near the bed, his elbow on the arm, his head resting in his hand, eyes shut. He looked worn. The room was silent. No-one had noticed she was back. She closed her eyes again, hoping to sink down again.

But this time consciousness would not play the game. She remained aware. There was a soft rustling sound, and then a cool hand was laid across her brow. When it was removed, she opened her eyes, and saw the white-winged face of a nurse bending over her. The face smiled. 'I knew you had woken. I heard your breathing change. You've come back to us.'

And then there was a flurry, and the nurse was replaced by Giles. Her hand – her limp hand – was taken up and squeezed, and Giles was . . . Was he crying? Not exactly, but his eyes were damp. 'Kitty!' he said. He kissed her hand. 'Thank God.'

She moved her lips, but no sound came out. She was tired, so tired.

'Don't try to speak. Arbogast says you are out of danger, but you must rest, rest. Good nursing and good food, he says, will bring you back to strength. Oh, Kitty, we thought we'd lost you!'

You did lose me, she thought, remembering how deep she had gone and how reluctant she had been to swim upwards. But why? Had there been an accident? She didn't remember.

Giles was gently pushed away by the white wings. Capable hands lifted her head, a cup was put to her lips. She was thirsty, and drank. Warm milk – comforting. She drank some more. Her head was laid back against the pillows. A little – just a little – strength came to her. She had to remember how to speak, to arrange her tongue and throat and summon breath, but she managed at last to say, 'What happened?'

'Don't you remember?' Giles asked.

Something in his voice warned her. It was so hard to think when it was all she could do to breathe in and out. She didn't want to think, but despite herself memory came creaking, limping back with a ghastly grin, the death's grin of a skull. She saw a red petal on a child's face; red petals, lots of petals, blood red on the gravel. Blood on the gravel – lots of blood. Her hands were resting outside the covers, resting on her abdomen. It was flat. She was flat and empty. The baby was gone.

Weak tears filled her eyes. 'I'm sorry,' she whispered to Giles. 'I'm so sorry.'

CHAPTER EIGHTEEN

He didn't understand. 'What do you mean? What are you sorry for?' He looked at her in concern. 'Please don't cry. My dear, what is it?'

She could only shake her head, slow tears seeping.

It was the nurse who intervened. She stepped up to wipe Kitty's face, and after a keen look said, 'Oh, sir – my lord! No, my lady, no – the baby didn't die.' Kitty looked at her in bewilderment. 'Sir, she thinks—'

Giles finally understood. 'No, Kitty, the baby's all right.' He pressed her hand to fix her attention. 'Listen to me – the baby's all right. He's small, but Arbogast says he's healthy. You can see him by and by.'

She looked at him with dawning hope. 'A boy? We had a boy?'

'Yes, and he's in the nursery doing very well. We have a wet-nurse for him, since you've been so ill. I'll have them bring him to you.'

But she turned her head away. 'Not now.' She was glad she had not failed, glad the child had survived, but she was too tired to feel more than that. 'Sleep now,' she murmured.

'Yes, sleep,' Giles said quickly. 'That's the best thing for you.'

She drifted away, only noticing, with the weary edge of her mind, that he let go of her hand before she had quite gone. She wished he hadn't.

★ ★ ★

'We thought you were going to die,' Alice said. Her face looked thinner, bleak from the emotions she had suffered. 'You lost so much blood. But Dr Arbogast says you will make it up – you can make new blood inside you, apparently – only it takes time, so you'll feel tired and weak for a while.' She didn't say that Arbogast had warned that the weakened body could fall prey to a host of other ills, and that my lady wasn't out of the woods yet, by any means. 'Lots of nourishing food, that's what you need, to build you back up,' Alice went on, and gave a small, tight smile. 'They keep making you custards and gruel and such, but I can't help thinking roast beef would serve you better.'

Kitty pressed the hand that held hers so tenaciously. 'I feel a little better each day,' she said, to comfort her. Then, 'What's the matter, Alice? What is it really?'

Alice broke. 'I feel so guilty! I was out and you were all alone. If I'd been there . . .'

'I told you to go,' said Kitty. 'And I'm all right. I will be all right.'

Alice hung her head. She had been at Axe's cottage, happy, enjoying herself, playing with Dolly and a new litter of kittens. Axe had offered her one for herself. And all the while . . .

'Please don't cry,' Kitty said wearily, 'or you'll start me off.'

'Sorry.' Alice blew her nose determinedly, and picked up her sketch-pad. Dr Arbogast had said the patient ought not to be agitated or upset. 'Look, I did a new drawing of Louis for you. It's rather rough, but he won't stay still for long.'

'It's lovely. Whose lap is that?'

'Afton's.' Alice giggled. 'He's taken such a fancy to him. Nanny can hardly contain herself – she doesn't think men ought to go into the nursery, ever.'

'Not even Giles?'

'Not even Giles. But she has to put up with *him*, since he pays her wages.'

*   *   *

Giles brought the new baby down to her – or, rather, he went up and commanded it, and Jessie followed him down with the baby tightly clutched to her chest.

'Still doing well,' he said, taking the bundle from her and placing it in Kitty's arms.

Kitty looked down at the tiny face, a wrinkled red apple surrounded by lace. Already she had got used to Louis and forgotten how small new babies were. Could something so small possibly be complete? She looked up. 'He's really all right?'

'Taking nourishment well, I'm told, and putting on weight. All things being equal, he should survive long enough for us to give him a name.'

There was no answering smile from Kitty, and he felt guilty, thinking she was not ready to be light about any part of it.

In fact, she was simply feeling blank. The precious moments of recognition immediately after birth had not been vouchsafed to her, and she had been too ill to hold the baby for a long time afterwards, and was not feeding him. She felt no attachment to him. 'It's good we had another boy,' she said.

She had done her duty. She had provided the House with a son and a spare. There was no need for any more. There was no more need for *her*, really. If she died now, it wouldn't matter at all. She sighed and let her head drop back on the pillow.

Jessie was quick to come forward. 'Let me take him, my lady. You're tired.'

'Yes, take him,' Kitty murmured. Poor little boy, she thought, and tears came to her eyes.

Giles was alarmed. 'I'll leave you to sleep,' he said; and left the room to send for Dr Arbogast again.

She asked to see Afton, and Giles sent for him. He came, looking his usual spry, dapper self, but with a shy hang of the head, never having been in a lady's bedchamber before. He didn't really know where it was proper to look.

But Kitty held out her hand to be shaken, and said, 'They tell me you saved my life.'

'Oh, no, my lady,' he demurred at once. 'I just happened to be there. Anyone would have done the same.'

'Not everyone would have been as quick thinking as you,' she said. 'So thank you, all the same. And for taking care of my little boy – Lord Ayton.'

Afton smiled. 'He's a fine lad, if I might be allowed to say so, my lady.'

'And grown fond of you.'

'His lordship kindly lets me go and see him now and then.'

'Were you never married, Afton?'

'No, my lady. The opportunity never came along.'

'I'm sorry. But if you'd married you might not have been here when I needed you, so perhaps there was a Providence in it. I – and my baby – owe you our lives.'

Afton was so overcome, Giles intervened out of mercy, and said, 'That will do, Afton, thank you. I'll ring when I want you,' and he bowed to Kitty and hurried gratefully away.

'He's a good man,' Giles said to Kitty, when he'd gone.

'Yes,' she said. 'What is his Christian name?'

'Do I know it?' Giles thought for a moment. 'Ah, yes, I remember. It's Stanley. Named after the explorer, I believe. Why do you ask?'

'I was thinking perhaps we ought to name the baby after him.'

Giles laughed. 'I don't think we can call our son Stanley – though it is the name of a venerable English house. But it has become rather "of the people", these days. Perhaps he could have it as a second name.'

'I would like that,' Kitty said.

'It would annoy my mother *so* much,' Giles said, 'which is reason enough for me. But what for his first name?'

343

'I don't mind. You choose.'

'What do you think about Alexander? I rather like it.'

'Yes, it's nice,' she said indifferently.

'And we had better honour our respective papas. People expect it. So, then – Alexander Stanley John William?'

'Mmm,' said Kitty, her eyelids drooping.

Giles smiled, and escaped to his work.

Nanny, with a new baby to brood over, was happy to acknowledge that Louis was becoming more active and could benefit from a run out of doors every day, and that her shape and the state of her feet made her ineligible to be the one to take him. That Mr Afton, she observed, was a very gentlemanlike man, p'raps from his close contact with the gentry. He also had a winning way with him and a twinkle in his eye – though she didn't say that bit aloud. At all events, his little lordship had taken a shine to Mr Afton, and it could do him no harm to be taken out when the weather was fine to run around and use up some of his energy.

'What a versatile man you are, Afton,' Giles laughed at him one morning. 'Valet, professional barber, and now unofficial tutor to the scions of the nobility!'

And detective, Afton added inwardly, though he hadn't got any further forward with his inquiry. But since his master was going out and wouldn't require him for several hours, he was going into Canons Ashmore to visit Thavey's.

It was a shop that sold all manner of second-hand things, from pocket watches to candlesticks, and was a byword in the village because it also served as pawn shop. Afton stood outside for a long time, looking at the display in the window of sad treasures – a tray of wedding rings, an array of service medals, a pair of red leather baby's shoes, a Toby jug, a framed photograph, a fringed silk shawl, a pair of Chelsea cats, a brass telescope – while trying to think of a way to frame his enquiry. In the end, he decided just to play it by ear.

Inside it was dim, low-ceilinged, and smelt of furniture polish. There were glass cabinets of treasures all around and diverse shadowy things hanging from the beams – Afton had to duck between a pair of dangling ice-skates and a pith helmet complete with chin scales. Behind the counter, a tall man in gold-rimmed glasses said, 'Can I help you, sir?' His expression was stern and his tone was not encouraging. Afton wondered if he'd had to deal with so much weeping and pleading over the years that he'd developed a carapace.

Afton tried an engaging smile. 'Just came in for a look around. I'm new to the area, but I've heard it said, "You can get anything at Thavey's," so I thought I'd see for myself.'

'I'm Thavey,' said the man. 'Were you interested in anything in particular?'

'Oh, my interests are wide,' Afton said. 'You take pledges, I understand. Do you keep the pledges separate from outright sales?'

'Depends on who's pledging. Some I know will be back come Saturday. Redeem it Saturday and pledge it again Monday. Some I can tell would like to come back but never will. What's your line, if I might ask, sir?'

'Barber,' Afton said. 'I might be in the market for a good razor.'

'I haven't any at present, though they do come in from time to time. Are you setting up here, in the village?'

Afton preferred not to answer that. He pretended to look in one of the glass cases. 'I've various hobbies, though. Quite interested in old coins. And stamps – do you do anything in the way of stamps?'

Thavey wasn't buying it. His sharp eyes had picked Afton apart and put him back together as something quite different from a wandering barber. 'Stamps are a specialist thing. I don't deal with 'em. And I don't deal with stolen goods. Everyone round here knows me. What's your game, Mr Barber-I-don't-think?'

Afton came clean. 'I'm trying to track down a missing stamp collection.'

'You're from up the Castle? I've heard rumours. If anyone took 'em, they wouldn't bring 'em to me. London's the place to get rid of something like that.'

'But if a person couldn't get to London?'

'I wouldn't know what a thief might do.'

'You could take a guess,' Afton suggested.

He thought for a minute, staring hard at Afton, who stared steadily back. 'You could try Pogrebin's, up at New Ashmore. He's not as particular as some. But I never told you that.'

'Of course not. I was never here,' Afton said.

New Ashmore was the settlement that had grown up around the railway, larger than a hamlet, but with no parish church, so it was not a village. There were rows and rows of terraced brick cottages, a couple of low-looking ale houses, and a flight of shops catering to basic needs. One of these had the three golden balls hanging outside. It was small and dark and there was nothing in the window but dust. Inside the space was choked with racks and racks of clothes, and the counter at the back had metal bars fixed above it all the way to the ceiling, suggesting the owner was not unfamiliar with the violence of the desperate.

Behind the bars, a figure emerged from some crepuscular haunt in the rear: shortish, a smudge of pale face between bushy dark hair and a massive dark beard. Afton suspected all the foliage was Pogrebin's defence, as Thavey's was his unyielding expression.

'What can I do for you?' the man asked, in a rich voice with a hint of some accent. The dark eyes were unfriendly.

Afton thought he was probably too well-dressed to be in here, raising suspicion. 'A friend of mine sent me,' he said. 'He pledged something and now he wants it back. Sentimental value, you understand.'

'Everybody's sentimental,' said Pogrebin. 'Why don't your friend come himself?'

'He's at work – can't get away. I said I'd come as a favour.'

Pogrebin sniffed, as if he didn't believe this but didn't much care. 'Wot's this thing he pledged, then?'

'A stamp album, bound in red leather. Have you got it?'

'Wot's he look like, your friend?'

'Tall, skinny, dark hair.'

'Face like a skellington?'

'That's him.' Afton suppressed a thrill. He was on the right track.

'He didn't pledge it. He sold it. Too bad for him if he wants it back.'

'He'll pay,' Afton said. 'With interest.'

Pogrebin bared unexpectedly white teeth in what was not a friendly smile. 'Too late. He can't have it. It's gone.'

'You've sold it on?'

'Reckons he can get more for it somewhere else now, eh? Too bad. Should have thought of that before. Sold is sold. If he didn't know the value of it, that's his fault.'

'Who did you sell it to?'

'None of your business.'

'Please. He's very attached to that collection.'

'I bought it fair and square and sold it the same. He was glad to get what I give him.'

'But maybe I could get it back, if you tell me who bought it.'

'London dealer. It was too rich for my blood. Specialist items like that, I sell 'em in London.'

'Specialist items? You mean stolen goods?'

The face tightened with anger. 'What's your game? Who are you? Are you police?'

'No, I'm just—'

'Get out, before I come out there and throw you out! And don't come here again.' As Afton didn't move, he went to the end of the counter and made to open up the flap.

'All right, I'm going,' Afton said. He didn't relish an encounter with the man who, though short, looked strong and, more to the point, capable of violence.

'And tell your *friend* not to come here again. I've done him favours enough. If he can't hold his tongue, he's a bigger fool than I took him for. Get out, I tell you!'

The interlude at Kincraig was coming to an end. Uncle Stuffy had announced that he was going to Italy at the beginning of September and closing up the house. The astonishment Linda ought to have felt at the announcement, that her mother clearly felt (he had never done such a thing before), passed her by. She was too concerned about her own future. The Tullamores would be going home, to Craigend near Perth – and had politely declined to take Arabella and Arthur, so she was probably going to have to take them back to Ashmore – unless another invitation miraculously appeared.

She had some hopes of Prince Usingen. Close observation on that first visit had convinced her that he was not interested in Rachel: he hardly looked at her, and took no pains to seek her out. So Linda had been assiduously cultivating him ever since, and she believed she was making progress. Usingen spoke to her increasingly as though there were some connection between them, and he even, she observed, seemed to be taking trouble to get to know her mother for her sake. It would, of course, be improper of him to address her so early in her mourning. The problem was to stay within reach of him until the end of her sixth month, at which point she would be able to indicate to him that a discreet courtship could decently commence, with a view to marriage as soon as the twelve months were up. And then – riches, security, and a proper social life. She felt she would do better in the wider courts of Europe than in the tightly packed circles of English society where she was already too much known.

The news had come from Ashmore about Kitty's new baby

– another boy, the lucky creature! – and her difficult lying-in. She was apparently very poorly and, if she survived at all, would be recovering for many weeks, requiring quiet, rest and good nursing. Linda had hastened to argue to her mother that it would be better for them not to go home – only to find that her mother had already come to the same conclusion.

'A second boy is good,' Maud said, 'and one is glad, but his birth is not of such great importance, and there is no need for me to be there. Indeed, given Kitty's frail state, we should hesitate to burden the household by returning.'

She did not say so aloud, of course, but she was thinking it might not be such a tragedy if Kitty were to succumb to her condition. Her fortune was already secured to the family, and while there might be more to hope for from Sir John Bayfield on his death, it was not a sure thing, and Giles could as easily find a new wife with another fortune – and preferably this time a female from their own rank in society, who would bring more credit to the family name.

In the mean time, she had to find somewhere else agreeable to go. She had tried to talk Fergus out of going to Italy, had even tried to discover why he *wanted* to go, but he was as uninformative as he was stubborn on the subject. He said only that he wanted to see what condition his house in Venice was in, and when she said an agent could just as easily do that, he shrugged and changed the subject. On raising the matter again, she had hinted that she would welcome an invitation for her and Rachel to accompany him, but he had merely laughed and walked away.

Meanwhile, Paul Usingen's attentions were growing so marked that she was afraid they would be noticed and arouse questions to which she was not sure she had any answers. Rachel was still on her hands, and while she *could* be packed off back to the Castle for a couple of months, there was still the prospect, if she did not get a suitable offer between now and Christmas, of having to chaperone her through another Season next year. What she *ought* to do was go back to the Castle and harangue Giles ceaselessly until he agreed to provide Rachel with a decent dowry, at which point all difficulties would evaporate: she would have her pick of suitors then. But the past year had tired her, and though she never normally shrank from a conflict, the thought of arguing with her unexpectedly mulish elder son filled her with *ennui*. Which meant she had to find somewhere else to go.

Then a letter came from her sister Vicky, announcing that the family was departing for southern France for six weeks. The announcement did not include an invitation, but that was not necessarily a problem. Once they were there, Vicky could hardly refuse to take them in.

The prince, obligingly, brought up the subject when they were out on a ride, pacing side by side and a little apart from the rest of the company. Usingen had evidently heard the news that Fergus was to close up the house.

'What will you do, then, when it is time to leave?' he asked. 'Or will you go sooner? I had thought you would be here the whole summer.'

'I thought so, too,' Maud said. Usingen was gazing at her admiringly, and she was aware that she presented more than usually elegantly on horseback, even though her borrowed mount was built for endurance rather than style.

'But you, of course, have many, many houses to choose from,' he went on. 'You, who must be welcome wherever you go. Do you yet favour one invitation over the others? Or do you go back to Ashmore Castle?' His tone revealed that he hoped her answer to that would be no. Of all places, the Castle was the least likely to provide him with access to her.

'I am minded to go to France. My sister and her family will be in Biarritz.'

His face lit. 'But that is of all places the most agreeable, and the company is always superior. Dear countess, you should go to Biarritz. I myself have been considering to visit. My sister Tilde wrote to me but last week asking where I would recommend that she take her children, and I said, "By all means go to Biarritz." She will take a large villa, and will like that I go to stay with her for as many weeks as I can spare. And if your sister will think to release you at any time, I know Tilde would be delighted to ask you to stay also. I am of the wish that she should meet you.'

'Your sister moves in the best circles, I suppose,' Maud said cautiously.

'Her husband, the Graf von Lippstadt, is connected to many great families,' he said simply.

'Ah, yes, I have heard of him,' Maud said. 'I think I will go to Biarritz. Rachel will benefit from the sea air.'

They had reached a prominence, and Usingen halted his horse, forcing Maud to rein in as well. The others were pulling further ahead. 'And you, dear countess, will you benefit?' he said seriously. 'If I ask you once again to marry me, will you give me an answer? I have proved my constancy, I think, and my dedication to your family.'

She felt a pang. If she kept putting him off, perhaps he would stop asking, and she didn't want that. She had pretty much decided that marriage to him was the way out of her difficulties. Now there was a second child at Ashmore, the line was secured and Kitty, if she survived, would be firmly ensconced. There was no place for her there. She wanted to be the mistress of her own house again, not a hanger-on. But there was the problem of Rachel. 'I would like to give you an answer,' she said, 'but my daughter is not yet betrothed.'

'That must not be a difficulty!' he cried. He tried to take her hand, but his horse, fidgeting, moved him further away from her at that instant and the gesture failed. He had to grab the pommel to rebalance himself. 'Dear countess,' he went on earnestly, 'only marry me, and I shall make sure *meine liebe Stieftochter* shall meet the best that Europe has to offer. She shall be married soon, *mit Herrlichkeit*, just as you could wish.'

'Yes,' Maud said. She could see it. A foreign noble – they were always impressed by English titles, and Rachel's beauty spoke for itself. A German prince, even a Russian grand duke would not be out of the question. Usingen was very rich, and if she married him he would pay to present Rachel in the best style. Visions of cathedrals, archbishops and coronets drifted through her mind.

'Yes?' he queried. 'Do you mean yes, you will marry me?'

'Let us see,' she said. 'We will go to Biarritz, we will meet your sister, and perhaps in a few weeks' time I shall be able to give you my answer.'

Usingen looked as though he wished to kiss her hand fervently, but his horse would not be persuaded to move closer to Maud's, which was a mare, and prone to biting.

The Tullamores were leaving two days before the closing of the house, at which time the Tallants would have to go. There was a final carriage outing to Loch Gynack for boating and a picnic, and Rachel and Angus managed to separate themselves from the party. They walked through a wood to a sheltered spot by the lake's edge where they could sit and talk.

'Even if you were staying, I couldn't,' Angus said gloomily. 'Father says there's work to do, and it can't be all holiday. We have to go home. But then in October he's taking me to Edinburgh to learn how the office there runs. That's what he says, at least, but I happen to know the Huntleys will be in Edinburgh in October, and I bet he's meaning to throw me together with Diana, in the hope that I'll go mad and propose to her.'

'You won't, will you?' Rachel asked anxiously.

'Of course not. I shall resist any attempt to marry me off, to her or anyone.'

'But what use will it be, if I'm abroad?' Rachel said in despair.

'It's only France,' he tried to comfort her. 'Biarritz is a holiday place. Nobody stays there for ever.'

'But who knows when I'll be able to come back? My aunt's going to be there, the one I stayed with last year, and my mother might decide to go back with her to Germany. And that horrid old prince is going to be there, and I'm afraid she wants me to marry him.'

'Remember what I told you, that the law says you can't be married against your will.'

'But that's in England. It might be different in Germany. And if I'm stuck over there, and can't get away, and they go on and on at me . . .' Her eyes filled with tears. 'I hope I can be strong,' she said, with a sob in her voice. 'I hope I can. But if I never see you again . . .'

'We'll write to each other,' he said, holding her hand against his chest. 'And if you thought that was going to happen, I'd come over and get you.'

'How could you, with no money of your own?'

'I'd find a way. But it won't come to that. We just have to hold out, darling. When they see that we won't change our minds, and can't be forced, they'll give in. They'd sooner have us married to each other than not married at all. We just have to be strong.' He drew her against him, and she rested in his arms, her head against his neck.

'When I'm with you like this I feel strong,' Rachel said. 'But I'm still afraid.'

'Just don't marry that old prince,' Angus said. 'Leave the rest to me.'

Rachel wasn't sure there was any 'just' to it. And she was afraid that when she was abroad and far from him, she wouldn't be able to get back. It all seemed black and hopeless.

But then there was kissing, and when she was kissing him, everything seemed a lot better. Surely they could not be kept apart for ever. *Surely.*

'Afton!' Giles said sharply.

Afton started. 'My lord?'

'I've asked you three times for my cufflinks.'

'I beg your pardon, my lord.' He stepped forward with the links and began to insert them.

'You were in an absolute daydream,' Giles remarked.

'Nothing so agreeable, my lord.'

'What is it, then?'

Afton hesitated, and decided the moment had come. He could not get any further alone. 'I have been investigating the disappearance of Mr Moss's stamp album, my lord, and I have hit a snag,' he said.

He told Giles the story so far, while finishing the dressing process. Giles listened, frowning, and at the end of the exposition said, 'It seems to me you have no proof at all. Your suspicion of Hook is based on nothing but dislike of him. I grant that he's a dislikeable fellow, but "a tall, thin man"? That could be anyone.'

'Indeed, my lord. *I* can't make him go and be recognised by Pogrebin, and I can't go and find the dealer in London who bought the stamps. I believe only the police can take the matter further forward.'

'The police?' Giles turned away irritably. 'You take too much on yourself. Why was it your business to go asking questions in the first place?'

'I beg your pardon, my lord. But there is talk and unease below stairs.'

'You put me in an awkward position. You've planted suspicion in my mind, without my being able to do anything to prove or disprove it. I don't want to suspect an innocent man – and I don't want to harbour a thief in my house. What the devil am I supposed to do with this knowledge?'

His mother, he thought, would magnificently ignore 'servant tattle'. Or would summon the chief constable and order him to investigate. Or would she just dismiss Hook out of hand? He wasn't sure. But he was not his mother. He couldn't act without due process. Should he confront Hook with the accusation? But if he was innocent, to be told he was suspected would be devastating. Speak to the chief constable? But that would be blackening Hook's name and, innocent or guilty, he would always be under suspicion after that. He put down his hairbrush with an impatient bang.

'You've put me in a *damned* awkward position,' he said again.

'I'm sorry, my lord.'

Afton finished putting things away in silence. But when he reached the door, he turned back and said, 'My lord? There is perhaps one thing that could be done, quite discreetly.'

CHAPTER NINETEEN

An enquiry by Richard found Mr Cowling conveniently in London. They met at his club.

'My lady wife is still away, at the seaside, with friends,' Cowling said, 'so I find myself a poor homeless thing, roaming the earth.' He smiled deprecatingly. 'There, I'm not often moved to poetry, but a house without its mistress isn't a home, in my view.'

'You may be right, sir. I have never yet found myself in your happy position of having a wife to miss.'

'You should get married. It's the best thing in the world for a man. It'd be the making of you.'

'Ah, but unfortunately I do not have an establishment to offer, or even a regular income.'

Cowling waved that away. 'Don't let that put you off. You've two hands and a good brain – you can find a way to earn a living. And a wife will be the spur to drive you on to make a success of yourself. But I don't suppose you met me here to talk about marriage. What's the matter? Something about the milk business? The Elthornes letting you down?'

'No, sir, not at all. Rather the opposite – they've been extremely patient. I've let them down on a couple of occasions.'

'Not producing enough milk?'

'It's not that. Production is going up slowly, and they're happy to increase their sales in line with my volumes. But

I've had some difficulties with the delivery side. Once it was a horse going lame, and having to find another at the last minute. And several times we've almost missed the train – once we actually did. The speed of the drays is too variable, even though we've improved the road. You can't get a horse along faster than its natural pace. And we can't start earlier to allow for delays because the milk won't be there.'

'Well, then, what's the solution?' Cowling said.

Richard saw by his amused look that he had already thought of it. 'Motor lorries,' he said.

'Aye, that's what I'd have said. In fact, I'd have gone that way from the start,' said Cowling.

'I've always thought of them as no more than a novelty,' Richard said apologetically. 'Good fun, but not reliable. I dare say you heard that I had an unfortunate tangle with a motor vehicle a while back.'

'Aye, I heard. Nina says you got a broken wing that's never mended right.'

'I'm afraid that's true. My left arm will never be completely sound. So I viewed motor vehicles in general with suspicion. And they were always breaking down in the early days. But you see many more on the road now – and not just private cars, commercial vehicles too.'

'Aye, lad, I know. I've heard some place in north London is to get a petrol-driven fire-engine next month, and once they have it, everyone'll want one.'

'How did you hear that?' Richard asked.

'Oh, I keep my finger on the pulse. And while I've always liked horses, I can see the use of motors.'

'I should think, as an industrialist, you would do.'

'You're right! I wouldn't want to go back to hand looms and women spinning by the fireside. I might even get a motor-car myself one of these days, for pottering about – though a carriage and pair is a lot fancier to look at, to my mind, more elegant. I'd sooner arrive at church on a Sunday

357

that way. But for everyday business use – well, you can't just stop a horse by the kerb, put the brake on and leave it. But, anyway, what did you want me for? Just my opinion, or is there something you want me to do?'

'Your opinion first,' Richard said, 'which I can see is favourable. And then your advice. I don't know where to go to buy motor lorries, or what are the best and most reliable makes.'

'And you think I do?' Cowling's eyebrows went up.

Richard smiled. 'I know that if there is ever anything you don't know, you very quickly find it out.'

'Oh, flattery, is it? Well, well, suppose I do make an enquiry or two, what then?'

'I hoped you might help me with the purchase.'

'You're after my money, are you?'

'Oh, no, sir! I didn't mean that. The estate is in good enough heart for capital outlay of that order. But I do know enough to realise that the innocent buying something he doesn't understand is always in danger of being rooked.'

'Well, you're not wrong there,' Cowling said approvingly. 'If I wanted to buy a horse, I'd ask someone like you to advise me. So you've come to the right man. I shall put enquiries in hand, and let you know what I find out. And mebbe come along with you when it comes to buying, just for a treat! Now, then, let's have some details. How many are you going to need, and what weight are they to carry?'

A club servant brought pen and paper, and they got to work.

Afton went round to the back door at Weldon House and, finding it open for the air, rapped on the glass panel and inserted himself politely halfway through. 'Hello! Anyone at home?'

A very small maid clutching a dishrag gave him a startled face, white with three dark circles – two eyes and a mouth – and said, 'Oo-er!'

The cook looked up from something she was stirring on the stove. 'Can I help you – sir?' She added the last in acknowledgement of Afton's neat and gentlemanly appearance.

'My name's Afton,' he said. 'Valet to Lord Stainton up at the Castle. I was rather hoping to have a word with Mr Moss. Just a friendly word, see how he's getting on. Everyone at the Castle misses him.'

'I believe you,' said the cook, eager to please now she knew how eminent her visitor was. 'Mrs Grape's my name. And we couldn't think more highly of Mr Moss, not if it was ever so.'

'He's a fine man, Mrs Grape. And the great expert in his calling.'

'Ooh, there's nothing he don't know,' Mrs Grape said eagerly. 'Any subject you like to name, Mr Moss knows all there is to know about it – don't he, Betty?'

'Yes, Mrs Grape.'

'Dinner's never dull here, I can promise you, with all the things he tells us. You should hear him talk about India, and elephants, and I don't know what else. All the long words and foreign names and everything, he's got 'em off pat. Hasn't he, Betty?'

'Yes, Mrs Grape.'

'Well, don't just stand there staring, child. Run and tell Mr Moss there's a gennleman to see him, a Mr . . .'

'Afton.'

'That's right. Hop to it! I think he's doing the dining-room.'

A little more of Afton's charm, and the servants' hall – their combined sitting- and dining-room – was made available for a private chat, while the other servants stayed in the kitchen.

'How are you settling in, Mr Moss?' Afton only knew the legend of Moss, but that was enough for it to seem strange to see him with a black apron over his shirt sleeves and waistcoat, sign that he was doing 'dirty work'.

'Very well, thank you,' Moss said, though his tone didn't match the words. 'It takes a bit of getting used to. My mistress is very kind and a true lady. But it isn't like the Castle,' he concluded bleakly.

But he perked up after a moment and wanted to know all that was going on up at the Castle, pathetically eager for detail. He had heard, of course, about the new arrival, and offered his congratulations. 'But as to a name, Mr Afton – I've heard conflicting stories.'

'Alexander,' Afton supplied.

'I did hear that, but didn't give it full credence,' Moss said sadly. 'Not a family name at all.'

'Well, second son, you know . . .'

'Not even really a Christian name – not an Apostle or one of the Blessed Saints.'

'There are saints with weird and wonderful names, you know, Mr Moss. Like Boniface and Adalbert.'

'Not *English* saints,' Moss corrected him firmly. 'And her ladyship, the mistress, how is she? I heard she was poorly.'

'Coming along, Mr Moss. She was very much weakened by the birth, but I believe she is not in danger, and should make a full recovery.'

Afton patiently answered his questions about the rest of the family, and then Moss came obligingly to where Afton wanted him. 'And below stairs – how are things going along?'

'Not as smoothly as when you were in command, Mr Moss. Somehow we haven't recovered our rhythm. We muddle along all right—'

'Muddle!' Moss was shocked.

'But there's no-one with your eye for detail.'

Tears came to Moss's eyes. 'I knew how it would be. I never would have left, if I'd had the choice. And to be putting someone like Hook in charge! A tyro, Mr Afton. The merest tyro. Thinks he knows everything, but it takes years and years to learn how to run a great house.'

'We were lucky to have you, Mr Moss. And we're lucky that you're not far away, so that we can come and pick your brains when we need to – at least, I hope we can. For instance,' he went on quickly, 'there's a little discrepancy we have with the plate-room book. The new inventory that was made up recently. I was wondering – his lordship was wondering – whether you would be so good as to have a look, just glance through and see if you can spot anything that's missing from it.'

Moss looked uncertain. 'Oh, I don't know, really . . . My duties here – I ought not to take time out. My loyalties to my new mistress . . .'

'I'm quite sure you remember every piece of silver in the closet, Mr Moss, with your magnificent grasp of detail. No-one has a mind like yours – you are much missed every day, you know.'

While laying on the flattery, Afton pushed the log gently at him, and Moss took it automatically, while still murmuring that he didn't know, really. As he began to leaf through it, his attention was caught, and he picked out pieces to comment on. 'Oh, the Indian epergne! We had that out for Lady Linda's wedding, filled with roses, pink and white. Looked a treat, it did! Made to commemorate the old Queen when she was named Empress of India. All the big houses had Empire parties that year . . . Ah, the silver name holders. Her ladyship – her dowager ladyship – never liked them. Thought it a vulgar idea. Like a boarding-school, she said once. And they're only plated, not the real thing . . . The silver chargers, now: they were for when they used to have *service à la Russe* in the old days. You took them off with the soup bowl. There *was* a service of fifty originally, for banquets, but there's only a dozen now. The rest got sold. Might as well have sold the lot, I say, because when would you use them, with only twelve at table?'

'It's the less often used pieces, Mr Moss, where the problem is. The real antiques.'

'Oh, we used to have a beautiful nef when I first came, old as the hills. Enormous great thing in the shape of a galleon, took two to lift it, and the detail! All the rigging and flags and little people on the deck, and even a tiny anchor hanging over the side to stop it rolling! Last used for the Golden Jubilee banquet, just as a decoration. Got sold since then, though, sadly. I've an idea it ended up at Waddesdon.'

'Just so. Could you have a look through, see if you can spot anything that's not been logged?'

'Hmm. Hmm. Wait a minute!' He was running his finger down the pages towards the back of the register now, and stopped, went back, went forward, and frowned. 'There should be two Charles the second silver sugar casters – they're not down here.' He went back and forward again, painstakingly. 'No, they should be on the list. I remember seeing them when we did the inventory, because I commented that I was surprised they hadn't been sold, given they're never used. Too big, you see. Got forgotten at the back of the cupboard, I suppose. I don't know why they're not on the list, because they're definitely there.'

'Thanks. I'll see the register gets corrected. Anything else?'

'Hmm. Hmm. Wait, now – yes, there should be a set of six silver-gilt berry spoons. George the second they were, James and Josiah Williams, 1854. We had them out for Lady Alice's christening, but not since. The silver of 'em was getting so thin, the edge was like a razor – you could cut your tongue on it. They were in a green morocco case with a black velvet lining.'

'Anything else?'

'I can't see any more, but that's enough, isn't it? Reflects very bad on me when the plate book's not kept up proper.'

'Well, mistakes will happen. This isn't your handwriting, is it?'

'No, it was William took the things out of the cupboards, I called out the descriptions, and James wrote them down. Hook, as he now is. How could he miss things out?'

362

'It's easy to lose concentration when you're doing a long job like that.'

'A good servant never loses concentration,' Moss said indignantly. 'But these youngsters – careless, sloppy work! In my day—'

The maid, Betty, poked her head round the door. 'Beg pardon, Mr Moss, front door. Cook says d'you want me to go?'

'Certainly not. I shall attend to it,' said Moss, heaving himself up.

'I'll slip away, Mr Moss, don't want to get in your way. Thank you for your help. And I'll give them all your regards up at the Castle.'

'Yes – yes, do. Very well,' Moss said vaguely, as he bustled out, his mind clearly flown to his present duties and the necessity of squashing lowly general maids.

Richard arrived at Golden Square and showed himself up – Mrs Gateshill, the landlady, was always glad of an excuse not to climb the stairs. He entered the room into what was plainly an Atmosphere. He looked from Molly Sands to her daughter Chloë, and said bluntly, 'What's happened?'

'Good afternoon, Mr Tallant, yes-thank-you-we-are-quite-well,' Molly prompted.

He shook his head. 'I'm not an idiot. I can see you're upset. Have you been quarrelling?'

'Of course not,' Chloë answered, before Molly could speak. 'Mother and I never quarrel.'

'We've had some news,' Molly said. She intercepted a look from her daughter, and said, 'He'll have to know sooner or later. And I'd like his opinion.'

'Well, then, I'll tell it,' Chloë said firmly. 'You'll try to make it sound bad.' She turned to face Richard squarely. 'Sir Thomas has offered me a flat.'

'What does that mean?'

'Now the new term has started at the college, he would like me to move into a flat he owns.'

'Just you?' Richard asked pointedly, with a glance at Molly.

'You've gone straight to the heart of it,' Molly said. 'When a rich gentleman wants to put a young girl into a flat—'

'"*Put*"? You see, I knew that's what you would do!' Chloë interrupted, with a spark of anger. Her usually porcelain face took on a touch of colour. 'Listen to *me*, Richard. He has a service flat in a block behind the Albert Hall. An elderly aunt used to live there, and when she died, he didn't dispose of it, in case he ever needed it—'

'To house his paramours?' Richard asked lightly.

'*No!* To stay in if he needed it – for instance, if a concert at the hall ended late and he missed his train. But, as it happens, he's never used it. It's spacious, and quiet, a bit old-fashioned, but comfortable. And before you ask, there's a live-in housekeeper, a very steady middle-aged woman, who would take care of me, so it's entirely respectable. And it has a seven-foot concert grand in the drawing-room.'

'Ah,' said Richard. 'Now I see the attraction.'

'Please don't be hurt. The piano here is splendid, and we're very grateful to you for buying it for us, but I need constant access to a superior instrument.'

'Don't you have that at the college?'

'I have to share with the other students. Sir Thomas wants me to work seriously on Schumann this term. He wants me to work towards a concert at the Queen's Hall, which he will sponsor, a concerto with full orchestra.' She looked at him with raised eyebrows, to see if he understood the full glory of it. 'It will be my public debut. And afterwards – perhaps there might be a trip overseas, concerts in Paris and Berlin.'

'You see?' Molly appealed to Richard. 'Would he do all this for her – at enormous expense – and put her in a flat, if he didn't expect something in return?'

'Mother!' Chloë coloured in anger.

'Your mother's right,' Richard said, trying to keep the atmosphere calm. 'Gentlemen don't lavish time and money on a beautiful young woman—'

'Beautiful!' Chloë said witheringly. 'What has that to do with it?'

'Everything, I'm afraid. You have no idea how shallow, vacuous and venal men are, even the best of them. Lavishing time and money, as I was saying, on a beautiful young woman for nothing but smiles seems unlikely. A man does not purchase an orchard without wanting to taste the fruit.'

'Don't be disgusting,' Chloë said, but without heat now. She was dismissing his opinion. 'You don't understand.'

'I understand that, even with a housekeeper, tongues will wag.'

'What do I care if they do?'

'You'll care if people won't come to your concerts because they think you're a fallen woman.' He saw that point, at least, strike home. 'If the flat is large and spacious, as you say, why can't your mother live there with you?'

'My point exactly,' Molly said.

'Because I need to be alone to work,' Chloë said. '*We* need to be alone to work. Having Mother fluttering around worrying about what people might think and watching every movement in case a hand accidentally brushes an arm—'

'As if I would!'

'You would. And then there'd be your pupils, coming and going, banging away at their scales and "Frère Jacques". How could I concentrate?'

Richard intervened before Molly could explode. 'Chloë,' he said seriously, 'this man means you harm.'

She looked at him for a long moment, a clear, rather pitying look. 'Oh, Richard, do you think I don't know about men's lust? Music is full of it. I'm not a child – and I know you'll say, "That's the point."'

'You anticipate me.'

'But I know *him*. He hides nothing from me. And I can control him. He will never do anything I don't want him to. He treasures my ability beyond anything else that might be in his mind. It's the music, don't you see? The music is everything. He would never risk that for a moment's base pleasure. And I would never jeopardise my career by a moment's inattention. I think,' she added thoughtfully, stopping Richard as he was about to speak, 'that he's rather afraid of me.'

Molly groaned and put her face into her hands, but Richard studied the beautifully sculpted face and calm, clear eyes before him, and after a moment he said, 'I think he might well be. I think I would be, if I'd had the misfortune to fall in love with you.'

She wrinkled her nose and laughed, suddenly human. 'Misfortune?'

'A man wishes to be first in the heart of the woman he loves,' he said seriously, 'and the best a man could ever be with you is second – to music.'

Molly emerged and looked questioningly from one to the other.

Chloë turned to her, becoming brisk. 'You will have to agree to this, Mother, because I shall be twenty-one in a few weeks and then I'll be able to do as I please. But I don't want to quarrel with you. Please try to understand. I shall be perfectly safe, I promise you. And perfectly respectable. And,' she concluded with the clincher, 'it's something I *must* do. I have to move on. I can't do what I need to do living here.'

'It seems,' Molly said stiffly, 'that I have no choice in the matter.'

'*Please*, Mummy!' Chloë begged softly, with the childhood word. 'Give me your blessing.'

And then they were embracing. 'Oh, my darling child,' Molly said, muffled in her hair. Then she set her back. 'If he should so much as *look* at you—'

Chloë smiled. 'He won't. But if he did, I promise you I

would come running straight back to you, and let you say, "I told you so."'

'*That* would not be much comfort.'

'Oh, I think it would be *some*, surely? And now I must go – I shall be late for my composition class. Richard, you will stay and comfort Mother, won't you? She's bound to want to talk about this for hours yet.'

'Go, you minx,' Richard said. 'I'll stay as long as I'm wanted.'

She whirled away, all light and movement like sunshine dancing off a river.

When they were alone, Molly said, 'Oh, Richard!'

'No, truly, I think she'll be all right. She's very level-headed.'

'He's Sir Thomas Burton, powerful, rich and famous. And she's just a penniless child.'

Richard gathered her in his arms, and held her close to comfort her. 'She's not a child. She's as old as her art. I think she could be right that he's afraid of her. She certainly frightens me.'

She looked up at him and sighed. 'Ridiculously, I know what you mean. Her talent is something far outside normal parameters. How could I have produced such a – a—'

'Goddess? You didn't, perhaps, once step out of time and visit some Arcadian grove to lie with Apollo?'

She laughed, and pushed him away. 'Foolish! Tell me again, do you really think she'll be all right?'

'I really think she'll be all right. But as there's nothing you can do about it anyway, it would be foolish to keep worrying, wouldn't it?'

'I'm her mother. Worrying is what mothers do.'

'You've never met my mother. She has never worried about any of her five children for a single second. Disapproved of us almost always, been annoyed, angry, exasperated often, but I think her most constant emotion towards us has always been indifference.'

'Poor Richard,' she said. 'You've never had the mother's love that every child ought to have. No wonder you're—'

She stopped, and he filled in for her lightly. 'Such a hopeless case? Well, my Mariamne, they say there is always hope while there's life, so I authorise you to dedicate your life to redeeming me. And in return, I promise to be an attentive pupil.' He stepped close, cupped her face in his hands, and kissed her softly. Her lips responded for an instant, but then she took his hands and determinedly removed them.

He accepted the rebuff – for now. He asked, 'What will you do, when Chloë leaves?'

'What do you mean? What should I do?'

'Will you stay on here? It's not the most comfortable of nests. It was never meant to be more than a bachelor's diggings.'

'It's enough for me.'

'I wish it weren't,' Richard said. 'I wish I had the means to support you.'

'If wishes were horses . . .'

'Beggars would sell them to buy a neat little house somewhere and ask the woman they love to marry them.'

It made her laugh. He always had to be sure to leave her smiling, for fear that if he was too serious, she would cut him off. He made light of his deepest feelings, so that she should not have to face her own.

'This is very unsettling,' said Giles. 'You're sure the pieces are missing?'

'Well, no, my lord,' Afton said patiently. 'I can't check what's in the cupboards. Hook has the key to the plate-room, and I can't ask him for it without a reason. He keeps it in his bedroom, which now has a lock on the door, so I can't even take it without his knowing. The point is that they're missing from the inventory. And Hook was the one who wrote it all down.'

'But it could still just be a mistake – a transcribing mistake,' Giles said, in frustration.

Afton said nothing, allowing the thought to develop. The log was not a hasty scribble, but a careful recording in best copperplate of something being dictated to Hook in Moss's precise and ponderous delivery. It was hard to think how he could simply have missed out entire items, unless deliberately.

'What did you tell him, when you asked for the plate book?' said Giles.

'I just said you wanted to look at it, my lord. It was not my place to explain your reasons or his to ask. He will have supplied himself with a reason. For instance, you might simply want to know what there is that might be sold.'

Giles thought, *I'm surprised there's anything left after my father's depredations*, but he didn't say so aloud, of course. 'I don't see that we are any further forward,' he said. He did not need to add, 'I'm sick of the whole thing,' because his expression said it for him.

'If I might presume to suggest, my lord?'

'Yes, anything!'

'Silver, particularly old silver, is a different matter from a stamp collection. Dealers keep a record of the pieces that pass through their hands. And the police could put out an enquiry about a particular item.'

'The police,' Giles said with dissatisfaction.

'Not the village bobby, my lord, but someone higher up.'

'The chief constable?'

'I'm sure he would be happy to help, my lord.'

Giles nodded. 'But we still need to know that the pieces are missing.'

'Any search would alert Hook, if he is guilty, perhaps provoke him into some rash action.'

'Then we'd know, wouldn't we?' Giles said.

On leaving Kincraig, the party went first to Ashmore for

Maud, without great enthusiasm, to inspect the new baby and congratulate Kitty. 'It's just as well you had a boy,' she told her briskly. 'Since you have made such a piece of work of it, you will be glad not to have any more.' She thought of adding a few words of advice about how Kitty should conduct herself when Giles took a mistress, but decided that was for Kitty's own mother to address. To Giles she said, 'I'm told your wife should be fully recovered by the time the families come back to the country, so you will be able to host the social events that will be expected. The timing, as it turns out, is good.'

'Why should you think I want to hold social events?' he asked, faintly amused, slightly affronted.

She raised an eyebrow. 'It is not about what you *want*, Stainton. It is what is *expected*. You have a position to keep up, and since you do not seem to care for Town life, it is more important than ever that you lead the county. You have a son to follow you, now. And I hope that Kitty will make more of a showing, now that she is released from childbearing duties. You cannot always rely on *my* presence to fill the gap.'

'Why is that, Mother? Are we not to have the pleasure of entertaining you this autumn?'

She knew it was irony, but it slid off her armour of certainty. 'My future plans are in a state of flux. And that is all I have to say on the subject.'

Alice was greeted tempestuously by Arabella and Arthur. She thought them poor, sad things. The vigorous outdoor life of Kincraig and the company of the cousins had helped them across the worst period, and given them colour, but they were unnaturally subdued. Coming back to the Castle had reminded them of the loss of their father, whom they had loved more than their mother, and the lack of other children promised a dull future in which to mourn him. Alice offered to take them out riding, and vowed inwardly to speak to Giles about getting them a governess. She did not want to find herself with them permanently on her hands. She had no hope that Linda would do anything for them.

She assumed Linda would be staying when the dowager and Rachel went off to France. She, Giles and Kitty – without speaking of it aloud to each other – were all gloomy at the prospect of having Linda heaving herself angrily about the Castle, complaining about everything, but saw no alternative. The estate at Frome Monkton was being wound up and the creditors paid off but it was clear there would be nothing left over, so Linda and her children would have nowhere to go. Ashmore Castle, her childhood home, would have to take them in; and, except for the times when it might be hoped Aunt Caroline would have her in London for a few weeks, she would be theirs for ever. And since she could not enjoy London gaieties while in mourning, she'd be at the Castle at least until the following June.

But Linda had no intention of being incarcerated at Ashmore. At the very first discussion of the trip to Biarritz, she made it clear that she expected to go too.

'Aunt Vicky and Uncle Bobo will be expecting me,' she said. 'They would take it as a snub if I were not to go.'

'You are in deep mourning.' It was Maud who pointed out the obvious. Giles had been feeling a guilty relief at the thought of her departure.

'I can't see that that matters, when visiting relatives,' Linda said briskly. 'In fact,' she added, buttering a roll, 'I don't think the rules of mourning need to apply when one is abroad, where one is not known.'

'Aunt Vicky and Uncle Bobo know you,' Alice pointed out innocently.

Linda scowled. 'But it would put a dampener on them to have someone in widow's weeds hanging around the house when they are there to enjoy themselves.' And she went on quickly, in the tones of sweet reason, 'I think it would present a very *odd* appearance, full blacks at a place like Biarritz, where everyone is in light clothing and bright colours. Of all things, I abhor making a spectacle of myself. We would be stared at, Mother, and I know how you hate that. No, I think on the whole it would be better if I leave off heavy mourning when I get there. I can wear lavenders and greys, and be decent.'

'Have you got any lavenders and greys?' Rachel asked, savouring the *petite marmite*, so unlike the lumpy cock-a-leekie soup that was the standard fare at Kincraig. When she was growing up, there had not been much difference between Ashmore and Kincraig food. Ashmore dishes were much more delicate now.

'I've some old things. But you're going to Paris first for clothes,' Linda pointed out. 'I can get new things there.'

Maud made a sound of annoyance. 'And how, precisely, will you afford new clothes? Or your ticket? You surely do not think I shall pay for you?'

Her eyes locked across the table with those of her daughter, and the air bristled with all that was unspoken. *Cordwell left you penniless*, said Maud's accusing gaze. *And Papa left you penniless*, said Linda's. Rachel looked timidly at Giles, and then at Kitty, knowing full well that all the lovely things she had sported at her come-out, and all the fun she had had, had been paid for by Giles, or rather by the estate, and therefore out of Kitty's fortune.

And Giles was thinking, Am I to be burdened with this ridiculous extravagance for ever? Why should I pay for their pleasures? Why can't they stay quietly at home? Ah, but that was not the delightful alternative it might seem, was it? When it came down to it, he would be glad to pack his mother and sister off to France, and peace by his own hearth came at a price.

In addition, he had an inkling that Linda's desire to go to France without her weeds had another motive. She couldn't like her status as his pensioner any more than he did. She probably wanted to marry again. She was only thirty, and not bad-looking, if rather scrawny. In Biarritz there was a good chance of meeting a rich, elderly widower – scores of them went there for the very purpose. Aunt Vicky was quick-witted when it came to matrimonial issues, and might well invite suitable candidates to be met and charmed – if Linda could remember how to charm. To get her off his hands for good! It was worth the cost of a few more outfits – in a year in which he had already paid for more outfits than he could count.

'I think Linda should go,' he said to his mother. 'She's looking quite pulled, you know, after the tragedy. The sea air would do her good. And if you are buying more clothes in Paris, one or two frocks for Linda won't make much difference. I believe they're much cheaper there than in London.'

Linda was as surprised as she was pleased, and for a moment couldn't think of anything to say.

Maud gave him a scalding look, realising she had been out-manoeuvred, and was to be stuck with Linda. She had never thought Giles manipulative – bluntness had been his leading characteristic. Had he learned dark arts since becoming earl? He met her eyes steadily, and she could read nothing from his expression.

Rachel, thinking Linda would not be much of an addition to the pleasure of the party, said, 'If Linda's coming, couldn't Alice come too? She never goes anywhere.'

'Oh, I don't want to go, thank you,' Alice said quickly. 'I like staying at home with Kitty and Giles. And Kitty couldn't do without me – could you?'

'I should miss you very much,' Kitty said.

'You're quite the walker, aren't you, Mr Afton?' said Mrs Webster at supper. 'Whenever you have your time off, you go out, tramping away like those ramblers you see of a Sunday.'

'I like to get a bit of fresh air,' Afton said. 'Our lives, Mrs Webster, are sadly confined.'

'I don't like the out-of-doors,' said Ellen. 'All mud and insects.'

'I like being in town better,' Doris agreed. 'Shops and buses and a bit of jollity, that'd suit me.'

'That's the trouble with a big house like this,' said Daisy. 'You're stuck miles from anywhere. My sister's in a place in High Wycombe. They have all sorts going on there, and dances every Saturday through the winter. All we got here is blummin' trees and birds and such.'

'But Nature, in reasonable measure, can be very restorative,' Crooks pronounced. 'The contemplation of God's creation . . .' He caught Hook's derisive eye and stopped. 'Where in particular do you go on your rambles, Mr Afton, if I may ask?'

'I'm still exploring the neighbourhood – being the new boy here. And while it may not be teeming with the sort of fun to amuse young ladies,' he smiled at Daisy, who blushed, 'it has some very interesting nooks and crannies. For instance, I've been poking about New Ashmore lately.'

'Nothing interesting there,' Rose said. 'Except the railway station.'

'But there's a very mysterious-looking big house called High Beeches, shut in with a high wall and lots of gloomy shrubbery. It could be the scene for a Gothic novel with a madwoman shut up in the attic. Or the haunt of vampires.'

The girls gave a frisson of delighted horror. 'Ooh, Mr Afton!'

'Vampires!' Hook snorted. 'You do talk rubbish.'

'I use my imagination,' Afton said blandly. 'For instance, there's a little shop there, dark and dusty, run by a strange man like a troll or a goblin, with a great bushy beard and piercing eyes. I can just imagine him eating unsuspecting small children and grinding their bones to make his bread.'

'Ooh, Mr Afton! Stop it!'

'Though it will probably turn out he's just a harmless,

374

rather shy soul,' Afton went on, looking at Hook. 'Burdened with an unfortunate face and a peculiar name – Pogrebin.'

'Oh, I've heard of Pogrebin's,' Mrs Webster said. 'Isn't it just a pawn shop?'

'It's a pawn shop, all right, judging by the three balls outside. I don't know what else it might be. What would you say goes on there, Mr Hook? Have you had dealings with the child-eating goblin?'

'I never go up there. Nothing to walk up a hill for,' Hook said tersely.

'Except the railway station,' Rose said. 'I've known you take a train sometimes on your day off.'

'Nobody's business if I do,' Hook snapped. 'If everybody kept their long noses out of other people's business, the world'd go round a lot quicker.'

'Which would not necessarily be a good thing,' said Afton.

'Isn't it the world going round that causes gravity?' Crooks said vaguely. 'Or is it the other way round?'

Mrs Webster looked amused. 'We need Mr Moss here to tell us. From his *A to Z of Universal Knowledge*.'

'Think of a merry-go-round. If the world turned too fast, we'd all get flung off,' said Afton. 'And go spinning out into the darkness, along with our goods and chattels. Or, indeed, other people's goods and chattels.'

Hook glared at him glitteringly. 'What the hell are you babbling about?'

Mrs Webster intervened, 'Language, please, Mr Hook. We don't use that word in the servants' hall.'

Hook opened his mouth to tell her to go to hell, then shut it again abruptly. He sawed savagely at the remaining slice of pork on his plate. Rose looked at him for a moment, then at Afton, and reached thoughtfully for the dish of green beans. The rest of the table had broken off into other conversations, but she was interested in the atmosphere between the two senior males of the below-stairs house.

CHAPTER TWENTY

'You going out, *Mr* Hook?' Rose always pronounced the honorific like an insult.

'Mind your own business.'

'Just a civil question. No need to get narky.'

'I'm butler in this house,' Hook said, with a look like black frost. 'The day I have to explain myself to the likes of you . . . Get back to your work!'

She turned away without a word. She found Afton in the valets' room, sitting at the table polishing the silver pieces from his lordship's dressing-table. Silver-backed hairbrush, hand mirror, and two clothes brushes. Stud bowl, bud vase, pomade pot, pen-holder. Large and small trays. She knew them all from the days when she dusted the room. All but the hairbrushes had been his old lordship's before.

'You don't have to do that,' she commented from the doorway. 'It's not a valet's job.'

'I like cleaning silver,' he said pleasantly. 'It's peaceful. Promotes thought.'

She leaned against the door jamb, folding her arms. 'What do you think about?'

'You'd be surprised. All sorts of things. Don't *you* think?'

'I think there's something going on between you and Hook,' she said conversationally. 'And since he's a nasty piece of work, and you seem like a nice sort, I'm guessing you suspect him of something.'

He looked at her cautiously, not knowing how far she could be trusted. She seemed to see it in his eyes, because she snorted, drew herself upright, and said, 'It's no skin off my custard. I mind my own business. But I don't like strife below stairs – everybody suffers. And he's just gone out somewhere, in a right snotty mood. At a time he shouldn't be going anywhere, with upstairs lunch nearly due.'

Afton jumped to his feet. 'Did he say where?'

'Not to me he didn't. *I'm* lower than dirt. You can catch him up if you hurry.'

'I don't want to catch him up.'

'But you do want to know where he's going,' Rose said, with a twisted smile. 'Don't tell me – I don't want to know. And I never told you anything.'

'Of course not,' Afton said, and was gone.

Hook had gone the back way towards the village, down Mop End – Afton saw him just disappearing behind the hawthorns that lined the path. There was no way to follow him on the same path without being seen. He would have to take a chance that the village was his destination, and go down the main drive. If he ran most of the way, he could get to the high street first and wait for him to appear from the footpath to Cherry Lane. There were always people around in the high street, and it would be easier there to follow covertly.

A valet's life did not include a great deal of running, but he was lean and wiry in build and had always walked a lot, so he was fitter than might have been expected. All the same, he was red-faced and sweating when he reached the bottom of the hill. He crossed the bridge and turned into the high street, not running now – it would have attracted attention – but walking fast. When he came in sight of the stile to the footpath, he took up position behind a large elder-bush, and pretended to inspect his nails. No-one looked at him more than casually, and he had time to cool down. Too much time?

Had Hook got there before him? Was he long gone? Time seemed to drag, and he felt like a fool. If he'd missed him . . . And what if he had a perfectly normal reason for going out? Or what if Rose was in league with Hook and had sent Afton on a wild-goose chase while Hook got up to mischief elsewhere?

But, no, there he was at last, the tall, thin figure unmistakable with its curiously jerky gait. Afton drew back entirely behind the bush and watched as Hook sprang nimbly over the stile, crossed the road, and headed up Church Lane towards New Ashmore. Afton's heart lifted, and he followed, letting Hook stay well ahead – his height made him easy to keep in sight. He was ready to jump into hiding somehow if Hook looked back, but he never turned, strutting rapidly up the hill . . . the hill he had said led to nothing worth climbing for.

Afton followed. He was relieved when his quarry turned in the opposite direction to the railway station, and elated when he stopped at Pogrebin's, pushed open the door and went in.

Pogrebin was not pleased to see him. His jetty brows drew down alarmingly. 'I don't want you in here,' he snarled at Hook. 'You're trouble.'

'*I'm* trouble?' Hook said in outrage. 'What've you been telling folk about me? I thought you were supposed to be discreet, Mr P. Now I've got people looking at me funny and asking questions.'

'You've been flapping your mouth off,' Pogrebin said. 'I shoulda known better than deal with a amateur like you. I had a feller in here asking about that stamp album, said you wanted to buy it back.'

'Buy it back? Course I don't!'

'How'd he know about it in the first place, eh? Tell me that, Mr Blabbermouth!'

'What did he look like, this feller?'

'Little feller, spry, like a squirrel cleaning its whiskers. Copper's nark for all I know. Said he was a friend of yours.'

'I haven't got any friends.'

'You led him right to me. I want you out of here, before you bring the peelers down on me.'

'That silver I brought you—'

'Gone. D'ye think I keep stuff like that hanging around?'

'All right, then. But I got something else for you.' He brought out from under his coat a silver charger, one from the set. They were rarely used, and who would ever count them?

Pogrebin raised his hands in a fending-off movement. 'I don't want to know! Get out of here – and take that with you! You're bad news. You're trouble. Get out and don't come back!'

'But I need the money. I might have to clear—'

'Rube!' Pogrebin bellowed. The curtain to the back room parted and there emerged a figure with a marked family resemblance to Pogrebin, especially in the hair and beard department, but twice his size. He was broad enough to block out the light from the back room. There was an awful stillness about him. His fists hung down by his sides, like dented tin cans. Pogrebin addressed him without turning his head. 'See this feller here? We don't like him, Rube. He's not nice. If you see him anywhere near this place again, you can smash him up, hard as you like.'

The monster spoke, in a boulderish rumble. 'Right, Dad.'

Pogrebin addressed Hook. 'Now get out. And if there's any more visits from suspicious fellers, if you've led the peelers to me, Rube here will come and find you, and kill you.'

Rube took a step forward, a gesture of menace, and Hook turned hastily and left. Outside he began to retrace his steps, his heart racing. He didn't doubt Pogrebin meant what he said. What he was unsure of was whether he'd decide not to depend on Hook's silence and send Rube anyway. Better safe than sorry, so the sinister uncle might think.

That blasted stamp album! Why'd he ever bothered with it? Take things that won't be missed, that was the rule. 'I got to clear,' he said to the air. It was time. He was sick of the place anyway. He had a decent bit put aside. He'd have liked more – he could have *got* more – but a wise man knew when the game was up. What with his lordship snooping over the plate-room book – and who put him up to that, eh? And Afton asking him twisted questions and Rose giving him looks . . . He hated them all, despised them, bloody fools and parasites that they were! And stopping out here in cow-country was a mug's game, when he could be living it up in a town somewhere. Paris, maybe – they said living was cheap there, and it'd seemed like a jolly place when he'd gone there with his lordship. It couldn't be too hard to learn the old polly-voo. After all, little kids spoke it in France. He'd—

'Hullo! What a coincidence, meeting you here!'

Hook jerked out of his churning thoughts as someone stepped out from a doorway in front of him. He was walking so fast, he slammed into the man who, though shorter than him, was solidly built. The impact jerked loose the silver charger, held under his coat against his side by the pressure of his arm, and it clattered to the pavement. Afton – it was bloody Afton! – stooped and picked it up. 'Well, well, what have we here? Didn't I just see you come out of Pogrebin's? Don't say he's started selling fine silver. Bought this as a present for your old mum, have you?'

'Get out of my way, you snivelling runt!' Hook snarled.

Afton placed a surprisingly strong hand on his forearm. 'I think you've got some explaining to do,' he said gravely.

'Not to you, dog face!'

'No, to his lordship. And then probably to the police.'

'Take your hands off me!'

'I don't think so,' said Afton. And was surprised by the speed with which Hook's fist came flying at him. It caught him – by luck, because it was a wild swing if ever he saw one – on the point of the chin, snapped his head back and knocked him over.

As he hit the pavement and heard Hook take to his heels, he thought, *The idiot! There's nowhere to run.* He yelled, 'Stop thief!' as loudly as he could. He scrambled to his feet, his face aching from the blow, and saw Hook running towards the railway station. Heads were turning, and two men and a couple of boys took off after him.

The cry was taken up, '*Stop thief!*'

'Nab him!'

'Trip him up!'

Afton started in pursuit, remembering to snatch up the charger from the pavement. He saw Hook throw a glance backwards, judging the closeness of the hounds. But there was a hue and cry now, and several large men, who had come out of the station, had strung themselves out across the road in front of him. To the right there was an unbroken row of shops. Hook veered left, where the road was bounded by iron railings dividing it from the railway.

With surprising agility he vaulted over the railings. The valet in Afton winced as he saw Hook's jacket catch on the spikes and rip extravagantly. The jerk of it made Hook stumble as he landed, but he regained his feet and looked around. There were people on both platforms of the station – no escape that way. And now the word had spread, and two porters, followed by other interested bystanders, were coming down off the platform and heading towards him along the side of the tracks. He turned the other way, running along the sleepers for speed.

Afton clenched his fists in frustration. He knew he couldn't get over those railings. All he could do was watch and hope that someone would catch him up, though he seemed faster than his pursuers. But the station master must surely have telephoned the police by now, and perhaps would telegraph ahead to the next station. Even if Hook climbed over the fence further on and disappeared, he was a fugitive now, and must eventually be tracked down.

Hook was fairly racing along the sleepers, miraculously not tripping or stumbling, his long legs eating up the distance while Afton watched helplessly. The tracks bent round a curve just ahead and he would soon be out of sight. He was looking back now as he ran, to see how close the pack was, but still he did not stumble. The man was surrounded by some magic.

Fortune favours the wicked, Afton thought.

The train came round the curve, going fast – an express, not a stopping train, Afton thought afterwards. Big and black was the engine at the front, a fire-breathing dragon, a face under a black cap leaning out from the driver's cab to look ahead. The whistle sounded urgently – phoop-phoop-phoop. Hook jerked his head round to look. And went to jump off the tracks to the side, to safety. And now, only now, stumbled, catching a hasty foot on the rail. And went sprawling.

Afton never knew what the noise was that he heard, whether his own shout, the howl of the engine passing, or the inchoate roar of a crowd of witnesses, whether the shriek was the whistle or the squeal of brakes or a man's scream. He was battered by a hot, gritty wind as the engine rushed past, carriages rattling after, all slowing now, too late. His heart was clenched with horror. He became aware that his hands were hurting as well as his face, and when he looked down, he saw he was clutching the charger so tightly the rim was cutting into his palms.

In the housekeeper's room, with the door shut, there was an oasis of calm. Mrs Webster served tea to Afton and Rose with

382

a timeless air. The uproar and festering curiosity of the rest of below-stairs was both behind them and shut out.

'You mustn't blame yourself, Mr Afton,' the housekeeper said.

'But I do,' Afton said glumly.

'He was a nasty person,' Rose said.

'And a thief, you tell me,' Mrs Webster added.

'But he didn't deserve to die,' Afton said. 'And not like that.' At least, he thought, it would have been quick – the engine wheel that had cut off his right leg had severed his femoral artery and he would have bled to death in seconds. So the doctor had told his lordship, who had told Afton.

'When all's said and done, it was an accident,' said Mrs Webster.

'But I feel that I drove him to his death,' said Afton. 'He looked back when he was running, like a fox looking to see how close the hounds were. If I hadn't interfered, he wouldn't have been running in the first place.'

'If he hadn't been a thief he wouldn't have run,' Mrs Webster pointed out. 'And it was his choice to steal. Have a ginger biscuit. Mrs Terry's trying them out. Mr Richard was always very fond of a ginger-nut, the hotter the better.'

'Everybody's been upset since Mr Moss's stamp album went missing,' Rose said. 'Now we know who stole it, we can all settle down. You did a good thing, Mr Afton. Theft below stairs is the worst thing – everybody gets suspecting everybody else and there's no peace.'

'I can't believe I ever suspected you,' Afton said, with a penitent look. 'I'm sorry, truly I am.'

Rose shrugged. 'You didn't know me. I keep myself to myself.'

'Well, I hope you'll forgive me, and that we can be friends now.'

'We'll see.' She took a biscuit and nibbled at the crisp rim. 'I like shortbread better, but these are nice, Mrs Webster. You should tell her so, 'case upstairs forgets to.'

'Hm,' said Mrs Webster. 'I wonder if ginger shortbread would be nice?'

'Wouldn't be so crisp, like this.'

'Anything with ginger in it is good, as far as I'm concerned,' Afton said, with an effort to be sociable.

'Let me top you up,' Mrs Webster said, wielding the teapot. 'You're still looking shaken, Mr Afton – and no wonder.'

'It wasn't a nice thing to witness,' said Afton.

'But you're not to blame yourself,' she concluded sternly.

Upstairs, in the small drawing-room, the chief constable was having much the same conversation with Giles, over tea and a slice of Mrs Terry's delectable Victoria Sandwich.

'You mustn't blame yourself, my lord. The man was clearly a bad lot and no loss to society.'

'But did he deserve to die?'

'That's not for me to say,' said the chief constable. 'But he'd have got hard labour for theft of that order, and there are those that say death is preferable to a long stretch of hard.'

'Do you know?' said Giles. 'I don't find that thought particularly comforting. It *is* my fault, in that I should have dismissed him long ago, when he refused to come to Egypt with me.'

'Dear me!' the chief constable murmured.

'Yes, rank insubordination, but I was angry enough to think I was being clever by demoting him. I thought it would be a worse punishment. I thought he would be humbled over time, see the error of his ways. What rubbish!' He rebuked himself. 'My mother would not have hesitated – she'd have dismissed him without a character.'

'Indeed she would,' the chief constable said fervently. 'A remarkably firm character, her ladyship's.'

Giles was amused to know that a certain class of people – of which the chief constable was one – worshipped the very qualities that made his mother impossible to live with: granite self-assurance, an unbending determination to have her way, and complete indifference to the feelings of anyone else. It was how they expected a great lady to behave and, by a circular logic, confirmed in their minds that she was, indeed, great.

'If I'd dismissed him, as I should have,' he went on, 'he wouldn't have been where he was for the train to hit him.'

'Well, my lord, if you'll pardon me, nobody can ever know what might have happened if this or that was the case. It's my opinion that he'd have come to a sticky end one way or another. Now, as to the stolen items—'

'The ones we know about,' Giles interpolated. 'God knows what else he might have taken over the years.'

'Indeed, my lord. But as far as we know it, I have some hope of recovering the silver for you, having had such excellent detailed descriptions of them.'

'Won't they have been melted down?' Giles asked, from the vaguest idea of criminal activity.

'Well, my lord, that is often the case, but with antique pieces the value lies in their age and rarity – the amount of silver in them wouldn't make up for that. So it's likely they were kept intact, which gives us a chance to trace them. We have a fair idea, within a hit or two, of the dealer involved. I wouldn't say it's a sure thing that you'll ever see them again, but there's a chance. The stamp album, now, I'm afraid that's a different matter. Not much hope there.'

'And what of the man, Pogrebin?'

'Ah, yes. A shady character, without a doubt. Our local people have had their eye on him for a long time, but haven't been able to nail him. This might just be the last straw for Mr Pogrebin and his sons – who are in it up to their necks along with him. If we find the silver dealer, we can put pressure on him to finger Mr Pogrebin. There is no honour among thieves, my lord.'

'Let's hope not.'

The chief constable finished the last morsel of Victoria Sandwich and daintily dabbed his lips on the napkin to remove possible crumbs. 'May I ask after the health of your esteemed mother, my lord? She is not in residence, I apprehend.'

'No, thank the Lord. The one good thing about this appalling business is that she and my sisters left for London and Paris the day before it happened. She would not have been amused by any of it.'

'No, indeed! That is a blessing. Safe in Paris, eh? Viewing the collections?' Giles looked blank. 'Isn't it in September that the great couturiers show their new designs? The House of Worth and so on.'

Giles was amused. 'How in the world do you know that?'

The chief constable reddened slightly. 'My wife is passionately interested in clothes, my lord.'

'Ah!'

'She reads a quantity of magazines. Not, of course, that I could afford to dress her in Worth gowns, but everyone needs a hobby, and she keeps a scrapbook of dresses she cuts out of the magazines.'

Giles felt suddenly sorry for him. 'Do have another slice of cake,' he said kindly.

Rose took the news down to Weldon House on her afternoon off. The weather was holding fine, and the paths were dry. September was nicer for walking than August – generally fresher. The sky seemed higher, pale blue veined with white, like the trails milk makes when a drop is spilled into water. The hedges were stuffed with sparrows making a cheerful racket, and she saw a blackbird sitting on top of a bramble bush, extracting berries from among the thorns with delicate, precise tugs. She picked one for herself, and it was sweet and tasted of childhood. Then she cursed herself for a fool, because there was a purple stain on the forefinger of her glove.

She didn't think much about Hook's violent death. He was gone, and that was that. She did wonder what would happen now, though. Hook had been only temporary butler – though he had arrogantly assumed he would keep the job for good – but a butler there had to be. She thought of a new man coming in, the friction that would inevitably occur until everyone settled into a new groove. Nothing had really gone right, she thought, since Mr Moss had left. She wished they could have him back. He'd had his faults, but so did they all, and better the devil you know, as the saying was. She didn't suppose he liked it very much at Miss Eddowes's, after the splendour of the Castle, but there was no way back, not with his heart being unable to stand the strain.

He was going to be upset about his stamp collection, but on the other hand, he'd be pleased that the police thought they might get the silver back. He was a very loyal old stick, she had to give him that.

Miss Eddowes was out, having tea with Mrs Brinklow at the Red House – Rose had some knowledge of her tea-visiting habits and had chosen the time accordingly – and Mrs Grape was 'taking the weight off her feet' in her own room until it was time to start dinner, so Moss was able to sit and talk to Rose without disturbing his conscience. There was a bench outside the back door, nicely shaded by one of the apple trees in the little orchard to the side of the house, and they sat there in the pleasant warm air, the sunlight dappling the ripening fruits, glowing dabs of amber and topaz.

Moss took the chief constable's opinion about his stamp collection better than Rose had expected.

'To be honest, I'd given up hope of ever seeing it again. I don't suppose it was worth much in actual money, but it was worth a lot to me. Twenty years I've been collecting them.' He sighed heavily. 'But I shall be glad if they get the silver back. I feel guilty – I should have kept a sharper eye on what Hook was doing.'

'Everybody feels something was their fault,' Rose said impatiently. 'What with Mr Afton blaming himself for Hook's death. He was a bad lot, Mr Moss, and he came to a bad end. I shan't shed a tear for him.'

'We are all brothers and sisters in each other,' Moss pronounced. 'Which of us is without sin?'

'I've never stolen anything in my life.'

'Ah, but when we come before the Great Throne at life's end—'

Rose had no patience with this line of speculation. It was bad enough having it on Sunday, without extra portions during the week. 'What we're all wondering,' she interrupted him firmly, 'is who is going to replace him as butler.'

Moss looked anguished. 'Ah, Rose, I wish it could be me. I dream sometimes that his lordship has come down to ask Miss Eddowes for my return, and I walk up the hill and take my old place . . .' His eyes were moist and he stopped to pull out a handkerchief and blow his nose. 'But the doctor said it's out of the question,' he went on.

'I suppose they'll have to go to an agency,' Rose said.

'What a dreadful thought,' Moss said, shocked.

'Don't see they'll have any choice. Trouble is, you never know who you're going to get that way. And you always wonder, if a man's out of work and having to go to an agency, if there isn't a reason behind it.'

'It's a pity her ladyship's gone to France,' Moss said. 'She knows so many people, she would probably hear of someone suitable. Her young ladyship doesn't have that sort of – of *web* of acquaintance, if I may phrase it so.'

'She's been busy having babies,' Rose pointed out tersely. 'Hardly been anywhere to make friends.'

'Indeed, indeed, I meant no criticism. And we are blessed with two male heirs.' Still 'we', Rose noted. 'How is the new baby?'

'Coming along slowly. And little Lord Ayton is flourishing

like a weed. Running about all over the place now. You never saw such a likely lad.'

She told him a few stories about the heir's activities, and then it was time to go. Moss got gallantly to his feet to see her off, and looked so wistful as he asked her to convey his regards to everyone that she said, 'Why don't you come up to the Castle some time and give 'em yourself? On your next afternoon off. Come up and have tea – everyone'd love to see you.'

The suggestion seemed to cheer him. 'I will, I will. I'd like to see Mrs Webster and Mr Crooks and the others. I'll take a little stroll up there next time I'm off duty.'

Nina left her luggage to be collected, and walked the half-mile or so to Wriothesby House, partly because Trump needed the walk after the long journey, and partly because she rather fancied stealing unannounced into 'the vicinage of her home', like Jane Eyre.

Bobby, her husband and children were remaining a few days in London and had urged her to stay too, but as they were residing not at an hotel but with a relative she felt awkward about accepting and declared she was expected at home. She sent a telegram to say she was coming, but seeing an earlier train when she got to the station, she took it, so there was no-one waiting for her when she reached Market Harborough.

The little town looked pleasantly familiar, and one or two people she knew gave her a smile and a nod as she passed. Turning in at her gate, she saw the façade of the house, like a friendly face, and thought again how beautiful it was. Trump suddenly remembered, and pulled at his leash, so she let it go, and he dashed away and in through the open front door with a single glad bark. So by the time she stepped in, Mrs Deering had appeared from the nether regions with such a welcoming smile she really did feel she had come home.

'Oh, madam, there you are! But we were expecting you later. We must have misunderstood.'

'I saw the chance of an earlier train and took it, that's all.'

'But there was no-one to meet you! Dear me, did you take a taxi?'

'No, I walked. It's no distance.'

'Well, the master's gone down to the factory. He was going to go on to the station afterwards. He'll be so put out to've missed you.' She lowered her voice confidentially. 'He's been so excited about you coming home, ma'am. Quite like a boy at Christmas, if you'll forgive me.'

'Oh dear, I didn't think of that,' Nina faltered. Would he be angry, waiting on the platform for no reason?

'Not to worry, ma'am, I'll send the boy down with a message. I expect you'd like some tea. I'll bring it to you in the drawing-room. Oh, there's a letter for you, come this morning.' She took it from the hall table and handed it over.

The drawing-room was pleasantly cool and smelt of lavender wax. The French windows were open onto the terrace, and the smell there was real lavender – bushes of it planted along the edge of the wall. Trump dashed out with a thousand things to investigate, and Nina sat on the stone bench in the shade of the house and read her letter. It was from Kitty:

. . . a dreadful shock, however little one liked the man. You will think me silly, but I was rather afraid of him. But now all the uproar is over, I am in hopes that the house will settle down and everyone will be happier. He was not a calming influence below stairs so Hatto tells me. I'm just grateful that my mother-in-law was not here – she left the day before it happened – because I'm sure she would have found a way to make it my fault.

Nina turned the page and read the descriptions of the new baby and his remarkable progress. Alexander. What a strange, but noble name, she thought. So Kitty had two sons now, and she had none. She read on, about Louis, how he was running around and climbing on things, and how he had taken an odd fancy to Giles's man Afton.

> I suppose now that I have done my duty [Kitty went on], I shall not have to have any more children, and will see less of Giles even than I do now. He is always busy about the estate and often I do not see him all day until dinner.

Nina contemplated the message here. Kitty could not be explicit in writing as she might have been if they were together, but the paragraph sounded wistful. Was she saying that she thought Giles would no longer come to her bed? Nina took her heart by the scruff of its neck and would *not* allow it to feel any gladness about that. Poor Kitty, who was so in love with him! Would it be worse, she wondered, to be married to him and hardly ever see him? No, she thought, Kitty still had the privilege of calling him her husband, and the right to demand certain things of him. If she, Nina, had been his wife, she was sure he— *No!* She would not think along those lines. She turned hastily to the letter again.

> Alice is my great comfort, always ready to walk with me or sit with me. I shall be able to be a better companion to *her*, because Dr Arbogast says I may now resume riding, as long as I stay at the walk for the first weeks. I can't express how much I'm looking forward to going out on my darling Apollo, whom I've hardly ridden since Giles first gave him to me. And riding at the walk will be no penance, when I can be taken by his four legs where my own two won't carry me! Alice, of course, would spend every waking hour riding if she could, so being with me will not be nearly so irksome as it must sometimes have been these long months of being housebound.

Trump came galloping in from the garden and dashed past her, barking, and she heard the rumble of male voices and realised her husband had returned. She jumped up and hurried to catch him in the hall, thinking that if he'd had a wild-goose chase, his temper would not be improved by having to come and find her.

But his face broke into a beaming smile as soon as he saw her. Behind him, Decius smiled too, and nodded a greeting, but she had no time to speak to him. She had to have her hands captured by Cowling's, and both her cheeks heartily kissed.

'Well, well, there you are! Safe and sound after all!'

'I'm sorry about catching an earlier train—' she began contritely.

'No, no, don't be! I'm with you the sooner, that's all that matters. Well, my dear, and how are you? You look positively blooming! Did you have a pleasant time? I've missed you so much. I've been like a poor old dog – haven't I, Decius? – sniffing about the house looking for his lost mistress! Nothing's the same when you're not here. Nothing's right. Are you glad to be back?'

Luckily for Nina, Mrs Deering said at that moment, 'I was just about to take madam's tea in, sir, and it's only a matter of putting two more cups on the tray.'

'I can't stay,' Decius said. 'I only came to pay my respects to Mrs Cowling, but I must absolutely dash.'

'I'll speak to you later,' Cowling said to him, linking his arm through Nina's. 'You'll dine with us? No? Then I'll see you early tomorrow. Yes, bring the tea in, Mrs Deering. I'm ready for a cup.'

In the drawing-room he led Nina to one of the settles and sat, drawing her down beside him and, with her hand firmly held in his, surveyed her face as though taking an inventory of her features. Nina felt awkward under such close scrutiny. She tried to deflect it by saying, 'I'm afraid I may be a bit brown. We were out of doors so much, and it's hard always to remember to keep one's face shaded.'

'No, no, you've nothing more than a bit of healthy colour. It suits you – you're looking more beautiful than ever. Oh, Nina, I've missed you so much!'

Mrs Deering came in with the tray, and he released her hand and got up to move a table into position for her. Nina watched, with a little cold feeling round her heart, because she knew she hadn't missed him, not a bit. She'd had a wonderful time with Bobby and her family: so much company, so many to talk to, and laugh with, such warmth, and family feeling; such conversation and games, such soon-familiar jokes and carefree larking. There had been sea-bathing, which she had never tried before, and now absolutely adored, and sailing, carriage rides to the famous sights, and dinners, and musical evenings, and dancing. And Bobby's brother Adam had flirted with her so skilfully, making her feel beautiful and special and just a *little* excited, without ever crossing the line. She had forgotten for most of the time that she was a married woman. She had forgotten Mr Cowling.

Now, as he bent to move the table slightly, a shaft of sunlight from the French windows struck his face, and illuminated it cruelly. She saw how old he was, with his indoor pallor and the bags under his eyes, the frown-lines across his forehead and the slackness of the skin under his jaw. Involuntarily her memory contrasted it with Adam's firm young good looks. Mr Cowling was well-dressed and neatly groomed; she noticed his hands gripping the table edge and they were clean and well-kept, the nails neatly cut. But they were not young hands. He was a nice, kind, older man, and she felt absolutely no connection to him, as though he were someone she happened to be passing in the street. *But she was his wife!* She was married to him, this random stranger, and must remain so for ever; she must live with him and endure his caresses, while her heart and her instinct told her to run away, run away far and fast and never come back.

He sat again beside her, beaming, and said, 'There! Shall you pour, my love? I've missed having you to pour my tea. You were away so long, sometimes I thought you were never coming back.'

She threw a sidelong glance at him – had he somehow heard her thought? 'Only eight weeks,' she said.

'Nine, I think,' he corrected. 'But a very long time, whichever it was.'

She concentrated on pouring the tea. There was thin bread-and-butter, and scones, and Dundee cake. Trump came up close, nose lifted to identify what was too high up for him to see. She handed Cowling his cup and plate, and poured her own, aware that he was staring at her minutely the whole time. And when at last she could no longer put off looking at him, she found his expression solemn – almost apologetic.

'I've had plenty of time, while you've been away, to think about things,' he said.

'Have you?'

'Yes, and I came to the conclusion that I've been a fool.'

Her heart contracted. Did he know – had he somehow guessed?

'A fool and a crosspatch,' he went on.

'Oh, no,' she demurred.

'How did you put up with me?' he said. 'Telling you off, scolding you like a puppy, smothering your happy spirits when I should have been rejoicing in them.'

She looked at him blankly, not knowing where this was going, her mind churning with various guilty thoughts.

'You're young and eager and free-spirited, my Nina, and I don't want to change that. I don't want to damp down that fire. If I did, it'd serve me right if I lost you – and I have to confess to you that there've been times these nine long weeks

394

when I've thought you'd be a fool to come back to me!' He gave a nervous smile.

She smiled back, and said, 'No, nonsense!'

'Aye, well, you get to thinking strange things when you're too much alone. It's not a long step from thinking how lucky I am that you married me and how I don't deserve you, to thinking some other more worthy feller might steal you away.'

'You mustn't think like that. I'm your wife – and *I*'m the lucky one.'

'Oh, my love,' he said, in a broken tone, and had his hands not been full, he'd have drawn her to him and kissed her. He looked troubled. 'I know I've not been a true husband to you – no, you don't have to deny it – and you'd be in your rights to despise me—'

'Joseph, please don't talk like that,' she said, using his name, as she hardly ever did, in the hope that it would move him. 'It's not true.'

'But I want to make it up to you, if I can,' he continued. 'And to begin with, I'm going to buy you a horse. You should have had one from the start, and I was a fool to listen to those spiteful old cats. No, don't say anything. I'd have had one waiting for you when you got back here, except that I thought you'd enjoy choosing for yourself. You shall have a horse, and ride whenever you want, and this winter you shall hunt too, if you like. And I might even hire a horse and come out with you now and again – though I'm not the world's greatest rider. And I'm going to try to arrange my work so I spend more time with you, and we'll be social and do things together. Dinners and balls and London trips – whatever you like. I want you to be happy, my Nina.'

'I *am* happy,' she said. Thinking about the horse she was to have, she put down her cup and leaned forward to kiss him heartily enough to convince him she meant it. 'You are much too kind to me,' she said and, the first kiss having been to his cheek, laid a second on his lips.

'No,' he said, seeming a little shaken. 'I could never be *too* kind to you. Nothing I do could be worthy of you.'

She felt so bad, all she could think to do was to kiss him again. Feeling his lips respond, his breath quicken, she wondered if he would come to her bed that night, and if, perhaps, he might manage what he hardly ever had. And how she would feel about it.

But he didn't.

CHAPTER TWENTY-ONE

It could not be said that Rachel was pining away. She did think about Angus a great deal, especially in the moments between getting into bed and falling asleep, when she liked to conjure his face and the feeling of his lips on hers. But she was young and full of life, and there was so much to do. There were carriage rides and promenades and boat trips; lunches, teas and dinners; the spa and the opera; card evenings and musical evenings and dancing – lots of dancing. She tried sea-bathing but didn't much care for it, and her mother said it was inelegant, so she didn't try it again. Instead, aware she looked very good on a horse, she rode in the park, and found she had started a little fashion for it.

Above all, there were lots of idle young men to flatter her, flirt with her, dance with her, and compete to ride beside her. When they went out in the carriage, they were halting every few yards for some or other gallant to raise his hat and stand chatting, asking their plans for the day, begging for a dance or a place beside her at cards. It would have taken more determination than Rachel had to remain miserable under such an onslaught.

Since the casino was closed, having been damaged by fire the year before and now under reconstruction, card parties were taking place instead at the various grand villas. Aunt Vicky, who enjoyed a little light gambling, hosted one every week. Many of the guests were of her generation and older, but she made sure to invite enough of the young hopefuls too. Few of them were English, and Rachel's French and German improved apace.

For Angus to write to her needed some ingenuity. He could not write openly, of course. He persuaded his younger sister Gussie to write to Alice at Ashmore – luckily they had been notably friendly on previous visits to Kincraig, united by a love of horses – and to enclose a note from himself to Rachel. Alice would then enclose the note in her letter to Rachel. The sisters had not been much in the habit of corresponding, but with the dowager away, no-one else thought anything of it. Giles agreed to have her letters sent to the post with his own without a second thought, barely pausing on his way out of the house to say, 'Yes, yes, of course. Just put it on the hall table with the others. Oh, and give her my love.'

Rachel had been more than two weeks at the Villa Eugénie before she received the first note from Angus. It was full of declarations of love, of precious do-you-remembers, and a mixture of hope and despair about the eventual outcome. Rachel read it every night and every morning, and was able to go out fortified, to meet the challenges of the day with gay smiles and flirtatious eyelashes. Not being a great hand with the pen, she did not reply immediately: she would have to write something to Alice as a cover, and *two* letters were harder work than she liked. So it was over a week before her reply to Angus set off on its tortuous journey. It didn't occur to Rachel how long he would have been waiting for reassurance from her by the time it got there. However, if she had shown eagerness to write back to Alice, her mother would certainly have been suspicious, so perhaps it was just as well.

Linda, freed of her children and immediate money worries, and looking better in greys and lavenders than she had in blacks, was enjoying herself. She preferred Europeans, with their more formal manners, to Englishmen, and there were several promising older men she thought might do. Her German was good, from childhood holidays with Aunt Vicky, and she was a good card player. And being relieved of the anxieties of the past ten years, she was eating more and filling out a little, and losing the hungry-cat look that had so repelled.

To begin with she was concentrating on the Prince of Usingen, who was still hanging around their party. Since she could see for herself that his attitude towards Rachel was fatherly, she concluded that it must be her he was interested in. What else could bring him so often to the villa, or have him hurrying to join their group at every gathering? She responded by attaching herself to him and letting him know, in the subtlest terms, that she would welcome his addresses. She found him a reserved and awkward sort of lover, and had to do all the encouraging herself, but the more she discovered about his fortune, the more she liked him.

She thought it a very good omen when he invited her to meet his sister and her husband at the villa they had rented; and she noted his thoughtfulness in including her mother, sister, aunt and uncle in the invitation. For herself, she would not have minded a bit more passion and a bit less propriety to get things moving along, but given her delicate position – her mourning was not widely known, but it would curtail her pleasures if it became so – it was probably just as well that he was moving slowly.

The sister turned out to be a mousy, frumpy thing, but Linda graciously encouraged her, staying by her side and chatting to her, asking about her children, and praising Paul's qualities – doing everything, in fact, to prove to Paul that she would fit into his family. Her mother, she noted, was more acidulous even than usual, and cast many black looks at her during the evening. Linda shrugged them off. Her mother was in a temper, she supposed, from having to talk all evening to Paul's sister's husband – a stout, moustachioed bore.

Probably she thought Linda ought to have sacrificed herself by taking him on instead.

It was at the casino evening at the Countess de Coligny's villa that Paul Usingen finally managed to corner Maud in a tiny anteroom between two salons and, drawing her into the shade of some rather outrageous crimson velvet curtains, held her hand in both his and said, '*Gnädige Gräfin! Endlich!* At last I have you alone. I am tortured daily to be near you and not to talk.'

'We talk every day, Prince,' she said.

'But it is not talk of the souls, only of the mouths.' She flinched a little at the word 'souls' and he hurried on, 'I have waited for you, as you asked me, but now I plead you: do not make me wait for longer. Give me your answer – say you will marry me. Have I not done everything you wished? Made myself pleasant to your family, carried myself with discretion? What more test must I pass? *Schone Dame*—'

'I am not beautiful,' Maud said, trying to pull her hand away, 'and to hear you say so makes me think you are not of a serious character.'

He looked surprised. 'But you are beautiful to me! I would not say so otherwise. Please, I do not wish to wait any more. I wish to take you home to Usingen and begin our life together. Whatever you wish shall be yours – horses, carriages, jewels. A great wedding in Limburg Cathedral – the whole world will come. I have proved myself steady, faithful, is it not? Now *meine geliebte* will reward me, I know.'

He looked at her with such hope that this most unsentimental of women would have found it as hard to reject him as an ordinary person would find it hard to kick a puppy. And, in truth, she was tired. Bringing out Rachel had worn her to the bone, and so far had not yielded the prize she had counted on. Usingen was willing to take on Rachel as well as her, and to find her a European noble for a husband. Rachel was growing flighty, and needed the discipline of a father. To get her well-married and off her hands was one reason to marry Usingen; to be free of money worries and mistress of her own house again was the other. And, really, what was there to wait for any more? He had said his sister wanted to go home at the end of the month. With her as chaperone, Maud and Rachel could go too. And Linda – who was growing more annoying by the day – could be sent back to England.

'Very well,' she said.

He looked so surprised she almost smiled. 'Very well? You mean yes? You will marry me?'

'Yes, I will marry you,' she said clearly. 'And as soon as it can be arranged. I thought perhaps Rachel and I could go back with your sister—'

She stopped because Usingen was kissing her hand passionately and murmuring endearments in broken German, and at any moment someone might come through the curtains, and she was not yet hardened enough to be caught dallying in alcoves with strange men.

'Say nothing of this,' she said sternly, 'until I have told my family.'

'But – but—'

'I shall not keep you waiting long. You may come to the villa tomorrow at noon.'

She nodded, withdrew her hand too firmly for resistance, and walked away.

Linda found her mother walking in the villa's garden before breakfast the next morning. It was a lovely day, the sky pale and clear with the promise of heat later, the air cool and green-smelling. Maud was trying to settle her agitated mind. She had said 'yes' so easily last night, but marriage was a big step, as was leaving the land of her birth. She was not regretting her decision, but she needed time to absorb the new ideas. The last person she wanted to see was Linda.

But Linda wanted to see her, and was as tenacious as ever Maud could be.

'I've come to the conclusion, Mama,' she said, falling in beside her as she strolled down the green path, 'that the Prince of Usingen is not in the least interested in Rachel. I don't think he was ever going to make an offer for her.'

'Indeed,' Maud said discouragingly. *Not now, not now!*

'So if you were expecting something of the sort, you will be disappointed.'

Maud said nothing.

Goaded, Linda went on, 'You must be wondering how I can be so sure.'

'I wonder nothing,' Maud said truthfully.

'I've been observing him with Rachel these past weeks, and he's attentive to her, it's true, but like a father, not like a suitor.'

Maud said harshly, 'I wish you would not talk so much, Linda. You give me a headache with your constant—'

'But he *is* a suitor,' Linda went on relentlessly. 'Nothing else would explain his hanging around us so much. And it's thanks to me.'

'What *are* you talking about?' Maud snapped.

'*I*'ve taken the trouble to encourage him, to bring him out, and his attentions to me are becoming so marked, I think even you must have noticed them. Of course, he has to be discreet, since I'm still officially in first mourning, but there's no disguising his sentiments. That's why I felt I should warn you that he won't be making an offer for Rachel. He is in love with *me*.'

Maud looked at her daughter at last and, seeing her self-satisfied smile, wanted to slap her, even while at the same time feeling a queer twist of pity. She felt no responsibility for the way Linda, or any of her children, had turned out

402

– that was what one had nannies and governesses and tutors for – but Linda seemed to her just then like a wounded thing, or perhaps something half formed. Not a whole person.

'You are quite mistaken,' she said. Time to put Linda out of her delusion. 'Paul Usingen has been taking the trouble to get to know you and Rachel as a compliment to *me*.'

'Oh, *Mother*, how can you—' Linda began, exasperated at such folly.

'He proposed marriage to me in June. I asked him to wait for my reply. I gave it last night. I agreed to marry him as soon as arrangements can be made.'

Linda stared. '*You?*' she said at last, in disbelief. Maud held her gaze steadily, and her expression turned to disgust. 'You? But – you're *old*! It's ridiculous! Getting married at your age? And you're a widow! Father's hardly cold in his grave, and you're going to—'

'Don't dare to invoke your father's name,' Maud said furiously. 'As if you ever cared a jot for his opinion on anything!'

'I care more than you, that's plain to see! What do you think he'd say about this if he were alive today?' The absurdity of what she'd just said tripped her up for a moment, but she recovered herself. 'You'll make a fool of us all! You'll make the family a laughing-stock! I won't have it!'

'*You* won't have it?'

'You can't care for him, anyway – he's old and ugly. You just want him because he wants *me*. You always spoil things for me. You could never bear to let me to have anything nice of my own. Well, I won't let you take him away from me! I won't!'

Her face threatened to crumple into tears, and Maud slapped it briskly, but at the last moment modified the blow to a light tap. 'Keep your voice down,' she commanded calmly. 'If you become hysterical I shall slap you hard. Now listen to me. The prince has asked me to marry him and I have said yes. It is all agreed. Any feelings you thought he had for you were in your imagination. And if you think it is seemly for a woman less than four months widowed to be publicly throwing herself at another man, you are no daughter of mine. You will behave yourself, or I will have you locked up as irrational.'

Linda gasped as though cold water had been thrown in her face. *Locked up?* Her mother would do it, too. Her eyes filled with bewilderment. 'But – but, I thought . . .'

'No, you didn't,' Maud said firmly. 'Now we will go in to breakfast and I will tell the rest of the family about my betrothal. And if you don't want people to pity you, you will pretend to be happy about it, and you will behave civilly towards the prince. We will forget we ever had this conversation. *I* certainly shall never mention it.'

She turned for the house. Linda trailed after her, but she soon straightened her back. What she mostly felt was anger, and anger was very sustaining to dignity.

Giles put his head round the Peacock Room door and said, 'I shan't be in to luncheon.'

Kitty looked up in alarm. 'You're not going out?'

'Didn't I tell you? I have to see Adeane and Saddler about the poaching.'

'But can't you do that another time?'

'No, because I have to see Bexley this afternoon with the evidence if we're to make a case.' Lord Bexley was the local magistrate. 'Why? What's the matter?'

'The person is coming this morning to be interviewed for governess,' Kitty said.

'Oh, Lord! I'd forgotten. You can interview her on your own, surely?'

Kitty was dismayed. 'You said you'd do it with me.'

'Interviewing servants is your job, not mine. You're the mistress of the house. I can't be expected to undertake everything personally. Anyway, it can't be helped. I have to see Bexley today, because he's going away tomorrow morning, and I have to see Adeane and Saddler first.'

'They're *your* niece and nephew.'

His brows drew down. 'Don't be petulant, Kitty,' he said. 'It doesn't suit you.' And he withdrew, and closed the door.

Kitty was still shy with strangers, and though she was getting used to taking decisions about the house, it seemed like too great a responsibility to be choosing a governess for Linda's children. She admired clever people, but felt inferior to them. She didn't even know what questions she ought to ask. What if she employed someone quite unsuitable? She would be blamed. Giles would blame her. Her mother-in-law would blame her. Linda would *never* let it go.

Her imagination had presented her with someone tall and stern, with a steely mind, who would barely be able to conceal her contempt for Kitty's weakness. But when she entered the library, the woman standing by the unlit fireplace was only of medium height, and quite pleasant-faced. And, on seeing Kitty, she smiled, and the smile seemed to have a hint of nervousness about it. Only then did it occur to her that the applicant might have been dreading the interview as much as her. Certainly, she had as much to lose.

It cheered her considerably, and enabled her to say in a firm voice, 'Miss Kettel? I'm Lady Stainton.'

'How do you do, your ladyship?' Miss Kettel said, taking Kitty's offered hand. And, yes, there was a slight tremor in the voice, which heartened Kitty more.

'Won't you sit down?' There were two upholstered settles, facing each other on either side of the fire. They sat and looked at each other. Miss Kettel seemed to be about forty, with crinkled black hair threaded here and there with grey, and grey eyes behind steel-framed glasses. Her figure was trim and she was neatly dressed in a two-piece of navy cloth, and a nondescript hat of black felt. Her face was oval, rather pale, and while you would not have called her plain, exactly, neither was she beautiful. Ordinary, was the adjective that came to Kitty's mind. Everything about her was ordinary. If you passed her in the street, or sat in the same carriage with her in a train, you would not spare her a second glance. And Kitty, who had always been regarded as beautiful, and had been, besides, an important heiress and had married an earl, felt an unexpected sympathy.

The silence had now gone on too long. Miss Kettel raised an enquiring eyebrow, and Kitty giggled. 'It's very foolish,' she said, 'but I haven't the least idea what questions I ought to ask you. I feel quite at a loss.'

Miss Kettel smiled, and her face, and particularly her eyes, were transformed. 'It *is* an awkward situation,' she agreed. She had a pleasant voice, for which Kitty was grateful. She already had two harsh-voiced women in the house and didn't need another. 'Well, ma'am, you might, perhaps, ask me for my references. Or you could quiz me about my experience.'

'Oh, I know about all that, from the letter the agency sent,' Kitty said, 'and you seem quite suitable. I can look at your references later. Shall I tell you about the children? Arabella is nine and Arthur is eight, and I'm afraid they're terribly ignorant. They haven't had a governess before, and no-one has given them any regular schooling, as far as I know.'

'As far as you know? Are they not your children, ma'am?'

'Oh, no – didn't they explain? They're the children of my husband's sister. She was recently widowed and she and the children have come to live here permanently. So they need taking in hand. They are nice children,' she added, 'but they may not take to schoolroom discipline straight away. They have rather run wild until now.'

'Who has been looking after them?'

'Servants, mostly. Though my sister-in-law takes them out riding, and plays with them sometimes.'

'May I ask when they lost their father?'

'In June.'

'Poor little things. They will still be shocked and grieving.'

Kitty liked the fact that she had picked up on that aspect of it. It seemed to her, now she thought about it, that no-one had really wondered how Arabella and Arthur actually *felt*. 'They have been living with a large family of cousins since the unhappy event, and I think the company has cushioned the blow for them,' she said.

'In my experience, Lady Stainton,' said Miss Kettel, 'children who suffer a bereavement may seem quite unaffected for a time, but the shock eventually reveals itself, often in ways one might not expect. But forewarned is forearmed. Is it possible to meet their mother?'

Kitty felt embarrassed. 'Oh – no, not at present. She has gone with some of the family to France. But she has never had a great deal to do with them. I don't think you will find that she has any tendency to interfere in the schoolroom.'

Miss Kettel smiled. 'You said, "I will find". Was it a slip of the tongue, or does it mean you have decided to engage me?'

Kitty smiled too. She had lost any nervousness around this nice, ordinary woman; and indeed, without realising it, had been assuming for some time that she would be the new governess. 'Will you take the position?'

'I will. Thank you very much.'

'Without even meeting the children?'

'They will have to take me on trust, so I shall return the compliment. I have enjoyed this interview so much, your ladyship, when I had been dreading it, that I'm sure I shall like it here. You are not, if you will excuse my saying so, what I was expecting from the words "Lady Stainton" and "Ashmore Castle".'

'And you are not at all what I was expecting, either – I'm glad to say,' said Kitty. 'Can you start straight away?'

She hoped it was going to be all right. She thought it would be. At all events, Alice would be glad.

Two horses cantered along the brow of the hill, one liver-chestnut, the other bright chestnut, each ridden by a neat, female figure. They stopped at the end of the ride to let the horses breathe. The clouds spun fast across the windy blue of the sky, changing the colours down in the valley with their shadows, so that the village stood out, now bright and confident, now huddled and dull. 'I think it's going to rain,' Alice said. 'Can't you smell it?'

'We'd better turn for home,' Kitty said. 'I think I've had enough now, anyway.'

'I've *never* had enough,' Alice said, but cheerfully, turning Pharaoh's head downhill. Apollo turned too, and seeing they were facing home, they bucketed a little and nipped at each other playfully. They could smell the rain too, and as far as horses can imagine, they saw warm stables and full mangers ahead.

'What do you think of this news of your mother's?' Kitty asked, checking Apollo, whose stride was longer. 'I haven't had a chance yet to talk to you about it. It was rather a shock.'

'It was to me,' Alice said. 'One doesn't think of one's mother as being someone who could get married.'

'But it's a good thing? You aren't upset about it? I mean, on your father's behalf?'

'Oh, no.' She paused, assembling her thought. 'I didn't really know Papa very well. He was just a name – like the King. And somehow I never thought of them being married anyway, my mother and father, not the way you and Giles are married. They were just – the earl and countess. As if it was a job. Do you understand what I mean?'

Kitty nodded. 'Was Rachel upset? You had a letter from her.'

'Surprised, I think. And relieved – she thought the prince was courting *her*, and she's jolly glad he wasn't, because she didn't want to marry him one bit.'

'It must be strange for her. She's been in the middle of it all. Did she never think the prince was courting your mother?'

'Apparently not,' Alice said. But she had not thought her sister particularly noticing. Ever since she'd started her come-out, she'd had nothing but clothes and dancing and flirting on her mind. 'She *is* upset, though,' she went on, 'not because of Mother getting married, but because she has to go with them to Germany, and the prince has promised to find her a husband there, which would mean she'd probably never come back. He knows some Russian archdukes, you know – she might even end up there.'

'That would be exciting,' Kitty offered doubtfully.

'But she doesn't want to go to Russia. She wants to come home.' She couldn't tell Kitty about Angus, because that would be breaking a confidence. 'But I dare say she'll get used to the idea,' she went on. Rachel had always had her mind fixed on a high marriage, and Alice didn't think her recent romance with Angus would survive the lure of coronets and ermine. Especially if Rachel and Angus were parted for a long time. Rachel was not the sort of girl to hold out against sustained pressure, especially if it were of the pleasurable sort. She thought poor Angus was doomed to disappointment.

'I shouldn't like to have to live abroad all my life,' Kitty said, looking around at the green hills and woods, and the roof and chimneys of the Castle just coming into view below, and thought of her two little sons. 'I have everything I want here.'

'I shouldn't mind travelling,' Alice said, 'but I'd always want to come home. Not that there's much chance of my travelling – except to Usingen. I suppose I'll have to go over there for the wedding. I just hope the prince doesn't want to keep me there like Rachel and get me married off. Which would please my mother no end, of course. She'd practically given up on me, which was a relief, but if the prince can scrape me off on some local landgrave . . .'

'She wouldn't make you marry against your will,' Kitty said.

'You don't know my mother. I must try and make Giles promise to say I have to come back straight after the wedding. Kitty, will you ask him, too? Say you need me here, that you can't do without me.'

'I'll say all of that, if you think it will help,' Kitty said. 'And I *would* miss you dreadfully, though I shouldn't stand in the way if you were going to a good marriage, with a husband you loved.'

'*That* won't happen. I'm going to be here for ever, being aunt to your children. So please tell Giles to order me home.'

'I will, I promise.' She looked sidelong at her sister-in-law, and saw how much Alice had grown up in the past year. Her face was a young woman's rather than a girl's – and just now, as she rode deep in thought, unaware she was being studied, it was a sad face. What troubles Alice could have she didn't know, but she was very fond of her, so she said hesitantly, 'Wouldn't you like to get married?'

Alice didn't answer for a long time. At last she said, 'To the right person, yes, I would. But it will never happen.'

'You don't know that.'

'I do,' Alice said calmly. 'And I'd sooner die than be married to anyone else. So here I stay.'

Anyone else? Did that mean she was in love with someone? Someone unsuitable? Kitty wanted to say: 'Marrying the man you love doesn't always work out like a fairy-tale.' Although, in her case, she would sooner have the crumbs from Giles's table than a feast from anyone else's. Poor Alice evidently believed there would not even be crumbs. She wondered who the man was. She couldn't ask . . .

410

Alice was saying something, and she came back from her thoughts. It was about the dinner party they were giving on Saturday evening. Kitty's parents were coming to visit for the Saturday-to-Monday, to see the new baby, and there would be guests in to dinner on Saturday to meet them.

'What was Giles fussing about?' Alice was saying. 'Something about wine.'

'Oh, because we don't have a butler, and Moss always chose the wines – proposed them, at any rate, not that Giles ever disagreed, because Moss knew every bottle in the cellar and Giles has no idea what's there.'

'He can always look at the cellar book,' Alice said sensibly. 'That's what it's there for.'

Kitty smiled. 'No, it's there for the butler to look at.'

'He should ask Afton to look at it and choose the wines,' Alice suggested. 'He's served in lots of great houses and I'm sure he must know a thing or two. And he seems such a sensible, intelligent person.'

She could not praise Afton too highly for Kitty. 'He's wonderful with Louis. And he knows a lot about gardens and plants, too. I had such an interesting conversation with him up in the nursery the other day.'

Alice laughed. 'My idea of Afton is that he knows a lot about anything you happen to be discussing at the time.'

'You think it's a trick?' Kitty said doubtfully.

'No, I think it's a talent. Shall we trot a little? I'm getting cold.'

Richard crossed the room to kiss his grandmother's hand. 'You'll never guess what I've just done,' he said.

'Something disgraceful, no doubt,' said Grandmère.

'No, no. I've just ridden on a motor-bus for the first time. I was happily walking when I heard it coming along, and couldn't resist.'

'And how did you find it?'

'Noisy, but otherwise perfectly bus-like. And I saw two more during the ride.'

'There are more every day, it seems,' said Grandmère, indifferently.

'You don't approve of them, I take it? You do not want to see the noble horse displaced by these dirty, stinking mechanical demons?'

'*Tiens!* Only a fool would think so. Railway trains had to come, and motor-cars have to come, and so the world goes. And,' she added, with delicate practicality, 'one would like to cross the street without dirtying one's shoes. What are you doing in Town?'

'Visiting you, *ma chère.*'

'*Evidemment. Et ensuite?*'

'I came up to see the motor wagons we ordered for the milk collection, which are ready, and to decide what colour they should be. I have decided they should have Ash Valley Dairy Company painted along the sides.'

'Ah, you are a company now! Yet you appear to me still a half-grown boy. And your hair is too long.'

Richard cocked his head. 'You seem somewhat out of temper, dear. Has something happened?'

'Lady Vane has happened. She called this morning *pour m'agacer.* The subject of Sir Thomas and his new "friend" was much on her mind.'

'Lady Vane hasn't *got* a mind.' So it was common gossip now, was it? He contemplated her face. 'Are you angry?' She 'pupped' her lips. 'Jealous?' he hazarded.

'*Ne t'inquiète pas pour moi,*' she said briskly. 'But what of you? Is your little heart bruised? Are you *écrasé?*'

'I've told you many times, *ma chère,* I am not in love with Miss Chloë. I am a little concerned for her – though she says she can control him. That he would never do anything she doesn't want.'

'That does not comfort me, even if it is true.'

'So it's the scandal that you mind, then? The *tracasserie*?'

'I am afraid for him,' she said, suddenly serious. '*Il est obsédé par son génie.*'

'She *is* brilliant,' he allowed cautiously.

Grandmère went on, her eyes distant, as though talking to herself. 'Of course, one always knew about his *grisettes*. A man must have his . . . accommodations. It is not of the least importance. They were nothing to me or to him. And it is long since I had any desires in that direction. Our relationship has long gone beyond such things. I was, with him, exactly where I wished to be. But now . . . but *this* . . .'

'What are you afraid of?'

'He is not behaving like himself. He talks about her to me. He never would have done so before. And the *appartement meublé* – what can that mean? On the one hand, it is as a man installs a mistress—'

'I don't believe they—'

'No. Not yet.' She raised her eyes to his. 'On the other hand, this particular *appartement* has not that look about it. A family property? It is too particular. *J'ai peur que ce soit différent.* There is danger here. I think— I *fear* he is falling in love with her.'

Richard could think of nothing comforting to say. He took her hand, and she let him.

'I can do nothing,' she went on. 'I am twenty years too old for him. And *she* is twenty years too young. He is at the age when men make follies. When they feel the cold breath of age on the neck and hurry towards the warm fire of youth.' Her eyes sharpened, focusing on him. 'I do not wish him to look foolish. The *tracasserie* – that can be lived through. It even enhances a man's view of himself. But I do not wish him to be made a fool. I have loved him a lifetime, almost. This child – is she a good girl? *Mais qu'importe?*' She answered herself. 'The world will decide and the truth will not matter. There will be hurt for all. *Tant pis!* But him – I care about him.'

'I don't know what to say to you,' Richard mourned. 'Except that I think the music is all she cares about.'

'*Ça se voit!*' she snorted. 'And the more hurt for him when he realises.'

'But he loves the music too. He wants to give her a big concert at the Queen's Hall.'

'I know.'

'A Schumann concerto.'

'Ha!' Grandmère laughed mirthlessly. 'He has *never* been able to play Schumann. He has not the subtlety. I have told him so for twenty years. What is this that you call it, when an old man gets a young creature to do what he cannot?'

'Is there a word for it?' Richard doubted.

'If there is not, it ought to be invented,' said Grandmère.

'What are all these tomes and magazines I see you reading?' Giles asked. He had passed the door of the Peacock Room on his way downstairs and saw his wife at the table with her head bent in study. So small and neat, with her soft curls and serious little face, she looked not like a mother of two but a good little girl at her schoolroom books.

Outside the autumn rain poured down with the air of never meaning to stop. Occasionally a gust of wind flung drops against the window with a noise like pebbles. Not a day for riding. There was a good fire in the grate, adding a mellow light to the greyness, and the room was cosy – so cosy that the dogs had found their way there. They apologetically beat their tails for him to say that they didn't *really* want to go out, but if he insisted . . . An additional attraction for them was the presence of Alice who, in a chair by the fire, had a pad propped on her knees and was sketching Kitty. Tiger had his head resting possessively on her foot.

Kitty looked up, her face lighting for him as it always did. 'They're about gardening.'

'I didn't know there were so many books about it.'

'Some are from our library, though they're very old. And some are borrowed – Mrs Brinklow is very interested in gardens. Mrs Bannister, too. And there's a magazine called *The Garden* – they had a lot of back issues at the rectory that they've let me borrow.'

Giles raised his eyebrows. 'How much can there be to say about gardens?' he said, in surprise. 'A garden is just *there*.'

Kitty smiled. 'But someone has to put it there in the first place.'

Alice looked up. 'You obviously aren't aware that there's a tremendous row going on in the gardening world,' she said severely, 'between two schools of thought. There's the classicists, who think gardens should be formal and geometrical, and the naturalists, who believe they should be flowing and wild.'

'Hardly any point in having a garden if it's wild, I should have thought.'

'Well, not really wild, just looking more as if it sprang up naturally. I understand the effect is even harder to achieve.'

'An artful artlessness? I can believe it,' said Giles. 'And which do you favour, my love?'

'Well,' said Kitty, 'I think it would be reasonable to have a mixture of the two.'

He laughed. 'Very diplomatic of you.'

Alice spoke up. 'Reginald Blomfield says gardeners think architects know nothing about gardening and architects think gardeners know nothing about design, and that there's a lot of truth on both sides.'

'Who is Reginald Blomfield?'

'He's famous,' Alice said reproachfully. 'He builds great houses and designs their gardens as well. He's an architect by training.'

'So I suppose he favours the classical garden?'

'Well, you would think so,' said Alice, 'but he does say there are some sites where a purely formal garden is out of the question.'

'I think ours is a case in point,' Kitty said.

'Because of the slope?' Giles hazarded. 'It's the reason we've never had much in the way of a garden.'

'The head of the other camp is William Robinson,' Alice said. 'Kitty has his book, *The Wild Garden*. He says a garden is not a house so it shouldn't have straight lines – the dead lines of the builder, he calls them. It should be all curves, like in nature. Flowing. And flowers all mixed up together.'

'Like an impressionist painting,' Kitty offered.

'It sounds messy. How would you keep it tidy?'

Kitty smiled a little. 'I think that's a question you're not supposed to ask.'

He smiled too. 'So where is all this tending?' he asked.

Kitty bit her lip. They had come to the point – and how would he feel about it? 'I'd like to ask Mr Blomfield to come and look at our site, and design a garden for us.'

'Not the wild fellow?'

'I think someone with architect training would be better, given the slope. And he has made a garden at his own house that's on the edge of a cliff, and I read that it's quite natural-looking. But the thing is, Giles, I expect he would charge quite a lot just for coming to look.'

Giles frowned. 'His fee for looking, I suspect, will be as nothing compared to the expense of actually *building* a garden on that slope. He saw Kitty's face fall, and said quickly, 'But if you want one, you shall have one. Go ahead and write to the fellow.'

'Really?' Kitty said, afraid to be pleased too soon. 'I think it will be *very* expensive.'

'I'm sure it will. But, thanks to you, we are not paupers any more.'

'I should like to do something for Ashmore Castle, to be remembered by,' Kitty said. 'Not just to live here and die and leave no trace.'

'She could be in the history books,' Alice said enthusiastically.

She put on a declamatory voice: '"The famous gardens at Ashmore Castle, which attract thousands of visitors every year, were the inspiration of the wife of the sixth Earl of Stainton."'

'Oh, Alice, don't,' Kitty said, putting her hands to her cheeks.

'Write to this Blomfield fellow,' Giles said. 'I care nothing about gardens, apart from kitchen gardens – I like asparagus and peas and a good peach if I can get them – but I know a lot of people do care, very much. You brought me your fortune to save Ashmore, Kitty. You should spend some of it on something you will love.'

With a genial nod, he walked briskly away, and the dogs, inspired by the movement, heaved themselves up and trotted after him.

That evening, when he was dressing for dinner, Giles found himself staring thoughtfully at Afton as he stood by holding his trousers ready, and finally said, 'Her ladyship made an interesting suggestion to me the other day.'

'Indeed, my lord?'

'Indeed, Afton. I see you standing patiently there, ready to pass me my breeches, and it occurs to me that being valet to a man who cares as little about clothes as I do must leave you with a lot of time on your hands.' Afton made no answer, merely looked at him enquiringly. 'There it is, you see,' Giles observed. 'That sagacity, that restraint. The analytical mind waiting until it has more information before venturing a remark. You should have been in the diplomatic service.'

'An impetuous man might conclude that you were trying to get rid of me, my lord,' Afton said.

'Perish the thought! If for no other reason, I couldn't deprive my son of your company.'

'A passing fancy, my lord. He'll grow out of it.'

'An impetuous master might conclude from that remark that you were hoping to be got rid of.'

'I meant only to reassure, my lord.'

'Look here, let's stop fencing. I can't believe brushing my jackets is enough for an able man like you, and since I should very much dislike to lose you, I would like to ask if you would care to take up the position of butler here. You look surprised,' he added. 'Did it never occur to you?'

'I assumed that you would advertise, or apply to an agency,' said Afton.

'But it would be disagreeable to everyone to have a stranger come in, after so many years of old Moss – aptly named, by the way, since he seemed to have generated spontaneously on the old grey stones. One can't imagine him actually being *hired*, or anything as prosaic as that. And if we did get in a stranger, who is to know how he would turn out? He might be dreadful, and there'd be months of upheaval and unhappiness. And believe me, Afton, I have too many things on my plate to want to have to worry about unhappy servants as well.'

'I haven't had the training, my lord,' Afton said.

'But you have served in great houses, you've seen it all done, you're an intelligent man. And I believe Mrs Webster is an excellent housekeeper and would surely give you any help you needed. There is a system in place, after all, and it's only a matter of keeping it going.'

'I can see some ways in which the system could be improved,' Afton commented thoughtfully.

Giles grinned. 'You see? You've already put yourself in the butler's shoes. I'm perfectly sure you could do the job. The only question is, would you want to?'

'I think it would be interesting, my lord. And I fully agree that a stranger of unknown peculiarities would be disruptive to everyone – myself included. But would the other servants accept me, knowing I'm not a butler trained?'

'Oh, you're a likeable fellow. You'd soon get on top of them. They'd be just as glad to have someone they know.'

'And who would valet you, my lord?'

'You would, at first. I'm sure you can combine the jobs.'

'It is done in many houses,' Afton agreed. 'Though not houses as large as this.'

'Well, we don't entertain much. And if we do start to entertain more, we'll get more help in. We need more footmen, anyway, having lost both Moss and Hook, and you can train one of them up to do the little valeting I need, if you get too busy.'

'I'm sure I can manage both, my lord – if you're willing to admit a few bumps along the road during the transition.'

'Good, that's settled, then,' Giles said, relieved to have the matter resolved so easily, after all the disruption and uncertainty. Afton, he thought, was strong and healthy, and ought to last him into old age. 'I'll tell her ladyship, and she can tell Mrs Webster – unless you would like a formal introduction to the assembled servants?'

'I think we can manage without that, my lord,' said Afton. 'Your trousers, my lord.'

CHAPTER TWENTY-TWO

Cyril was the only one below stairs to express opposition. He had been Hook's acolyte, trained by him, modelling himself on him, and Hook's violent and shameful death had affected him more than the others, who had been shocked, excited, but not deeply moved. He felt that the solid foundation of his world had rocked. Hook not only snatched by death but shown up to be a bad person, now reviled by all, not someone to look up to and emulate. When Hook had reached the heights of butler, Cyril had seen his own career mapped out. Now he was left directionless, bruised, resentful.

'*He* can't be butler!' he declared, when Mrs Webster made the announcement at the servants' dining table.

Webster gave him a quelling look. 'It's the master's decision.'

'But he's too short! Butlers have to be tall – footmen, too. It's bad enough with Sam being short,' he said, casting Sam a contemptuous look, 'but if we're going to have a squatty little butler as well, we'll be the laughing-stock. How can we hold our heads up in the neighbourhood?'

'Nobody wants your opinion,' Rose said. 'It's how a man does his job that matters, not what he looks like. Sam's all right.'

William, who hardly ever spoke in company since his troubles, looked up and said in a low, slow voice, 'Well, I like him – Mr Afton. I think Mr Moss'd approve of him too. He's . . .'

he searched for the right word for the particular quality Afton had that he liked '. . . he's sort of serious.'

'He's quite funny too, though,' said Ellen. 'He makes me laugh sometimes with his stories.'

'And I like when he sings,' Sam said. 'Ever such a nice voice, he's got.'

'I didn't mean serious like that,' William said, floundering for lack of vocabulary.

'You mean he has *gravitas*,' Dory suggested. She had over-heard Mr Sebastian saying so to Richard as they walked along the corridor past her room.

'What's that mean?' Cyril asked suspiciously.

'Weight,' said Mrs Webster.

'He ain't got weight,' Cyril said. 'He's a skinny little bloke. And he's *too short*!'

Afton came in at that point, saving Mrs Webster from a pointless discussion. 'All serene?' he asked, generally but of her in particular.

But it was Rose who answered. 'We understand congratulations are in order, Mr Afton. We're all very pleased you'll be taking Mr Moss's place.'

'Thank you, Rose – and everyone,' he said. Of course, he might have been standing outside listening, but he gave a twinkling sort of smile that seemed to encompass all shades of opinion. 'Better the devil you know, eh?'

The rain had passed over at last, and everything was green and dripping. The sky was a plumy blue and the sunshine was glorious, turning a thousand drops of water into quivering, glinting gold beads. Pharaoh was glad to be out, and titupped along, flicking his ears back and forth, pretending to be scared of anything the breeze moved, for the sheer pleasure of shying and putting in extra dancing steps.

During the dowager's extended absence, Alice's groom Josh had finally given up his determination to stop her riding alone. The foot he had broken months ago still troubled him, especially in damp weather, and he had a cough that never entirely went away, which tired him out. He had enough to do in the stable without trailing after Lady Alice in all weathers, knowing he wasn't wanted. He still, for form's sake, adjured her to ride only on Stainton land, and she still, out of old habits of obedience, gave her promise. Thus honour was satisfied, and he could retire to a warm tack-room for a smoke and a cup of tea and complain to his fellow grooms that the younger generation didn't have the standards *they* had grown up with.

Alice took Pharaoh for a good long ride, round by Shelloes, then up along the tops before coming back down through the woods and turning towards Castle Cottage, to arrive at just about the time Axe Brandom would be looking for his luncheon. This was not, of course, a meal like luncheon at the Castle, but a bite of bread and cheese to stave off hunger between his distant breakfast at half past five and his dinner, which he generally took around half past three or four.

It was a glorious and painful delight to her to visit Axe, one that, lately, she had felt she must ration. It had taken her a long time to realise what those feelings were that she had towards him. She had been a child when she had first started calling on him, then at his old cottage down at the Carr. She could look back now and see that Alice as the simple, schoolroom creature, mad about horses and dogs, lonely for company and conversation, who had found in Axe someone who actually saw her as a person, and just, simply, *liked* her. It had been fun to go there and chat with him, play with his animals, watch him whittling exquisite little models out of odd bits of wood, help him with some of his tasks.

But lately, so gradually that she hadn't noticed the transition, that had changed. To be with him eased something taut in her, which became more irksome month by month. He had become her place of happiness. And the odd, quavery feelings she sometimes had when she was near him – the yearnings for something while not actually knowing what it was: she had slowly begun to recognise them for what the grown-up world called 'love'.

She had known about love only from stories: Paris abducting Helen and fighting the Trojan war for her; Romeo and Juliet braving their families' wrath and dying for each other; heroes in fairy stories facing terrible ordeals to win the princess. It was something that happened only once in the character's life and was all-consuming and everlasting.

In real life, love seemed something different. She had an idea that Kitty loved Giles, but did he love her? They seemed to live quite separate lives, and it was hard to imagine them clasping and kissing and groaning and dying for each other. Her mother and father – no. Linda and Cordwell – doubly no. Rachel had been 'in love' with Victor Lattery the year before, and there had been kissing and tears, but how could one have a noble passion for someone like him? And it had not been for ever – Rachel had got over him very quickly. There had been all that flirting in Germany and London, and even though she was now 'in love' with Cousin Angus, she was still dancing as if nothing had changed.

Perhaps in real life it was not like the stories. But if 'love' meant wanting to be with someone all the time, feeling utterly content just to be near him, treasuring every aspect of him, his physical self, his character, his abilities and habits and speech . . . If it meant seeing in magnified detail the brush of his eyelashes on his cheek as he bent over a piece of work, the slanting sunshine lighting the golden hairs on his arms . . . If the scent of his skin was like an old memory that filled you with longing . . . If you yearned to trace with your finger the shape of his lips . . . If the word 'home' with all its connotations of comfort and belonging had come to mean him and where he was . . .

Two days ago, kept indoors by the relentless rain, she had

stared at her reflection in the mirror in her bedroom, and said aloud, 'I love him. I love Axe Brandom.' And though she had been suspecting it for a long time, the words spoken had made everything coalesce. She was not in the habit of looking at herself. If she stood before the glass while pinning on her hat it was the hat she saw, not her face. She had no strong mental image of her appearance. But now, suddenly, Alice became a real, solid, flesh-and-blood person, and she looked, and despaired. She loved Axe, in the way that she supposed grown-ups loved each other when they declared love and married each other lovingly. But she could not and must not love him. She must not even let him know how she felt, because he would be horrified and embarrassed and would probably tell her not to come any more. And she *ought not* to go. But one glimpse of her life without him in it was enough. She *had* to see him. But she must somehow continue to act like the pony-mad little girl he had been comfortable with, suppress the longings, behave normally around him and everyone else. She must keep an iron control over herself.

In bed, alone, at night, she could let go. She had her drawings of him – dozens of them now. She could pore over them, gaze her fill, think about him as freely as she liked. And cry. Crying was a luxury. Best to do it at night, so that her eyes and face would have returned to normal by the morning.

Now, after an absence of many days, she was going to visit him. In a few minutes, she would see him, and he would smile, and talk to her, and she would feel his hands on her waist as he jumped her down from the saddle. These were her treasures, to keep her alive until the next time. Pharaoh, catching her gladness as they neared the cottage, danced a little, tossing his head; then he caught the scent of the place, and let out one of his devastating whinnies, bracing his sides and shaking her in the saddle.

Alerted by the sound, Axe was waiting in his yard when

424

she rode in, and her heart leaped with joy as his face lit in a welcoming smile.

'You'd better not ever try and sneak up on someone,' he said, coming to Pharaoh's head. The chestnut butted him hard in the chest, then stuck his nose into Axe's ear and fluttered his hair with nostrils and lips.

Alice said, 'He's glad to see you.' She leaned towards him to be jumped down and felt his big, strong hands take her without hesitation – licensed to touch her in this intimate way by long custom.

'And what about you, Lady Alice?' he said. Her feet were on the ground, but just for an instant he did not release her. 'Are you glad to see me?'

Her heart was beating like a caged bird. If only those words meant something! 'Of course I am, or I wouldn't have come,' she said, and heard with amazement how ordinary and prosaic she sounded. *I should have been an actress*, she thought.

He let her go and was attending to the horse, and Alice's attention was demanded by his terrier, Dolly, who came bustling up for her share of caresses, and then by a half-grown Cyprian cat, who leaned against her legs and stuck his tail straight up like a poker. 'Is that one of the kittens?' she marvelled.

'They grow up quick,' he said from under the saddle flap, where he was loosening the girth.

'Oh, you have ducks!' she exclaimed, straightening up as a flotilla of five white Aylesburys came waddling from round the side of the house to investigate, heads imperiously high, making sarcastic remarks to each other from the sides of their beaks.

'Our Seth's Mary put a clutch under a broody hen for me. I'm partial to a duck's egg. Long as I can keep the foxes off 'em. Building 'em a house next to the cart shed. Have to shut 'em in the scullery at night until it's ready.'

'That must be messy.'

''Tis. But better that than heads and feathers all over everywhere and no eggs.'

'Nature is cruel,' Alice said, following him as he led Pharaoh over to the stable and tied him to a ring.

He looked at her. 'Nature is natural. Cruelty doesn't come into it. It's humans that are cruel. Humans've a choice to behave otherwise.' She nodded, bathing in his blue eyes. 'Was just about to have a cup of tea and a bite. Want to join me?'

'Yes, please,' she said. She might have been saying 'yes' to the Cup of Life. He gave her a curious look, head tilted, then turned away to the cottage. *Be more careful*, she told herself.

She sat at the table, with the cat on her lap purring like an engine, watching him set out bread and cheese and make the tea.

'How are you getting on with *Great Expectations*?' she asked.

'Getting along. That Miss Havisham, she's a queer one. I reckon she couldn't have been right in the head even before the wedding. Shutting herself up like that's not a reasonable way to behave, even with a broken heart.'

'Don't you think so? If you loved someone so very much? And you were all alone. Being alone is very hard.'

'But she's not alone, is she? She's got the young lass, and Pip to visit, and the lawyer fellow, and I dare say there'll be servants in the house. She's not alone like, say, old Miss Oadsby down at the Carr. She's got no-one at all, never sees a soul from one day to the next. Never married because she had to take care of her mother, and when her mother died – what? must be fifteen year since – she was left all alone. Just her in a damp cottage. No, I don't reckon Miss Havisham has got much to complain about. She could buck up if she put her mind to it.'

'Funny, I was thinking the same,' Alice said. 'Self-indulgent, that's what I thought. She's watching herself being tragic, like watching a play.'

He smiled. 'But here we're talking about her as if she was

a real person. So that Dickens has done a powerful job of inventing her. I can see all the people in the story in my mind's eye, just as if they were real. That makes him a good writer, doesn't it?'

'I'd say so. I love being able to step into a story, like stepping into a house, and just *seeing* it all around you. If you like Dickens, I'll bring you another one when you finish. He wrote loads.'

'As long as you don't get yourself into trouble, taking them.'

'I won't,' she said.

'Big goings-on up at the Castle,' he said.

'Which ones?' she said.

'His lordship's valet taking over as butler.'

'Oh. How did you hear about that?'

He smiled as if she should have known. 'The Castle servants in the churchyard after service, talking about nothing else.'

'Was it glad talk or the opposite?' she wanted to know.

'Bit of glad, bit of surprise, bit of doubtful, but nobody's unhappy,' Axe told her. 'He's generally liked, is Mr Afton. But they didn't see it coming, him being only a valet.'

'Well, but after all, Hook was valet before he became butler.'

'Ah, but Hook was footman first, and that's the usual way up the ladder – footman, under-butler, butler. That way you know the job.' He brought the teapot to the table. 'Shall I pour?'

'Yes, please.'

'Strong, not much milk. I know.'

'Giles says Afton's so intelligent he'll learn the job in no time.'

Axe gave an amused snort. 'Don't tell your footmen that. People don't like to hear their jobs are so easy anyone can learn 'em in five minutes. They like to think a lifetime of experience can't be replaced.'

'Well, ours aren't very experienced, except for William, and he's too dull to want to be butler. Anyway, Kitty says Mrs Webster will tell Afton anything he needs to know. And he's served in big houses all his life – he's bound to know what the duties are.'

'And there's no chance of Mr Moss coming back?'

'No. I think that's what everyone would have liked, but no.'

'I see him walking Miss Eddowes to church Sunday, holding the umbrella over her. Seems like he's got a sweet billet there. She's a nice lady. Shame she never married. She was the prettier one of the two sisters.' Axe had been boot-boy in the Eddowes household long ago. 'And she inherited a good bit from her father, so she could have married anyone. But some folk just aren't made that way. Same with horses. Lord Bexley at the Grange – old Lord Bexley, I mean, not the current one – had a prize mare, beautiful creature she was, bay thoroughbred, that he wanted to breed from. Any foal of hers would have been worth a fortune. But she wouldn't let the stallion near her. Tried her with different studs, but she just wouldn't have it. Some females are made that way, for God's own purposes, whatever they may be. Nothing to be done about it.'

He pushed her mug across to her. She had already cut a piece of cheese, and now laid it carefully on a slice of bread, taking care to line up the edges. 'I sometimes wonder if perhaps I'm like that,' she said.

He looked at her bent head, as she was apparently completely absorbed in what was on her plate, and his smile, had she been able to see it, was tender and sad.

'You? No, not a bit of it,' he said. She glanced up, then quickly down again, as one snatches a hand away from an unexpectedly hot surface. 'Give it time,' he said. 'Things change sudden, and you've no inkling about it beforehand. Hear what happened up at Shelloes a week past? Young Danny Gregory was playing on top of the haystack with his brother.

He fell off, landed on a hayfork and one of the tines went into his heart. Killed him straight off.'

'Oh, how dreadful! I hadn't heard.'

'Point is, nobody knew that morning it was going to happen. Life hits you sudden, like lightning – sometimes bad things, sometimes good. And you're too young, begging your pardon, my lady, to be saying "never" about anything. Like some pickle with that? Got a jar of our Ruth's apple chutney, go nice with the cheese.'

She laughed. 'From life and death to pickles.'

'Too much serious talk's not good for a person.' He got up and went to the dresser to fetch the chutney. 'Heard a rumour,' he said, coming back and sitting down, 'about your mother going to be married again.'

'However did you hear that?'

'Is it supposed to be a secret? Marriage is a public thing.'

'Well, I think we're not talking about it yet.'

He gave small, cat-like smile. 'Someone's talked, because I heard it in the village.'

'Who from?'

'Not saying. It's true then?' He studied her a moment. 'Do you mind it?'

'Mind? No, of course not,' she said. He continued to regard her, chewing impassively, watching her think. 'I think it's strange,' she allowed at last, 'and I don't know anything about the man, but she must love him, I suppose, because she doesn't *need* to get married. And if it makes her happy – that can only be a good thing, can't it? I don't think she was ever happy before, not while I've known her.'

'Sounds funny, you saying "not while I've known her", as if she wasn't anything to do with you.'

Alice didn't know how to answer that, and said nothing. She knew what he meant. She had seen the Brinklow children, who had been playmates of her and Rachel, with their parents, and they had all seemed glued together and intertwined. She

429

saw him preparing another question, and prompted him: 'What is it?'

'I heard she was going to be living in Germany with this chap, your mother.'

'Yes. He's a German prince. He lives near Frankfurt.'

'Does that mean you'll be going to live there as well?'

A quiver of pleasure ran through her, because it sounded as though it mattered to him whether she did or not.

'I don't know if she'll send for me,' she said, 'but if she does, I'm going to ask Giles to say I have to stay here. He's the head of the family, so he can insist if he wants to.'

'So you don't want to go?'

'Not at all.'

'Don't want to marry a German prince yourself?'

'I *love* Ashmore,' she said, suddenly passionate. 'I never want to leave.'

'You will, one day,' he said, and it sounded sad. They were silent for a moment. Alice drank tea. He cut another slice of bread. Then he said, 'I got to take a load of logs up to Topheath Farm when I've finished luncheon. With Della and the cart. Want to come with me?' Her expression as she looked at him was his answer. 'You're not wanted at home?'

'Nobody wants me anywhere,' she said. Then added daringly, 'Except here.'

'You're always welcome here,' he said. 'While you want to come. That'll change. Other things'll come into your life. Other people. And you won't want to come here any more. But that's all right. That's the way things go. Pass that chutney, will you?'

From life and death to pickles. Too much serious talk wasn't good for you. He must know as well as she did – better than she did – that she shouldn't be here at all. Why did he let her come? Because he liked her? Because he felt sorry for her? A mixture of the two, probably, she thought. And it was best they shouldn't get talking too seriously, or she might say things that were best not said. The things she really longed to say. And whether he welcomed them or rejected them, it would break something.

It all happened surprisingly quickly. Decius heard of a horse and went to see it, liked it, and arranged for Nina, with Bobby accompanying her for the extra support, to go and try it. Nina loved it, the sale was arranged, and within a week everything was in place. A groom was found by recommendation – an odd-looking, short, bow-legged, rubicund man with black hair and a faint Irish accent – and with the help of Deering he cleaned out the stables in readiness. Another horse was found locally. Fodder and straw were delivered from a nearby farm. And Wriothesby House took delivery of Jewel, a six-year-old, fifteen-two thoroughbred gelding, black with one white coronet and a small white star, and Nankin, a sixteen-hand gelding of no particular breeding, brown with four white stockings.

Daughters, the groom, said that Nankin was 'a dacent steady harse,' and that Jewel was 'a little beauty, so he is'.

Mr Cowling said, 'I'm glad it's black. A black horse looks very smart, especially with you being so fair.'

'I love him,' Nina said. 'Thank you *very* much. It's more than I deserve.'

'Nonsense. I'd give you the moon if I could get hold of it.'

'Oh, I'd sooner have Jewel, thank you. The moon would be awfully in the way.'

He chuckled. 'Ah, you like your little jokes. But, now then,' his expression changed, 'I want to be serious for a minute.' He looked at her, not quite sternly, for there was a hint of apprehension in it. 'I'm not going to *order* you to ride side-saddle, but I am going to *ask* you to. This other business won't do, Nina, it really won't. To please me, will you promise only to ride side-saddle?'

Nina was so delighted with her horse, and touched by his generosity, she hadn't the heart to argue. Bobby would call her weak and be exasperated with her, but – at least for now – she couldn't and wouldn't fight him.

'I promise,' she said.

On her first ride out on Jewel, she was accompanied by Bobby, and by Clemmie on a hireling. Bobby's groom Hoday rode behind with Daughters to take care of all three.

'And he's taken out a subscription to the hunt for me,' Nina said. 'He's quite thrilled with the idea. I wouldn't put it past him to have a photographer waiting at the first meet to capture me in full fig.'

Clemmie smiled. 'He's a dear! You're very lucky, Nina.'

'But it was rather unscrupulous of him to make you promise not to ride across,' Bobby said. 'Catching you at a weak moment when you were soft with gratitude.'

'You can't call it unscrupulous,' Nina protested.

Bobby shook her head. 'You'll have to work on him. I was counting on the three of us hunting astride this season. Then, with Mrs Anstruther, we'll make a real impact. You're with me, aren't you, Clemmie?'

'You can't ask Nina to defy her husband,' Clemmie said. 'It's all right for me, because I'm not married. Mrs Anstruther is a widow, and your husband is very modern-minded.'

'But it's not *reasonable*!' Bobby proclaimed, frustrated. 'Riding side-saddle is unnatural and dangerous. The only impact you can make that way is impact with the ground when you come a cropper and break your back.'

'Oh, don't,' Nina protested.

'Julia Caldwell, November 1899,' Bobby said relentlessly. 'Her horse came down jumping a bullfinch on Langdon Hill and she was trapped underneath. She never walked again. She died of pneumonia a few months later. Pimmy Galloway, February 1901—'

'Enough, Bobby,' said Clemmie. 'You don't need to convince us.'

'I know I don't. But we all need to keep working to convince the men. Riding side-saddle is all part of the same thing, the denial of equality, like denying us the vote. How much longer are we going to wait for simple justice? Did you know people have been arguing for women's suffrage for forty years, ever since John Stuart Mill got into Parliament? Forty years is a lifetime! And I don't want to wait for another forty – I'd be too old to enjoy it. At that rate I might not even live to see it.'

'Perhaps we should join the NUWSS,' Clemmie said, and translated for Nina. 'The National Union of Women's Suffrage Societies. Millicent Fawcett founded it, to draw together all the scattered societies to make one more effective force. My father knew her mother's father in London. She's a wonderfully strong woman and she has very good connections.'

'What do they do?' Nina asked.

'Oh, hold meetings and get up petitions to try to get MPs to support the idea. We could even start up our own branch here,' Clemmie said, in her mild, unemphatic voice.

'Meetings! Petitions!' Bobby exclaimed scornfully. 'How can you change men's minds that way?'

'What would you do?' Nina asked, amused. 'Throw stones at them?'

'It's the best we can do,' Clemmie said. 'Great changes always take time. You're too impatient, Bobby.'

Nina grew bored with the subject and said, 'Shall we canter along here?' She heard a shrill bark and looked back. 'Oh, bother, there's Trump. I asked them to keep him in the kitchen, but he must have got out somehow and followed me.'

'If we canter on, he won't be able to keep up and he'll go home.'

'Oh, poor thing! He'll think I don't love him.'

'Dogs don't think like that,' Bobby said. 'He'll be all right. Let's see how fast Jewel is. I'll race you to the Five Beeches.' And she gave up politics for the moment, in favour of equitation.

Mr Blomfield wrote back to say he deeply regretted that he was so completely engaged in a project he would not be able to come and look at Ashmore until the following spring, but if Lady Stainton would indulge him with her patience he would be delighted to wait upon her then. Alternatively, his trusted assistant could come immediately and do the initial survey, make notes of her requirements and report back to him.

Kitty was young enough not to want any delay, so she wrote to say an immediate visit by the assistant would oblige her.

He came on a fine day in November, when they were enjoying a goose summer: soft, settled days with gentle warmth at the zenith and mists at either end. Kitty was surprised to see such a young man: at first glance he looked no older than her, though when she saw him close up she realised that he had one of those boyish, young-looking faces and in fact was probably in his early thirties. Still, she had thought of all gardeners as being wise and weathered greybeards, so he was refreshing. He was tall, with a face that seemed always on the brink of smiling, thick wavy brown hair and very blue eyes. 'Henry Fenchurch, your ladyship,' he introduced himself. 'Mr Blomfield is sorry not to be able to come himself, but I am well acquainted with his ideas and methods. I have assisted him on half a dozen great gardens. I assure you—'

Kitty was quick to put him at ease. 'Please don't apologise. I'm very pleased you have come. Will you take some refreshment?'

He smiled, showing excellent teeth. 'If you will excuse me,

I would rather walk round while it's fine. I've learned by hard experience not to take English weather for granted. You have a gardener to show me the ground?'

'Oh, but I was expecting to show you round myself, so that I can tell you what I want.'

'So it is really *your* garden? Your plan entirely?' He seemed pleased by the idea.

'No-one else is much interested,' she confessed. 'My head gardener loves vegetables and fruits, and my husband is the same – he doesn't see the point in growing things you can't eat. But he knows I've always wanted gardens here, and he's happy for me to have them created the way I want them.'

'Well, then, let's go and look, and you can tell me your vision,' Fenchurch said.

'I don't know how practical my vision is,' she said, leading the way out.

'But that is what I'm here for,' he said. 'To understand what your imagination sees, and find a way to create it.'

'You don't mind, then?' she said shyly. 'I thought great gardeners expected to have a free hand. To make the garden –'

'– in their own image?' he anticipated. 'Well, that is often the case – perhaps usually the case. To paint on an empty canvas is satisfaction in one way. But to interpret someone else's dream, to pluck it from the empty air and make it real – what a privilege!'

She laughed, feeling strangely at ease with him. 'I believe you would agree with me whatever I said.'

He smiled back. 'We'll see. You may be sending me away with a flea in my ear in half an hour's time.'

'I'm sure I won't.'

First they strolled about the small formal garden at the back of the house, where they were joined by Peason, the head gardener. He eyed Fenchurch suspiciously, and gave his opinion that the slope behind the house was too steep to do anything with, and that there was no point in setting her ladyship up for disappointment.

'I've got my hands full with the kitchen gardens,' he concluded. 'And her ladyship wants more glass – grapes, nectarines, melons. Might even manage a pinery, my lady,' he added beguilingly to Kitty. 'I haven't never tasted a ripe pineapple, but they do say it's a wonder of a fruit. Wouldn't mind trying my hand at that.'

'Yes, that would be something special,' Kitty said. 'You're doing a wonderful job, Peason, and I'm especially glad for his lordship's sake, because he's such a delicate eater. Fresh fruit and vegetables make all the difference to him, and to his health. But I want my pleasure garden as well. It won't take away from your kitchen gardens, I promise.'

Peason's face set in disappointed lines, like a dog watching a door closing, and he stayed silent as Fenchurch asked Kitty what she imagined beyond the little parterre.

'Do you think it's too steep?' she asked meekly.

'You can garden anywhere, even on a cliff face,' Fenchurch said. 'This is not too steep by any means. I think it will lend itself admirably to terracing.'

'What does that mean exactly?'

He described it with gestures. 'You dig away some of the hillside to create a level area, with a retaining wall in front and behind to hold the hill in place. And repeat the process upwards as often as you wish.'

'I would like it to look quite natural, if that's possible.'

'Of course. The plots you create can be any shape, and the retaining structures can be hidden by plants, or incorporated into rockeries. All the shapes you create can be curved, meandering, overlapping, so that they fit the contours of the ground. No need at all for straight lines. Same with the planting – the shrubs and flowers in sinuous sweeps, blending with the shape of the plot, just as they do in nature.'

'Straight lines are necessary for hoeing,' Peason objected.

436

'How can you get the weeds out from between the plants if you don't have straight lines?'

Fenchurch looked at him indulgently. 'That's the beauty of this sort of planting – you don't have to weed. The plants cover all of the ground, no bare earth.'

Peason shook his head at such folly, and Kitty intervened: 'Every time I look at this hillside from my window, I imagine what it would be like to have a stream running down it, with little pools and waterfalls, perhaps.'

'Oh, Lady Stainton, you have made me very happy! Of all things, I love to introduce water to a garden – and with a fall such as this, there are so many possibilities. And,' he added eagerly, 'I took the liberty of studying the Ordnance Survey maps of the area, and it seems that you have two natural brooks coming down this hillside, the Shel to the south and the Wade to the north, either or both of which could be diverted to provide the water. It makes it so much easier to have water coming down a hill if you don't have to pump it up there in the first place.'

Peason said. 'And when you've dug away half a hillside, sir, where d'you think you're going to put all that soil?'

He gave his answer to Kitty, his eyes dancing with excitement. 'I couldn't help noticing on my way up here from the station that you have a fine downhill slope on the other side of the house. Two very large terraces, given over to lawn and perhaps a few carefully placed shrubs and trees, would greatly improve the aspect, and provide agreeable places to walk and sit.'

'It would be like having a park,' Kitty said. 'His lordship's mother always complains that Ashmore has no park.'

'And that, my friend,' Fenchurch said to Peason, 'is what you do with half a hillside.'

'Dig it out from the back and pile it up at the front,' Kitty said. 'That's so clever.'

'Rather in the way they make railway lines,' said Fenchurch.

'The earth dug out to make a cutting is piled up to make the next embankment.'

'Is that so? I never realised!' Kitty exclaimed.

Peason shook his head again, but this time more in wonder than disapproval. 'The things you can do nowadays,' he said. 'If you'll excuse me, my lady, sir, I got to tend to my archi-tokes.' He knuckled his forehead and stumped away.

Fenchurch bade him a civil farewell and, when he was gone, said to Kitty, 'Strange how many gardeners have diffi-culty with the word "artichoke". My father's gardener, when I was a boy, called them ratchet-cocks. Shall we go and look at the front now?'

'Were you always interested in gardening?' Kitty asked, leading the way. He was so easy to talk to, it was like chatting to Nina.

'You look very handsome in evening dress,' Molly said. 'You should always wear it.'

'Yes, especially when out hunting,' Richard said. 'It would shorten my valet's life considerably, though. He regards a minute smudge on a dress boot as a dagger to the heart – think how he would react to several pounds of moist loam. You, however, look beautiful in anything.'

She looked stern. 'You cannot have thought what you are saying. A woman spends several hours dressing with the utmost care for an evening at the Queen's Hall, and you tell her it doesn't matter in the least, she'd do just as well in her day dress.'

He laughed. 'You know quite well that's not what I meant. I suspect you are talking to hide your nerves. Are you nervous, O mother of the soloist?'

'Of course I am, especially as I haven't been able to see her for a week. She forbade me to visit – said she couldn't be distracted from her final preparations.'

'Oh dear, "final preparations" sound awfully hangman-ish.

Along the lines of the last meal and confession to the prison chaplain. Is she scared to death?'

'Richard!'

'Sorry! Just trying to distract you. I think I must be nervous too.'

'Well, you were responsible in the beginning for bringing her to Sir Thomas's notice.'

'Yes, it's all my fault. I'm never sure whether to applaud myself or curse myself for that.'

'Applaud, on the whole,' said Molly, serenely. 'I am feeling a great deal better about it all now. It's a wonderful opportunity for her to study under him. And for the rest, she seems very happy. I believe she was right when she said she could keep him at a distance. I'm sure in my own mind that he is not trying to make her his mistress – hard though it is to believe.'

'Hmm,' said Richard. Of course, not moving in those circles, Molly was not exposed to the gossip, instalments of which he got from his grandmother. Fortunately the musical world and the world of the *ton* were not interconnected at a deep level. Most of the leading hostesses regarded concert music as a very peripheral part of London life – far down the list from opera and ballet, which themselves fell well short of the theatre. Consequently, musicians were far less interesting and important to the average *grande dame* than her hat-maker. But Sir Thomas, of course, was a very well-known public figure, so there had been gossip.

'Shall we go?' he said. 'I have a cab waiting outside.'

'How extravagant you are.'

'I didn't want you to catch cold walking to the rank,' he said. 'Can't have you sneezing during the quiet passages. Especially as we're in a box, and all eyes will be on us.'

'In a box?'

'My grandmother has a box for every concert. I told her I was bringing a guest.'

He had been putting her wrap around her shoulders, and now she pulled back from him, turned, and stared.

'Richard, no!' she said angrily. 'Not on any account! What were you thinking?'

He was taken aback. 'I was thinking that there's plenty of room – the box seats eight, and there will only be Aunt Caroline and the Levens besides.'

She was furious. 'You want me to accept your grand-mother's hospitality, sit in her box and chat with her? *I was her son's mistress!*'

He was taken aback. 'I'm sure she doesn't know about that.'

'*I* know about it! And I'd bet she does. How could you even *think* it would be all right?'

'If it comes to it, her lover is your daughter's patron, but that doesn't seem to trouble you,' he said, a little petulantly.

'That's a different matter entirely, a relationship between artist and patron. If you can't see that you're an idiot. But for me to sit beside your grandmother in a social situation, her guest, obligated to her . . . How could you be so thought-less as to suggest it? Have you no sense of etiquette? Have you no sense *at all*?'

'Enough of that,' he said, angry too now. 'I won't be spoken to like a child.'

'Then don't behave like one!'

They stared at each other in a brittle silence, which became an appalled one. They had never quarrelled before.

He tried to find a firmer ground of reason to stand on. 'You refine too much on that old relationship. No-one knows about it, and if they knew they wouldn't care. Men in that position have always taken mistresses, and he's dead now anyway—' She winced at the words, and he cursed his clum-siness. 'I'm sorry. But the point is, it's over and done with.' She didn't answer. 'You have to go to Chloë's concert. Look, you don't have to sit in the box. I'll go to the ticket office

440

when we get there and buy two stalls seats. I'll make some excuse to Grandmère. Please don't go on being angry with me, or it'll spoil the evening.' He touched her arm tentatively. 'It's Chloë's evening. We mustn't forget that.'

She turned to him with a sigh. 'Don't wheedle.'

'But it's what I'm good at,' he urged.

She almost smiled. He was very hard to resist. 'Just understand, Richard Tallant, that I cannot meet any of your family, not now, and not ever. I am outside society. That cannot change.'

'We'll argue about that another time,' he said, pulling the wrap round her shoulders.

Sir Thomas was nothing if not a showman, and to build up anticipation he had arranged the concert so that the piano concerto was the whole of the second half.

As soon as the conductor and soloist had left the platform, Richard jumped up and ushered Molly through the pass door, which he had located during the interval, not forgetting to slip something to the attendant to ease their passage and direct them to the dressing-room.

Chloë was alone, still clutching the huge bouquet of flowers that had been presented to her on the platform. She was alight with excitement from the performance, her eyes brilliant, her usually pale cheeks flushed. Her elation was so palpable Richard almost expected flames to shoot out of her head.

Molly couldn't speak and could only lay a hand on her daughter's arm.

'You were wonderful,' Richard said simply. 'But I'm a layman when it comes to music. Were *you* pleased with your performance?'

'It was – almost unbearably exciting,' Chloë said, her voice vibrating with emotion. 'Like riding a wild horse – ten wild horses! The power, the speed, the elation! Oh, my God,

Richard, I can't describe it! Playing is exciting always, always – but with an orchestra, a full orchestra . . . ! Sixty musicians! The power, the sound, and I control them all!'

'I thought the conductor controlled the orchestra,' Richard said.

'But I controlled him. You don't understand. In a concerto, the orchestra must follow the solo part. The conductor must take his cues from the soloist. She has the reins of it all in her hands. All of it! Oh! I shall never, never . . .' She pushed the flowers into her mother's arms in a gesture that clearly did not really see her, and sat down. 'I'm in a dream. I'm in Heaven.'

Richard met Molly's eyes above the flowers. He could feel the power radiating out from Chloë, and not for a moment did he think she would ever allow anything to happen that she did not want. The elegant, important, rich, famous Sir Thomas could get no foothold on the shining carapace that enclosed Molly's daughter. 'You see,' he said to her, 'the soloist controls the conductor.'

Before she could speak, the door opened, and Sir Thomas came in: a tall man, handsome, well-built, big in evening clothes, big with success, hot from his exertions, displacing more air than with his physical self alone – his 'presence' was at least a whole extra person's worth, so that Richard felt himself pushed back, and Molly took a step away towards a corner, instinctively effacing herself. Behind Sir Thomas a dresser hovered, pushing a towel into his hand so he could mop his face; and behind *him*, other lurking figures, the one in evening clothes the hall's manager perhaps, and who knew who else? A person like Sir Thomas rarely moved without an entourage.

But Chloë, Richard was glad to note, did not stand up at his entrance, though she looked at him with a ravishing smile and something of intimacy in her eyes. It was almost lover-like – it was certainly the look between two people who were very close – but Richard had the wit to remember that her excitement was all about the music and the performance, and to interpret it in a different way. Chloë and Sir Thomas were sharing something vivid and vital and excitingly important to them both, but it was not something the average man ever shared with a woman. It was a piano concerto, with orchestra, and he would never know what that felt like.

'My dear.' Sir Thomas claimed her hand in both of his and kissed it almost reverently. 'What a triumph!' he said. 'Never have there been thirty minutes of such impassioned virtuosity. You have arrived, my dear, you have arrived. By tomorrow the world will know it.'

Oddly, Richard saw that his words were not further elating her but bringing her down to earth. In a flash of understanding, he saw that she had been in a different place where the musicians, including herself and Sir Thomas, had no physical form, but were part of the incorporeal thing that was the music. Now he had reminded her that they were human after all, and she didn't like it. He suddenly felt much more cheerful, and wanted to tell Molly that she had nothing to worry about. Chloë would never fall under Sir Thomas's spell. As far as she was concerned, he didn't have one. He felt almost sorry for the old boy.

'Now we must go and talk to our patrons, and the press,' Sir Thomas was saying, 'and then we shall go with a select party to supper at the Savoy.' His roving eye discerned Molly – whom he had probably taken for a dresser – and with a jerk of recognition he said, 'Servant, ma'am. You must be very proud. And, er, Mr . . .'

'Sir Thomas,' Richard said tormentingly.

'Yes, yes, of course you must both join us.' He dropped them like a used towel and returned to Chloë. 'A few minutes, my dear, just to refresh your face and tidy your hair, and then upstairs. I'll send Hayter to fetch you. Don't keep us waiting.'

★　★　★

Richard left Molly for a few minutes' privacy with Chloë, and slipped out into the foyer to mingle with the crowds and hear what they were saying. He discovered that, while it was to be supposed they were music lovers, most of them spoke, like other members of the *ton*, only about their own affairs and people they knew. Intellectual analysis of the performance they had just witnessed was not to be expected.

But he did hear a few comments.

'Astonishingly good.'

'Remarkable playing.'

'So young, too. Quite a prodigy.'

'I loved that tune in the last movement. Pom-pom-ti-tiddle-om-pom-pom. How did it go?'

Less welcome comments too.

'I've heard that she's in Sir Thomas's keeping. Yes, an *appartement meublé* no less!'

'It's shocking, an old man like him and a young girl like her.'

'Well, what can you expect? Ballet girls and actresses and musicians, all the same.'

'It's Lady Burton I feel for.'

'Yes, poor Violet. She's not at all well, you know.'

'There's really something rather *off* about a young female performing in public.'

'Oh, I agree! I shouldn't like one of *my* girls to expose herself like that.'

Then his gentle sifting through the throng brought him face to face with his grandmother.

'Where have you been?' she demanded crossly.

He had forgotten to go and make his excuses during the interval. 'I was sitting in the stalls. I wanted a closer view.'

'One does not view a musician. One hears.'

'I'm not an aficionado like you, *ma chère*. I need to engage my sense of sight as well. And then I went along to the dressing-room to congratulate Miss Chloë.'

'You are quite the stage-door Johnny.'

'Her mother was there. Sir Thomas came in and invited us all to supper at the Savoy.'

'Yes, he has invited me and the Levens as well. Caroline was already engaged elsewhere. I think I will not go, however. I am tired and want my bed. Where is your guest?'

'Gone. Listen, *ma chère*, I think you ought to go to the Savoy.' He *had* to show Molly that it wouldn't matter. And she would not make a fuss in a public restaurant. Besides, he now had another reason. 'I've been listening to people talk.' He waved a hand round the foyer. 'Not good talk.'

'One cannot be governed by the opinions of imbeciles,' she said irritably. 'I have had *une expérience transcendante*, and I do not wish to have it shattered by worldly chatter.'

Richard said urgently, 'Yes, dear one, but I think you should go all the same. It would be better if the imbeciles were reminded that Miss Chloë is Sir Thomas's *protégée* only, and that the position of *amoureuse* is already filled.'

She looked at him thoughtfully for a moment, then said, 'You are not so *insensible* as you pretend. Hmm. *Il parait que j'ai un petit creux*. Perhaps an omelette, or a little *foie gras* would suit me after all. Give me your arm, and make a way for me through *cette foule*.' She waved a disparaging hand at the superbly dressed gathering of the capital's top people.

'This *foule* of fools,' Richard improved.

She gave him a little smile. '*Une foule de fous*.'

'Throng, host, multitude, congregation,' he said. 'It always amuses me that "congregation" comes from the Latin word for a flock of sheep.'

'But these are more like a pack of hounds,' she said. 'And when hounds go rushing off after something new, it is called a riot, this I know.'

CHAPTER TWENTY-THREE

The rain had stopped by the time the service was over, and Moss stepped out into a world of drips and sparkles and a little spiteful wind, the sort that gets down inside your collar and shakes raindrops from trees just as you pass under.

He was not strictly needed to carry the umbrella over Miss Eddowes on the short walk home, but he waited anyway. There was something dignified and nicely old-fashioned about a lady being accompanied by a male servant when she walked abroad. It had been the custom of his youth. No young lady would have been allowed to go and look at the shops without a footman following; and though he was a butler, not a footman, he was beginning not to mind these gradations of service in the way he had. It was pleasantly relaxing to be in a small household like Miss Eddowes's. As long as things were done properly – and he made sure they were – it didn't matter so much who did them. They all served the one mistress, after all. His old self would have been surprised to hear that thought from his new self, but so much had happened to him this year. He had lost so much, and was now in the way of being grateful for what he had retained.

The recent rain had stripped the last of the autumn leaves from the trees, and the bold colours were gone now, leaving a grey world and a distinctly wintry aspect. He wondered what was usually done about Christmas in the Eddowes household. He hoped there would be some entertaining. He thought of Christmas at the Castle, and how he had always made the punch for Christmas Eve from his own recipe. He'd be glad to make it again for his new mistress. Everyone had said his punch was the best they'd tasted. He remembered the occasion, during the old lord's time, when the Earl of Strathmore had been pleased to say . . .

He was jerked out of his thoughts by the sight of the Castle servants streaming out of the south door, having come down from the gallery where they always sat – and more particularly by the sight of Ada, arm in arm with one of the other maids. Mildred, wasn't that her name? He felt a painful tightness around his heart as he looked at that dear little face, pale and pointed, and the few strands of transparently pale hair he could see under a brown velour hat. His Ada, his love, on whom he had longed to pour out the treasures of a lifetime of learning and doing. He was staring, he knew, but he couldn't stop himself.

She saw him now, and stopped, and the other maid glanced up, then detached herself from Ada's arm and stepped aside. The other servants streamed past with curious glances, and Ada stood looking up at him, as fragile and tremulous as a fawn.

'How – how are you, Mr Moss?' she asked at last.

Love surged through his heart like a tidal bore. Her sweet interest in him was balm to his spirits. 'I am very well, thank you, Ada. And how are you? How are things up at the Castle?'

'All right, thanks,' she mumbled shyly. She wished he'd move aside and let her go, but he seemed to expect her to say something, so she said, 'We got a new butler now.'

'So I heard. Mr Afton. I hope you're all helping him to settle in.' She blushed and looked down, lost for a reply. 'You all like him, I hope?'

'He's nice,' she mumbled. She scraped her brain for something to say. 'He sings, sometimes, when he's working. He's got a nice voice.'

'Sings?' Moss said doubtfully. That wasn't the behaviour of a butler. At Christmas, leading the carols in the hall, perhaps, or at church, but in the *house*, while *working*? 'Well, I expect he has his own way of doing things.,' he concluded, not to undermine Afton's authority.

'He's not like you, Mr Moss,' Ada agreed, and he chose to interpret this as regret.

'Things change, I'm afraid, life brings changes, and we have to change with them.' There was a famous Latin phrase *Omnia mutantur, nos et mutamur in illis*, and he toyed with quoting it, but wasn't sure he had the wording exactly right. He'd look it up when he got home. Miss Eddowes had a book of quotations and sayings in the drawing-room bookcase. Instead he said, in a softened tone, 'I hope you didn't take any harm from our outing in the summer, which had such an unfortunate ending.'

'Oh, no, Mr Moss,' she said. Then, 'I *was* a bit scared . . .'

'I'm sure you conducted yourself properly, just as you ought,' he said. 'I've always thought you a very well-behaved girl, Ada. I've been thinking lately that I might come up to the Castle one day, perhaps take a cup of tea with you all, see how you're getting on. Do you think I'd be welcome?'

'Oh, yes – I'm sure . . .' she mumbled. She shifted from foot to foot, longing for escape.

He lowered his voice. 'Would *you* be glad to see me, Ada?' he asked. She stared desperately at her shoes, her cheeks rosy. Moss gazed, longing to press her to his heart. Her little head like a flower, the milk-white stem of her neck, the entrancing smell of soap and starch . . .

And then a large, loutish fellow came up behind her, had the temerity to slide his arm through hers, and leaned in to whisper something in her ear, with the hint of placing a kiss upon it. Outraged, Moss cleared his throat harshly, and the boy jerked up his head, pulled his arm away and snatched

448

off his hat with a look of consternation. 'Oh, Mr Moss!' Moss stared unrecognisingly. 'It's George, Mr Moss. Third groom up the Castle.'

'Is it, indeed?' Moss said discouragingly.

But Ada had taken courage from her swain. She relinked their arms, drawing him closer. 'Me and George are walking out, Mr Moss. Regular,' she said proudly.

'George and I,' he corrected automatically, causing Ada to stare with incomprehension. 'You should say, "George and I", not "me and George".'

'Yes, Mr Moss,' Ada said, grateful to discover it was only a matter of grammar and not some appalling misunderstanding.

And Moss, speared through the heart, turned away, saying, 'I must look for my mistress.' He didn't want to think about that horse-smelling rustic walking out with Ada, holding her hand, perhaps kissing her with his rubbery lips. *And Ada letting him!* Even encouraging it . . . Any particle of the dream he had been harbouring withered and dropped from the branch. He felt old and tired.

'Shall I tell Mrs Webster you'll be coming up the Castle?' Ada asked, emboldened by his turned back.

'We'll see,' Moss said. 'We'll see.'

But he would not be going up there, he knew. It was the fairy castle up in the clouds from which he had been banished by an evil spell. His life was down here now, at the bottom of the hill. The word *hubris* drifted through his mind, and he resolved to look it up when he got home. Home, to Miss Eddowes's.

Richard's excuse was that he wanted to see how the milk collection was going, and discover whether there were any snags to smooth out. But, really, he just wanted to ride along for the fun of it.

He picked one of the motor-wagons at random, and

discovered that the driver, Jobson – a young, eager man with a bright-eyed passion for machinery – called it a '*lorry*'. Richard had known lorries hitherto as those flat, four-wheeled hand wagons used in railway stations to move luggage about, but it seemed as good a name as any.

'How is it going?' Richard asked him, as they rattled along the road beside the river.

'Pretty well, sir,' said Jobson. 'Daisy's a good old girl, haven't had any trouble with her so far.'

'Daisy?'

'The lorry, sir. Named her after my dad's old carthorse that I used to ride back from the field when I was a nipper.'

'Ah. Good name. She's not an old girl, though – practically brand new.'

'I know, sir. Just a figure of speech. The road's not so good, though, further up the valley. Slows me down, going round the pot-holes – don't want to ruin her springs.'

'I'll look into that. It was all supposed to have been done.'

'It's the cold weather, sir. Frost gets into any little crack, widens it. Next thing you know, it's worn into a hole. Got to keep on top of roads all the time, sir.'

'I'll take that into account,' said Richard. 'You seem to be getting up a good speed here, though.' Jobson seemed to be pelting along. Richard was not yet entirely at ease with motor-transport. His first experience had not ended well for him.

'Road's good this end,' said Jobson. His large hands gripped the wheel firmly, trembling with the vibration of the engine, and he stared ahead keenly like a sailor on the look-out for whales or tidal waves. 'I like to push along, get a bit ahead of time, case we meet a flock of sheep somewhere.'

At the first stop, Richard saw the estate carpenter, Gale, at work on the milk platform. He looked up. 'Morning, Mr Richard!'

'What's the trouble?'

'Some damn fool in one of they motor-cars took the bend too fast in the dusk yestreen, and slammed into it. Cracked one of the supports. Saw Mr Whitcroft in the Dog and Gun last night and he mentioned it, so I thought I'd come down and get it done first thing, 'fore it got any worse.'

Even while he was speaking, Jobson had jumped down and grasped the first of the churns, which was sitting on the side of the road.

'Ought to move this here platform back a bit,' Gale said. 'Just a foot, so's it doesn't stick out. Want a hand, son?'

As soon as the churns were in place, Jobson leaped for his seat again, nimble as a charioteer, and with a cheerful shout of thanks to Gale, they were off.

He was plainly already a familiar sight, as people stepped hastily off the road onto the grass edge, and waved to him as they passed. At the next stop, a child was waiting beside the churn platform, and handed a small parcel to Jobson, saying, 'Ma says please can you put this into the post office when you're done, and here's tuppence for the post, and,' she drew another package out of her apron pocket, 'a piece of her currant cake for your trouble.'

'Can't your mother get into the village herself?' Richard asked, from the cab window, while Jobson dealt with the churns.

She looked up at him, squinting against the light. 'Her leg's bad again, please sir. I've stopped off school to help with the little 'uns.' She lingered to watch Jobson – the fascination of the new. Richard leaned out of the window to look back as they moved away, and saw her waving him vigorously off as though the lorry was an ocean liner.

When they got to the bad part of the road, Richard saw for himself how it slowed matters down. 'Damnit, the road-menders couldn't have done a very good job. I'll have to get them back, and make sure they're supervised this time.'

'Can't bump the old girl about too much,' Jobson said.

451

'Not just the springs, but your milk'd turn to butter, sir, by the time I got it back to the station. Oh, now what's this?'

A horseman was coming along the centre of the road, and having just got up speed, Jobson was forced to stop.

'It's Lord Shacklock,' Richard said. 'I recognise the horse.' A groom was riding behind him, and edged his horse out of the way, but his lordship's mount was snorting and goggling at the unfamiliar dragon, and skittering in the nerve-racking way horses had, swinging first his quarters then his head across the road as his rider tried to keep him from bolting.

'Better go really slowly,' Richard said to Jobson. 'I'll get down, hold him.'

'Ah, Tallant,' Lord Shacklock called, as Richard slid himself out of the cab. 'Well met, sir. I'd like a word or two, if you don't mind.'

'It's going to put me out of time, sir,' Jobson said, 'if I have to wait for you.'

'Don't worry,' Richard said, as he closed the door. 'You go on, do your job, I can walk home from here.'

The horse shied from his hand, but as soon as he had hold of the rein it dropped its nose and seemed grateful for the reassurance. The lorry came creeping forward. There was one bad moment when, resenting being held back, the engine backfired with a noise like a gunshot and the horse jerked so hard in affront that it almost sat on its haunches. But then it was past, clattering and clanking away down the lane, and as peace returned the horse consented to stand still.

Still holding the rein in a precautionary manner, Richard looked up at Lord Shacklock and said, 'You had something to say to me?'

'About this milk scheme of yours.' Shacklock, a long, bony, choleric man of sixty, was staring after the lorry. 'Ash Valley Dairy? Bit presumptuous, ain't it? Sounds as if you owned the whole damn' valley.'

'I'm looking to the future,' Richard said. 'Not to owning

the land, of course, but to the time when every man with a herd sells his milk through me. And I thought it had a certain ring to it – Ash Valley milk.'

'Ring be damned. Whatever made you think of such a thing?' Shacklock said scornfully.

The horse was still twitching, shifting its forefeet, chumbling the bit and sending a generous stream of foamy saliva down Richard's sleeve. He bore it patiently, and stroked the bay nose with his other hand. 'I was taking drawing-room tea with a lady in Golden Square one day, and she was mourning the fact that you couldn't get decent milk in London. I thought, Hey-ho, I have milk, and there's a fast train straight from Canons Ashmore to Marylebone – the plan wrote itself, really.'

'But you think it can pay?' Shacklock said crossly.

'There are millions of people in London all wanting milk,' said Richard. 'I can't see how it can fail.'

'Hmph. Well, I've been hearing things. People are talking. M'groom said Gregory of Shelloes has bought his wife a new hat, said it was milk-money. That something to do with you?'

Richard smiled. 'I haven't seen the hat in question, but I'd say it was. In order to get the thing moving, I've taken on all the costs of setting-up, and I'm paying the farmers straight away. I couldn't expect them to wait for their money. But the price I'm getting in London is such that I think we should have cleared the costs and be making a small profit by the new year.'

'But is this Stainton's scheme, or yours?'

'It's my brother's scheme, of course, but I'm running it for him. He has enough to do with the rest of the estate. He's given me full powers.'

'Good God,' said Shacklock, not very flatteringly. He used the end of his crop to rub his nose thoughtfully, and finally cleared his throat. 'Everyone with a herd, eh? You'd better come up to the Park and tell me about it.'

'You're thinking of joining the scheme?'

'Steady the Buffs! Should need a lot more information about it before I decided. But perhaps, perhaps.'

Richard concealed his elation. 'I'm sure we'd be happy to have you with us,' he said. 'But something would have to be done about your section of the road. Can't have the lorries shaken about too much once the milk is on board.'

Shacklock harrumphed. He was notoriously bad at keeping up his roads. To divert the subject he said testily, 'Lorries, lorries, what the devil are lorries?'

'The motor-wagons that collect the milk and take it to the station. Speed is of the essence, as I'm sure you understand, which is why we went with motor-transport.' He freed one hand to pull out his watch. 'I must be on my way, now your horse seems quiet. I'll pop into Ashridge Park some time when I'm passing with a few facts and figures, shall I?'

'Tomorrow, at noon,' Shacklock said, taking back the initiative and, before Richard could say whether that was convenient or not, wrenched his horse away with rein and heel and sent it on down the road at a butcher's trot. The groom, as he passed Richard, rolled an eye at him in what might have been disdain, though it might just as well have been sympathy.

Mr Cowling came out into the stable yard to see Nina off when she hunted Jewel for the first time. 'You look very nice, my love,' he said, with satisfaction. 'Very smart indeed. Very ladylike.' He realised that might sound like a veiled criticism, and added, 'Just like you always do.'

Nina smiled and said, 'Thank you,' but she wasn't feeling quite comfortable. Of course she liked new clothes, and of course she enjoyed dressing up, and when her maid Tina had finished with her and she looked into the long cheval glass (a recent present from Mr Cowling) she liked what she saw: the elegant, well-fitting habit, the top hat with the veil, the gloves, the ivory-handled hunting whip. She had liked being helped to mount by her very own groom, had adored having her very own horse for the first time in her adult life. But as her husband admired her appearance, she suddenly felt like a child's plaything, a doll for dressing up. She could imagine a gigantic little girl stooping over her, picking up her and her toy horse and dotting them along the bedroom floor in a pretend trot to an imagined meet.

She shook away the thought, scolded herself for being ungrateful, and leaned forward to stroke Jewel's handsome black neck. 'He's quite excited,' she said. 'I think he knows what's coming.'

Cowling looked a little anxious. 'You will take care, won't you, my love? Don't go taking any risks. Or jumping any big hedges.'

'I'll be careful,' she promised. 'This is the first time I've hunted him, so I don't know how he'll react. And as for hedges, I never overface a horse. Don't worry.'

He smiled again. 'I always worry. But that's because I love you.'

She had nothing to say to that, nodded a goodbye to him, gathered the reins, and set off.

The meet was at Ferndale, the home of Mr and Mrs Burham Andrews, a short hack away. There was already a crowd there, and Jewel flung his ears forward and snorted in excitement at the sight of so many horses. The men had mostly dismounted and were standing in groups chatting, or engaging one of the mounted ladies in conversation, while grooms walked their horses about. The first person she saw was Bobby, mounted side-saddle on Zephyr. She came across to Nina at once.

'I know, I know – I'm a coward! But Clemmie isn't hunting today, and then I heard Mrs Anstruther wasn't coming out – she's had to go and visit a sick aunt or something of the kind – and with you defecting from the ranks I didn't quite have the brass to do it alone. So here I am being meek and womanly, and if we have a fast run and I break my neck over some tremendous bullfinch I shall blame you.'

'You'll be dead, so you won't be able to blame anyone,' Nina said.

'Oh! So cruel, and so young!' Bobby exclaimed. 'How is Jewel? He looks excited.'

'I think he must have hunted before. He seems to know what's coming.'

'Well, it's a good day for scent, so let's hope we have a run,' Bobby said. She looked Nina over critically.

Various people came up to say hello to Bobby, who was a well-known and popular member of the hunt. She introduced those Nina had not met elsewhere, and there was desultory chat about the weather, the prospects for the day, and the price of lamb. Mrs Burham Andrews came over on a raking chestnut that was already trying to pull her arms out, and after a few sentences was forced to move him away as he tried to bite both Zephyr and Jewel.

'I foresee fun ahead. I know that plug,' said a familiar voice, and Nina looked down to see Adam leaning against Jewel's shoulder and smiling up at her. 'Fellow called Cossey hunted him with the Cottesmore two or three seasons ago and couldn't hold him. Why on earth Cora Andrews bought him I can't imagine.'

'Oh, hello, Kipper.' Bobby heard her brother's voice and turned round. 'I was just talking to Foxton about it. Cossey gave up hunting it and had it broken to side-saddle, and his wife's been riding it, apparently with no difficulty. Quietened down with age, I suppose.'

'Unless it's just hunting that makes it mad,' Adam said.

'But shouldn't someone warn her?' Nina said, feeling they were taking it too calmly.

'I already have,' said Lord Foxton, appearing from the other side of Zephyr. 'But she's confident she can manage, so all one can do is sit back and watch the entertainment. I recommend you ladies, however,' he went on, embracing Bobby and Nina with his gaze, 'to keep well clear of them. Nice piece of horseflesh you have there, Mrs Cowling. How does he go?'

'I haven't hunted him before. But he's fast, and a clean jumper, so I hope we shall have a good day.'

'I'll stick close to you,' Adam said, 'just in case you have any trouble.'

'What are you hunting, Kipper?' Bobby intervened. 'Tallyrand? Then you're in no position to promise Nina anything. Once Tally hears the gone away,' she told Nina, 'he's gone away, and there's no stopping him.'

'I can manage my horses, thank you,' Adam said loftily.

There was a call of 'Hounds, please! Hounds, please!' and the pack arrived. Jewel went tense, quivered all over, and snorted with excitement. His ears were so pointed they almost crossed. Adam put a precautionary hand on the rein, but Nina still had contact with his mouth and read his mood. 'He's all right. Just interested,' she said.

'Yes, aren't we all?' Adam drawled, looking up at her. But she was watching the huntsman and whips and didn't hear him.

The day was cold but not bitter; damp, a little misty; and it should have been good for scent. But the first two draws were blank, and apart from jogging between coverts, Nina had nothing to test Jewel, or her ability to hold him. Mr Cowling would have been pleased, she thought – nothing to alarm him, or ruffle her perfect appearance.

She was sitting on Jewel a little apart at the third draw, listening to hounds working. Jewel had passed from excitement to boredom, and apart from jangling his bit as he chewed it and occasionally scraping the ground with a hoof, he was quiet. Adam rode his big bay up beside her, glanced

457

back at Daughters, waiting a little way off, and said, 'Is your groom to be trusted?'

Nina looked puzzled. 'I haven't had him long, but he came with a good reputation. Why? Have you heard something about him?'

Adam grinned rather wolfishly. 'How literal you are! I didn't mean in that way. Can he be trusted to keep his mouth shut?'

'About what?'

'I was thinking this is slow work. I'm pretty sure they're going to draw a blank here as well – yes, you see, they're pulling hounds out now. I can think of better things to be doing. What say on the way to the next draw, you and I slip away through the woods? I know a charming little inn over at Mersitone where there'll be a good fire and something agreeable to drink and eat. Where we can be cosy and talk to our hearts' content.'

Nina was half thrilled, and half appalled. She stalled him. 'What on earth would we talk about?'

'Ourselves – the most interesting subject in the world to two attractive young people. But if you don't feel like talking, there are other things.' He touched the back of her hand with the handle of his whip, then ran it back and forth like a caress.

Now she was uncomfortable. She moved her hand away. 'You mustn't say such things.'

'Why not? No-one can hear. And don't pretend you haven't been thinking them. I've seen the way you look at me.'

'You're mistaken,' she said awkwardly. 'I don't look at you in any particular way.'

'You look at me like a woman who needs loving. You have the wistful look of a cat at the window, watching the birds fly by, unable to get at them through the glass.'

'Don't be absurd. I do not,' she said. 'And you mustn't talk to me like this. I'm a married woman.' He only smiled, and she added, 'Besides, I *am* loved. My husband loves me.'

'But you don't love him.'

She turned her head away. 'Stop it,' she said, low and angry.

'And in any case,' he went on, unabashed, 'I'm not talking about the sort of love an old man can give a lovely young woman in the prime of life. You need loving properly, thoroughly. Every woman deserves that. I should like to kiss you until your lovely face has that expression of astonished bliss – like the cat that has got at the cream.'

He was handsome and familiar and she was young and lonely. She felt a pang deep in her stomach, of excitement and longing. She had never been loved, in the way he meant, and it shocked her that he recognised it. She was shocked, too, with her own reaction. Just for a moment she wanted him, and the betrayal that represented made her angry with herself, and angrier with him.

'I have no wish to be kissed by you,' she said bitterly, and it was true. The yearning feeling in her stomach was for Giles, and that was yet another betrayal. 'Leave me alone. And never speak to me like this again. I'm a—'

Even then he was not abashed. 'You're a married woman, I know. You're my sister's bosom friend. I assure you I'm interested in your welfare, that's all. Friendship and kindly concern are my motives.' He turned his horse, preparatory to moving off. 'Look, they're coming out – we're on the move,' he said. Talleyrand began to circle on the spot, ready for action. He spoke in broken phrases when his face was towards her. 'I can – be patient. When – the fruit is – ripe, it comes off in your – hand without a tug.'

I'm not fruit! she thought, gathering Jewel's reins and preparing to follow. But just then, she rather was. It wasn't natural for a healthy young woman to live as she did, unmated and unfulfilled. She didn't want to want Adam, but she was afraid that if she encountered him at the right moment in the right place, something might happen.

On the way to Germany Giles and Kitty stopped off in London to see Aunt Caroline.

'Why does she have to get married at this time of year?' Giles complained. 'She could have waited until spring.'

'I believe the prince doesn't want to wait,' Caroline said mildly.

'What possible difference can it make to him? Why must he hurry to secure her? I don't suppose there are any rivals for her hand, and she hasn't any money.'

'Don't be so cynical, Giles. You have not considered that he might be in love with her.'

Giles was about to explode – *In love? With my mother?* – when he caught Kitty's anxious eye and realised how rude that would be. But, of course, both women read it in his face.

'You're not quite fair to poor Maud,' Caroline said. 'She had to be mother to all of us from a very early age, and run the house too, and Papa was never appreciative. Now she hasn't any cares of that sort, she can be less . . . forbidding. And consider, she is probably a different person when she's with the prince.'

'Hmph,' said Giles, unable quite to believe it. But he managed to say, 'I hope she will be happy with him. I'm surprised she's satisfied with such a small wedding. You'd think she'd want our whole tribe to share her triumph.'

'She said in her letter she thinks it would look ridiculous at her age to have the sort of wedding she was planning for her daughter. So it's to be close family only.'

'But you're not going?' said Giles.

'She knows I can't bear the cold at any price. I'll see them in London next year on their bridal tour. Vicky and Bobo will be there, and she says Stuffy is going over from Venice, though I haven't heard anything from him about it.'

460

'What on earth is he *doing* there all this time?' Giles asked. 'Almost three months, he's been away.'

'Renovating his house – that's all I know. Of course, we don't know that he's been in Venice the whole time. You know what he is for wandering. There are plenty of English people living in Italy he might visit. In any case, I don't expect he knows how long he's been away – he doesn't have a very firm grasp of time. But you can ask him at the wedding what he's been up to, if you really want to know.'

He shrugged it off. 'Mere idle curiosity. Well, Aunty, I suppose we had better be leaving if we're to catch that train.'

'*Have* you got plenty of warm clothes, my dear?' Caroline asked Kitty. 'It can be colder in Germany than you can imagine.'

'I think so,' Kitty said.

'Well, but let me lend you my sable muff. Just ring the bell, and I'll have my maid bring it down for you. I know they're old-fashioned, but you can't think what a comfort, when you're travelling. You look apprehensive, my dear.'

'Oh, I'm not worried about the journey. I just don't like leaving the children.'

'It's only for a week or so,' Caroline said. 'They won't have time to miss you.'

'But I'll miss them,' Kitty said.

'How sweet,' Caroline said vaguely. What was there about little children to miss, she wondered. That reminded her of something she had meant to say. 'By the way, Giles, when you come back, I do wish you would insist that Linda goes with you back to the Castle. I'm afraid she's settling in here as if she means to stay for ever. And it's not as if she's an agreeable companion. Nothing is ever right for her. She complains about everything.'

'Is she upset not to be going to the wedding?' Giles asked.

'Upset is not the word,' said Caroline, grimly. 'You'd think it was the greatest treat in the world she was missing. And,'

461

she remembered, 'you're not *supposed* to have treats when you're in deep mourning.'

It was a long and miserable journey, which Kitty beguiled by thinking about her garden. Mr Blomfield had sent preliminary drawings, suggesting how it might look, which had enchanted her so much that she was thinking of having Gale make a frame for one of them, and hanging it on the wall of her sitting-room. Just in case it never came to pass.

Because Blomfield had also sent a preliminary list of large works required and a first estimate of the cost, and it was a lot. A very great deal. She had not shown either the drawings or the estimate to Giles yet, for fear that he would say it was out of the question. She didn't want to hear the absolute veto yet. She wanted to indulge herself a little first, thinking about it: the twisting path that wound its way up the hillside, the little grassy spaces where one could rest, the shadowed ferny glades, the rockeries and shrubberies, the tall flowers and the ground-huggers, the stream tumbling whitely over stone lips into little pools . . . In her imagination she walked there, strolling and admiring and breathing in the scents, until she reached the top were there was a grotto in which a spring, the source of the stream, leaped from a stone mask in the wall, and a little white temple with a bench where one could sit and look over the whole valley. That last bit was not in the drawings – she hadn't mentioned it to Mr Fenchurch in case he laughed at her.

When they got home from the wedding, she would have to talk to Giles about it, find out if there would be a yes or a no. Otherwise it could never move forward. But she would hold off until then, and hug her dream to her in leisure moments, and in that drowsy half-world just before falling asleep at night, when girls think about their lovers.

It occupied her during the worst of the journey, during the last part of which she was profoundly grateful for Aunt

Caroline's muff, and only wished there were a muff for feet. The carriage drive from the railway station was almost the last straw: at least the scenery dashed past when you were in a train, but the two horses pulling the carriage seemed to be built for strength rather than speed. They pulled up at last before the main door of the Usingerhof, plain and flat-faced, which looked like an oversized English Georgian country house that had littered a large number of wings, annexes and attachments. A vast array of unlit windows slept above and a closed great door seemed to mock their chilled weariness. But as they trod up the shallow steps, it was flung open to them by a stout, white-haired major-domo in a uniform that featured many brass buttons. Moments later they were in a large hall, brightly lit, and with an enormous fireplace in which what looked like an entire tree was burning briskly.

A kind-looking, mousy sort of female, whom Kitty took to be the housekeeper, came forward to welcome her, and though she was speaking German, she was plainly saying nice things and inviting her to take off her outer garments.

And then Maud was there, a strange Maud wearing a new and more flattering gown and with her hair arranged differently, giving her a softer look. Still, she spoke with Maud sharpness. 'In English, please, Tilde. Lady Stainton does not speak any German. So, Kitty, here you are. Giles. You are a little ahead of time. German railways are most efficient. But Stefan drives so slowly you must be frozen. I will have tea brought immediately. I have not yet managed to make many changes here, but I have at least taught them how to make tea. Oh, this is the prince's sister, Matilde von Lippstadt,' she mentioned, almost as an afterthought. 'How are my grandsons?' she continued, before Tilde could complete a murmur or shake a hand.

'Flourishing,' Giles answered. 'Is everyone else here?'

'No, you are the first. The prince is still in his business-room with the steward. I'll have him sent for.'

And then a small whirlwind entered the room from under the great double staircase and flung itself on Giles. 'Oh, you're here, you're here! I'm so glad. I was afraid you wouldn't come!'

Giles gently detached his sister and, holding both her hands, set her back a little to look at her. 'Such a greeting!' he said. 'Anyone would think you hadn't seen me for years.'

'It *feels* like years,' Rachel said passionately.

He saw the change in her. She looked thinner. Some of her sparkle had dimmed, and the marks of discontent were in her face. 'What's the matter? Have you been ill?' he asked.

'Of course she hasn't,' Maud said sharply. 'Too many late nights, that's all. Baumann, have the bags taken up and have tea brought at once. We've put you in the Homburg Room. Come to the fire, Kitty. Rachel, don't slouch in that disagreeable way. Stand up straight.'

It was plain to Giles that his mother's character had not yet undergone fundamental change. The prince's sister was nominally the lady of the house, but it was Maud who already ruled the roast, and Tilde barely spoke a word, though she did what she could by way of smiles and nods to make her guests welcome.

After Aunt Caroline's warnings, Kitty was glad to discover that the house, while large, was wonderfully warm in comparison with English houses, despite the cold outside. In conversations over the next two days, she learned that this was largely thanks to Tilde, who in the last two years had overseen the installing of double windows everywhere, and tiled stoves in all the rooms, which gave a much more comprehensive heat than open fires. The great log fire in the hall was for cheerfulness, and it was there, she learned, that most gatherings took place. It was hard to feel the same about gathering around a stove, though they were pretty with their different-coloured glazed tiles, some in cream, some green,

464

some deep burgundy red, some – Kitty's favourite – in Delft blue-and-white.

That first evening, the prince came hurrying from his meeting as soon as he was called, and welcomed them warmly. He, too, seemed to have undergone improvement, which Giles put down partly to new clothes but mostly to happiness, which seemed to radiate from him to such an extent that Giles was forced to conclude his aunt had guessed right. Amazing though it might seem to one who had grown up under her shadow, Usingen was in love with his mother.

Aunt Vicky and Uncle Bobo arrived next, and finally Uncle Stuffy, and a very cheerful dinner followed, featuring *Kartoffelsuppe* – a potato soup; carp with *grüne Soße*, a green sauce made of sour cream and a variety of herbs; *Rippchen*, which were spiced pork cutlets; a strong-flavoured game bird, which the prince said was capercaillie; and *Sauerbraten*, marinaded venison, which was served with dumplings. The food was tasty and hearty, and Giles was surprised at how much his mother ate – it accounted for her slightly less angular appearance. There was plenty to drink, and everyone seemed to be in a good mood – except, Giles noticed, for Rachel, who drooped unhappily and didn't join in the conversation.

They didn't sit up late, as the travellers were tired. As Kitty had already discovered, when she went up to change, she and Giles were to share a room, either from a mistake or because it was the German custom. The enormous, high, white-covered bed had a vast carved headboard in black oak, which reached all the way to the ceiling and was a riot of plants, animals and gargoyles. There were no blankets. Instead they were to sleep under a *Federbett*, an enormous thick quilt filled with duck down. It was so light in weight compared with the layers of blankets at home that she feared she would be cold, but it was actually much warmer – deliciously so. It was strange to have Giles in bed with her, but they were both so tired, they fell asleep at once.

She woke at some point in the night, and found that in sleep he had rolled over against her, and had flung one arm over her. His closeness and touch and warmth were blissful to her and she drifted back into a happy sleep. When they both woke early in the morning, it seemed the proximity had worked on him, too, for he drew her to him and kissed her; and then, without words or awkwardness, they made love, for the first time in a year.

Though the wedding was not to be large or grand, the prince was the local lord of the manor so it was a serious matter. On the day itself, the servants were in a state of suppressed excitement, while a stream of messages, flowers and supplies came to the door from an early hour.

The prince's other sisters – Sofie Waldsolms and Klara Rosbach – who lived within twenty kilometres of Usingen, arrived with their husbands, and a favourite cousin, Leonie, Princess Surova, the widow of a Russian noble, who was staying with them. As well as German and French they all spoke good English, which made conversation inclusive. They seemed to be stout, prosperous, richly dressed people, though Maud's expression suggested she thought they were not elegant. A sort of nuncheon had been prepared for everyone, a vast array of cold meats, cheeses and breads, and the newcomers tucked in with journey appetites while chatting cheerfully, their cheeks rosy, their mouths and hands busy. Maud only picked, then excused herself to go up and dress.

Everyone had gathered by the fire in the great hall when she came downstairs, looking elegant in a jacket and skirt of pale lavender silk over a cream blouse of Brussels lace. She wore a triple strand of very fine pearls – the bridegroom's present to her – with matching earrings and bracelets, lavender suede gloves, and a large cream-coloured hat, wide as a boat, decorated with ostrich feathers and silk roses.

The prince, in morning coat and grey trousers with a white

camellia in his lapel, looked by far the more nervous of the two, but Giles was both touched and a little uneasy to note that his mother seemed not her usual monument of icy calm, but just a little fluttered. In consequence, she seemed younger and, to his astonishment, almost beautiful. As she was a widow, there were no bridesmaids, but Rachel had a new dress of pale blue trimmed with narrow white fur, and a wide upturned hat of pale blue filled with wax flowers, and would have been very pretty if it weren't for her beaten-down look.

The carriages were sent for. Outside the church a crowd of locals had gathered despite the cold, to cheer and wave handkerchiefs for 'their' prince, marrying at last. He paused on the steps to wave back, his eyes full of tears. Giles thought he was moved by the tribute, though it might just have been the cold wind making them water.

The service was long and, of course, in German, and the church was cold. The small number of guests made it seem overlarge, echoing and unwelcoming. Kitty, her hands deep in the sable muff, tried to concentrate on the moment, but her mind kept drifting back to that very, very warm and downy bed, and Giles, and the thought that they were to have two more nights in it.

After the service and the cold church, it was back to the lovely warm house and the wedding feast that the servants had been preparing while they were out. The best of the local families had been invited, for even a small wedding must be celebrated, and the nuptials of an Usingen were of import beyond his family. In the great hall there was room for all to stand and chat and drink champagne, before being called to the dining-table.

Giles, glass in hand, did his best to circulate and talk to everyone, aware that as head of the bride's family he had certain responsibilities. Soon he came up against Uncle Stuffy, already on his third glass, and looking mellow.

'Extraordinary thing of Maud's, this,' Stuffy said, by way

of greeting. 'Getting married again. I mean, I'm in favour of marriage in general, but she's already done it once – you'd think she'd have had enough, after your father.'

'Perhaps it's a case of love,' Giles said, not entirely ironically. The prince, standing by the fire with his bride, holding court, looked to be in rapture, while Maud seemed fairly pleased with herself, and certainly had a bit of colour in her cheeks.

'Even if they like each other, marriage is going a bit far,' Stuffy said. 'I've overheard some of the locals on the subject – they're not too pleased, given Usingen's never been married before and has no heir. The heir presumptive is some cousin called Adelbert, or some such name, who's not popular, and they've been hoping Usingen would bring home some rosy Gretchen in breeding prime. But Maud – if she's not past child-bearing already, she soon will be.'

Giles was uncomfortable with this line of conversation and changed the subject. 'What can you have been doing in Italy all this time?'

Uncle Stuffy's face took on a smile that was not just serene, but almost smug. 'Italy's lovely at any time of year,' he said. His eyes twinkled, as though he was enjoying a joke at Giles's expense. 'As you ought to know – spent enough time there, haven't you?'

'I didn't go for idle pleasure. I was studying,' Giles pointed out. 'And working.'

'Nothing idle about pleasure, if you go about it properly. Takes it out of you. But in any case, *I* was working. Seeing to the renovating of m' house in Venice. Got into a bit of a poor state over the years, from neglect.'

'I didn't even know until this year that you *had* a house in Venice. You never went there, did you?'

'Forgotten about it.'

'How can you forget an entire palace?'

'Shan't do so again.'

'And what will you do with it when you have renovated it?'

'Oh, something will occur, I expect,' he said, his eye wandering. It fell upon his niece. 'What's going to happen to little Rachel, now Maud's married? How does her step-papa feel about her?'

'An odd thought. It hadn't occurred to me before that Usingen is her step-papa,' Giles said. 'She's not looking very happy about any of this.'

'No, she's very mumpish, poor child. But he's as rich as Croesus, I understand, and well-connected. If he exerts himself to get her a husband, I can't see how he'd fail. He might even stump up a dowry for her.'

'It's not his job to do that,' Giles said, crossly because he was sensitive on that subject.

'Well, it's not yours any more,' Uncle Stuffy said, clapped Giles's shoulder, and eased himself away through the throng.

CHAPTER TWENTY-FOUR

Mr Bland sank half of the pint in one extended swallow, as though he had a long thirst to satisfy. Sebastian took only a sip at his. He enjoyed a glass of local Brakspear's ale by the river when he was at his house in Henley, but he had no idea where this stuff came from. It had an acrid taste that went with its yellowish hue. The random thought came to him that it probably looked much the same when it left the body as it did going in.

The other denizens of the Blue Posts seemed to be quaffing it without distress; but probably they had other priorities than taste.

Bland wiped his mouth and said, 'Well, sir, you'll be pleased to know I have found your quarry.'

Sebastian felt a little bolt of shock in his stomach. So it was starting at last! 'Indeed? That's good news.'

'The trail was a long and twisted one – I don't suppose you want all the details?'

'You may cut the to end. Where is he?'

'In Brighton, where a lot of London villains end up, in my experience. They seem to feel they can hide there almost as well as in the Smoke, and find clients just as ready for fleecing. I don't know if you are acquainted with Brighton at all, sir?'

'I have visited it once or twice,' Sebastian admitted. 'I can't say I know it well.'

'There's an area of old Brighton commonly called The Lanes – a warren of narrow streets and alleys, full of shops and pubs and low eating-houses. And other amenities.' He gave Sebastian a knowing look and a nod. 'Not a fashionable area, as you might say, though the smart young bucks like to carouse there for the dare of it, show their colours, splash their rhino about and prove their manhood.'

'It's a common habit among young men without enough to do.'

'You're right, sir. I should say it's not *all* rough – there are plenty of honest small traders there – but it's a poor area. The sort of place where you find a pawnbroker on every corner, and there are more shops repairing things than selling them new.'

'I understand. And what is Hubert doing there?'

'He has a small shop. Second-hand clothes – what they call a shoddy shop – and tailoring repairs. Much what he was doing in London, but to a different set of customers. No carriage trade there. Local folk don't have much money to spare, and one suit has to last a man his life. Don't suppose he's making much of an income. He lives above the shop. There's a woman living with him—'

'He's married?' Sebastian said sharply.

Bland gave a mirthless smile. 'I didn't say anything about marriage. She doesn't look the marrying sort, if you take my meaning. And I reckon he's drinking. I saw her going in at eight of a morning with a jug and it wasn't full of milk.' He paused and surveyed his client with a bright-eyed look. 'So, what would you like me to do next?'

'There's no doubt it's the same man?' Sebastian asked.

'There's always doubt, sir, but as far as I can ascertain. Still calls himself Jack, though there were several versions of his surname when I spoke to local people – Hubert, Herbert, Hewitt, even Hubbard. That's not unusual when you're among people who don't write things down much. But there are no breaks in the trail, and it looks like the same man. Same trade, same drinking habits.' Another considering look. 'Do you want me to speak to him? Ask him anything?'

'No,' said Sebastian. He was thoughtful. He had not entirely thought out what he meant to do when, or if, he tracked down his quarry. The quest itself had been enough to begin with, to use up his frustrated energy. And in a large country of thirty million people, he had not reckoned Bland's chances of finding one man very highly. He must be a singularly good bloodhound, Sebastian thought, to have followed the trail to its conclusion.

But now he had him, what *was* he going to do with him? Actually, he had half hoped the trail would end with the information that Hubert had drunk himself to death. As long as he was alive, Dory could not remarry. But perhaps he might at least make sure the villain never tried to find her, never came near her again.

'This requires thinking about,' he said at last.

'Just as you wish, sir,' said Bland. He slipped a folded piece of paper across the table. 'There's his direction, at any rate. And if you want me to do anything more, you know where to find me.' He stood up, finished the rest of his pint – probably it slipped down more easily when you were fully vertical – and was leaving. But he paused. 'Word of warning, sir. He's not well thought of locally. Too quick with his fists. He'll pick a fight, they say, just for the pleasure of it. And he might be in his cups a lot of the time, but that doesn't mean he can't hit straight. You often find with those habitual drunks that it doesn't slow them down or spoil their aim. Wouldn't do to underestimate him, sir, that's all I'm saying.'

'Thank you. I haven't decided yet what to do, but I shall be careful.'

Bland nodded neutrally, and was gone. Bland by name and bland by appearance, within a few steps he had blended into the throng. He seemed, Sebastian thought, to dislimn like a ghost at cock-crow.

★ ★ ★

472

As long as they were in France, Rachel had been content – concerned, certainly, about how she and Angus were to manage to be married, but not deeply worried. Something would happen, or he would contrive something, she was sure. Meanwhile, she was having fun, and agreeable young men were vying for her company. Her enjoyment was only intensified by her love for Angus, her assurance that he loved her too, the excitement of waiting for his secret letters.

All that changed when they moved to Germany. Instead of Aunt Vicky and Uncle Bobo's cheerful company and their near genius at arranging entertainments, there was to be only strict Mama and dull Prince Paul and his sister. And Usingen was so far away! In Biarritz, she had felt only a hop, skip and jump from England, but now she seemed to have been dragged into an infinitely distant foreign land, a wilderness from which return would be impossible. The little town held no attractions for her, and all around were the woods, the sinister lakes, the un-English-looking rivers, the forbidding forested mountains on one side and the vast empty meadows on the other. Everything was too big and, with the onset of winter, bleak. How would she ever get back? Would she ever be *allowed* to go back? She was a helpless prisoner in a giant's castle and her misery grew day by day. She understood for the first time the force of the word 'exile'.

It wasn't until the day after the wedding that Giles had the opportunity to speak to her privately. As she left the room after breakfast, he caught up with her, tucked her hand under his arm, and said, 'I've found what I think is the warmest spot in the house. Come and see.'

It was a small conservatory, with a stone-flagged floor, built on to one side of the back of the house, at the end of a long dim passage. It was only about ten feet square, not meant for sitting in, but to over-winter delicate plants. It faced south to catch whatever sun there was, and it had hot water running in pipes around the walls. Small plants sat on

473

trestles under the windows, while larger ferns and palms stood in pots on the floor. It smelt of warm, damp greenness, like an English riverbank in summer.

'Now then,' Giles said, turning to face her, and pushing closed the glazed, metal-framed door behind her, 'tell me what's going on. Why are you looking so miserable?'

Rachel stared at the floor, scuffing the flag with the toe of her shoe. Giles was so much older than her, and she had hardly known him before her father died. In her mind he ranked among the grown-ups. She didn't know how far she could trust him. But then the desperation of her plight broke through the barriers.

'Oh Giles, I hate it here! Oh, please don't let them make me stay! Please let me come home!'

'I thought you'd been enjoying all your travels these past two years,' he said. 'The Wachturm and then France, London, Scotland, France again. All the clothes – my God, the clothes! – and the balls and everything else. It's a young woman's dream, isn't it?'

'It *was*,' Rachel admitted miserably. 'But it's all changed now, you must see that. Now that Mama's married Paul, the prince . . .' Rachel shuddered and stopped.

'Is he unkind to you?'

'Oh, no, he's . . .' She stopped, wondering how to explain. 'He tries to be nice, I do see that.'

'What, then?' She shrugged helplessly. 'It's your mother? Well, she's always been difficult. She was difficult with me.' No answer. 'Anyway,' he tried, 'won't she and the prince be going off on a honeymoon now?'

'Wedding tour,' Rachel corrected automatically. Her mother had strenuously objected to the word 'honeymoon', saying it was not appropriate to people of her and the prince's age.

'Wedding tour,' Giles allowed. 'She won't be taking you with her for that, I presume.'

Now she looked up, eyes desperate. 'You don't understand!

She wants to get me married. It's all she cares about. And Paul – the prince – goes along with it to please her. They're going on the tour to visit all his cousins and relatives – he has *hundreds* of them, all over Germany and Romania and Russia and Greece and I don't know where else. And they're going to pick out one of them to marry me. I've heard them talking about Count This and Prince That. Mama's mad for it. There's a Russian prince, Paul's nephew I think, that they're especially keen on. Oh, Giles, I don't *want* to marry a Russian prince!'

'Really? I'd have thought you'd like to be a princess,' Giles said, bemused. Wasn't this what all the debutantes talked of and dreamed about – who could get the highest prize in the marriage stakes? 'Russian princesses have the most jewels and furs and fine horses, you know.'

'I don't want to live in Russia. It's so far away. I don't want to live abroad and never come back. I want—' She stopped herself, unsure of what his view of Angus would be. 'I want to come home,' she ended miserably. 'Oh, Giles, please talk to her. Make her let me go.'

He was uncomfortable, seeing how upset she was, though he thought her fears exaggerated. A good marriage, from what he gathered, had been her ambition as much as her mother's. Why should that suddenly change? It was probably, he thought, just the depressing effects of the Usingerhof and winter. Once she was travelling again, seeing new places, meeting new people, she would cheer up. 'Unmarried girls have to live with their mothers,' he said. 'That's the way of it. I can't interfere.'

'You're head of the family.'

'But you were left to your mother's guardianship, not mine. I'm not your father.'

'No. I've got a stepfather now,' she said, in a low voice.

It affected him. 'Are you really miserable, dear?' he asked gently. She nodded, staring at the floor again. He reached out and took a long drooping curl of fair hair in his fingers – so soft, almost like a baby's hair. 'If I asked her to let you come home, and even if she agreed, there's nothing at Ashmore for you. We don't entertain much. You wouldn't have all the dances and outings and everything you've got used to. I'm afraid you'd be very bored, and then you'd be unhappy, stuck at home with nothing to do, and nothing to look forward to. It's not much of a life for a female, you know, if she doesn't get married. Wouldn't it be better to trust your mother – and the prince – to find you an agreeable husband? Then, once you were married, you'd have the freedom to do what you wanted. And there'd be children – you'd like to have children, wouldn't you?'

She looked up, her face suddenly calm and firm. 'I want to get married. I want to have children. Just not some foreign lord's. Please let me come home, Giles. You could insist.'

'If you're really serious about this,' he said, 'I'll ask her. But if she won't budge, there's nothing I can do. I don't have any influence over her.'

'But you'll try? *Really* try? And it has to be today.'

'Yes, of course. We're leaving tomorrow.' She stared at him insistently, and he said, 'I'll go and find her now.'

'*Thank* you,' she said profoundly. 'I know you can beat her. You think you don't have any influence, but you do. She can't control you, and she knows that. She doesn't like people she can't control.'

Rachel almost ran to her room and shut herself in, and got out the most recent letter she'd had from Angus. In it he said, in reply to the fears expressed in her last letter, that if necessary he would come and fetch her; that if they threatened her with marriage he would come and take her away. It was a lovely vision, and when she was alone with the letter and her memories of him, it was comforting, but when she compared it with the reality of her mother and the prince, it had no substance. It was just a fairy story. If she could have run away, she would have, but in the middle of Germany, in the middle of winter, with no money to pay for fares or food, no idea how to get home – no real idea even where she was – no, that was a fairy story too. Some Rachel somewhere might have been hardy and resourceful enough to do it, but not this Rachel.

Giles thought it would be difficult to get his mother alone for a talk, but in fact she came with him readily when he approached her, and led the way to a pleasant room she had already acquired for her private use. She had fitted it out, with furniture chosen from the rest of the house, as a sitting- and writing-room.

She was glad of the interruption, bored with the conversation of Vicky and Tilde, who talked about nothing but the wedding, who had said what to whom, and who was related to whom in what degree. She suspected Giles had nothing agreeable to say to her – when did he ever? – but at least it was a change.

'Well?' she said coolly.

'It's about Rachel,' he began.

'Indeed. And what have you to do with my daughter?' she asked forbiddingly.

'I've been talking to her. She's very unhappy. She's afraid you and Usingen mean to marry her off to some foreign count – a cousin of Usingen's, or something like that.'

'Oh, really!' Maud exclaimed. 'What does she suppose we've been doing these past two years but prepare her for marriage? A process in which she has taken enthusiastic part, I may say.'

Giles felt awkward. 'I *did* say that to her. I told her being unmarried is no fun for a woman in the long term.'

'She knows that. The fact of the matter, Stainton, is that she took a fancy to one of her cousins when we were at

Kincraig, and now she thinks she's in love with him, and sees herself as the tragic heroine of some romantic story.'

'Oh. She's in love?' That explained a lot.

'She wants to marry him, but I haven't gone to all this trouble and expense to throw her away on a nobody.' She left out the annoying consideration that Tullamore didn't want Angus to marry Rachel either. 'You need have no apprehension,' she went on. 'It's a passing phase, and as soon as we are travelling again and meeting new people, she'll be back to normal.'

'Are you really taking her with you on your honey— your wedding tour?'

'You don't suppose I would leave her here alone?'

'No, but newly married people generally—'

'Usingen and I are not seventeen. We are quite capable of maintaining civilised relations with people apart from each other. And as we will be visiting some very suitable relatives of his, it is sensible to take Rachel along and introduce them. Someone will take her fancy. When she sees how they live – when she has a taste of court life – she will see her own place among them, and this nonsense about Angus will fade away.'

Oh, it's Angus, is it? he thought. He remembered him vaguely from the ball – a well-built, fair young man. The thought crossed his mind that they would make very pretty babies, and he was surprised at himself.

'I think,' he said judiciously – it was no use offering his mother emotional arguments – 'that it won't do much good showing Rachel to prospective suitors when she's in this sort of mood. She's unhappy and depressed. All she'll do is put them off. First impressions last, you know.'

He saw his mother take the point. 'What are you proposing?' she asked, with a hint of impatience.

'Perhaps she's just over-tired. I suggest Kitty and I take her home with us for a rest. We'll have a family Christmas, and then it will get very quiet. When she discovers how dull it is at Ashmore, she'll soon start pining for the sort of life you're offering. She'll come back to you refreshed and ready to fall in with your plans. And, meanwhile, you and Usingen will have a little time together to get to know each other.'

'We know each other quite well enough, thank you,' said Maud, but he could see she was thinking about it. 'We *could* alter the order of our tour,' she said, after a moment. 'Visit the relatives with no eligible sons first. But Usingen says we must see Petersburg in the snow, which means by February, before the thaw. You could have her for Christmas and through January.'

'January is a *very* dull month,' Giles said encouragingly.

'Very well. You may be right, Stainton. This might work in all our interests. Of course,' her gaze sharpened, 'I look to you to see that there are no clandestine meetings between her and Angus. Or correspondence.'

'Of course,' said Giles.

'Then I shall speak to Usingen. It will mean letters to be written, telegrams to be sent. A great deal of trouble all round.'

'But worth it, for your daughter's happiness.'

'Happiness is overrated,' she said. 'Many people get through life perfectly well without it.'

'All the same—'

She waved him away. 'You may go. Ring the bell on your way out, and I will send for Usingen now.'

Giles obeyed, noting as he left that it was for the prince to attend on her, not vice versa. Start as you mean to go on was a good precept for married life.

Alice thought it was lovely having Rachel back, and to have Christmas to plan for – like the old days, but better, because their mother had never been a great one for Christmas. Even Linda, annoyed at having been dragged away from London, where she had been perching since being sent back from Biarritz, cheered up at the thought of some festivities, threw herself into planning, and took more notice of her children than for many years past. She even begged them a holiday from Miss Kettel to take them out riding – Miss Kettel, harbouring a cold, was glad to give in and take to the big armchair by the nursery fire, with a shawl and a novel and a handkerchief sprinkled with friar's balsam.

Alice enjoyed long, cosy talks with Rachel – at least at first, until all the new matter had been gone through. But when it got to the point where every conversation became about Angus, when even playing with the babies became coloured with the putative future babies of Angus and Rachel, she began to be aware that having her sister at home and constantly demanding her attention curtailed her freedom.

She wanted to go and see Axe. She had a new book to lend him – *The Call of the Wild* by Jack London – which Giles had bought months ago and finally finished. She had borrowed it from him on her own behalf and had galloped through it. She thought Axe would enjoy it because it was about animals. And she had a Christmas present to give him – a sketch she had done of him, which she had been almost satisfied with. She had tinted the drawing with water-colours, and framed it, using the frame, glass and backing from an old print from the day-nursery. The print was an Ernest Nister of Little Boy Blue asleep in the hay with his horn on his lap. The print had torn slightly as she got it out, and she'd had to conceal it in her dresser drawer, but without remorse. She had always despised it, thinking the boy poor-spirited for letting the sheep wander, perhaps into harm's way, while he dozed stupidly. You always put your animals' comfort before your own, as she had been taught by Giddins when put astride her first pony at the age of three.

A day came when a grey sky and bitter cold outside had Rachel and Linda both retreating to the Peacock Room to share Kitty's good fire. They all had work – Kitty embroidering a bib for Alexander, Rachel pin-tucking a blouse for herself, and Linda fiddling with a piece of crochet, which she had been intending as a hat for one of her children but, since it seemed to have a mind of its own and kept going out of shape, might end up as a scarf instead.

Alice watched them for a moment, contemplated drawing the group, and then, restless, said, 'I think I'll go for a ride. Does anyone want to come?'

'Too cold,' said Rachel, without looking up.

Linda didn't even reply. Kitty looked up and smiled, but said, 'Not me. Are you sure you want to go out? It's not a nice day at all.'

'Can't stay in,' Alice said. 'I've been sitting too long.'

She had underestimated how cold it was. When she stepped out of the side door, the nearest one to the stables, the freezing air bit her, like a spiteful dog, and she gasped as the first breath seared her lungs. The stable yard was deserted, the grooms all having retreated inside. Even the yard dog was inside his kennel and declined to come out or bark. Someone must have alerted Josh to her presence, because he came limping out of the tack-room, letting out a cloud of smoke. They had lit a lamp in there, probably more for the warmth than the light, but its yellow glow spilling onto the frost-rimed cobbles made the grey day look darker.

'I'm going for a ride,' Alice told him.

He hunched into his collar and said, 'It's too cold, my lady. I think it's going to snow.'

'It's not. And I'll be warm enough when I'm moving.'

'D'you want me to come with you, my lady?' Josh asked, clearly hoping for the answer no.

She almost said yes, just to tease him, but that would not answer her purposes. 'No. And you don't have to saddle Pharaoh – I'll do it myself. Just hand me out his tack.'

Josh hesitated, clearly tempted, but said, 'I'll do it, my lady.'

Pharaoh, annoyed at being dragged from his warm stable, laid back his ears sharply as he was led out, and nipped, his breath making clouds. When Josh pulled up the girths, he cow-kicked. While Josh tried to throw her up into the saddle, he skittered about, his hoofs slipping on the cobbles, and when she was up he tried to nap back to his stable. But she was glad she'd decided to go out. The cold was exhilarating: her cheeks stung with it, and she wanted to gallop.

'Looks like snow, my lady,' Josh said again. 'You don't want to get caught in it.'

'I'll turn for home as soon as the first flake falls,' she promised. 'But I don't think it will. It's too cold for snow.' And she turned the reluctant Pharaoh and drove him firmly out through the gate and into a canter up the hillside.

The sombre sky was like pewter, and the sun, reaching weakly for its winter zenith, showed as a swollen red ball through the indigo brush-strokes of bare branches. The last part of the route to Castle Cottage was under the lee of the woods, and by then rider and horse were warmed up, though Alice's hands were burning with cold. She turned down the track under the trees at last, and into an eerie stillness and twilight. Pharaoh's hoofs made no sound, and the birds were all silent, huddled away somewhere.

But there was sound coming from the cottage, the intermittent thud and crack of logs being split; and at the same moment she smelt the delicious tang of woodsmoke. As she rode into the yard, Dolly gave a single welcoming bark to announce her, and Axe came out from the smaller barn.

'Wasn't expecting any visitors today,' he said. 'Colder'n a witch's curse.'

'Josh says it's going to snow,' she replied, halting Pharaoh and loosing her foot from the stirrup.

'Might do,' he said. 'Hard to say.'

'I said it was too cold to snow. Anyway, I've been cooped

up indoors for days. My sister's back, and she had so much to tell me, I had to sit and listen to her.'

He stood his long-handled axe carefully against the door frame and came to jump her down. He was a patch of cheerful colour in the grey day, wearing a red woollen shirt – he had taken off his jacket when the exercise made him warm.

'My hands are frozen,' she said. 'The rest of me's all right, though.'

'Give 'em here,' he said. She pulled off her gloves and held out her hands, and he folded them between his own, which were hot from the axe-handle. 'Bet ol' Pharaoh didn't like coming out.'

'He tried to bite Josh, then he tried to kick him.'

'We'll put him in with Della, she'll like the company. Hands all right now?'

'Yes, thanks. Have you been out today?'

'Course we have. Bit o' cold don't stop us. Ready for a cup of tea now, though.' They led Pharaoh towards the stable. 'Heard Lady Rachel was back, and his lordship and her ladyship. Weren't long in Germany, were they?'

'You always know everything,' she marvelled. 'I think the birds must tell you.'

He gave his most cat-like smile. 'How was the wedding?'

'Rachel said it was odd. I can imagine – it's strange to think of one's mother marrying someone else.'

'She's not that old, your mother.'

'It's not age so much as – well, they sort of come as a set, you know, mother and father. When you've grown up with them.'

'I expect we'll see him here some time, your mother's new husband. Prince of somewhere?'

'Usingen. It's near Frankfurt.' His smile said he didn't know where Frankfurt was, either. 'They'll be in England some time next year. They're doing a sort of grand tour of all their relatives, and he has a lot, according to Rachel, so it'll take a while before they get round to us.'

483

She spent a few minutes petting Della, then had to say hello to Cobnut, who was in the barn, and the cats who were keeping him company. 'Like a hot-water bottle he is to them,' Axe said. 'Sit on his back when he's standing up, then when he lies down they curl up along his belly.'

'I expect they keep him warm, too,' Alice said.

'True. Nothing so warm as a cat on your lap of an evening.'

Inside the house it was warm and welcoming with the fire glowing in the range and the kettle steaming thoughtfully on the slow plate. Dolly hurried past them straight to the hearth. Another cat, a smart ginger tabby, that had slipped in with them, darted into the scullery to see if there was anything left in Dolly's food bowl, then stalked daintily, with a slight swerve to rub Axe's legs, to the fire, sat down beside the dog and started a thorough wash.

'What's in the satchel?' Axe asked, as she pulled it off over her head.

She showed him. 'A new book for you. I'll take back *Oliver Twist* if you've finished it.'

'Not quite,' he said. 'But 'nother couple of these long evenings'll do it.'

'I'll take it next time, then.'

'What's this new book?'

'I think you'll like it. It's about sled dogs, somewhere up in the north of Canada. About one in particular that has all sorts of adventures. It runs away and joins the wild wolves in the end.'

He took it with a sort of cautious reverence, the way he always handled books, which touched her. 'Are you sure it's all right, me borrowing all these books?' he asked, not for the first time.

'Nobody else reads them,' she said. 'And I know you'll take care of them.'

He laid the book carefully on the dresser before filling the pot from the kettle, putting it on the table, and taking down the cake tin. 'See what you think of this,' he said, removing the lid.

She peered in. 'Fruit cake. It looks good. Which one of your sisters made it?'

'Made it myself. First effort. Might be terrible.'

'I'm sure it's not.'

'Had a duck egg that was cracked so I thought I'd give it a go. Something else in that bag of yours?'

'Yes, one more thing. It's a present for you. For Christmas.' She got out the picture. 'I hope you like it,' she said shyly.

He looked at it for a long time. She had drawn it in the summer, when he was sitting outside mending a bit of harness. His head was bent, his eyes down, and his hands at the bottom of the picture were just visible holding needle and palm. His sleeves were rolled up to the elbow, and his shirt was open one button at the neck. The light that day had been gold-green, strong sunshine filtering in through the leaves of the lime tree at the side of the house. She had remembered that when she coloured the drawing, so his skin was golden, while there was a greenish tint to his sun-bleached, red-gold hair. She remembered the exquisite, piercing smell of the lime blossom.

'I remember that day,' he said. Then, 'You're amazing good. Good as those Old Masters. You ought to be exhibiting in London.' He looked up. 'Thank you,' he said softly. 'I'll treasure this all my life.'

The words were wrong, as if it had been a going-away present. She wanted to say, *But I'll be here! Treasure* me*!* She looked at him with a sort of foreboding, devouring him with her eyes against future famine. He seemed to glow, large in his little cottage, more solid, more real, more absolutely *there* than anyone else she knew. The rest of the world was an unconvincing shadow beside the intensity of his presence.

Their eyes met, and for a long moment she felt belonging pass between them. Then he coloured slightly, and turned

485

away in shyness. 'I'll put a nail up after, hang it between the windows where I can look at it all the time.' He turned away, shy with emotion, took the picture to prop it carefully on the dresser. 'Sit down and have some tea,' he said gruffly. He paused with his back to her, and she wondered for a shaky moment if he was crying.

When he came back to sit, one hand was curled round something. 'I did this for you. Funny, you bringing me a Christmas present, cos I made this for a Christmas present for you.'

She held out her hand, and he deposited onto it a little carved wooden object, a cat curled up asleep. It was all curves, as a sleeping cat is, and fitted perfectly into her palm. The detail was beautiful; the warm smoothness of the wood invited caress.

'It's old ginger there,' he said, unnerved by her silence. 'He's a great sleeper – hardly ever does anything else.' He looked at her anxiously. 'It's just a little thing I did, to pass the evenings.'

'It's beautiful,' she said. She looked up. '*You* ought to be exhibiting in London.'

He laughed, breaking the tension. 'Can't see that National Gallery doing an exhibition of my silly bits. What'd they call it? Brandom's Whittlings?'

'They could do worse,' she said. 'In the British Museum, for instance: Aunt Caroline took us there once, and there's a whole gallery of glass cases filled with little bits of broken pottery. Some bits so small you can't even tell what they were bits of.'

'Is that right? Broken pottery?' He cut her a slice of the cake and pushed the plate across to her.

'Terribly old, thousands of years, but it didn't make them any more interesting. Mm, this cake is very good.'

'First effort. Do better next time. How are things up the Castle? Your new butler settling in all right?'

They chatted comfortably through cake and two cups of tea and a variety of subjects. There were never any awkward silences with him, Alice thought. Talking to him was as easy as breathing. Then Axe glanced at the window and said, 'Time you started home, if you don't want to be out in the dark. No moon tonight. Want to help me shut the ducks in? Then you ought to be off.'

Outside the cold seemed to have intensified: it was like an actual weight on the air. The ducks were good and ready to be shut in – most had already retreated inside their new house, and the last stragglers waddled along at the first call, commenting on the weather as they bundled through the door.

In the stable, Della and Pharaoh were dozing together, Pharaoh's chin resting on Della's withers. He looked distinctly annoyed at being rousted out of his warm bed for a second time. Alice slipped the bit back into his mouth and buckled the cheekstrap, while Axe saddled him. Then she went to look out of the door at the darkling day, resting her folded arms on the closed lower half. It looked as unwelcoming out there as it was homelike indoors. As she watched, a little bit of white came twirling past. 'Oh dear,' she said.

'What's that?' She felt Axe come up behind her, felt the heat and weight of him displacing the emptiness, felt – or imagined she felt – his sweet, warm breath on her neck.

'I told Josh it was too cold for snow, but I think it's starting.'

They stood in silence, watching as more flakes fell, black when they were high up against the grey sky, turning white as they came past.

'It's not much,' she said. 'I don't think it's settling.'

His hands came down on the top edge of the door, one either side of her, as he looked out over her shoulder. 'It will do,' he said. 'Ground's cold. If it gets any heavier . . .'

Perhaps I should stay, she said. But not out loud, only in her head. She felt him breathing behind her; she felt his thoughts. Almost without volition, she turned on the spot, within the gateway of his arms, and as if it were an automatic reaction, he closed them round her. She looked up into his face, etched with the uncanny stormlight. Every part of her, from her skin to her soul, ached for him. He gave her a quizzical look, but she felt the inevitability that cradled them. A slight lift of her chin was all it took to tilt them over the edge. His lips were on hers, soft, tasting of him, somehow known, though this was the first time. Hers were ready, longing. A stream of piercing sweetness passed from him into her. She wanted all of him, she wanted everything. She yearned to get closer to him, closer yet. She wanted to climb right inside him and never come out.

In her imagination, in a fraction of second, like a landscape illuminated by lightning, she saw the snow become a blizzard, too heavy for her to go home, saw them hurrying into the cottage, saw her staying the night, sleeping in his bed, saw him joining her there, saw them twined and blissful and together.

Then she would never go away again.

It was *right*.

The kiss paused for breath, she moved her head slightly so that her cheek was against his warm cheek, and the last sane part of her mind said, *What am I doing to him?*

If she stayed, a Rubicon would have been crossed. She would never be able to go back.

And they would destroy him.

She wanted it. She wanted it with every drop of her blood. But she must not, could not do that to him. It was not too late. One kiss, the madness of a moment, never repeated, put out of their minds. Dragging her cheek away from his was like ripping off skin. She could hear him breathing as though he had been running. But she turned away, breaking the lock of his arms, and said, 'It's not too heavy yet. I think I can get home all right.'

Her voice didn't sound like hers – remote, weirdly normal.

And his didn't sound like his as he said, 'Best leave right away, then.'

Best for both of us if you go away and don't come here any more.

No. Best for him, certainly. But for her – exile. To live in a strange land, among strangers, for ever. *He* was home, but she must leave him. She must go away.

They were unnaturally natural in the last few moments as he tightened Pharaoh's girth and she led him out and he threw her up into the saddle and helped her find the stirrup. She gathered the reins, and could hardly see him through the tears. She thought that if he said he was sorry for kissing her, she would die. But he did not mistake her. She was not upset because he had kissed her but because they had stopped. He knew, and she knew he knew, and it was the only comfort in that desolate moment.

CHAPTER TWENTY-FIVE

'I hate not being with you at Christmas,' Richard said.

'It isn't really any different from any other day of the year,' Molly said.

'And I hate it when you're reasonable. It *feels* different, and don't pretend you don't know what I mean.'

'Oh, the romance of significant dates! Well, if it's any comfort to you, I shan't be alone. I shall be going over to spend it with Chloë. The housekeeper, Mrs Mackie, will be cooking us Christmas dinner, and apparently she's a very good cook.'

'And will the moustachioed villain be there?'

'If you mean Sir Thomas—'

'Who else?'

'He'll be in Surrey, spending Christmas with his wife, entertaining all the local dignitaries. They always have a big dinner on Boxing Day, so I'm told, and invitations to it are much prized.'

'Let's hope Lady Violet keeps him until Twelfth Night at least. What's the flat like? You never did tell me.'

'Large rooms, but gloomy, all in the Victorian style: heavy dark furniture, red flock wallpaper, a red velvet cover on the mantelpiece with little bobbles all along the edge – do you know the sort of thing?'

'I do.'

'The old aunt's what-nots are everywhere. Sir Thomas

never removed them, and Chloë, of course, doesn't even see them, so there they sit, to be meticulously dusted every day by Mrs Mackie. Who is my main comfort.'

'What's she like?'

'A Scots woman – '

'So I gathered.'

'– in her fifties or sixties. She was housekeeper to the old aunt. Very respectable. And she seems determined to maintain the proprieties. I couldn't exactly discuss the situation with her – after all, she *is* employed by Sir Thomas – but I hinted as much as I could and she made a granite jaw and assured me that she would take "*verra* guid care of the young lady". And she said, "You need have no fear, Mistress Sands, of any queer goings-on as long as *I* keep hoose here."'

Richard laughed. 'You should be on the halls, Mrs Harry Lauder! But, seriously, I'm glad to hear Chloë has a Cerberus.'

Molly didn't smile. 'I'm afraid even Mrs Mackie won't be able to stave off scandal if this plan goes ahead for a foreign tour next year. If he shows her off around Paris and Berlin, no-one will have any doubt. There'll be no keeping a lid on it.'

'But there'll be a large entourage, won't there? It won't just be two of them in a sleeper compartment?'

'He'll take a secretary and a dresser with him, and possibly some other servants, but—'

'Well, then you should go, too, as Chloë's dresser. What could be more respectable than to have her mother with her?'

She smiled now. 'Considering how you would hate me to go abroad, it shows greatness of mind on your part to suggest it.'

'I shouldn't hate you to go abroad, if you went with me. *En épousailles*, perhaps. My uncle has apparently just discovered he owns a palace in Venice. Perhaps he'd lend it to us. The Ca' Scozzesi, it's called.'

'The Scottish House?'

'You see? More Scots. Entirely respectable.'

'I'm not sure one wants to be entirely respectable on one's honeymoon,' she said teasingly. 'Not that I've ever had one.'

'Neither have I. Which makes me believe all the more firmly that it's something we should try for the first time together.'

She sighed. 'One day you'll wear me down. If only Chloë were safely settled . . . But we'd have to live abroad. The scandal of marrying your father's mistress would ruin you in England.'

'*Late* father's *ex*-mistress. And how can I convince you that nobody would know or care?'

'They'd *know*, my dear. People have an uncanny knack of always knowing the one thing you want to keep concealed.'

Giles had been in London, consulting the banker, Vogel; and Richard, who had gone up on undisclosed business of his own, met him at Marylebone and travelled back with him. The train rushed black through a frozen landscape of black and white. The sun was a wobbling scarlet ball, sinking towards the horizon behind streaks of lavender cloud like smoke, against a chilly pale pink sky.

Richard and Giles were bundled in their greatcoats against the inadequacy of railway heating. Richard offered his brother a cigarillo, and they both lit up. Giles sighed out the first smoke and said, 'Well, at least the finances are looking satisfactory.'

'That's good to hear.'

'Your milk scheme—'

'*Our* milk scheme.'

'As you please – it's taken up some capital this year, and it's not making a return yet—'

'But it will. Especially if Lord Shacklock comes in. I don't care for the man, but his involvement will encourage other farmers to join, and obviously the more we have on board the better. It's greater volume that will bring in the profits.'

Giles smiled. 'To hear you talking like this! Can you really be my wild brother Richard, or has a sorcerer exchanged you with a metamorph?'

'Oh, I'm still Wild Richard underneath. But I have to be serious and weighty to beat Shacklock down to a reasonable price per gallon. He seems to think we should be so grateful that he deigns to sell us his milk that we'll pay him whatever he asks.'

'I thought the herd was really his wife's hobby?'

'It was to begin with. I think she saw herself as a sort of Marie Antoinette, playing milkmaids with nicely washed cows dressed in ribbons. The reality of the other thing that comes out of cows was probably too harsh a descent to earth. At any rate, her interest has waned, and Shacklock is looking for a way for it all not to be a waste.'

'She's a lot younger than him, isn't she?'

'Yes, and a lot prettier.' Richard grinned. 'Rather a man-eater, from what I observed. If I have to have much to do with her, I may need to take a bodyguard with me, in case she sees the old wild Richard and not the new serious one.'

'You *wouldn't?*' Giles began to exclaimed.

'Of course not. On our own doorstep? And Shacklock's the sort to reach for his shotgun if anyone's caught tampering with his property. Look how he peppered that poacher last winter! Besides, she doesn't appeal.'

'You *have* changed.'

'But you were saying the finances are sound?'

'Despite all the capital outlay, on the milk scheme and around the estate, we're doing very well. The jam scheme is bringing in so much money, Vogel's having to look for new places to put it. And that's despite our mother trying to ruin us with clothes for Rachel.'

'Ah, Rachel. I'm glad to see she's perking up a little. She looked very pulled when she came home.'

'Too much dancing.'

493

'Probably. But now Alice is moping about something. Am I doomed always to have one sister up and one down?'

'You have three sisters.'

'Linda's always the same,' Richard said. 'Down, down, down.'

Thinking about the up-and-downity of his younger sisters, Richard went looking for them when he got home. Rachel was in the great hall, helping to decorate the Christmas tree that had been brought up by the woodsman while he and Giles were out. The children were in a state of wild excitement, dancing about wearing coronets of tinsel, and quarrelling over who was to put the angel on the top. Since Linda had a firm hold of it, Richard guessed she would keep that privilege to herself. Miss Kettel, for once not trying to contain them, was chatting earnestly to Uncle Sebastian about Dickens, her eyes fixed intently on his face. Kitty stood watching the scene, with Louis in her arms.

Rachel stood on a chair and carefully disposed glass ornaments. She seemed happy, and either exertion or pleasant anticipation had put colour into her cheeks. Alice was not there. The tree was something that in previous years she would have been sure to be involved in, and it added to Richard's feeling that something was troubling her.

He found her in the old schoolroom, which she and Rachel had long used as their sitting-room. There was a fire in the grate, and its red contrasted with the grey snow-light from the windows, making a little glowing cave around the hearthrug. Alice was sitting there, looking through a sheaf of drawings. The dogs had found her, and were basking side by side on the rug. They heaved themselves to their feet and came to greet him, swinging their tails, their yellow eyes shining wolfishly in the firelight.

Alice gave a quick glance over her shoulder, then turned back to her drawings, shuffling them so that those on top were underneath. He noted the subterfuge, as he had also noted the glint of what might have been a tear on her cheek, and the quick swipe of her sleeve that removed it.

'I've just got back,' he said. 'What are you doing up here all alone? Are you coming down? They're decorating the tree without you.'

'There wasn't room for all of us round it,' Alice said, her voice sounding normal. Far too normal, as though it were an effort.

'But your eye is needed. After all, you are the artistic one of the family.'

'Kitty's artistic. She does lovely embroidery. You should see the buttercups and daisies she's done on Alexander's bib.'

Richard walked round and sat in the fireside chair so that he was facing her. 'You don't need to put on a show for me,' he said. 'I'm your brother, and I know when you're upset about something. Can't I help?'

'I'm not upset,' she said. 'Just—'

'Yes?' She didn't answer. He held out a hand. 'Can I see?'

She looked at him to gauge how serious he was, then separated and handed over a wedge of sheets – not including the ones she had moved to the bottom, he noted. He went through them slowly, studying her work. Figure studies, landscapes, some still-life groups, mostly in pencil or charcoal, but some colour-washed. 'These are very good,' he said, in surprise. He had always known she liked drawing, but he hadn't realised how much she had developed. There were wonderful dogs and horses in various poses. The human studies – Uncle Sebastian reading, spectacles slipping to the end of his nose, cigarette between his fingers; a man digging in a vegetable patch, foot on spade and back bowed; Afton polishing silver, faintly smiling at his own thoughts; the back view of a maid hanging up a dress, stretching to reach – they were not only lifelike, but seemed so alive they might have moved and stepped out of the page. 'You're *very* good,' he said, looking up. 'I had no idea.'

495

She shrugged shyly at the compliment. Then she said, 'I can draw – sometimes I think quite well. But I want to paint. I feel as if I can't really get any better without some instruction. There are techniques – there must be – but I don't know them. I keep doing the same things again and again, not moving on. It's frustrating.'

'These look pretty good to me.'

'But I want to be *better*.' He waited, hoping his silence would invite her to expand. At last she said, 'I have to get away.'

'Get away?'

'I've spent all my life here. I want to go somewhere and *do* something.'

'You'll have your Season next year, I suppose.'

'I don't want one. And it won't happen now Mother's married and gone. She was the only one who cared about that sort of thing, and she never wanted it for me anyway. I wouldn't have paid for all that dressing-up. I'm not pretty enough.'

'I think you're beautiful,' he said, not just loyally, but because just then it was true.

She waved a hand, cancelling the remark. 'Oh, all that's just – it doesn't *matter*. It's not—' She stopped.

He tried to help her along. 'Well, then, what do you *want* to do?'

She looked at him with an urgency and, at the same time, doubt that impressed him with her seriousness. *Something* had happened to her. He wished he could have had a look at the drawings she didn't want him to see.

'I don't suppose it's possible. Oh, but, Richard, if it *were* . . . Do you think you could talk to Giles, ask him, perhaps tell him it would be all right? I don't suppose he cares much what happens to me anyway, but he might think it wouldn't *look* right – as though *that* matters! But it's what I want, more than anything in the world.'

'You haven't told me what *it* is. *What* do you want to do?'

'Go to art college. Don't say anything yet! There's a place in London, the Slade School of Fine Art, where women are taught on the same basis as men. They have wonderful teachers, and people who study there become famous, famous artists! It's all completely respectable,' she said, on a descending note, as though knowing it would be forbidden.

'Where is this school?'

'In Bloomsbury. Near the university, and the British Museum. You know University College takes women students?'

'It hadn't occurred to me to wonder.'

'Well, it does, so there'd be lots of other women all around in the area, studying – decent, respectable women. For me to be there wouldn't be anything odd or outlandish that anyone could point a finger at.'

'Where would you live?'

'I could stay with Aunt Caroline, if she'd have me – it's no distance at all. I could walk, or go on the omnibus, and come home at night so everyone could see it was respectable. Oh, Richard!'

'You really want to do this?'

'I'm desperate to go!' she said, and her face looked fined-down and bleak, as if some unhappiness had stripped away the last of childhood's plumpness.

'Well, cheer up, chick,' he said. 'If it's that important to you, I'm sure it can be managed. I don't see why Giles should mind in the least – it's not as though you want to go on the stage.' He thought briefly of Chloë, and contrasted the ambitions of the two. But Chloë was older, of age, and could do as she pleased. Poor little Alice was still a prisoner.

'Would you ask him for me?' she asked, a perilous hope in her eyes.

'We'll ask him together. And we'll take your drawings to show him. I don't suppose he realises how good you've got.'

He handed them back, watched her sort out the ones she

didn't want seen and push them casually under the armchair out of sight. Then she got up. 'Can we do it now?'

'Why not? They must have brought tea, so he'll be in a good mood. Come on.'

Tea had been brought into the great hall, and the whole family was seated round the table when Richard and Alice arrived, preceded by the dogs, who raced to Giles, almost knocked over the milk jug with an ecstasy of tails, then sat one at either side of him, leaning suggestively, noses cataloguing what was on the table.

Giles had been telling the good news about their financial solidity. Halfway through the exposition, he thought he should perhaps have waited until Linda wasn't there. She looked as though she was gathering herself for an appeal, and Richard arrived just in time to forestall her.

His arrival forestalled Kitty, too. She had been on the brink of mentioning her garden plans. If there was spare money, perhaps Giles would think it could be afforded – or, at least, some of it. But she could wait, and talk to him tomorrow, or whenever they were alone. Nothing could be done until the spring, anyway – and if he was going to say no, she'd rather keep her dreams for a bit longer.

Richard passed around Alice's sketches, and gave everyone time to pore over them. Then, while Alice stared determinedly at her feet, he dropped the bombshell of her request.

Linda was the first to speak. 'Good heavens, what an idea! A Tallant becoming some kind of Bohemian? We'd never live it down.'

Giles frowned. 'These drawings are very good – but good enough?'

Kitty said, 'I think they are.' Giles looked at her. 'You know we studied fine art at Miss Thornton's.'

'I remember. You surprised me by knowing about impressionism.'

'Until then, he thought young ladies only liked pictures of kittens, and little girls feeding ducks,' Richard said, with a teasing look at his brother.

'Well,' Kitty went on, ignoring him, 'for what my opinion is worth, I think Alice has a real talent.'

'Having a talent doesn't mean you become a professional,' Linda said. 'There's a difference between taking part in country-house dramatics, and going on the stage.'

'Painters are not the same as actors,' Richard said. 'Great artists are welcome guests in the finest salons. They even get honours. *Sir* Peter Lely? *Sir* Thomas Lawrence?'

'Men, not women,' Linda said. 'Women don't become great artists.'

'Angelica Kauffman? Elizabeth Siddal?'

'Oh, Richard, do stop saying names,' Linda said crossly, not having heard of either of those two. 'A girl of Alice's age can't go to art school. I'm sure they don't take girls anyway.'

'The Slade School does,' Alice said. She addressed Giles, and told him all the things she had told Richard.

He listened quietly, then asked, as Richard had, 'Is this what you really want?'

'Yes,' she said, putting all her force into one word.

'You don't want to have a Season, like Rachel?'

'Please, no!'

'Well, I dare say art-college fees won't come to as much as all Rachel's clothes did, to say nothing of the ball. If you're sure, then I see no reason why you shouldn't go.'

She ran to him, put her arms round his neck, and pressed her cheek to his.

'We'll have to ask Aunt Caroline if she'll have you,' he said.

'Oh, Giles! I can't believe it! I can really go?'

'*I* have no objection,' he said.

'Mother will never agree,' Linda said. The temperature cooled.

The joy faded from Alice's face, but then she squared her shoulders and said, 'She doesn't care about me.'

'She cares about the family name.'

'But there's nothing *disgraceful* about it!' Alice protested.

Giles intervened. 'I expect she can be brought round. We'll look into it. I'll get Markham to make some enquiries – he's the man for finding things out. We don't know yet if they'll take you, of course.'

'For a fee, they'd take *me*,' Richard said.

He still wondered about those drawings she didn't want him to see. His guess would be that they were of some male figure, and that his youngest sister was suffering from a bad case of unrequited first love. Going to art school was rather an extreme way of dealing with it, but he couldn't see that it would do her any harm – and, not being a boy, she couldn't 'list for a soldier.

Rachel felt so much better now she was in England, as though it gave her some small amount of control over her life. It was a relief to be away from her mother and the prince – and to be closer to Angus. He had written of his delight that she was back, and had given his reassurances that he hadn't changed and that all would be well.

His next letter, however, was more alarming. His father had been putting pressure on him to agree to the marriage with Diana Huntley.

Sir Gordon had summoned Angus to his study and told him that the usual family gathering would take place at Craigend at Christmas, and the guests would include the Huntleys. 'And I expect you to get on with proposing to Miss Huntley,' he concluded sternly.

'But, Father—'

'No more of that! No more "but, Father"! You are making a show of me. Sir Philip is starting to ask pointed questions. All this shilly-shallying is insulting to him *and* to the girl. I want it done before the Christmas party breaks up. I've agreed with Sir Philip that the wedding can take place in April. Easter is very late, on the twenty-third, so it had better be before that. The dowry will be partly in cash and partly in property, and Sir Philip is giving Miss Huntley, as a wedding present, a handsome house in Edinburgh, where you will live – in Queen Street, as it happens, just a few steps from my offices, where you will take up your position as my deputy. So you see, everything is falling most satisfactorily into place.'

'But, Father, I don't love her,' Angus said desperately.

Tullamore made an impatient sound. 'Love is not for young people to decide at a dance. Love is for grown-ups, Angus. It develops over time, when two people are well-matched and are set up in a proper, sensible fashion. Miss Huntley is suitable in every way. You and she will have everything you need, and you will be very happy together.'

The substance of this Angus told Rachel in his letter.

But I am determined not to ask her. Her father and mine can arrange what they like between them but if I don't ask her it can't happen. And I believe that if I am steadfast in refusing, they will have to give it up in the end. Then I'm sure Father will agree to my marrying you. But you must be steadfast too, my darling love, and not let them bully you into marrying anyone else. Promise me you will stay true to me. Remember, they can't force you to marry against your will.

Rachel felt that she was safe enough at Ashmore, for with her mother abroad, no-one else had any interest in finding her a husband. The danger would be if her mother came home or, worse, if she summoned Rachel to go back to live with her abroad. Once she had left the country, everything would be harder, close to impossible.

'If they try to make me go abroad,' she wrote to Angus, 'I will run away and find a way to get to you.'

Angus thought of Rachel trying to get to Scotland – gentle, helpless Rachel, with a carpet bag and a few shillings, becoming stranded somewhere because she hadn't enough for the full journey, left without the means to get to him or to contact him. It was enough to make him shudder.

He wrote back: 'If you think there is any danger that you will be sent abroad, if they even start to talk about it, tell me at once and I will come and fetch you. Promise me you won't try to run away on your own.'

Rachel happily promised, and into her mind came the image of Angus, like Young Lochinvar, riding up on a white horse, sweeping her onto the saddle before him, and galloping away. Even if it didn't happen *precisely* like that, it was quite satisfactory, and freed her mind from worry so that she could enjoy the Christmas season. Kitty, glad not to be pregnant for once, was full of energy and was planning lots of entertainments at Ashmore, and there was hunting, and parties at other houses, including a grand ball at Ashridge Park, Lord Shacklock's seat. He was bound to invite people down from London, and there would be a chance for her to wear one of her expensive London ball gowns.

But she also enjoyed less exalted Christmas activities, like gilding walnuts to hang on the tree, and making paper chains with Arabella and Arthur. Miss Kettel showed them how to fold paper into a multiple thickness, then cut it in a certain way, so that when you unfolded it, it made a chain of angels holding hands. It was pleasant to sit by the fire with the children, in a plain dress and with her hair down, and do simple, childish things, and not have to worry how she looked or what anyone was thinking of her. The dogs came, flopped, and snored; Miss Kettel told them all stories; Alice sat nearby and drew the group. Then Kitty would come down with the babies, and Louis would run wild with excitement, while Alexander goggled at the shining tree, and reached out a starfish hand for one of the swinging ornaments. And Uncle

Sebastian would play the piano – wheeled in from the state drawing-room to the great hall for the season – and they would all sing.

Having a horse had made all the difference to Nina's life. She hunted twice a week, which used up more than two days, because the day after a hunt was spent in a happy languor of mental and physical tiredness. Mrs Anstruther had not appeared, being apparently detained with the sick relative, and in her absence Bobby had not found the courage to hunt astride, so there had been no friction for Nina, no danger that she would be cajoled into doing something that would upset Mr Cowling.

On non-hunting days she usually rode with Bobby, on one of her horses if Jewel was resting. Sometimes Clemmie joined them, and the three of them rambled far afield. Mr Cowling liked to see her happily and innocently occupied, and was even talking about buying her a second horse, after Aubrey Wharfedale had described to him the disappointment when a person's only horse went lame and couldn't be hunted.

And when she wasn't riding, she often went out walking with Trump, having all the energy of nineteen to use up. Evenings were occupied with entertaining or being entertained. Mr Cowling loved to play bridge, and Nina was sharp enough to make a useful partner, though she could never quite feel the passion for it that some obviously felt. There were dinners, too, and musical soirées; and when nothing else had been arranged, she could always walk up to Welland Hall, with Mr Cowling or alone, and join in a family dinner, and games.

She was occupied; she was mostly happy. But there were still times when she paused, and looked at herself and wondered, *Is this all there is?* What would happen when the hunting season ended? Ordinary riding was a pleasure, but hunting stretched every nerve and muscle and fibre to the limit, and left you drowsy and relaxed all the next day. Taking that out of the equation would leave a void to be filled – with what?

When she allowed herself to think beyond the moment, she was uneasy. She felt cut adrift from life, as if everyone else had found the thing that made it all make sense, while she hadn't an idea where to look for it. Bobby was happy – there was no doubting that her life fulfilled her. Clemmie – though it was less easy to be sure, because she didn't give much away – Clemmie seemed happy. All the women she met at all the parties they attended seemed happy. And, after all, what else was there? When you were a girl, you prepared yourself for marriage, you worked towards it, longed for it. And once you had it, that was supposed to satisfy you for the rest of your life. No-one ever told the unmarried girl what happened afterwards. You journeyed to the place called Marriage, and there the story ended. Close the book.

But there you still were, wondering what to do with yourself.

She woke early on Christmas morning and lay in her warm bed staring into the darkness and thinking all these things. *Can this life go on?* Just like this, year after year? She had a huge desire to run away – but run away where, to what? Running away *from*, rather than *to*, could only end badly. She was comfortable, safe, cherished where she was. It was a lot to give up. But she felt as though a cloud was forming, one of those low purple bars on the horizon that portends a storm. *Could this life go on?* She had felt the ground tremble under her.

She must have fallen asleep again, because she was woken by the mouselike sounds of the maid lighting her fire, little rustlings and scratchings. Christmas Day. Apart from church, she would be alone with Mr Cowling all day. He was the provider of all this comfort, her downy bed, the fire in the grate, the servant to light it, the horse in the stable – even

504

the little dog, who took the opportunity to dash in when the housemaid went out and jump up on the bed to greet her with the passion of a night's absence. So she would do her best to make today pleasant for Mr Cowling. It was ridiculous to be discontented, and downright naughty to be ungrateful.

She wore one of his favourite dresses, a dusky rose barathea, long-sleeved, high-necked, with a ruched bodice and a trimming of coarse cream lace on the neckband, bodice and sleeves. With it she wore the pink kid shoes with the jet bead decoration that he'd had hand-made for her. She would lift her skirt just enough as she walked so that he could see them, and it would please him.

Tina did her hair, she put on pearl earrings, picked up the parcel she had left wrapped and ready by the door, and went down.

He was there already, waiting by the drawing-room fire for her, so that they could go in to breakfast together. 'Merry Christmas,' he said, greeting her with a kiss, looking her over keenly. 'I like that gown. I'm glad you wore it, because here is your present. Open it!'

He seemed tense with pleasurable anticipation. From the size and shape she guessed it was jewellery. It was what he liked best to buy her. He watched her, hungry for her reaction, as she removed the paper and opened the box. It was a hair ornament of glittering pink stones.

'You see?' he said gleefully. 'Something made you wear a pink gown today! It was meant to be.'

'It's beautiful,' she said. 'What are they?'

'Pink diamonds. Normally I wouldn't buy them, because they're not as good as white or blue, or even yellow. But these are such a good colour, and of exceptional clarity and brilliance, I couldn't pass them up. And you look so pretty in pink.'

'I've never seen pink ones before. How lovely! And how kind you are.'

'Nonsense, not kind at all. Let me pin it on for you. There now. Oh, very handsome! Those diamonds must be feeling very proud, being worn by a lovely woman like you.'

She laughed, because she knew he wanted her to, and then said, 'It makes my present to you seem very dull, I'm afraid. Here – with my love. Merry Christmas, Joseph.'

He unwrapped the parcel, being careful not to tear the paper, and coiling up the string from thrifty habit. It was a book, very recently published: *The Theory of Business Enterprise* by Thorstein Veblen. It was about the clash between the two great impulses, of business and of industry – which Nina had not realised were different things. According to the author, business was the making of profit, and industry was the making of goods, and the two things were in conflict with each other. All this she knew because Decius had told her about the book and what it concerned, and had said that Mr Cowling would love to have a copy.

She looked anxiously now at his face as he turned a page or two. 'I hope it isn't a disappointment. I was thinking of a cigarette case, but then someone said you'd been longing to read this—'

He looked up, smiling. 'Let me guess: someone whose name begins with a D? I happened to mention to him . . . Oh, my! Disappointed? I couldn't be more pleased! A cigarette case wouldn't have been as – personal as this. This is something you've really thought about. Thank you, my darling.'

She laughed with relief. 'I'm glad it's you who has to read it, and not me.'

'Oh, Nina,' he said, and between the first word and the second his voice went from elation to sadness. He put the book down and took both her hands in his.

She wanted to say, *Please don't. Don't say anything about disappointment. Not now.*

But he did. He said, 'I know this isn't what you expected from getting married. You were fresh to life, full of hope and ideas . . . Lord knows, I never expected you to say yes in the first place. But I thought I had the – the wherewithal to make you happy. I meant you to be, you know. And I've failed you.'

'No,' she said. 'No.'

'It's not the way I wanted it to be. And there doesn't seem to be anything to be done about it. But I want to make it up to you – or, at least, make it come out all right for you. As right as it can be. So I've a suggestion.'

'Please don't,' she said. 'Please don't say any more.'

He lifted a hand. 'Hear me out,' he said. 'This is not easy for me to say, and it won't be easy for you to hear. And you might be shocked. You might be offended. But before I say it, I want you to know that I love you, more than ever, and though I know you don't love me the same way, I think you are fond of me, a bit – aren't you?'

'Oh, Joseph!'

'So this might be the solution – the thing that'll make it come out all right. With good will on both sides, I think it could.'

In her distress she couldn't find any words. And taking her silence as consent to continue, he told her his idea.

It was not easy for the telegraph boy to get his bicycle up the hill through the remains of the snow, and since Uncle Stuffy had sent the telegram from the station before mounting the train, it gave barely enough time to put the horses to and get down to Canons Ashmore station to meet him.

Rachel was in a panic. 'He didn't say Mama was with him, did he?'

'No,' said Giles. 'It just says, "Arriving by the 1.55. Please meet."'

'But it doesn't say it's just him. It might be both of them. All three of them.'

'Why should Mother and the prince be travelling with Uncle Stuffy?' Giles said patiently. Rachel dithered on the spot, like someone preparing to bolt. 'I assure you, if Mother was coming back she'd have said so. We've only sent two horses to meet Uncle Stuffy. She'd expect four, you know that. She wouldn't risk being met without due ceremony.'

'Oh,' said Rachel. 'I expect you're right.'

'We'll put Lord Leake in the Waterloo Room,' said Mrs Webster to Afton. 'Thank goodness we've got enough good sheets now. Once when he came he got a sides-to-middled sheet because that was *simply* all we had, and he sent McGregor down to request a different room.'

'McGregor's his manservant?'

'Yes, and look out for him. A more savage temper there never was on a human being. I had nightmares about that sheet for weeks afterwards.'

Afton smiled. 'I'm sure you didn't. I can't imagine anything flustering you.'

'I wasn't flustered, just frost-bitten. Now I must go and speak to Mrs Terry about dinner tonight. He's a great diner, is Lord Leake. We can't give him hashes. The leftover pie is all right – her pastry is so good it will carry it – but there will have to be a joint.'

'We've pheasants enough in the game larder,' Afton pointed out.

'But he'll expect a joint as well as game. Someone will have to go down to the butcher. Who can you spare, Mr Afton?'

'You can have Sam. He's intelligent and quick.'

'Then he can see if the butcher has any sweetbreads, as well, for a savoury. Lord Leake is very fond of fried sweet-breads.'

'You'd better let me have the menu as soon as possible, so I can look out the wines,' said Afton. 'Is it usual for his lord-ship to descend like this, without notice?'

'No,' said Mrs Webster, 'it isn't. He's a great one for his

comfort, likes to be sure everything's in place for him before he arrives. And it's a strange time to be coming. Wherever he goes for Christmas, he arrives well before and stays until well afterwards. I hope it's not bad news.'

'People generally send bad news by letter or telegram, don't they?' Afton said comfortingly. 'They don't dash down to deliver it in person.'

'Perhaps not,' Mrs Webster said doubtfully, then shook herself. 'We'll know soon enough, I dare say. Send Sam to me in the kitchen right away, will you, and I'll give him his instructions once I've agreed with Mrs Terry. She'll want to make a special sweet for him, too, I expect.'

'Lucky man,' said Afton, turning away.

'Well, it's nice to cook for someone who appreciates it,' said Mrs Webster.

It was too cold for the family to assemble outside on the steps to greet Uncle Stuffy. They waited for him in the great hall, where there was a good fire. Rachel fidgeted on the spot as she waited to see if he was indeed alone, and Kitty threw her a compassionate look. There were sounds of arrival outside, murmured voices, and then he was there, pulling off his heavy, fur-lined gloves and the travelling-cap with the lappets and handing them to Afton. His face was wreathed with smiles. *Not bad news, then*, Afton thought. He could tell them that down-stairs.

Giles came forward to shake his hand, Kitty at his elbow. 'What a pleasant surprise, Uncle. How nice to see you. Did you have a pleasant journey?'

'I've only come from London. Wretched train, no heating, but I had my big rug so I was all right. McGregor tells me some Scotch feller has invented a patent glass bottle in a metal case that uses a vacuum to keep liquids hot. Don't ask me how that works, but it means you could carry hot tea or soup with you on a journey, for when the train has no restaurant car. Excellent idea. Have to get one of those if I'm going to be dashing back and forth at all times of year.'

'And will you?' Giles asked.

He chuckled. 'Looks quite likely. Given the situation.'

'What is the situation, Uncle Stuffy?'

'No more of that "Stuffy" nonsense, if you please! I'm Fergus, or Lord Leake from now on. Got to have a bit of dignity. Stuffy's not a name for a married man.'

'But you're not married,' Giles said, bewildered. 'Are you?'

'As good as. On the brink – head in the noose. Engaged, at any rate. It's all official, you know. Just the wedding to arrange.'

'Who—' Giles got as far as asking, and broke off as someone else came into the hall. Rachel gave an audible gasp.

The newly designated Uncle Fergus looked over his shoulder, and said, 'Look who I picked up at the station! He came down on the same train, but he was in third class for some reason, so I didn't know. Spotted him on the platform when I got out, otherwise the silly lad would have had to walk up to the Castle, because I noticed when we went through the yard that there was no cab there. I told him, "There'll be a carriage waiting for me, no sense in ruining your boots. Nothing worse than water-marks on leather" – am I right, Afton?'

'Yes, indeed, my lord,' Afton said, passing Lord Leake's outerwear to the waiting William so that he could help divest the newcomer.

Angus looked worn, disarranged from travel, and distressed. 'I'm so sorry to burst in on you like this, without notice,' he said to Giles, and encompassed Kitty with an apologetic glance.

She was quick to reassure him, recognising a crisis to be dealt with. 'It's quite all right. You're welcome at any time,' she said. But the question was all over her face: *What on earth are you doing here?*

Tiger and Isaac were fawning over Angus, severely

510

hampering his attempts to get out of his greatcoat. He looked whitely past Kitty at Rachel, who burst into noisy tears.

'Now, now, now,' Fergus said to her. 'None of that. Don't want any waterfalls when I'm trying to deliver my good news. Didn't you hear me say that I'm going to be married?'

Kitty was telling Afton in a low voice to have a room prepared for Angus. Rachel was trying to staunch her tears with a handkerchief and Angus was staring at her, biting his lips, while Linda was staring at Angus, evidently about to bark the question Kitty had only thought. And William had dropped one of Fergus's leather gauntlets, and Tiger had pounced on it, obviously meaning to worry it to death.

'We heard you, Uncle,' Giles said, feeling he was caught up in some vaudeville burlesque. 'You didn't pick up anyone else on the way? I'm not going to see a troupe of clowns or performing dogs come tumbling through that door next?'

'What? What?' said Fergus, staring at him blankly. 'You think the circus is in town?'

'You haven't told us,' Giles said, with desperate patience, 'whom you are going to marry.'

But he had a horrid feeling that he knew.

Return to where it all began with the first novel in Cynthia Harrod-Eagles' Ashmore Castle drama series, set at the turn of the twentieth century.

1901. When the Earl of Stainton dies in a tragic hunting accident, Giles, the eldest son of the noble Tallant family, must step forward to replace him as the head of the family. But Giles has avoided the Castle and his stifling relatives for years, deciding instead to forge his own path away from the spotlight. Now, he must put aside his ambitions and honour his duty to the family.

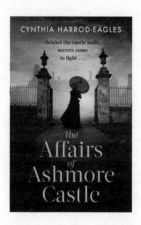

The second in the Ashmore Castle historical family drama series, set at the turn of the twentieth century. Behind the doors of the magnificent Ashmore Castle, secrets are waiting to be uncovered . . .

1903. Giles, the new Earl of Stainton, is struggling to bring his family's estate back to order after the death of his father, and he has little time to spare for his young pregnant wife, Kitty. She lives in fear of her mother-in-law, who won't give up the reins of the household. Will she ever truly be mistress of Ashmore Castle? Perhaps if her coming child is a boy, that will change the balance of power . . .